ACOLYTE

TEMPRIS
BOOK
2

STEPHANIE FISHER

For Travis.

-

You are the Ten to my Rose, the Danny to my Clara, the Rory to my Pond.

Together.

Or not at all.

CONTENTS

MAP

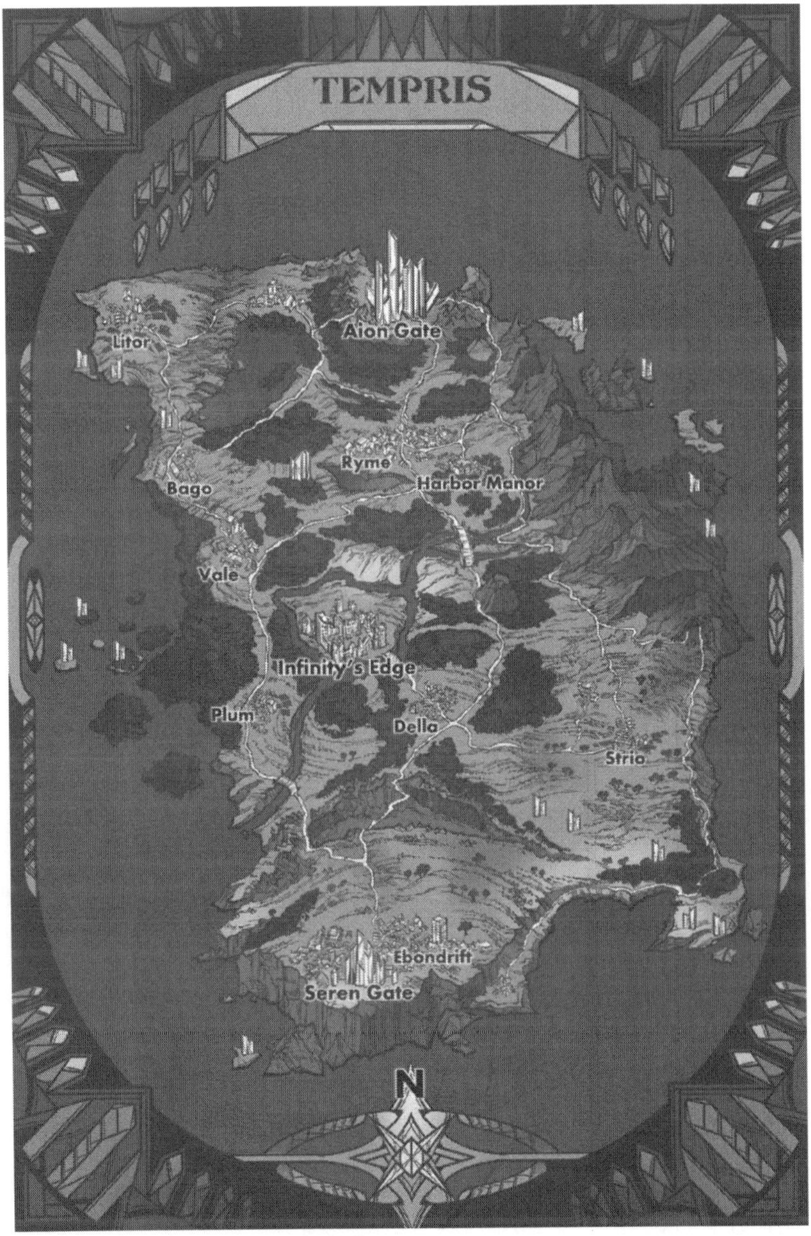
TEMPRIS
Aion Gate
Litor
Ryme
Harbor Manor
Bago
Vale
Infinity's Edge
Plum
Della
Strio
Ebondrift
Seren Gate
N

PROLOGUE

Carin had always hated executions.

She hated the brutality, the needless cruelty. She hated the nearly feral thirst for violence radiating from the crowds that would inevitably gather. The smell of blood and urine, the harsh clamor of steel mixed with shouts and screams and pleas for mercy. Since the Schism, there had been many executions. Some would say too many. Others, too few.

As she stared at the motionless body lying in a pool of blood and filth in the middle of the old barn, she sincerely hoped that tonight would be different. She had always hated executions, more so now that she was to be the executioner.

Bloodshot eyes blinked open, the yellow irises nearly lost beneath the patchwork of bruises and swollen flesh. The man groaned, his cracked lips parting. Even though Carin couldn't decipher the broken, garbled stream of words that fell out of him, she knew his meaning: water. Just a few drops, enough to wet his tongue, to wash away the taste of blood and bile. It would be a mercy.

Carin glanced at the trough shoved into the corner but remained seated, perched on the edge of an empty stall door. "Vaughn," she warned, pulling her cloak tighter as another drip of rain leaked through the roof and trickled down her neck, soaking the few wisps of honey-colored hair that had escaped her braid. It was always raining on this damned island. "I have orders to discipline you if you don't stay quiet. Our master is almost done reviewing your testimony about the incident in Vale. It won't be long now."

Vaughn groaned again, his burly shoulders trembling. He had been tied here for three days now, denied food and water as he was routinely beaten and healed and beaten again. That was the consequence of failure. And while Carin didn't know the exact details of what had happened with this man, she knew why he was here. The time mage and Vaughn's inability to detain her was all anyone in the outpost was talking about.

Another moan. Another feeble whimper. But then, Vaughn quieted, his head slumping to the ground.

Thank the Shards, Carin thought. She didn't want to have to beat him again. If he survived his interrogation, he likely wouldn't forget the things she had already been made to do.

The barn door creaked open, and the low hiss and patter of the storm raging just outside the thin, rotting walls intensified. Lightning streaked the sky, and for half a heartbeat, night turned into day.

Carin scrambled off her perch, then dropped to one knee. "S-sire," she stammered, wincing at the slight squeak in her voice. No matter how many times she met their master face-to-face, no matter how many hours she stood in his presence, she would never get used to that fog of dead air that seemed to follow him. It was like a miasma, sickly and suffocating and inescapable.

The door slammed shut, the sound almost lost in the peal of thunder that boomed overhead, and a hooded figure, little more than a shadow in the flickering light of the storm, stood at the far side of the barn.

Unmoving. Silent. But watching.

Just like he had been watching that night in the tavern. The night her life had changed.

Heavy footsteps echoed, and Carin's lungs began to burn. She couldn't stop her body from trembling as she ducked lower to the ground, pressing her cheek against the trampled hay and excrement that littered the floor.

A gentle hand caressed her hair, and she flinched, her whole body shaking. "Lady Fenmar." The voice was soft, too young for the predator that lurked beneath that heavy, black-furred cloak. "Rise, child."

Carin scrambled to her feet, ducking her head and failing to completely suppress the shudder that ran through her when the figure continued to observe her. Though his height was decidedly average, his build slight, that aura of emptiness was searching. She could feel its tendrils brushing across her skin, coiling around her body like a snake preparing to devour its prey.

The aether in her blood shivered when she felt him withdraw.

The hood obscured his eyes. When he smiled, his full lips parting, it was merely a flash of too-white teeth in the shadows. “Has he given you any trouble?” the man asked, his voice crisp and cultured, almost amiable. As though he were inquiring about the weather or commenting on the rain.

Carin glanced at the man still bound and gagged on the floor. His yellow eyes were round and frightened, and he watched, taking in every breath, every movement. “No, Sire,” she said. “He’s been quiet.”

The man chuckled. “Lady Fenmar, *Carin*.” She hated the hand that landed on her shoulder. “How long have we known each other now? How long have we been here, on Tempris, working together for the betterment of our people?”

Too long, Carin thought, catching a glimpse of her sleeve. When she had first come to Tempris, her tunic had been new—bright carnation pink to match the color of her eyes. The pigment was nearly gone now, washed away by months of sun and rain and sweat.

“Sorry,” she whispered, swallowing hard. “Aneirin.” The name felt like ash on her tongue.

Aneirin gave a satisfied nod before stepping across the room and crouching in front of the man. “Well, Vaughn.” He grabbed a fistful of dark hair, pulling the shadow mage’s eyes to his. “Shall we get started?”

Aneirin made a gesture, and Carin rushed forward, placing an old, rickety chair behind him before skittering a safe distance away.

Aneirin swept his cloak to the side, revealing a formal frock coat made of deep blue satin and trousers to match. His face remained hooded as he lowered himself into the chair with effortless grace. “You may show your respects,” he said, and pushed a boot forward.

Vaughn struggled, flopping awkwardly as he tried to inch his way forward with both his arms and legs bound tightly behind him. When he was able, he placed his lips upon the polished leather of the man’s boot. “Sire,” he whimpered pitifully. “Have mercy, Sire. Master. I did not know that the girl—”

“And I still do not believe you.” Aneirin gestured idly, barely more than a flick of his finger. “Carin? If you would be so kind.”

Carin approached the shadow mage, doing her best to ignore his increasingly desperate petitions for mercy as she pulled a small dagger from the sheath at her waist. Its wooden hilt felt warm against her chill skin, and her expression remained stoic as she dragged her palm across the blade. So much of shadow magic was tied up in bloodletting—all shadow mages eventually learned to ignore the pain.

Blood welled around the cut, and she channeled her aether, slowing her body’s natural healing as she crouched in front of the man. Grabbing his hair, for he had yet to cooperate with anyone that had approached him, she thrust her palm into his mouth, using her magic to bolster her strength when he began to struggle. Eventually, she felt something catch, like a gentle tapping on the inside of her thoughts. He’d swallowed. Not much, barely a drop. But it was enough.

Enough for her to tug at that little piece of her magic, to send her aether coursing through his veins, infecting every part of him.

She gave a silent command, and he swallowed. One mouthful. Two. She pulled back, standing to her full height. Her heart thumped, her stomach turned, but as she gazed down at this traitor, at the blood smeared across his lips, cheeks, and chin, she thought only about the spell and the very next step.

Her mind curled around his, invading every dark corner, every hidden recess. An entire lifetime of memories and thoughts and secrets laid bare before her.

She retreated. His mind wasn't hers to pillage. That would be their master's privilege.

"He's ready," Carin said, and stepped back. "He'll tell you whatever you want to know." She continued to watch, taking in every movement and twitch. Even though Vaughn's magic had been drained slowly and methodically over the last three days, he was older and more powerful. He could still put up a fight if she let her guard down.

"Good." Aneirin crossed an ankle over his knee. "Now, Vaughn. Tell me about the time mage."

Vaughn resisted at first, but a tug on the spell was all it took to set him babbling. About the human girl that had snuck into the Vale relay, about her warning to Ryme, about the spells inscribed on her arm and what they concealed. On and on, the details spilled out of him.

Occasionally, she felt a faint nudge of resistance, so she would delve deeper, digging in her claws and prying apart those memories he seemed so reticent to share. Forcing the words past his lips.

Desire. Lust.

He had wanted this girl. He had known what she was, sensed the magic in her blood from the beginning. But he had still wanted her because she had reminded him of someone else. Someone he couldn't have. They were so similar, and he just wanted a taste. One little taste before he had to turn her over.

It was that single moment of cruel stupidity that had cost him. Carin saw the gun, felt his memory of that cool barrel pressed against his chin.

The pain of that single gunshot to the head reverberated through her.

And then the explosion of energy and light and magic that erupted from the girl—just the memory was enough to leave Carin blind and breathless, grasping at the spell.

The time mage, little more than a child, had caught him unaware.

Vaughn was panting when he finally finished the full account, and blood streaked with spittle dripped from his open mouth. He looked up, his eyes wide and pleading. He had stopped struggling against his bindings, and his body lay prone.

Aneirin didn't speak for several long moments. His fingers drummed against his thigh as the lightning flickered, a low rumble of thunder quickly following. Carin found herself taking a step back as she felt the aether around him begin to ripple.

Finally, Aneirin rose from his seat and began to circle the panting shadow mage, still kneeling in a patch of blood-soaked hay.

"Now *that*," Aneirin mused, "is a very different story than the one you originally told me."

Even the storm raging outside quieted, holding its breath as the predator homed in on its prey.

"So, if I am to understand you correctly," Aneirin went on, "the first time mage to appear in over two centuries stumbled into your post like a gift from above, and instead of trying to woo her, instead of using charm and tact to play on her sympathies—you attacked her; you attempted to rape her; and then, worst of all, you *lost* her." Aneirin ticked off each sin on those bony, too-pale fingers.

Vaughn rasped, "But Sire—"

"Shut him up!"

Carin flinched at the snarled command, quickly tightening her grip on the spell.

Vaughn whimpered, and then quieted.

Aneirin clenched and unclenched his fists. His attention flicked to Carin. "Tell me—how long have I been planning this assault?"

"Two and a half centuries," Carin mumbled hoarsely. Although the war had been raging quietly in the background for far, far longer. Their master—or rather the thing inside him—was old. Older than the oldest immortals, older than she could even begin to fathom. He had been planning his revenge, plotting to bring down the heavens, since before time began.

"Yes," Aneirin crooned with an almost imperceptible nod of his head. "Two and a half centuries since we lost our last time mage. Two and a half centuries since we forfeited what would've been complete control of Tempris. It has taken two and a half centuries to regroup, to build our army, to choose our moment."

With a sweep of his cloak, Aneirin crouched, tucking a finger underneath the shadow mage's chin and forcing his eyes up. "Vaughn," he said, almost gentle. Vaughn started to shake in earnest. "I have no need for sentient stupidity. So, I'm going to give you one chance. One chance to tell me something—anything—that might convince me not to turn you into one of my puppets. Tell me, Carin." Another flash of those teeth. "Would you recommend *ascension* to our friend here?"

Carin clamped her lips together and shook her head. Even after a year, she could still feel that gaping hole in her anima, where a piece of her soul had been carved out, the wound left to fester. She had never wanted to come to Tempris, to join this cause. She had only been at the tavern that night because Asher had dared her, said that she was too prim to ever step foot in a common bar.

But Aneirin, who had called himself something different back then, had found her and made his offer. And when she refused, he had taken away her ability to say no. He had turned her into one of his ascended, that piece of her soul passed around to his cronies like a leash.

"I didn't think so," Aneirin said, then turned back to Vaughn. "With that in mind—what have you to say in your defense?"

Carin loosened her hold on the spell, just enough for him to speak. Vaughn gulped in a breath. "I think I know where she went," he said in a rush. "I lost her at the old palace. There was a portal. Inside the gates. And then Breena—"

"Breena?" Aneirin asked.

Vaughn nodded. "Yes, Sire. Breena Venwraith."

"I was told she died."

"I have reason to believe that she bound her anima inside the enchantments concealing the girl's magic."

"Why would she do that?" Aneirin asked. "Why would she protect a time mage? Breena Venwraith was assigned to protect the High Lord of Water. It was not her mission to search for the Time Shard."

Vaughn began to tremble, and once more, Carin felt a tug of resistance. She twisted her claws deeper, and the shadow mage groaned. "Her daughter." A pained gasp. "The time mage was the child of Breena Venwraith. Corinna—though I suspect that is not what the girl is known by now.

"I lost them at the gates of the palace when Breena opened a portal. I fought, Sire. I tried to recover the girl, but Breena… she summoned fairy fire. She used the spirits of the dead to steal the girl away."

Vaughn whimpered as the hand gripping his chin moved to his neck.

"I am very disappointed, Vaughn." The hand began to tighten. "So very disappointed."

"We just need to lure the girl out." There were tears in Vaughn's eyes now, streaking the blood on his face. "There has to be something she cares about. Something we can use to draw her out of hiding. We just have to figure out what that is."

That sagging hood tilted, as though considering the proposal, and the fog of dead air, suffocating in its emptiness, quaked. Carin took another step back when she felt that hollow void brush against her.

"We don't even know who this girl is," Aneirin said. "How are we supposed to gather information on a person without a reliable name?"

"Please," Vaughn begged. Carin could feel his fear through the hold she still had on his mind. "There was a transmission. The girl managed to contact Ryme on the relay system. Vale's outpost was destroyed, but Ryme may still have a recording. We might be able to find something to identify her."

Aneirin clicked his tongue. "That's not good enough."

"There's more!" Vaughn sobbed as the smell of urine permeated the air. "Please. Please wait, there's more. When the enchantment matrix containing her magic shattered, she went somewhere. She projected her anima."

Aneirin released his hold on Vaughn's neck. "Who was the anchor?"

"A boy," Vaughn panted. "I was still trying to work my way free of her magic at the time, so I couldn't follow properly. But I saw a flash. It was a boy pulling her through."

"Would you recognize him?"

Vaughn nodded eagerly. "Without a doubt. And if we get the boy, the time mage will follow. I'm sure she'll come for him."

Aneirin's fingers still hovered over the shadow mage's neck while he deliberated. After a long moment, he said, "You have made things far more difficult than they needed to be. However" —he rose— "for the moment, you are still more valuable to me as you are."

Aneirin gave a slight nod as he straightened his cloak, and Carin released the spell. Vaughn slumped to the floor, wheezing as he sucked in gasps of air.

"Well then," Aneirin said, idly picking at the sleeve of his coat. "I guess this means we're off to Ryme."

"We, Sire?" Vaughn shoved Carin away as soon as she cut his bindings.

"Yes," Aneirin replied. "I want this time mage, and since you can no longer be trusted to act on your own, I will be seeing this matter through personally."

Aneirin jerked his head, and Carin bowed, grateful for the chance to leave. As she heaved open the barn door and stepped out into the darkness and rain, she sent up a silent prayer to the Shards. For the time mage. For this island. For the home she'd left behind.

But not for her. After the things she'd done, it would be a mercy to join the dead.

CHAPTER I

-From the personal notes of Azura Raine, High Lady of Time

The world ended today. By my own hand.

I shut down the gates.

I take full responsibility for every death, every lost colony, every life inexorably altered. I say a silent prayer for my friends who will have to live in the world that comes after, and now I go freely into my exile.

I deserve far worse than an eternity alone.

The door was locked.

And truthfully, Talya Caro wasn't sure why she had expected anything different. Every door she had tried in this damned place was locked. The windows even had bars. Beautiful, filigreed bars made of gold-painted iron—but bars, nonetheless.

Taly took a step back. The door was a great, massive thing made of carved oak that swirled together in nonsense patterns. A subtle shimmer covered the surface like a veil. The handle was made of gold.

She reached out one more time, as if something might suddenly change—

And then immediately snatched her hand away, hissing, "Shit, shit, shit," as well as other more colorful curses when her fingers continued to tingle.

The door wasn't just locked. It was sealed with warding magic, and there were only two reasons to use warding magic.

The first was to keep things out. The second to keep things in.

In this case, she was more inclined to believe it was the latter, confirming her rising suspicion that she was now, indeed, a prisoner.

It wasn't just the door that had led her to this conclusion, rather a collection of variables, all gathered within the handful of minutes since she'd awoken, tucked in with care in a massive bed piled with pillows and quilts. If the circumstances didn't seem so dire, she might've been impressed by the list of problems she'd managed to acquire in so short a period.

The most problematic being that she didn't know where she was. Or how she had gotten here. She was clean, her hair washed and braided, and someone had replaced her smoke- and bloodstained leathers with a gauzy nightdress—but she couldn't say who. The last thing she remembered clearly was meeting a woman claiming to be the Time Queen, and then... nothing. Just darkness.

A long line of windows spanned one wall of the apartment, curving in a way that reminded her of a tower. Just beyond, rolling green hills rose in the distance. It was summer, warm and sunny, lovely in the way that all Tempris summers were undeniably lovely.

That was also a problem.

It had still been spring when she'd left Ebondrift. Still cold and raining when she'd been dragged into that swirling portal, taken from a place that had been left to ruin and deposited at the gates of a palace that was too shining and new to exist anywhere on the ramshackle island she called home.

It was as if she had been plucked from one place, one *time*, and transported somewhere else, and that was a very big problem.

"Breathe," Taly murmured, squeezing her eyes shut. Yes, this place was impossible. That woman was... impossible. But she wasn't dead (yet). And she hadn't been recruited into some unknown, undead army (yet).

On the other hand, she was at the Time Queen's palace, being held in a locked room by the most vilified woman in all fey history. A woman that had committed wide-scale genocide of every known species in the Fey Imperium, whose actions had precipitated a centuries-long hunt for anyone unlucky enough to be born a time mage.

Which Taly was now. A time mage. *Fey*.

Turning from the door, she let her eyes drift over the room. She had two choices: she could stay and wait, see what her captors wanted and hope they meant her no harm; or, she could escape, and then figure out the solutions to all of her many problems from the relative safety of anywhere else.

She preferred option two.

Escape.

The word solidified in her mind as Taly strode further into the apartment. She was trapped and alone with no plan and no way out. Dread began to creep in, but she pushed it back, murmuring under her breath, "Just think about the next step." That's what Ivain had always said. "Don't panic. Don't get bogged down in the details. What's the next step?"

That was easy. She needed shoes. And weapons. Real clothes would also be nice, and she already had an idea where to find them.

The rooms flowed from one to the other, separated only by thick velvet curtains draped across each open doorway. There was a parlor, a music room, even a small library with an attached study—and inside the bedroom, hidden behind a panel that swung open when pressed, Taly found a corridor that ran around the back perimeter of the apartment, leading to those rooms that were typically set aside for personal use.

The carpet was soft beneath her bare feet as she made her way down the hallway, each side lined with more doors, all of them locked save for two. The first led to a washroom that was as grand as everything else in the apartment, and the other... well, it wasn't what she had expected to find, though Taly wasn't sure why she bothered being surprised as she stood wide-eyed and gaping in what had to be the largest closet she'd ever seen.

There were rows upon rows of corsets, and ballgowns, and dresses of every style and color.

Fashions she recognized, others she didn't, and some she had no words to describe.

It was all entirely impractical, of course. Too heavy and restrictive to allow for fighting or running.

Still, she thought, picking at the skirt of a nearby dress that looked as wide as a tent. It was a lot of fabric. Good quality too. Thickly woven.

Taly smiled as an idea began to form. The doors and windows were locked, but there had been a terrace. From what she could tell, she had been put in one of the palace towers. It was a long way down, but still... that was something she could work with.

Running her fingers along sleeves and ruffles of silk and lace, she picked up a pair of shears that she found tucked in a sewing basket along the way. Then, choosing a random gown, she began cutting the jeweled satin into strips.

When she'd reduced the dress to nothing but ribbons, she grabbed another, then another. She braided the delicate fabric, tied the woven cords end-to-end until she had the beginnings of a rope that she felt confident would hold her weight.

Never thought I'd be here, she thought as she ripped another dress off the rack. Granted, she had read her fair share of stories about princesses trapped in tall towers. Both fey and mortal alike had a strange fascination with locking their women up at high altitudes. But she'd never expected to find herself stuck in an actual tower, imprisoned by an evil queen.

But then again, her life had taken a lot of strange twists lately, so she kept cutting and ripping and weaving until she was surrounded by the decimated remains of dresses that, though lovely, would go on to serve a far better purpose than accompanying some snobby fey noblewoman to some equally pretentious ball.

Inspecting her makeshift rope, Taly jerked her head. “This’ll have to do,” she said, and stood, tugging off her nightdress as she set off in search of boots, pants, anything that didn’t have ruffles or lace. There was a flicker to her right, and she jumped, fumbling for the shears, for any kind of weapon, only to… stop.

And for a moment, she forgot about escaping from towers and evil queens as she turned to face the woman standing only a scant few feet away.

“Shards…” Taly whispered, slightly dazed when the woman’s lips moved in time with hers. She had known she looked different, had seen her reflection at the river’s edge. But here, in the light of day, utterly naked with nothing to hide behind…

A stranger. She hadn’t been prepared to see a stranger staring back at her from beyond the glass.

Lifting a hand, Taly traced the unfamiliar arch of her ear, then pulled at the skin of her face, trying to find something, some piece of her old self, that had escaped the transformation unscathed.

The color of her hair, the shape of her chin—those were still the same. And, maybe… yes—her nose was still just a little too long, and there was a bump on the bridge from when she’d fallen down the stairs as a child.

But everything else…

Her skin had turned a few shades paler, and her body, though curved in all the ways that a woman’s body should be curved, looked thinner. Prominent cheekbones, brows that arched in a way that was decidedly inhuman, and her eyes... No longer a human gray, her eyes were the color of storm clouds and smoke, steel and steam. In the dim light of the closet, they nearly glowed.

Taly took a breath—in and then out. *Clothes*, she reminded herself. She needed some real clothes, something a little sturdier than a nightdress or a ballgown.

Muttering a truly foul string of curses and feeling slightly better for it, she turned away from that beautiful, alien creature and began rifling through a large dresser set against the wall. There were drawers of lacy underwear, nightgowns as delicate as cobwebs, and more jewels than she had ever seen in a single collection.

After several minutes of frenzied exploration, she opened a drawer and smiled. "Finally." Simple, sturdy clothing—perfect for traveling.

She shimmied on a pair of leggings, shrugged on a shirt—both black—and then dug through the racks and racks of fine clothing until she found a lightweight, leather coat. Everything fit like it had been made for her, but she didn't let herself think too hard on that fact.

Since she hadn't found any weapons, she tucked the sewing shears into a pair of boots that were still too new to be comfortable and fastened her hair into a bun using jeweled pins that looked sharp enough to sting if it came down to a brawl. Then, grabbing her makeshift rope, she made her way back to the terrace.

There were two doors leading to a wide stone patio that wrapped around the whole of the tower. Each was ornately carved, inset with a long oval of leaded glass, and both were unlocked.

Probably because it was well over 300 hundred feet to the ground and jumping off the side of a tower was an objectively terrible idea.

Oh well.

A veil of that same warding magic surrounded the terrace, and it dimmed the sun, casting the entire area in shadow. Taly smirked a bit as she ghosted a hand across the slight shimmer that fell just inside the gray stone railing. Now that she was outside, that was an easy problem to fix.

Pulling the scissors, Taly crouched, levering up a loose stone. Rows of silver wiring ran underneath, and a few snips were all it took to have that veil dissolving, letting in the unfiltered light of day.

The sun was near blinding, and she flinched back into the shadows, holding up a hand.

Fey senses for this new fey body, and Shards, it was like she'd been living her entire life with a bag over her head—one that had suddenly been ripped away. Everything was too loud, too bright. Blue was now *blue*, and red was *red*. A balmy, summer breeze caressed her skin, bringing with it the smell of jasmine and freshly cut grass—the smell was so strong, it almost made her choke.

Breathing through her mouth, Taly forced her eyes open. The sky stretched out around her, and the gardens surrounding the palace were in full bloom, speckled with bright bursts of color. It chafed against her senses and made her head ache, but she staggered to her feet. She needed to hurry. There was no way to know when someone would come to check on her, and she needed to get into place.

Keeping her head down, she tied one end of the rope to the railing, letting the other dangle over the edge. And then instead of throwing herself off the side of a tower to what would most certainly be her death, she retreated back inside. This was the part where the princesses always got it wrong. Because the point of making a rope out of something like bedsheets or, in her case, dresses, wasn't about escaping. It was about making your captor believe you had.

Taly hurried to the front room, to the door that would open when someone came to see if she was awake.

Which she was, and she made sure they knew it by knocking and rattling the handle. The warding magic snapped against her skin, like a thousand tiny ants all stinging at once, but she ignored it. Her hands were still tingling as she slipped behind one of the heavy velvet curtains.

From somewhere within the apartment, a clock ticked away the seconds as Taly began to wait.

It didn't take long for the door to open, and metal clanked as something large and heavy lumbered past.

Mechanica armor, Taly thought, pressing her back flat against the wall. It had to be. She couldn't think of anything else that would sound that large or that heavy.

The armored suit moved farther into the apartment, but Taly didn't move. She didn't even dare breathe as she listened for its footsteps.

Stone grated, and she knew it had found the open terrace doors and clipped wires. The cloth rope had been left in plain sight, and when those heavy, lumbering footsteps reversed, rushing from room to room and back through the front door, Taly knew that her warden now believed her to be somewhere else in the palace. Maybe even splattered on the ground.

And since there was no reason to lock an unoccupied cage... Taly allowed herself a smile when she peeked from behind the curtain to find that the front door had been left wide open.

She didn't give herself time to revel in her victory as she half-ran, half-leapt down the spiraling steps, careening round and round until she hit the landing below.

Another hallway—lit with windows that spanned all of one side. She gave it a passing glance as she turned and—

Two hulking metal creatures spanned the length of the hallway, and Taly whirled only to find two more blocking her path.

A rough metal hand clamped down on her shoulder, and Taly yelped, twisting and pulling the shears from her boot in one fluid move—

Only to realize that this "weapon" would do very little against the thing that towered over her.

Against any of those now crowding around her.

At 10 feet tall, the Mechanica suits were bulky yet polished, and under any other circumstance, Taly would've thought them beautiful. Each piece of gold plate was inlaid with whorls of glistening blue, and the helms were decorated with metal horns twisted with silver.

But as they slowly advanced, caging her in, all she could see was the deadly blades on those horns and the cannons set into the gauntlets as they flashed red and white.

"I'm glad I set guards," said a surprisingly light female voice. "Her Majesty warned me that you were slippery."

Taly retreated a step, uselessly adjusting her grip on the shears as her back hit the wall.

"My Lady," that voice said again. The center one, though Taly couldn't be certain. The helms covered their faces. "I apologize for my tardiness. We did not know when you would wake."

When Taly didn't answer, just continued to grip those scissors like a lifeline, the center one stepped forward, metal clanking. "My Lady—"

"Stop calling me that!" Taly snapped. They were toying with her. She was sure of it. "Whatever it is you're here to do, just get on with it. Stop stalling." Her voice cracked.

The Mechanica tilted its strange, metal head, glancing at the others as it said, "As you wish, *Madam*." Like it was the form of address that was the issue here, and they had all just committed some grievous sin.

It took a step, then another, each one scraping harshly against the polished marble floor.

"Shit." Taly held the scissors out in front of her. Her hands began to shake.

A metal arm extended, and she braced herself for what was sure to be a murderous blow…

That never came.

Taly opened one eye, only then realizing that she had closed them. Still clutching her scissors, she could do nothing but gape as the group of Mechanica awkwardly bent at the waist and... *bowed.*

"The Queen respectfully requests your presence at tea," the woman in the center suit stated tersely.

Taly blinked. "What?"

"*Tea,* Madam," the woman repeated. A brief pause, and then the center suit shuddered. The pieces of armor clanked together loudly as it rose, the other armored suits quickly following. "Her Imperial Majesty has requested your presence at tea."

Taly was suddenly glad for the wall at her back, how *real* it felt when everything else was spinning out of control. A private audience with the Time Queen was the absolute last thing she wanted in this place that made no Shards-forsaken sense. This was the woman responsible for the Schism. A Genesis Lord. A High Lady. No sane, rational person would agree to this, and even though her grip on reality was starting to feel dangerously tenuous, she still considered herself to be both sane *and* rational.

"T-tell the Queen that I decline," Taly said, mustering that politeness Sarina had worked so hard to instill in her. "Respectfully."

"That is not a suitable answer," the woman in the center suit replied.

"Then I guess it's not a request." The words were out before Taly could think better of them.

The woman hesitated, then said, "Forgive me, Madam. The Queen respectfully *demands* your presence at tea."

"And if I still don't go?" Taly argued mulishly.

"Then I suppose I will be forced to carry you."

The Mechanica reached for her then, its metal body stiff and unyielding, but Taly flinched away, stabbing at it with her scissors.

It paused. "Do we make you uncomfortable, Madam?"

"Yes." Taly eyed the two cannons embedded in its metal gauntlets. "You could kill me in an instant. Of course, you make me uncomfortable."

The suit bobbed its head, the movement graceless and uncoordinated. "I apologize, Madam. We will make adjustments."

All around her, metal began to shiver and clank. The helmets were the first thing to fall, hitting the floor with sharp cracks. The arms came next as their whirring joints slowly spun to a stop and slipped out of socket. The legs shuddered, and the plating on the torsos began to cave as Taly watched the five hulking Mechanica abruptly collapse in on themselves, crashing to the floor in a tangled heap.

Tendrils of blue energy floated in the newly empty space, swirling chaotically as they began to take shape, forming themselves into the shape of a woman. Her face was smooth and featureless, and her dress looked like smoke as it clung to her nearly transparent form.

Behind her, four perfectly round orbs, each one as large as a child's head, hovered expectantly.

Fairy fire.

Spirits. Just like the ones she'd seen at the gates of the palace, the ghosts her mother had summoned to fend off Vaughn.

"Is this more to your liking, Madam?" the woman asked.

Taly blew out a slow breath, willing her heart to settle. "Strangely… yes. I still feel like you could kill me if you wanted to, but this is better than a giant suit of weaponized armor being powered by a ghost." Sensing that these things weren't going to hurt her—at least not yet—she took a tentative step forward.

"What are you exactly?" Taly asked as she began to circle the woman. "You don't look like the fairies that brought me here. Or like them." She nodded at the four orbs that still hovered nearby, silent.

The woman's head followed her, twisting at an unnatural angle. "I am the same as my brothers and sisters. I am a spirit, a manifestation of anima. However, unlike many of the fairies you will encounter here, I have chosen *not* to pass through the mists that separate our two realms. Your world degrades us, whereas this place preserves what is left of our generative force. Because of this, I still have my mind. I am nearly the same now as I was when I died, simply lacking a physical body."

"Who were you when you were alive?" It seemed like a reasonable question to ask a ghost.

"That is not important," the woman replied. "For now, you may call me Leto. I have been assigned to be your attendant during your stay. If there is anything you require, you need only ask."

Taly finally lowered the scissors. "I would like to leave. Can you show me the way home?"

"That is not possible."

"Why not? Am I a prisoner?"

"No," Leto answered matter-of-factly, her head still held at that impossible angle. "You are a guest of the Queen, and you will be given the freedom to roam the palace after you have spoken with Lady Raine. I apologize for any unease you may be feeling at present. That is my fault. I had hoped to be there when you awoke so that all this might be explained, but I was called away."

Taly shuddered at the thought of waking up to that hulking suit of armor looming over her bedside. "What about my weapons?" she asked, even if she already knew the answer. Her dagger, her pistols—each one a gift, a reminder of Skye. "A friend made those for me. I'd like them back."

"You will be allowed to arm yourself after you have spoken—"

"With Lady Raine." Taly scowled, shoving her scissors back in her boot.

"I'm so glad you understand," Leto said. Taly jumped when the fairy's body abruptly snapped back into its proper configuration. Smoke curled around her phantom form, slowly dissipating. "If that is all, Madam, I must start preparing you for tea. Your current garb is insufficient."

Taly kept a wary eye on the fairy as she was gently herded back up the stairs and through the apartment, ticking off the facts in her head. She still didn't know where she was, and she didn't know if there was a way out. She was unarmed and trapped inside this tower with the ghost of a woman she didn't fully trust. She was defenseless, and her magic—the one thing she might be able to use to protect herself—had gone quiet inside her. Not a spark, not an ember, not a single vision.

What's the next step?

That's what Ivain had always said, and in this case, it was easy. She needed to speak to the Lady Raine. After that, she would be in a better position to find a way out.

"Okay, Leto," Taly conceded, knees wobbling as she followed the woman into a small dressing room decorated in shades of blue and gold and pink. "You win. I guess I'm going to tea with the Time Queen." It sounded even more absurd coming out of her mouth than it had in her head.

Leto gave her a suspicious glance, as if she didn't quite believe Taly's sincerity—then inclined her head. "Very good, Madam," she said, drifting across the room. Her ethereal hands moved aside several draped panels of sheer blue gossamer, revealing yet another set of doors.

Ones Taly recognized.

That were already standing open.

Shit.

The fairy paused at the threshold, gazing into the ruined mess that used to be the closet. Shredded remains of fabric dusted the carpet, and empty hangers still swayed on the racks. Several drawers had been overturned, their contents spilled across the floor.

Leto turned, and even beneath that smooth, featureless face, Taly knew that the spirit wore a look of shock.

"This," Leto clucked in a way that sounded strangely like Sarina, "may take longer than I expected."

Somehow, Taly mustered a sheepish grin, shrugging as the fairy turned and began sorting through the wreckage.

CHAPTER 2

-An excerpt from When the Bridges Fell: Letters from a Lost Island

They're calling it the Schism now—the day the world broke apart. Most people, if you ask them, will say they remember the flashes of light, or the explosions, or the way the ground around the gates began to fall away. But me—I was at home that day, far away from any of the gates. All I remember is the ash. I thought it was snowing at first, but then I remembered it was summer.

-Author and recipient unknown. This letter is part of an unclaimed collection discovered after the evacuation of the mountain pass villages.

Taly's boots clicked on the gold-and-white checkered marble as she followed Leto down the darkened hallway. The ghostly woman drifted ahead of her, glowing softly. Her light expanded to fill the space, casting everything in shades of pale blue.

Leto had been circumspect in the information she gave. Tea was to be served in the Water Maze, though Taly had no idea what or where that was. And aside from the Queen and the fairies and now *her*, the palace was uninhabited. Something that seemed as absurd as it was wasteful for a place so large and grand.

Taly had read once that the Infinity's Edge complex boasted over 1,500 rooms, and those were only the ones that had been officially mapped. Enchantments were woven into the very stone, spells that made time and space twist and fold in on itself, concealing even more rooms and more treasures. It would be easy to get lost in such a place. Before the Schism, Ivain said that at least one person would go missing inside the palace every week.

Some were never found.

Taly took a long breath—in and then out—but her fingers still shook as she smoothed her hands over the supple velvet that hugged her waist. Growing up as the Marquess Castaro's ward, she was no stranger to finery. Sarina had always made sure that Taly's wardrobe was full of the latest mainland styles—pretty, feminine clothes made of rich fabrics that would've been better suited on some fey beauty. And yet it all paled in comparison to the ensemble Leto had cobbled together from the tattered remains of her tower closet.

A formal frockcoat spun from shadows and threaded with stars, a silky tunic as blue as the sea—both perfectly layered and draped over a pair of steel-gray leggings that flaunted every curve. Sapphires dotted her ears, and water magic darkened her lashes. A simple diadem painted a streak of silver through the graceful riot of golden curls that spilled over her shoulders.

She looked like a noble, like some proper highborn lady one might find roaming the halls of the Dawn Court, surrounded by a flock of sycophants and fellow courtiers. After spending so much of her life learning to accept her human imperfections, to stop idealizing the flawless beauty of the fey, seeing that beauty reflected in herself now… she still wasn't quite sure how that made her feel.

After what seemed like an eternity, they came to a long receiving hall flanked by doorways, columns, and little alcoves. Like everything else, it was empty, though it was easy to imagine lords and ladies milling about, each one waiting for an audience with the Queen. A set of massive oak doors stood at the opposite end, opening on silent hinges as they approached.

Taly blinked, raising a hand to shield her eyes as she stepped into the bright light of day. The formal gardens stretched into the distance—a kaleidoscope of color punctuated by gently rolling lawns of green candy-colored grass. The air was warm and fragrant, thick with aether.

So unlike the Tempris she knew, where even on the best days, highborn fey would still walk around gasping and complaining about the quality of the air.

They continued to walk, down pathways and stairs, through grottos and groves. Taly was sweating by the time they came to a large reflecting pool. Heavy bricks of white moss-covered stone formed a twisting path across the smooth surface, and a raised platform lined with trellises covered in bright-blue ivy floated in the center.

A water maze, Taly thought, almost smiling. And the trellises no doubt formed their own kind of labyrinth, one that occasionally reordered itself so that no one ever memorized the path. The fey loved puzzles, but they bored easily. They would never build something as static and unchangeable as a common garden maze, which is why it came as no surprise when Leto gave a command, and the blocks immediately regrouped, rippling the water as they scraped against each other to form a straight line.

Across the path and through the wide, wooden arch leading into the trellises, the leaves pulled back to let them pass and then closed behind them as they walked further into the maze. It wasn't long before Leto stopped beside a natural break in the hedges, inclining her head.

"I must leave you here," she said. "Her Majesty wishes to greet you alone."

Leto didn't wait for her reply before turning and drifting back through the hedges.

Taly watched her go, her heart thundering too fast and too loud in her new fey ears. She was tempted to run, even if the still-functioning part of her brain knew that would do her little good.

What's the next step?

Talking to the Queen. If she wanted to go home, that had to come next.

So, Taly took a breath, clenched her fists at her sides, and then stepped into the clearing.

Inside, a woman stood in a circle of white stone. Her ebony hair fell down her back in waves, and the pale pink of her dress shimmered in the sun. She wore no crown, nor any jewelry except for the pendant at her neck. A crescent moon set inside an unbroken circle—the symbol for the Time Shard.

The woman's face lit up when she caught sight of Taly still lingering at the edge of the clearing, and she rushed forward, arms extended. "Finally!" she exclaimed, beaming from ear to ear. "I was getting worried!"

Taly backpedaled, but the Queen caught her, pulling her into a bone-crushing hug.

The Lady Azura Raine was a giant of a woman—taller than Skye, maybe taller than Ivain—and even in heels, the top of Taly's head barely grazed the woman's chin. She kept her arms firmly at her sides, her body stiff. When the Queen took a merciful step back, her eyes flicked up and down in a way that made Taly feel as though she were being weighed and measured and somehow found lacking.

"Have you been eating well?" the Queen clucked with what seemed like genuine concern flashing behind those strange golden eyes. "You're thinner than you were the last time you visited. I'm always telling you: good nutrition is important. It shouldn't take you *three days* to recover from a little aether depletion."

The Queen squeezed her shoulders, and Taly squeaked, managing to wriggle away. *Three days*? She'd been asleep for three days? That couldn't be right.

The Queen followed Taly's retreat, still talking. "I've seen you in all manner of states, my dear—covered head to toe in blood, out of your mind from poison, and let's not forget that wyvern you left splattered across my throne room. But you've never been so low on aether that you just *collapsed.* I daresay, you had us all dreadfully worried. Especially when you wouldn't wake up."

Taly's back hit one of the trellises. That would explain why she couldn't remember anything, though it pained her to imagine collapsing right at the Queen's feet. If this woman had wanted her dead, that would've been her chance.

A small comfort, she supposed.

The Queen abruptly grabbed Taly's arm, looping it through her own. Taly was still too shocked to put up much of a fight as she was dragged from the clearing and into the hedges.

"Your Majesty," Taly finally managed to say. "I think—"

The Queen let out a sharp bark of laughter. "Since when do *you* call me *Your Majesty*? It's Azura. Or Az, if you feel so inclined. I keep forgetting this is your first time here, especially now that you look a little more like yourself."

"I don't know what that means," Taly mumbled weakly. She didn't understand any of this. Couldn't figure out just how this woman thought she knew her.

"As for Vaughn," the Queen went on, and it took Taly a moment to follow the rapid shift in subject, "he's always been a bastard. Ever since he was a child. And I know that's a horrible thing to say about a child, but, in his case, it's true. Your mother was the only one that could ever stand him for more than five minutes. Maybe that's why he took her betrothal to your father so badly. Shards, I really thought he was going to make a scene at the wedding. We all did."

Taly's thoughts were a jumbled mess, and she could feel a dull ache setting in behind her eyes as the Queen flitted from story to story. Azura knew about Vaughn and seemed personally acquainted with both her mother and father? Taly hadn't even been aware she still had a father. Her memories from before the fire were scattered at best. Little more than a tangle of half-remembered dreams already worn away by the passage of time.

They finally came to a small wooden and glass gazebo, and the Queen was still babbling—something about a blowfish, a bottle of tequila, and a top hat.

And Taly… well, she didn't particularly care about the blowfish or just how it had found itself inside the bottle. She was still trying to figure out just what a "*bachelorette party*" was and why this was something her mother had wanted when she found herself being pushed to sit on a gnarled wooden bench. Azura took a seat across from her, arranging her skirts beneath a matching table before she began picking at a tower of brightly colored pastries. There were cookies laced with frosting, cakes stuffed with cream, candied fruits, pocket pies, and little dots of chocolate and caramel everywhere.

"And that's when I said" —Azura paused to take a bite from a frothy cream puff— "Venny—he always hated it when I called him Venny. So I said,

Venny, Breena is a quality woman. You're never going to win her over with things like flowers or jewelry. If you want to woo her, get her the thing she really wants, the thing that *all* women *really* want. A dagger—sharp but still small enough to be worn to a ball."

Azura took another bite. "The gowns were so dreadfully tight back when your parents were courting. It was almost impossible to wear more than a few throwing knives beneath your skirts, never mind a decent short sword. Although, Breena... well, she was a creative one. I once saw her hide a rapier in a place where a rapier had no business being." The Queen laughed, then paused, her expression sobering. "Is there something wrong?" She eyed Taly like there was, indeed, something wrong. "Why aren't you eating? I've never known you to turn down sugarberry tart before."

"I... um..." Taly reached for the piece of pink quartz around her neck, glad that Leto had let her keep it. Her mother's necklace. She felt the familiar divot in the center as she rasped, "Sugarberries are fine." More than fine. She loved sugarberries—had, on more than one occasion, forced Skye to escort her through the Seren Gate to the nearby town of Marin for the First Harvest Festival just so she could gorge on sugarberry confections.

But that begged the question: how did the Queen know that?

How did the Queen know her at all? Taly had never been inside the palace before, much less met the woman that used to sit on its throne.

"I'm confused," Taly said, even though it felt like an understatement. She was more than confused. She had lost the thread of the conversation a long time ago—alongside her grip on reality. "Who is Venny? And how did you know my mother? How do you know Vaughn?"

Azura's lips pursed, and she carefully set the half-eaten pastry in her hands on a delicate golden plate. "Oh, dear," she murmured. "Oh, dear, dear, dear, dear, dear… You said you would know next to nothing when you got here, but I didn't think it would be this bad." Azura fixed her with a look. "Am I to understand that you don't know who your parents are?"

Taly shook her head.

"Or why you're here?"

Another shake of her head.

"Or who's invading your island?"

That was also a good question—one Taly also didn't know the answer to.

She shook her head.

"I can only assume then," Azura said, "that you know nothing about our arrangement."

"Why would I have an arrangement with a terrorist?" The words were out of her mouth before she could stop them, and Taly's stomach gave a sickening lurch when the Queen raised a brow.

"I see that mouth of yours has always been a problem." Azura leaned back in her chair, smiling. "If I'm being perfectly honest, my dear, I was hoping that was one aspect of your personality that developed later in life. Shards only know how many problems it's caused."

Taly chewed on her lip. Azura wasn't wrong. Sarina was always telling her to think before she spoke.

Azura sighed and pinched the bridge of her nose. "I suppose we'll start with the basics," she said as if it pained her to do so. "You, my dear, are a time mage. Not the first to be born since the Sanctorum started hunting our kind, but thanks to your mother's ingenuity and a little intervention on my part, the first to survive to adulthood."

Taly stared at her palm, the place where that little moon-shaped scar used to be. The skin was smooth, unmarked. The runes, what little had remained of her mother's enchantments, had been wiped away. "My mother made me look human."

Azura shook her head. "Your mother didn't just make you *look* human. She made you bleed like a human, grow like a human, move like a human. She had your body so convinced it was mortal, your blood used iron instead of aether. Or at least it used to, until the spells began to break down." Azura reached into her pocket, producing a small shadow crystal that she placed in the center of the table. "The anchor for your mother's spells. I thought you might like to keep it. The enchantment matrix was so old that once I removed it, what little magic was left crumbled."

Taly reached out a trembling hand, carefully picking up the crystal. She had carried this with her for fifteen years without knowing it. It felt strange to be holding it now—one of the few items of her mother's she had left.

Azura went on, "You've been here before—many times, along with your entourage. However, due to the unusual nature of this place, we're a bit out-of-sync—chronologically speaking, that is. You never show up in the right order."

"What does that mean?"

"It means that while I've known you for a very long time, you do not know me. Not yet, at least.

Time mages experience the world differently, especially in places like this where the normal rules of time and space don't apply."

Taly clenched her hand around the crystal. An anchor—this had been an anchor, and that's exactly what she needed now. "We know each other," she said. Not a question, though she still couldn't quite wrap her head around the concept. She grasped at a flicker of memory, something Azura had said at the gates. "Are we friends?"

"Of course."

"But you committed genocide. How could I ever be friends with you, knowing what you did?"

Bold words—far bolder than she felt.

But the Queen just chuckled, looking at her with the fondness one might hold for a pet. "And there's that mouth again," she said. "And that frown. You know, I'm always telling you—it doesn't matter if you're immortal, you're going to get wrinkles if you keep frowning like that."

Taly's brows nudged together even further, deepening said frown. "You're insane."

"Yes," Azura replied easily. "And if you ask me, that's better than…" She waved a hand in the direction of Taly's face. "Whatever *that* is. You're always so serious. Always need to know every little thing. You're always saying *'Azura, this isn't the time'* or *'Azura, that's inappropriate'* or *'Azura, please stop rambling; you're giving me a headache.'* You're always so predictable, and I'm not saying that just because I can see the future." She pointed an accusing finger. "You, my dear, are a fun-killer."

"I am not," Taly snapped back. Shards, how had they gotten here?

"Yes, you are," Azura countered childishly. "In fact, by the authority vested in me as the High Lady of Time, I dub thee *'Lady Caro, Killer of Fun.'* There—now it's official." She pouted, reaching for another cookie. "No wonder Skye always looks so bored when he's here. Poor boy probably never gets to go out and play—not with Lady Fun-Killer attached to his hip."

Taly shook her head. She wasn't going to ask. Didn't care about this madwoman's ramblings. "Look," she said, placing a hand flat on the table, "I don't know how I got here, or even where *here* is. And to be perfectly honest, I don't give a shit. About any of it—you, the Schism, this future version of me that apparently has no problem with the fact that you killed millions. I just want you to send me home."

"Don't be ridiculous. You can't leave."

"So, I'm a prisoner then?" Taly arched a brow, amazed that her voice remained so even.

"A prisoner?" Azura barked out a laugh. "What makes you think you're my prisoner?"

"I was brought here against my will, and now you won't let me go. Even by the loosest definition, I'm pretty sure that makes me your captive."

"You know," Azura said, tapping a finger to her lips, "you said that you were going to say that. Well, not *you* you. The other you—the one that grows into someone worth knowing. And granted, I didn't believe you— *her?* —at the time. After all, our visits are always so pleasant, and she made a special trip just to make sure your rooms were prepared. Brought along the loveliest bottle of brandy. Actually, now that I think about it, that's probably how she talked me into loaning you so many of my jewels."

Taly eyed the ring on her finger—an obscenely large emerald surrounded by a nest of gold. She hated wearing rings, but she'd been drawn to it immediately. It was the same color as Skye's eyes. "Are you insinuating that I'm complicit in my own captivity?"

"Well, you did ask me to train you, so… yes—it seems that your current state of *captivity* is entirely your fault, and that makes me feel quite a lot better, so thank you. Given your age and unusual set of circumstances, your education will be unorthodox, to say the least. I was starting to feel marginally guilty, and it was a very unpleasant emotion."

Taly leaned back. "I asked you to train me," she murmured to herself.

Though it didn't stop Azura from muttering, "Have we really not established that yet?"

"And if I said I no longer wanted your help?"

"Oh, I gave my word, dear. I never go back on my word."

"But you gave your word to me. A future version of me, but still me, and I'm telling you, *right now*, to let me go. You're not breaking any vows."

Azura paused, considering. "Well, that is a conundrum," she said at last. "Oh, it makes my head hurt. Are you the same Talya Caro as the one I know, or are you different, in which case which woman's wishes take precedence? Would the fabric of the universe come crashing down if I allowed you to deviate from the path I know my friend is supposed to follow, or would the timelines stabilize? Would there be an entirely different universe that grew from the divergence, with another you and another me?" There was a pause, and a sly smile slowly spread Azura's lips. "You would know these answers if you had even a basic knowledge of time magic."

Shit. She'd walked right into that one, albeit unknowingly. "I want to go home," Taly tried again.

"Don't be ridiculous." Azura reached for an empty plate. "You will stay here," she said, piling the plate high with an assortment of cakes and cookies, "until I say you can leave."

Taly eyed the plate that was placed in front of her. Her stomach gave a vicious growl, reminding her that it had been literal days since she'd last eaten. "And when will that be?"

Azura began to fill her own plate. "Eat, dear. You really are nothing but skin and bones. Any thinner, and I'll be able to see right through you."

Taly obeyed, taking a shaky bite of what appeared to be sponge cake. Something in the back of her mind cataloged the taste and texture—both more exquisite than anything she remembered from her human life. "You still haven't answered my question. How long do you intend to keep me here?"

"And there goes Lady Fun-Killer again," Azura said, waving her fork imperiously. "Can't we have one conversation where you don't try to talk business? The humans have a saying about all work and no play, and even though they don't get many things right, they were right in this one instance, so *eat*, my dear. You're going to need your strength."

Something rattled from behind the hedges, and Azura's eyes abruptly flicked away. "Finally!" she exclaimed, smiling brightly. "The tea is here! But... oh my." Her expression wilted when Leto drifted into the clearing pushing a gilded tea caddy. "Why aren't you wearing your uniform?" she whispered, glancing at Taly nervously. "It's her first time here, remember? She's not used to seeing all of you just… floating around."

The ghostly woman bowed. "Forgive me, Majesty, but the armor caused her Ladyship great distress."

"What?" Azura looked to Taly, then reached into a pocket hidden inside the seam of her skirts, pulling out a worn, leather notebook. Loose leaves of paper had been stuffed between the dog-eared pages, and stains spotted the spine. "Oh dear…" she muttered as she frantically rifled through the pages. "Oh dear, oh dear, oh… Here it is!" She tapped the page. "It says right here: *no armor*. Leto, why didn't you remind me?"

"I did, Majesty."

"Fairies lie, Taly." Azura shoved her plate away, making room for her journal on the table. "No one told me! Absolutely no one, and I just wanted everything to be perfect." She turned the page. "What else have I forgotten?" Another page. "Tell me, Taly—what else have I forgotten?"

"I… I don't know." Taly glanced at Leto, who just shook her head, turning away as she busied herself with the tea. "I've never been here before. In fact, I still don't know where *here* is. We haven't covered that yet."

Azura sniffed as she reached for a lavender tea cake. "We're in a garden, dear. Shards, you didn't mention just how slow you used to be."

Leto poured the tea with a practiced hand, serving the Queen first before offering Taly a teacup painted with gold. She eyed the amber liquid warily before taking a tentative sip, sighing at the taste. Reysang tea—one of her favorites, though the flavor seemed off somehow. Stronger, more nuanced than it would've been to a human tongue. She could taste the minerals in the water, the slight tang of gold from the rim of the cup. She could even taste the smoke from the ovens that had been used to dry the leaves.

Leto leaned down and began whispering in the Queen's ear.

"It's that late already?" The journal snapped shut. "My, time did get away from me today." Azura rose from her seat. "We need to go. *Now.*"

Taly let out a yip when Azura reached down and yanked her to her feet. The teacup flew from her hands and promptly shattered on the white paving stones. "What the hell is going on now?"

The Queen said nothing as she proceeded to march them back through the garden and across the stone pathway that bridged the reflecting pool. Leto followed close behind, still pushing the tea caddy and what little remained of the pastry tower.

"Oh, dear," Azura muttered. "I was hoping to avoid this conversation for a few more days, but I always seem to lose track of time when we get to talking."

They started back up the avenue, the palace rising in the distance. Even though it was nowhere near sunset, the sky was already turning dark, the remaining light rapidly waning.

Taly jerked her arm, but Azura's grip held firm. "You're hurting me," she bit out, stumbling on the main stairs. She would've fallen, but the Queen dragged her back to her feet.

With each step, Azura's back seemed to straighten, her expression turning colder. "While you're here," she said, not a bit out of breath, "there is just one rule. Do not leave the palace after 18 bells. Lock your doors. Lock your windows. Do not go outside. If you leave the palace's protection, I will no longer be able to guarantee your safety."

They burst through the main doors of the palace, barreling through a dense throng of fairy fire waiting on the other side. There were hundreds of them, and their smoky blue forms filled the vast chamber, bell-like voices echoing off the walls in a deafening clamor.

Halfway across the hall, Azura finally released Taly's arm, and she lurched back, rubbing at her bicep and what would surely be a bruise come morning. The Queen looked different than she had before. Her entire demeanor had transformed and hardened, every trace of softness gone. She held up a hand, and the fairies abruptly quieted—like an orchestra following a conductor's command.

"I just want to go home," Taly said in the silence. "Please, just... just send me home. I don't know who this person is that you think you know, but it's not me."

The Queen began to circle her, heels clicking on the checkered marble floor. Taly swore she felt the ground shudder.

"You are a time mage, Talya." Clear, precise words, devoid of warmth but not unkind. "And I am your High Lady. For a human, that means very little. I realize that. But you are no longer human, and if it is my wish that you stay here and train, then you will obey."

"And what if I don't?" Taly raised her chin defiantly. "You can make me do a lot of things, but you can't make me obey."

Azura's answering smile was a thing of frightening beauty. "Is that so? Well then, far be it from me to *force* someone into my care." Her tone was far too sweet. "If you really value your life so little," she said, waving at the wide double doors that still hung open, "then by all means."

Taly's eyes went wide. This woman made no sense. She was erratic, unstable, inconsistent... "But you said—"

"Forget what I said," Azura chirped imperiously. "Go. Before I change my mind and decide to let you spend the night in my dungeon."

"Majesty," Leto interjected softly. She stood off to the side, her ghostly hands gripping the tea caddy. "Is that—"

"Do not interfere, Leto," Azura warned. The fairy hung her head.

Taly searched the Queen's expression, but it was a look she knew all too well. She had seen it countless times, plastered on the faces of the highborn nobility. Pleasant and deceptively blank—it was a look that gave away nothing.

Taly took a cautious step towards the door, ignoring the hushed whispers of the fairies. Between staying here with an all-powerful god of a woman whose sanity seemed to be teetering on the edge of a fathomless abyss and going home—she chose home.

Yes, there was the Sanctorum. And Vaughn. And the shades. But she would deal with those problems as they arose. There were plenty of places to hide on the island. She would figure out a way to get by.

Another step. When Azura made no move to stop her, Taly broke into a sprint, heading for the door and the freedom waiting just on the other side.

Beyond the towering arch, dark clouds streaked a blood-red sky, and the scent of smoke carried on the wind. Thunder rumbled from every direction.

Taly stopped just outside the door, eyes on the horizon.

Lights flickered in the distance, too bright to be stars, too sparse for city lights.

Snow began to fall from the sky.

Except… no. Not snow.

Taly held out a hand, watching as something downy and black fluttered into her palm. “Ash,” she whispered.

And then the world exploded.

The sound was deafening, the wash of light that devoured the land near-blinding.

And it repeated, over and over and over again.

The air clogged with ash, and Taly choked. The ground shook, and she began to stumble. The stairs to the palace were falling away as the land buckled and broke, destruction rolling in from every direction.

There was another mighty *boom,* and Taly’s legs buckled as she began to fall, thrown sideways—

A rough hand grabbed her by the collar, and she barely managed to stifle a scream as she was yanked back onto her feet and into the palace, away from the door and the rain of chaos that was quickly unfolding.

It was silent inside the palace. Completely still. The explosions still rumbled, but it was like distant thunder.

"You're safe," the Queen said softly, *soothingly.* It was only then that Taly realized she was shaking. "We are all safe so long as we stay inside the palace. Look."

Taly looked to where she pointed. Beyond the doorway, pillars of smoke speared the air, and violent flashes of white light cracked open the sky. Ash swirled in the air and pelted the ground, but it all stopped at the palace doors, as though there was an invisible line.

"What is that?" Taly breathed.

Azura gazed impassively out the doorway. "That was the reason I told you not to go outside. And before you ask, yes—that will be happening every night."

"Every night?" Taly edged farther away from the door. "How? Why?"

"Oh, did I forget to mention?" Azura watched her retreat. "This is a time loop."

"A what?"

"*A time loop*," Azura repeated, enunciating each word as though she were talking to a small child. "Imagine time as a length of string. Now, if someone were to cut out a portion of that string and tie it in a circle—that's where we are. This is a single day, repeating over and over without end."

Taly worked her tongue, trying to translate thought into speech. But the words wouldn't come. She was paralyzed, rooted to the spot. Helpless to do anything but watch as the world outside crumbled and burned.

"Which day?" Azura offered. "You were about to ask it. Or wanted to."

"Which day?" Taly parroted weakly.

Azura gave a soft, sad sigh, her eyes still on the door. Like she wanted to look away but couldn't. "This is the day the world ended. By my own hand."

Those words settled in her like a stone, and for a moment, Taly stopped seeing the vast marble hall, the rolling destruction at her back. She stopped hearing the explosions, the ones she now realized weren't really explosions.

They were gates closing abruptly, each one a bridge connecting two worlds separated by time and space. Without the proper shutdown protocols, the two sides of that portal would crash back together, forcing all the air and physical matter that used to occupy that artificial space in-between away in one explosive outburst.

There was another blast, louder than all the rest. Closer.

She knew now why they called it the Schism. It sounded like the ground, like the very world, was breaking apart.

"So, all this time," Taly said, mustering anger in the absence of courage, "you've been here? While the time mages were being hunted, while the Sanctorum was destroying the island—you were *here*? Reliving… what? Your greatest triumph? Time Queen victorious because fuck everyone else?"

"I would hardly call this a triumph," Azura said. The ash was collecting on the ground outside, piling up against the veil of protective magic. "More like an unfortunate necessity."

Taly sneered. Millions of people had died that day; the world had never been the same. And this woman talked like it was little more than an inconvenience. "You're a monster," she spat.

"I know."

The words were so soft, Taly almost missed them.

Azura finally turned away from the door. "This is what I'm talking about," she said tiredly. "You're always so serious, always making me talk about things I'd rather not revisit. Lady Fun-Killer you are, Vanquisher of Joy. Maybe I should get you a little sash. Those do eventually come back into style."

A sudden giggle bubbled up, and Azura waved a hand as the fairies began to chatter and disperse.

Outside, chaos reigned.

"You will not escape," Azura called back. Her steps were slow and measured as she retreated down the hall, a row of fairies trailing behind. "It's pointless to even try. There are many doors and pathways that lead in and out of this place, and I control every single one. I decide who comes and who goes, where and when. You're here until I say you can leave."

Taly ran after her. "And when will that be?" she asked, not even trying to hide the desperation in her voice. "How long do you intend to keep me here?"

Azura paused, and for a moment, Taly thought she wasn't going to answer. That she would deflect the question the same way she had in the garden. But then she said, "When you earn your third training designation, I will send you home. You have my word."

Taly stumbled to a stop in the middle of the hall. "But that could take years," she rasped. Skye had been 16 when he earned his third seal—that was 11 years of training, and he'd been a special case. He'd had Ivain—one of the greatest living shadow mages—working with him day in, day out. It took most fey far longer.

She'd be forgotten by then. Given up for dead by all that knew her.

Azura's expression softened. "Don't worry. Time moves differently here. Skye and the rest of your family—they'll hardly notice you're gone.

"And speaking of family…" Her eyes dropped. "I almost forgot." Without warning, Taly's necklace was ripped away.

"No." Taly grasped at the necklace, frantic. "That was my mother's."

Azura held the chain just out of reach. "And who do you think gave it to her?"

Taly stopped reaching. She barely felt it when the tears began to fall. Her mother's necklace. The Queen had managed to taint even that.

The Queen once again turned, offering no explanation as she began to walk away.

"You seem tired, Madam." Leto's voice was melodic and soothing, and she placed a gentle hand on Taly's shoulder. The buzz of aether made her teeth sing. "Would you like to retire for the night?"

Taly nodded wordlessly, allowing herself to be pulled to the side, towards a door she didn't recognize.

"Everything will look better in the morning," one of the fairies whispered sympathetically as they passed.

"She's really not that bad," another chimed.

"Yes, she is," came a tinkling mutter. "But you get used to it."

A murmur of agreement rippled through the crowd.

But Taly had already stopped listening.

She was trapped.

That thought kept repeating in an endless loop.

She was trapped in a strange place with an even stranger woman. Trapped until she could complete a task that could take years.

As she trudged after Leto, she felt each one of those years opening up in front of her, a dark, yawning chasm from which she couldn't escape.

CHAPTER 3

-From the personal notes of Azura Raine, High Lady of Time

Her name will be Talya, and she will be just a girl, chosen because she was unlucky enough to be born when I needed a champion.

His name will be Skylen, and he will be just a boy, chosen because he was unlucky enough to fall in love when I needed a sacrifice.

I hope that one day they will be able to forgive me for the things that I have done. For the things that I will force them both to endure.

Skylen Emrys, future Duke of Ghislain and acting commander of the Gate Watchers, leaned against the parapet of the compound wall, staring out into the gray haze of morning.

It had been five days since the attacks began, and the city of Ebondrift spread out before him—a broken husk. The winding streets were littered with rubble, doors of nearby buildings hung askew, windows had been broken. Just below, what used to be a bustling market square lay in ruins, a few tatters of smoke-stained cloth the only hint at what had only a week before been a colorful sprawl of canvas awnings.

The situation had only grown worse since Taly went missing. They were being attacked nearly every day with lethal precision, and the leadership was still fractured on whether to stay or go. The holdouts wanted to stay in Ebondrift, but, as Skye had continued to argue, that wasn't an option. Their supplies were rapidly dwindling, and, as last night's battle had once again proven, their walls had been breached.

The skirmish had been brief but devastating. The shades had somehow managed to infiltrate the underground tunnels beneath the compound, and due to a mistake in the guard rotation that Skye still couldn't explain, the entrance beneath the keep had been left unguarded.

The first few minutes were a slaughter. Since the lower levels of the keep stayed warmer in the winter months, mortals and magicless—those more prone to disease—had been assigned to the undercroft. Almost twenty men died within the first few minutes, and the shades were already slicing through the mortal camp by the time a nearby contingent of mages was able to push back the swell of undead. Skye and a few others had spent the rest of the night clearing out the tunnels and trying to find out who had dismissed the guards.

The search had been fruitless so far. Despite Kato's suspicions and Taly's abrupt departure, there were still traitors in their midst. Which meant that even if Taly was in league with their enemy—albeit unwillingly—she wasn't the only one.

"You look like shit."

Skye snorted, turning to face the dark-haired woman trudging up the stairs behind him. Even after five days of trying to restore order in a world gone mad, Eula was a sight. Her hair was coiled neatly around her head, and despite the dark shadows beneath her eyes, her scaled leather armor was clean, the sword at her waist polished to a shine.

When faced with conflict, some people crumbled. Eula, however—she just worked harder and longer and worst of all, she made it look easy.

Skye picked at a streak of dirt on his sleeve. After spending all night down in the tunnels beneath the keep, he'd only had enough energy to wipe away the blood before redonning his armor and preparing for the day ahead.

"Good morning to you too," he said, forcing a smile.

"I thought you said you were going to try to get some sleep after last night," she chided, coming to stand beside him.

Skye grimaced. "You're right. I did say that." And, to his credit, he had tried. But just like every night before, he couldn't bring himself to go back to a room and a bed that still smelled like *her*. Taly. His friend and the woman that always seemed to be leaving him behind.

"Skylen," Eula said, and he had to resist the urge to roll his eyes. He knew that tone. All the women in his life had somehow mastered *that* tone. "We have a long day ahead of us, and you're our commander. We need you at your best."

It wouldn't matter, Skye almost said, but thankfully didn't. Eula was just doing her job, trying to account for the variables they could control. And if she wanted to believe that a few hours of tossing and turning might make any damn difference, he saw no harm in letting her. The journey to Ryme would be long and dangerous, and they weren't ready. But the longer they stayed, the more they opened themselves up to further sabotage, maybe even another attack.

By now, they were both tired of building funeral pyres, each one larger than the last.

"I'm fine," he said.

"No, you're not," Eula immediately replied. "You're thinking about Taly. You're wondering if you did the right thing."

Skye's jaw clenched, and he leaned forward, watching as the first of the wagons began rolling out of the gates. He'd told Eula the same thing he'd told all the others—that he had sent Taly to find the relay. It was a lie, of course. But nobody had questioned him. Not to his face, at least.

"It might have been a mistake," Eula said after a moment, misinterpreting the guilt in his expression. "But I believe in Taly. She's smart, tougher than anyone gives her credit for, and she's good with a gun. I'd bet good coin she's already found her way to Ryme, and when she finds out how much you've been worrying, she'll laugh herself silly."

Skye attempted a smile. He hoped, but he knew she wasn't going to be there. He knew because she wasn't really his scout. She wasn't heading for the relay. She had left him behind, lied to him about why, and all the evidence that had come out since then… Kato had discovered spells inscribed on her arm, a web of shadow magic hidden beneath a glamour so complex, it was nearly undetectable. And while he didn't know the substance of those spells, there were so many terrible things a shadow mage could do to another person. Ways to take away their free will, to make them act against their family and friends. To erase the memories of those trespasses.

Taly was working with the enemy. He truly believed that, as much as he believed that she had been forced into the role unwillingly. And while that distinction might not matter to the people who had lost their homes, their families, demanding that blood be repaid with blood—it did to him. Which is why he had lied for her. Protected her. And once they made it to Ryme, once he delivered these people to safety, he would be free to go find her—and bring her back kicking and screaming if that's what it took.

"As for your brother," Eula went on, "he's still convinced Taly is a traitor."

"Still?" Skye asked. He had done everything he could to assuage his brother's concerns. He had told so many lies.

Eula nodded. "Yes. I've been told he's been questioning the ensigns, and even though I don't think it was his intent, rumors are starting to spread. About you. And Taly." She gave him a meaningful look.

Skye swallowed, turning back to the market square down below. "I see."

"Yes," Eula sighed, frowning as she followed his gaze. The first of the wagons were being wheeled out of the compound gates, only half loaded.

Skye said, "Rumors have brought down entire households, and we can't afford to be divided right now. Is this going to become an issue?"

Eula shook her head. "Surprisingly, no. I think it may have actually increased your popularity among the ensigns. Taly is a beautiful human, and you're a highborn noble—they think it's one of those cheap coppershop romance novels, and for now, I don't see any problem giving them something better to talk about than the army of corpses trying to beat down our door. Your brother, however..."

"You think there's a problem?"

"Yes... No... Maybe?" Another sigh. "Kato—he means well, but there's too much anger there. Too much misguided loyalty. He's convinced himself that Taly is a threat to this island and this organization, and I'm not sure what it's going to take to change his mind. I'm afraid that if he keeps poking at this issue, he might do some real damage. Something more severe than a bit of gossip."

Skye pressed his lips together. Kato's suspicions were valid, and a part of him respected his older brother's attempts to do what he thought was right. It was honorable, if inconvenient.

Eula placed a hand on his shoulder. "We're going to get through this," she said, though Skye couldn't be certain if it was for his benefit or hers. "Let's get these people back to Ryme, and then, once we're safe, once we find Marquess Castaro and start trying to sort through this mess, I'm going to help you find your girl. Even if she didn't make it to the relay, she's still a damned hero for trying."

Skye snorted, leaning against the parapet wall as he watched Eula make her way down the walkway, towards the stairs. "Taly's not *my* anything," he called out, "and I'm pretty sure she would skin you if she ever heard you refer to her as belonging to anyone for any reason."

Eula gripped the staircase railing, smiling over her shoulder. "Maybe," she said. "But I have a feeling that, in this case, she might not mind." That smile widened in a way that made Skye distinctly uncomfortable. "Just a bit of friendly advice—the next time the two of you decide to go at it between the library stacks, be a little quieter. That's how rumors get started."

Skye cleared his throat, resisting the urge to tug at his collar when he felt his neck start to flush. "I'll keep that in mind," he said, not bothering to come up with a lie. He was done trying to pretend he wasn't in love with his best friend—the girl he had known since she was six and he was ten.

A clamor rang out from inside the keep, followed by a shout. They both looked towards the sound of the commotion.

Skye asked, "Is that—"

"Yup." Eula sounded tired. It was the Riette sisters—the final two holdouts of the Gate Watcher leadership still arguing to stay at the compound. The youngest was becoming increasingly hysterical, demanding to speak with the *"damned person in charge."*

That was Skye, and he felt a stark sense of relief when Eula gave a weary shake of her head and said, "I'll take care of it. You just make sure you're ready for today. Take whatever time you need, do whatever you need to do. I know it's been hard, especially with Taly not here and Kato trying to stir up trouble. I know you weren't expecting to become a leader so soon. But you stepped up when we needed you, Skye. And you've done well. As well as anyone could've done with the same shit situation. Leaving is the right decision. Don't let anyone make you doubt that."

"Thank you," Skye said, and meant it.

Even if it did little to stop him from doubting.

CHAPTER 4

-From the personal notes of Kato Emrys

The 1st day of the month Janus, during the 251st year of the Empty Throne

My brother is lying to me. I'm sure of it. He says that he sent the human girl away—that the enchantment matrix I discovered was a known quantity, created to cover the scent of a few healing spells. And yet the more I dig, the more people I question, the more the variables don't add up.

No one saw her leave, and she didn't requisition any supplies. There was no escort assigned to see her to the edge of the city. Even disregarding my other suspicions, I find it unlikely that my brother would've sent this girl on such a mission so unprepared.

I will admit, there's a part of me that wants to believe Skylen's story. I liked her, this Talya Caro, and Shards know it's been a long time since I could say that about anyone. But I can't shake the feeling that my brother is hiding something. Not with the way I saw him looking at her. Our kind do not love easily. We are too long-lived, too territorial, and even though it's been centuries since I sent Sarah away, I still remember that feeling. I remember how much it burned—how easy it would've been to sacrifice everyone and everything, including honor.

I won't let Skylen go down that road. Not when there are so many lives at stake. So, I will continue to investigate. Play the villain, if need be. Even though the human is already gone, beyond our ability to retrieve, if my brother has allowed sentimentality to come before duty, then he is unfit to lead.

The sun continued to rise, and the refugees filed out of the compound, wending between the line of wagons in the early morning mist. If the final count was accurate, 2000 men and women had decided to make the journey.

For most, the choice had been easy. The Gate Watchers' compound had been breached; its walls were crumbling. The few that had decided to stay would be defenseless, with no weapons, no supplies, and only a handful of trained fighters. Skye had tried to convince them to come—had kept trying until the compound gates closed behind them, locks sliding into place.

To no avail.

As they slowly moved through the broken city, checking alleyways and empty buildings for shades or anything else that might be lurking, Skye sent up a silent prayer to whatever might be listening. With fewer people, fewer resources, hopefully, the compound would no longer be a target.

Hopefully, he hadn't just doomed them to die.

They made it out of the city and onto the main highway without incident; the few groups of shades they encountered were easily dispatched. Away from the coast and up through the southern grasslands, the carts groaned and rattled.

Skye had ordered the Gate Watchers to strip the city of everything that might be useful. The main aether core was packed away safely, as well the compound's flash cannons. Food, supplies, spell books, enchanting tools—they'd brought anything they might need should they make it to Ryme only to find that there was nothing left.

Midday came and went. They were making good time, and by some stroke of luck, the protective wards lining the highway were still intact. Skye might've felt optimistic if he wasn't currently ankle-deep in mud.

"Shit," he grunted when his boots slipped. He sunk even further into the mud as he readjusted his grip on the edge of the wagon. The jagged metal bit into his skin. "Shit, shit, shit."

A similar string of cursing drifted from the other side of the wagon, followed by a "Ready?" Eula's voice was thin and punctuated by heavy gasps.

"Yeah," Skye panted. He pulled at the meager supply of aether in the air, using it to bolster his strength. His lungs burned, his muscles ached, he couldn't remember ever being this Shards-damned tired. The fatigue had become a physical weight, dragging at his every step.

But he couldn't stop, couldn't let himself break. These people had trusted him with their lives—he wouldn't let them down.

The wind was biting cold, but the sun felt hot. Skye wiped at the sweat collecting on his brow, not caring about the streaks of mud left behind.

"Lift."

At Eula's command, Skye dropped into a crouch and heaved, lifting the wagon out of the mire. The fatigue coupled with the truly massive weight of the wagon and its cargo had his knees shaking, threatening to give way.

"Almost there," someone called from the front. The horses bucked, pulling against the reins as a young water mage led them forward. Even though the rain had let up, parts of the road were still flooded. This wasn't the first time they'd had to stop to free one of the wagons from a ditch.

Eula cried out, and the wagon jerked as she lost her grip. With a rumbling groan, Skye shoved his shoulder into the side of the cart and pushed. Sweat soaked the shirt beneath his armor. His hands were bleeding, and something in his bicep tore.

But he continued to push, to pull, to lift.

More aether. The air was so thin; it was getting hard to breathe.

The wagon lurched before falling back.

Another jerk—Eula had resumed her position.

More mages fell in beside him, and they all began to push, groaning and grunting, slipping in the mud.

Just keep moving. The words Skye had repeated to himself so many times he'd lost count. There was always more to do, someone that needed something. The knocks on his door, the taps on his shoulder, the never-ending litany of questions and concerns and complaints.

But he kept moving forward, never stopping, never resting.

Little by little, inch by inch, the wagon began to move until—

Skye grunted when the cart abruptly pitched forward, and he stumbled. Several of the mages gave similar cries, slogging through the mud as they continued to push.

Rubbing at the rapidly healing cuts on his palms, Skye stepped to the side, content to watch now that they had managed to free the wagon from the watery ditch.

Crescent Canyon was only a few miles up the road, and the terrain was already becoming more densely wooded as they moved out of the grassland and back into the forest. People milled about, catching their breath. Like him, they were coated in a combination of sweat, mist, and mud. The sick and injured rode on top of the wagons, some taking refuge underneath tattered tarps that billowed in the wind. Everyone else walked.

"We can't keep going like this," Eula grumbled, coming to stand beside him. Mud stained the leather of her boots and armor, and her hair had become disheveled and flecked with dirt. She clucked her tongue as she took in his hunched shoulders and labored breathing. "How's your aether?"

Nudging at that well of power inside him, Skye teased out a tendril of magic, snaking it around one of the shadow crystals slotted into his armor. He pulled at the aether stored within, pushing it into his blood. The burning in his lungs immediately began to soothe; the aching pain in his arms and legs abated.

Standing up a little straighter, he gave her a strained smile. “Just fine.”

Eula’s lips curled into a familiar frown, but the reprimand never came. “If we keep up this pace,” she said instead, “we can make it to Della by nightfall.”

“Good,” Skye replied just as someone shouted from the front of the line. The wagons began to edge forward, the wheels slinging dirt and muddy water onto those walking too close. The horses groaned, struggling beneath the massive load, and a few shadow mages took up positions behind the carts and began to push. For not the first time that morning, Skye wondered if they should’ve left the flash cannons behind. While they would be useful in a fight—an absolute Shardsend if Ryme’s defenses had been compromised—they were heavy.

Skye and Eula walked alongside the horses, not caring about the sprays of water that soaked their already-damp clothing and armor. The week had been full of hard work, and spring on Tempris was always wet and miserable. Anyone that lived on the island for any length of time eventually got used to the rain.

“Shards, this is awful,” a new voice griped. Skye turned, his scowl deepening when he saw another familiar face jogging to catch up.

“Report, Kato,” Eula snapped at the brassy-haired fey. The stern noblewoman was known for her patience, but even she was starting to crack beneath the strain.

"The potholes are filled," Kato said as he fell into line beside them. His leather armor was almost identical to Skye's, with the emblem for House Ghislain—a dragon surrounded by swirls of shadow magic—set into the breastplate. A plain blue canvas coat protected him from the rain, and a simple but well-made sword with a row of fire crystals running the length of the blade hung from his belt.

Skye glanced back at the gaping, watery pothole in the middle of the road. Thankfully, the other carts were managing to steer the horses around the ditch. "You missed one."

Kato blew at an unruly lock of hair that clung to his forehead. "No, we didn't." He banged on the side of one of the carts. "These things are just so damned heavy that the sand isn't doing shit. And since you're still insisting that the earth mages need to save their aether to fortify the camp tonight rather than helping us fix the roads, this is what you get."

Skye and Eula shared a look, both choosing to remain silent as they continued to march. Most of the earth mages were already exhausted. The week's hardships had brought with it a steady stream of sick and injured, and it would've been foolish to waste their aether on something so easily fixed with simpler, non-magical methods. Even Kato knew this, was capable of understanding, though he would never stoop so low as to be agreeable.

"I hope that if it comes down to it," Kato said, smiling in a way that made Skye bristle. He didn't trust that smile. Didn't dare trust the man. "This crazy idea of yours works. Bringing along the flash cannons *might* have been a good idea—if you hadn't sent away the only person that knew how to fix them."

"I might not know as much about firearm crystal circuits as Taly," Skye said, his heart twisting just at the mention of her name. That had no doubt been his brother's intent. He was always poking at that wound. "But I'm hardly inexperienced. They'll work."

"Oh, well that makes me feel better." Kato turned to Eula. "Doesn't that make you feel better? Skye thinks that these rust buckets will work. Never mind that they haven't been fired in centuries."

Skye resisted the urge to bare his teeth. "Maybe if you had *deigned* to help me this week instead of spending your nights drinking and gambling with the ensigns, we might've had time to test them. But since you didn't, you don't get to complain."

Eula shot a disapproving glare at the lanky noble. Kato was tall and thin—just like Skye. They both resembled their mother in that regard, though that was where the similarities ended. "Was that really the best use of your time, Marshal?"

"I believe so," Kato replied easily. "Ensigns have the best gossip, and since everyone just seemed to forget that we had a traitor in our midst, I took it upon myself to do some investigating."

"We didn't forget," Skye said. Not with the attacks they had continued to weather, the people they had lost.

"Perhaps I misspoke then," Kato said. "You didn't forget. You just chose to do nothing."

Skye glanced at his brother. "Eula," he said, never taking his eyes off Kato. He inclined his head, listening to the shouts sounding from behind them. "I think they're having trouble with the horses at the back of the caravan. Would you mind checking?"

Eula looked first to Skye, then to Kato. She sketched out a shallow bow. The two brothers had been butting heads all week, and she was smart enough not to come between them.

Skye listened to her footsteps as she marched to the back of the caravan. When she was out of earshot, he said, low and cold, "I thought I told you to drop this. Taly is not a defector—she's my scout."

That bastard was still grinning. "I didn't say anything about Taly."

"You didn't need to. You've been skulking around, asking questions, and spreading rumors. Did you really think it wouldn't get back to me? People are already on edge without you going around stirring up trouble, Kato. And yes, *this*—" Confronting him in the middle of the road when they both needed to be focused on keeping these people safe. "This is what I call stirring up trouble."

Kato gave a low chuckle, and Skye wondered briefly if he could get away with killing him. The island had been invaded by dead men. What was one more?

"Gossip is a funny thing," Kato said. "Most of the time, it's just pointless blather, told and retold, distorted by exaggeration, disinformation, and misrepresentation. However, in my experience, there's always a small kernel of truth, if you know how to find it. You would know that if you tried a little harder at court. Dealing with other nobles can be tedious, but you get very good at figuring out when someone's hiding something."

Skye tried to look unaffected. "Do you have a point?"

"You sent Taly away."

"That's right." The lie came easily—just one of many.

"So, if that's the case, why were you asking about her at the gates?"

"What?" Skye stopped abruptly, and two lowborn fey walking close behind nearly collided with him. They paled when both brothers turned their way, mumbling wary apologies as they shuffled past.

"The guards that were on duty that day," Kato went on. "I played a few hands of cards with them earlier this week. They said you were asking about a blonde human female, early 20s, below average mortal height. I wonder who that could be?"

It wasn't the first time Kato had pressed him about Taly, testing the hastily constructed web of lies he'd spun to keep the events around her departure a secret. Each time, Skye gave him the same story. And each time, Kato had no way to prove him wrong.

But that hadn't stopped him from digging.

No matter.

Skye began to walk forward. "I had a moment of weakness." Another lie. She had run, and he had tried to stop her, thinking he might be able to catch her before she got through the gates.

But she had already been gone, and the rains had washed away her scent. Even if he had been able to follow, if duty hadn't leashed him to that compound, there had been no way to track her.

"Ever since we were kids," Skye added softly, "I've done everything that I can to protect her." That part was true. She had always been younger, smaller, *mortal.* The first time she scraped a knee, he'd thought she was dying, especially when she just kept *bleeding.* At only ten years old, he'd never seen anything like it. "Those old habits are hard to break. Even if, rationally, I knew that sending her away was the right decision."

Kato's nostrils flared, as though he could smell the deceit. Like he had said, the most convincing lies always contained a small bit of truth. "Understandable."

No smile. No amusement. Skye could already see him changing tack, and he braced himself.

"It's just," Kato began, almost hesitant. "Circumstances being what they are..." That there were dead men lurking in the shadows, and she was just a human among them. The concern in his brother's eyes almost looked genuine. "It's just a little heartless, I suppose. You've been jabbering about this girl since you were ten, and I... I guess I thought you cared more. That's all."

Skye pushed down a growl. Oh, he *cared.* He *more* than cared. He loved that idiot human more than anything in this world and the next, and every day since she'd been gone had been agony. Sheer, unending torture as he wondered where she was, what she was doing, if she was injured, still alive or dead or... worse.

He wasn't sure what he would do if he ever met a shade with her face. Even if she'd been turned into a monster, he wasn't sure if he could kill her.

A chill breeze gusted through the trees, and a collective rumble of displeasure rose from the caravan.

Skye stared straight ahead. Continued to put one foot in front of the other. Kato's words had found their target, but that didn't mean he had to pick up the bait.

Kato's voice followed him. "You think she's still alive, don't you?"

Ignore him, Skye thought as something inside him began to wail, growing louder and louder, drowning out the sounds of the caravan. *Just ignore him.*

"I suppose it's possible," Kato went on. "Unlikely but... well, let's do the math, shall we? The trip to the relay and back should've taken what? A day on horseback? Maybe two? It's been five days now and not one peep. Sure, she could've made her way to Ryme instead of coming back to Ebondrift, but with shades roaming the woods... What chance would a mortal have if there was trouble? Humans are weak. They bleed easy. They *die* easy."

Skye's throat constricted, and he counted his breaths, his footsteps, anything to keep those words from sinking in. "If you have a point, then I suggest you make it."

"I just want you to admit it."

"Admit what?"

"That you lied," Kato said simply and without malice. "That you didn't send her away. That you've been covering for her because you know she's hiding something, even though you have no idea what that something is."

"You're reaching. Making baseless assumptions. I've told you everything I know."

"And I still don't believe you," Kato countered easily. "I want to. Don't get me wrong. But c'mon, Skye—we both know she's dead. She was dead the moment she set foot outside the compound gates, and if you're telling me the truth, if you really sent her for the relay—then you sent her to her death. That little human you only ever wanted to protect—her blood is on your hands."

Skye took a steadying breath, willing the anger to ebb out of him. He wouldn't give his brother the reaction he so desperately wanted. Not here. Not in front of all these people.

"Tell me the truth, little brother," Kato drawled, still twisting that knife deeper and deeper. "Taly was very pretty, but don't throw away your honor just because some shardless bitch let you get your cock wet."

His anger snapped, and Skye saw red.

His body was already moving, already closing the distance—

A hand clamped down on his shoulder, a bone-shattering force that held him firmly in place.

"*Stand down,*" Eula snarled at Kato, flashing her teeth when Skye yanked himself out of her grip.

"Why?" Kato hissed. His hand began to drift towards the dagger at his waist. "Because he's my commander, my future Duke? The heir to my household, so I should just fall in line like a good boy even when I know he's *lying*?"

Letting her aether flare, Eula lunged, punching Kato square in the nose. It was swift and brutal, and Kato staggered back. "Yes," she barked. "For all those reasons and more. You might be a son of Ghislain, but right now, you're under my command. And his." A glance at Skye.

"And you will not endanger this mission or these people with petty squabbles."

Kato held up his hands. "I was just expressing some concerns—"

"Concerns that have already been dismissed." Eula fixed him with a stare, thunder in her expression.

Kato, wisely, backed down.

"The scouts just came back," Eula said, still not taking her eyes off Kato. "We've cleared the road ahead, and there are more potholes. Get to work."

Kato gave a huff, wiping at the trickle of blood seeping from his nose. For a moment, it looked like he was going to say something.

But then that smile slipped back into place, just barely concealing that hidden edge lurking underneath. He gave a merry salute before disappearing into the crowd.

Skye turned to Eula, arching a brow.

She shrugged. "What? Just because you shouldn't go around punching people doesn't mean I can't. I'm your Lt-Commander, and he's my Marshal. I call that discipline."

Skye's lips twitched, but he didn't smile. Or laugh. Couldn't bring himself to. "Did anyone—"

"No one heard. At most, this will look like a disagreement between brothers, and considering that the two of you already have a reputation for animosity…" She shrugged. "Kato at least had the good sense not to go around flinging accusations with shadow mages in earshot."

Except for Eula. He'd probably assumed she already knew.

"You don't need to explain anything," Eula said, sensing his thoughts. "I don't know why Kato won't let this be, but I've known you and Taly your entire lives. Every level of hell would freeze over before either of you would betray your island, your people, and especially, each other."

Skye's chest tightened to the point of pain. The blind trust, the faith… He had no words.

Eula looked to the front of the caravan, where the last group of scouts were emerging from the forest. Their faces were lined, their clothes wet and ragged—but they signaled the all-clear. It was safe to proceed to the canyon.

"Why don't you go out with the next wave of scouts?" she suggested. "Stretch your legs, clear your head a bit. It'll be good for you."

It was tempting. He was starting to feel antsy. Claustrophobic. "Are you sure?"

A nod. "I can handle things here. You should go."

Skye didn't need to be told twice. He began weaving his way through the crowd, stopping briefly to grab a scrying communicator off one of the returning scouts. He hit the forest, passed through the wards—

And then he was running.

The world became a blur of color, but he channeled his aether, willing his legs to move faster, faster, *faster*.

We both know she's dead.

The words still echoed.

Her blood is on your hands.

Kato was a bastard, and he'd been poking for a reaction. But he'd also been right. Because Skye… he hadn't been there when she needed him. Hadn't listened when she'd tried to tell him something important. He'd pushed her aside, and now… now she was gone.

Into the enemy's hands.

If she died, it really would be his fault.

Instinct guided him forward—cataloging sound and scent and sight. The caravan was safe, defended. But they needed to keep moving forward.

So, pushing even more aether into his legs, Skye savored the sting of the wind, the smell of the earth, as he flew through the forest, making his way to Crescent Canyon.

CHAPTER 5

-An excerpt from A Time Mage's Field Guide to Dream Symbology

The Sight is a rare and coveted gift, and for those few that possess the ability to peer into the future, reality begins to take on a new shape through the simple act of dreaming. While the future can never be determined with complete accuracy, dreams allow the time mage to see possible eventualities months, sometimes even years, ahead of the event in question. Details, of course, change based on the accumulated effects of individual choice. A dream on the eve of battle may hint at victory, but a last-minute decision to go right instead of left, an accidental fall, or even a misfired shot can become pivotal, thereby skewing the expected outcome.

The future, by its very nature, is inherently malleable, and it is generally advised to take a time mage's dreams as a prediction and guide for future actions rather than true divination.

The first thing Taly noticed was the quiet.

Neither gentle nor easy—it was oppressive, almost like a physical thing crawling across her skin. It was the kind of quiet, the kind of charged stillness that came from being in a place that was better left undisturbed.

Towering walls of gold surrounded her on all sides, and if she looked closely, she could see that instead of stone, each partition had been fabricated from countless threads weaving, tangling, and snarling together into a dense web.

She inhaled, somehow relieved when the rasp of her own shallow breathing reached her ears.

"Hello?" Her voice echoed, and Taly touched a finger to a nearby wall, watching as it rippled out into infinity. "Is anybody there?"

There was no answer.

Her thoughts scrambled, and her senses felt dulled. She knew she should probably feel panic. Especially when the walls began to realign themselves, moved by an unseen hand. But all she could muster was the faintest trace of confusion as she picked at her nightdress, her unbound hair. As she tried to remember where she had been, where she was going, and why she didn't have shoes.

Sound and light began to bleed through the gossamer threads, and then, so abrupt that it left her staggering and gasping for air, the landscape snapped into focus.

Screams pierced the air, and the shuffling of thousands of feet shook the ground. A swarm of people, covered in mud and blood, their skin slick with rain, writhed as they pressed together on what looked like a bridge.

Taly immediately recognized the woven net of branches and steel that formed a tunnel around the canyon bridge. Storm clouds painted the sky, and a dark chasm loomed below. Walls of red stone stretched to the east and west.

"The Riftway," she said, her voice swallowed by the wailing din of the crowd. She was back on Tempris, standing in the middle of the bridge that spanned Crescent Canyon.

Which meant—a dream. She was dreaming. She knew that instinctively, even if the realization felt muddy and faraway.

Shields clanged in the distance, and she began to press her way forward, making her way to the south side of the bridge. The crowd frothed and writhed in their panic, and even though their bodies were little more than smoke, forming and reforming around her, it was like trying to swim through a wall of water.

"Shore up that line!"

Taly jolted at the familiar voice, so full of exhaustion and rage.

Skye.

She began to run, not caring about the ghosts that still streamed past as her feet hit solid ground. The bridge was behind her now. A rank of heavily armed mages pushed back the crowd, and just beyond, streaming through a break in the wards and swarming the road—

Shades.

They used no careful formation as they slashed and hacked at the retreating refugees, pushing their way through a rapidly crumbling defensive line of mages.

And there, in the middle, shoving the wounded out of the way of the oncoming horde, was Skye. There was a scrape on his neck that wasn't healing—the blood so bright against the blackened gore that streaked his skin. And instead of a sword, he wielded a long staff. Men and women stumbled around him as the shades broke through their ranks, and he reached down, pulling a young black-haired boy to his feet and pushing him to the center of the sloppy formation.

"Skye!" Taly screamed as panic—true fear—wormed its way inside the dazed indifference that still muddled her senses. Something was pulling her forward, like a tether, some sort of invisible rope.

"Behind you!" she screamed again, even though a part of her knew it would do her little good. She was a wraith, nothing more than a spectator, and all she could do was watch as Skye ducked to grab at another scrambling mage—only to take a dagger straight to the gut.

His armor tempered the blow, and even though he was already recovering, rapidly turning on his heel as he adjusted his grip on the staff, that slight blip in his attention had cost him. Another shade leaped onto his back, clawing at his face just as a third grabbed at his legs. He struggled, still swinging that staff that glowed both red and blue, but more began to pile on top of him, eventually wrestling him to the ground.

"Serves you fucking right," a familiar voice said from somewhere behind her. Kato. She glimpsed a flash of brassy hair. There was shame in those amber eyes.

Then he was gone, swallowed by the crowd.

A scream. A flare of magic.

"Skye!" Taly was still reaching for him, still struggling against the crowd that seemed more solid and real with each passing moment. This couldn't be happening. Skye couldn't die. She refused to believe that there was a reality that existed where he could die and leave her behind.

When she was thrown to the ground, she began to crawl, blood staining her hands, her nightdress, her hair. It felt warm and sticky and far too real—same as the pain she felt as she was trampled and kicked from all sides.

By the time she reached the place where Skye had been, the shades had moved on, already on the bridge. It was chaos behind her, the screams growing louder as people began jumping into the canyon, choosing one death over another.

But Taly didn't care. About any of it. Not as she began to dig, wrenching away the bodies—some she recognized, others she didn't—until she found him. His breaths were coming in gurgling gasps, and his eyes stared at the sky.

"*Em*," she tried to say, but she couldn't breathe over the great shuddering sobs that broke out of her. One of his eyes was gone, the entire left side of his face destroyed. But that wasn't the worst of it. Not nearly as bad as the gash that split him from sternum to hip, so deep that blood and entrails were leaking out of him.

"Skye, please," she tried again, but he didn't turn. He just stared up at the clouds as the rain began to fall.

As she began to scream his name and grope at that giant, gaping wound, fingers twisting in his innards as she tried to piece him back together.

His blood soaked her skin. The light in that single green eye began to fade.

She knew the moment that he was gone, and that something of her had gone with him.

Taly was still screaming when the world grew dim.

Still screaming when she wrenched awake.

She screamed until her voice went hoarse, and she became aware of soft sheets and the smell of flowers and the lack of screaming outside her own.

She stopped, her entire body shaking as she cracked open her eyes.

The soft violet light of the first moon spilled through the windows, punctuated by the occasional flash of blinding white as the world outside rattled and shook.

The palace. She was at the palace, not Crescent Canyon. And Skye…

"A dream," she rasped. "It was just a dream."

A horrible, terrible dream that had felt far too *real…*

Taly pulled the blanket firmly around her shoulders, curling on her side as she willed the images to fade. "It was just a dream," she whispered, too afraid to close her eyes.

She'd always had bad dreams. For as long as she could remember.

"It was just a dream."

So, why could she still smell blood?

"Just a dream, just a dream, just a dream," she chanted.

But her body continued to shake.

Skye stood at the edge of the cliff, a reckless thrill shooting through him as he peered into the yawning expanse. Pebbles knocked loose as he shifted his weight, and the wind whipped at his hair and clothing, howling, pushing him closer to the edge.

Crescent Canyon stretched across the landscape, following the path of the city for which it had been named. Once a sprawling, underground metropolis, Crescent City had collapsed during the Schism. The rubble had been cleared away long ago, but the soft-colored rock was still peppered with holes, and gaps, and tunnels that had once been homes, and stores, and roadways.

Some gates, like the Aion and Seren Gates, weren't online when the Time Queen forcibly closed the bridges between the worlds. They survived with little damage and minimal loss of life, while others, like the five gates that now lay at the bottom of the canyon, had been open. The aether surge the Queen had used to override the safety protocols had immediately shattered the Crossroads—that artificial space between worlds where the fey had built their bridges.

Those that were there that day always said that the flashes of light came first. Then the explosions, the smoke, the fires. There had been no signs of impending danger. Nothing to hint at what was to come as people gathered on the bridges, fanning out through the markets that spread around the gates.

Very few had survived the blasts, though places like Crescent City…

When the gates exploded, the city collapsed, swallowed by the land. Half a million people died in Crescent City alone. There were five more underground cities scattered across the island that had also perished.

Tearing his eyes away from the jagged pillars of crystal that still jutted from the canyon floor—all that was left of the Primus Gate—Skye began picking his way along the edge of the cliff. He could see the suspension bridge in the distance, just around the bend. Spanning the narrowest section of the ravine, it was a web of tangled vines and living timber, reinforced with steel and cable and mesh. Since the aether on the island could fluctuate drastically, Ivain hadn't dared build a bridge using traditional methods. During a depressive swing, when the aether could get so thin that each breath felt like fire, the floating air platforms common in places like Arylaan and Thanos would fall from the sky. So, the Marquess had borrowed the design for the Riftway from the humans, mixing their technology with just a hint of fey magic to create something truly unique.

Most mainland fey believed it to be an abomination. Skye thought it was genius.

A heavy curtain of trees crept forward, butting up against the rocky cliffside, and Skye reluctantly turned away from the canyon. The area was clear, and he hadn't seen any sign of danger since he left the caravan. It was time to head back.

Gravel crunched and leaves hissed as he pressed himself between the trees. The forest was dense on this part of the island, and he would have to move slowly. There would be no room to run, nothing to help him shake off the nervous energy that still simmered just beneath the surface.

He wasn't sure how he could be so restless and so tired at the same time. It was like his body thought it could run away from that aching hole in his chest that seemed to grow larger with each passing day, not knowing that it was a part of him now. Would follow him until he found—

Taly.

Skye sighed. Even if he tried to push her out of his thoughts, she was always there. Her laugh, her scent, her smile—the memories would inevitably sneak up on him when he wasn't paying attention, and the pain would begin anew.

A twig snapped in the distance, and Skye refocused his aether, tilting his head and listening, scenting the wind.

No footsteps or obvious signs of a predator. No unusual pockets of silence. The air smelled of moss and loam, rain and wind. A stream trickled in the distance.

Nothing seemed out of place.

Though…

Skye reached for his magic, something tickling at the edge of his senses. It was instinct, a feeling that—

"Skye, you there?" Eula's voice filtered through his earpiece. "We've reached the next waypoint. The canyon is in sight. Are we safe to proceed?"

Skye loosed a breath, punching the button on the comm strapped to his waist. "Affirmative. The eastern sector is clear."

"Good." Eula's tone was clipped, and Skye could hear Kato grumbling in the background. "We're moving. Meet us at the bridge."

"Will do."

Skye continued, heading west, back towards the main highway and the caravan that would be gathering around the bridge. A breeze rustled the leaves high overhead, shaking loose a flurry of delicate white petals that drifted around him like snow. He looked up, searching for the characteristic tangle of blue thorns twining through the upper branches.

Pixie slippers. That wasn't the real name for the tiny flower—just the name Taly had picked out when they were children. She thought the petals looked like little shoes.

Skye rubbed at his chest. There were too many memories. Too many reminders. And what if Kato was right? A human on an island full of shades? Even if she was working with the man, woman, or thing responsible for creating them... What if she had already served her purpose? What if she had already outlived her usefulness and—

"Huri, Cora, and Sela have returned." Eula paused to bark out an order. "They're standing by."

"Good, that's everyone." Skye stopped to swat at a butterfly that flew too close. Its wings were edged with charcoal, making it look like it was made of smoke. Soot sprites. Taly had read a story once about how they were supposed to bring good luck, and ever since, she had made a point of catching them whenever they went camping in the woods. "Send out the next wave of scouts. If the area on the other side of the bridge is clear, keep moving forward."

"Sire."

The comm clicked, and for a little while, there was only silence.

After an hour of walking and picking his way through the underbrush, the forest began to thin. Skye circled back around to the canyon edge, squinting as he emerged from the tree line. Eula was reciting a long list of status updates through the comm, and he could see that she had already started moving the carts across the bridge.

His eyes flicked to the other side of the canyon. Another thick line of trees rustled in the breeze, and a stag darted between the foliage, its antlers catching on the leaves.

That can't be right.

Skye looked again. Then raised a hand to his ear. "Stop the caravan," he said as something ghosted across his skin—the faintest whisper of foreign magic.

"What?" came Eula's reply. "Are you sure? The scouts gave the all-clear."

"Yes," he said. Because this late into the spring, the deer would've shed their antlers. It would be months before they grew back.

Skye stepped carefully along the canyon edge. "Can't you feel that?" It was the same thing he'd felt before, that tickle just outside the reach of perception.

"Feel what?" Eula asked, voice tinny and faraway.

Skye rubbed his fingers together. It was almost like a film, like oil or soap. "It's water magic, Eula."

His comm gave a painful screech, and moments later, shouts sounded in the distance.

"We have shades!" an ensign squawked through the comm. "At the back of the convoy. They're coming from the forest!"

Skye's body reacted before the words fully registered, and he was already running through the woods, ignoring the scrape of brambles and thorns. He pushed more aether into his legs, willing his body to go faster.

The screams grew louder as he sprinted towards the Riftway and the battle unfolding at Crescent Canyon.

CHAPTER 6

-An excerpt from the Tempris Daily News

The 27th day of the month Ishin, during the 6th year of our Lady Raine

Nearly 30,000 people gathered at the gates of Infinity's Edge to witness the maiden flight of the Arabella, the first prototype airship of its class to be co-developed by the Fey Imperium and the Draegon Hierarchy.

Commissioned by Her Supreme Imperial Majesty, Queen Raine, the Arabella is a scouting vessel optimized for low-aether environments. She is scheduled to be turned over to Commander Adahy, currently stationed on Earth.

The forest melted into color and light and motion as Skye pumped his legs, willing his body to move faster.

Screams echoed in the distance, and every channel on the comm was clogged with disjointed chatter as the Gate Watchers tried to regroup. The shades had come from the rear. *Hundreds* of them—streaming from between the trees, pressing in on the caravan as it neared the bridge. They had broken through the wards protecting the roads, traveling through areas that had previously been scouted and determined safe.

An army hidden among the trees. How the hell had they missed that?

Faster, faster, *faster*... Skye had always loved to run, loved the way magic and adrenaline would mix as he flew through the air.

Now, he felt only dread as he pushed his body forward, as the highway wardline shimmered up ahead, coming up fast.

Moments later, he exploded from the tree line, nearly toppling a young woman as he skidded to a stop.

A crowd of people surrounded him, frantic as they tried to push towards the bridge. Their screams churned the air, a droning whine punctuated by the sharp clang of steel against steel that sounded from their flank. Fey and mortal mingled, indistinguishable in their desperation and panic.

"Shit," Skye cursed, trying to shove his way through. He could barely move his arms, hardly find enough room just to breathe. To the south, the sounds of battle continued to rise and fall above the roar of the crowd, and bursts of fire and ice flew into the air. He craned his neck, but he couldn't see more than a few feet over the roiling crush of bodies pressing in on him from all sides. None of the faces looked familiar. Even though he could still hear their voices trickling in over the comm, he couldn't see Eula or Kato or any of the other Gate Watchers in the teeming mass.

Higher ground—he needed higher ground.

Gritting his teeth, Skye let the crowd push him back to the edge, and once he had enough room to move freely, he jumped, grabbing a low-hanging branch of a nearby tree and hauling himself up.

Seconds later, he was perched nearly forty feet off the ground.

The southern roadway was a sea of confusion, stirred by unseen currents and flowing towards the bridge like a river. The people pressed together, desperate to stay within the confines of the wardlines and the limited protection they still provided. He could just make out the dark blue of the Gate Watchers' coats peppering the crowd, waving their hands as they tried to steer the refugees away from the edge of the canyon. The carts had stalled, and several earth mages were perched atop the hulking mounds of supplies and weapons, their hands glowing green as they sent out waves of calming magic.

"Eula," Skye barked into the comm. "Status report."

"Sire." The words were clipped. "They're still attacking from the rear. We've got the fire and water mages in formation, but they won't be able to hold them back for very long. They're going to be overrun. Most of our shadow mages were already across the bridge and scouting the northern side. We've hailed them on the comms, but the bridge is blocked with civilians."

Skye's attention cut to the south, and a quick tug on his aether had his eyes shifting, his pupils going wider. There was a second of near-blindness, and then the details of the battle raging in the distance snapped into bright focus. He could see a thin line of mages feeding aether into a towering wall of magical fire, pushing back against the dark wave of creatures that lapped at their flank. Smoke rippled the air, but Eula was right. They wouldn't be able to keep that up forever. The flames were already beginning to sputter and fade.

Skye pressed a key on his comm, filtering out the chatter. "How many shadow mages are on the north side?"

"Nearly half," Eula grunted, already out of breath.

Skye looked to the northern side. A steady stream of refugees flowed from the bridge, fanning out along the canyon edge. He squinted, quickly recognizing the gruff man that stood on the other side, directing traffic and barking orders to a small rank of shadow mages. Kane Harin. He was a fire mage. Lowborn, but he had a head for strategy. Enough that he had managed to bring more than a few highborn to their knees during one-on-one combat. "Let's keep them there for now. We don't know if more forces are hidden on the north side of the canyon. Tell Harin to take over and dig in."

Skye turned back to the battle raging down below. "Where's Kato?"

"Here," Kato's voice buzzed through the comm. "I'm on the bridge moving south to reinforce Eula."

Skye spotted the familiar shock of brassy hair moving against the swell of people rushing onto the bridge. "Wait," Skye said, eyeing the massive tarp-covered wagons that lumbered towards the entrance. The flash cannons.

Kato immediately stopped, his body glowing violet as he channeled enough aether to keep from being swept away. "Make it quick."

"I can see you from my position. I'm closer to Eula, so it's going to be easier for me to reinforce our flank. I want you to circle the wagons near the mouth of the bridge on the south side. If you can set up a defensive perimeter and get the flash cannons online, Eula and I can retreat back to your position once everyone is on the bridge."

"On it," Kato said. There was no mockery, no derision. A small mercy. At least his brother could stow his attitude when it mattered.

The comm clicked, and Skye saw the crowd begin to part as Kato shoved against the throng of people, this time cutting a path to the wagons.

Skye dropped from his perch, refocusing his aether and hitting the ground with a hard thud. The magic spread through every cell and sinew, and he barely felt the impact from the forty-foot drop as it rippled up his legs. Then, he began to sprint toward Eula's position, moving along the edge of the wardline and weaving between the crowd.

Reaching inside his coat, he produced a length of leather-wrapped wood no longer than a handspan. He thumbed the button set into the side, holding the grip away from his body as each edge unfolded. Wood and metal hissed, sliding and scraping until the stave was as long as he was tall.

They had figured out early on that cutting weapons were useless against an enemy that was impervious to pain. Though they may have once been men and women formed from flesh and blood, death had tempered every weakness. Remove an arm or a leg—a man would fall, blinded by the pain. But a shade... a shade just kept moving, kept swinging and fighting and clawing and tearing. The only way to stop them was to crush their bones. The only way to kill them was to shatter the crystals lodged deep in their chests.

Skye could feel the pull of the shadow crystals concealed beneath the leather grip, and lines of blue and red gemstones began to flicker as aether flowed through the mass of wiring carved into the surface of the wood. "Eula, I'm right behind you," he said, giving his staff a few experimental sweeps as the crowd began to thin. Each end was tipped with iron, sharpened to a point. "Get the shadow mages into formation and be prepared to pull the casters back."

"Yes, Sire," came Eula's clipped reply.

Skye could see the shades now. Just beyond a rapidly dwindling barricade of blue magical fire, they flowed through a break in the wardline, as monstrous as any Skye had seen. Decayed flesh sagged off rotting bone, veins spiderwebbed beneath waxy pallid skin, and jagged cuts peeked through tattered scraps of cloth and leather that might once have been armor.

Countless and wild, there was no formation, no order to their rank. The enemy shades crashed into the soaring wall of heat and ash, waving spears and swords that were more rust than metal and bellowing out their rage.

Eula hung back, her body awash with shadow magic as she marched behind a trembling assembly of fire and water mages, pushing the ones that attempted to run back into formation. Most of them were young, two centuries or less—the sons and daughters of the lesser nobility back on Lycia. They had been trained to move with grace and ease through the ranks of noble society, a far different kind of battlefield than the one they now faced.

Unfortunately, a week of combat training had done little to make up for this deficiency in their education.

The shadow mages were already falling into line in front of the casters, standing steady and holding identical staves that flickered red and blue. Occasionally, the wall of flame would gutter, turning to smoke, but the few shades that rushed through were quickly struck down, first with fire and then with ice. That was something else they had learned during that first battle with the abomination. Fire made the shades panic, and ice made them shatter.

Skye took up position beside a stout, black-haired boy that looked to be a few years younger than him. "Eula? Get ready to drop the wall and fall back."

"Yes, Sire," came Eula's response, followed by a shout from somewhere behind him.

"On my signal!" Skye's aether flared, and he gripped his staff. Similar flashes of violet light repeated around him as the shadow mages began to shuffle nervously. "Now!"

The wall extinguished, and Skye gave a shout, launching himself forward. He felt the lingering heat of the blockade, but the protective wards woven into the lining of his armor immediately activated. A thin coating of frost slithered across his skin, the cold pushing back the heat in a hiss of steam as he barreled straight through the heavy cloud of smoke still curling through the air.

A heartbeat later, he emerged on the other side, unharmed, and the scent of rot slammed into him.

The black-haired boy at his side staggered at the smell, but Skye grabbed his shoulder, pushing him forward as they crashed into the horde. The shades rushed the shadow mages, quickly huddling into a dozen individual battles.

Skye swung his own weapon as a small group peeled away from the main skirmish and converged on him. Their emaciated bodies tangled together, and they stabbed the air with long spears, trying to skewer him.

They were fast. Strong.

But he was faster—*stronger*—and he neatly side-stepped their attacks, using aether to speed up each motion.

A click of a button activated the fire crystals in his staff, and the shades began to shriek and thrash as bright bursts of flame flared to life, licking at their feet and devouring flesh and bone.

Another step. Another swing. Another press of a button. Skye felt a chill ripple through his staff as lines of frost began to trail each sweep. The shades abruptly quieted as ice replaced fire, and their bodies shattered completely when he aimed a direct blow to the center of their chests.

Skye smelled the tang of iron before he felt the rush of wind, and he instinctively brought his stave up, barely managing to catch the dagger aimed at his head. Metal sliced his neck, but it was a glancing blow.

The shade yanked its blade from the wood, stumbling as Skye dropped and swept its feet, stomping the heel of his boot into its chest as he whirled to face another.

Blood sprayed, and gore splattered. But the shadow mages held the line, following Eula's measured retreat as she continued to direct the casters and their ongoing volley of fire and ice. She was aiming for those places where the shades had begun to regroup. A few shadow mages were caught in the salvo, but the wards in their armor flickered, turning fire to smoke and ice to steam. The black-haired boy that had made a point to stick close to Skye got a little singed, but nothing his aether wasn't already working to heal.

Or trying to. All around, mages were bleeding, but not healing. Including himself, Skye realized abruptly. That scrape on his neck was still trickling blood.

Skye ducked and swung, and the steady stream of aether he'd been channeling flickered. The realization hit him like a brick to the face. "They're using rysine poison!" he shouted to the other shadow mages. Their wounds were never going to stop bleeding. Not until they were completely drained of aether. "Fall back and get medical attention!"

Eula covered their retreat as they ducked behind the line of casters, and the wall of flame immediately went back up as two earth mages rushed forward, their hands already glowing green with healing magic.

Panting and sweating, bleeding far more heavily than he'd realized, Skye craned his head as one of the earth mages began prodding at his neck. "Kato, report," he said into his comm.

There was a screech of static, and then, "The civilians are on the bridge, and we almost have the barricade in place." A pause. There was nothing but panting on the other end. "I'm having trouble with the guns. Some of the wiring was dislodged during the trip, and I don't know how to fix it."

Skye replied, "Are you honestly telling me that after working on the Mechanica for nearly two decades, you can't figure out how to fix a cannon that uses technology older than you are?"

"This isn't a fucking suit of armor!" Kato snapped. There was a blip in the comm, followed by a garbled stream of cursing. "...the hell! Taly made this look easy."

Skye peered through the smoke at the shades still flinging themselves into the flames. There were too many of these things. Even though they had managed to break through the enemy's ranks, they wouldn't last. Shades never tired, never stopped to tend to their wounded. And considering the circumstances, the terrain... "Kato, you need to figure it the hell out. We can't take much more of this."

Eula was still snarling orders. The shadow mages were still bleeding. And because the barricade still wasn't completed, as soon as the earth mages signaled that the poison had been cleared, Skye gave the order to rejoin the fray.

Metal clanged. Bone crunched. Every muscle in Skye's body barked with fatigue as he continued to swing and cleave and push against the endless tide.

We can't keep this up, he thought. Not at this rate. They were burning aether too quickly. He could already feel the stinging in his lungs.

A terrified howl sounded above the din. The black-haired boy had tripped, and the shades converged on him before he'd even hit the ground.

"Shore up that line!" Skye shouted as he rushed to grab the boy, wrenching him back to his feet. But more mages were still falling. A woman—tall and sturdy—yelped as she went down, and Skye was already moving in her direction, already reaching for the bloodied hand that clawed at the ground when someone grabbed at his collar and yanked him back.

"What the hell?!" Skye sputtered, thrashing as Kato dragged him behind the line of fire and water mages. The woman was being swarmed now, the shades piling on top of her as she continued to scream, and scream, and—

Her screams stopped.

Skye snarled, but his brother gave him another hard shove. "Don't go getting yourself killed just yet." Kato glanced back at the rapidly widening pool of blood, and Skye followed his gaze, fighting back the nausea that shuddered through him. The shades were frantic as they jabbed and jostled each other, ripping the woman's body apart. Those that couldn't get near enough for even a mouthful of flesh began to lap at the blood pooling on the pavement.

Thank you, was what he should've said, but all Skye could manage was a panted, "I didn't know you cared."

Kato huffed. "I don't," he said, wincing as he pressed a finger to his bloodied lip. "But if you die, oh fearless leader, then chances are, we all die. Let me take over here. I've got the wagons circled, but the flash cannons still won't come online. As much as it pains me to say it, I can't fix them. You, however, can."

Fair enough. Skye gave his brother a curt nod, pressing a button on his staff that had it retracting in on itself. He stowed it inside his coat and then ran for the bridge.

A row of carts circled the entrance, the tarps pulled away to reveal a row of gleaming metal barrels. He had to jump to clear the elevated mounting platform, and his hands flew over the console as he began keying in the startup sequence.

The old gun hummed and shook, and something below his feet rattled ominously. Skye breathed a sigh of relief when the lights on the control panel flickered to life. Dropping to the ground, he grabbed a red-haired fire mage that stood nearby, barking instructions as he pushed her onto the platform. He didn't wait for her reply as he ran to the next gun.

The smell of smoke and charred aether permeated the air, and a red glow began to coalesce around the barrel of the first cannon. Moments later, a chorus of cheers rang out among the mages as a trail of condensed fire blazed a path through the horde.

Skye didn't stop to celebrate, running for the next cart. There were five wagons on this side of the bridge, which meant five cannons. If he could get them all running, it might be *just* enough to give them an edge.

The second cannon, loaded with ice, shivered and died. Forcing his hands to steady, he tapped one of the gauges before dropping to his knees and prying open the console. It was an easy fix, and relief shot through him when he felt the gun kick underfoot as it began to sputter and groan. Without looking to see just whose sleeve he'd grabbed, he shoved another mage behind the controls.

Skye continued down the line as metal and magic lurched to life. Flesh sizzled. Bone melted. The shades fell to the ground in waves, their bodies reduced to ash and cinders.

For the first time in what felt like hours, hope bloomed in his chest. Kato and Eula were reforming the shadow mages, covering the casters' retreat behind the line of flash cannons, and Skye finally felt comfortable turning his attention to the north.

"Harin?" Skye turned a dial on his comm, trying to tease out the right frequency. "Harin? Report."

The comm crackled—nothing but static.

Skye looked to the north. Refugees were huddled around the entrance to the bridge, and the ramp was stuffed from end to end, not a scant patch of pavement visible between the press of bodies. The suspension web blocked his view of the other side.

"Harin?" he tried again. "Come on, answer me, Kane."

But there was no answer. Just static.

Skye's heart lurched. Throwing one last glance to the crowded ramp, he took a running jump off the platform, reaching for the tangled net that encircled the bridge and hauling himself up. He moved through the dense web, over the crowd and across the canyon. The people below murmured and cried, and Gate Watchers lined both sides of the bridge, pushing back against the swell of people and trying to keep the jabbing and jostling to a minimum, lest some poor soul get shoved right off the side. Several carts had been caught halfway across the ramp, and from this distance, they looked like islands of wood and steel set adrift at sea.

Skye was halfway across the bridge when his comm began to squawk. "Help!" a young woman pleaded. Maka—Skye had met her just yesterday when she had been tending to the horses. She was one of the shadow mages that had been sent to the north side. "They're in the trees! They're coming from the forest! We're surrounded!"

"Harin!" Skye barked. "Report!"

"Emrys?!" Harin's voice was gruff and laced with pain. "Where the hell have you been? We've been trying to hail you for the last twenty minutes."

What?

Eyes wide, Skye turned the dial on his comm, sending a hail to the other side, to Kato or Eula or anyone who might have been listening.

But there was no answer. Just more static followed by hollow silence. The signal was being blocked. Something on the bridge was interfering with their comms, which meant—

Skye shook off that train of thought. There would be time for questions later—time to figure out just how their enemy had managed to conceal themselves. How they had known the day and time the caravan would be crossing the bridge.

Reaching for a piece of steel trussing, Skye pulled himself up, climbing higher and higher and higher—high enough that he could see past the walls of black dirt that jutted from the ground around the northern bank. The earth mages looked ashen and pale as they tried to fortify the hastily constructed blockade. Some were on their knees, and others were being propped up by lowborn and mortals who could do little more than offer small sips of water and whispered words of encouragement.

Just beyond, in the small ribbon of highway that cut a path through the forest—more shades. A never-ending ocean of rotting limbs and gnashing teeth.

Climbing through the net, Skye made his way south, just far enough that Eula's voice began filtering through the comm. "We have shades to the north," he said, letting his weight rest on a nearby vine. "Hundreds of them. The earth mages are holding them back, but they're going to be overrun if they don't get backup."

"What?" The whine of the flash cannons mixed with the hiss of static nearly drowned out the single-word response. Kato's voice sounded in the background as Eula gave a shout. An explosion *boomed* to the south, so fierce it made the bridge begin to sway.

"Skylen," Eula panted as the low growl of the blast began to taper and fade, "We can't—"

"I know," Skye said, checking the handful of shadow crystals that clacked together in his pocket. "Stay where you are and continue to push. I'll go north and reinforce Harin—see what I can do. There's something blocking the comms, so as soon as you have the south side secured, send up a flare and start moving the civilians off the bridge. We're trapped right now with nowhere to run. Use those guns and give us somewhere to go. Understood?"

There was a brief pause, then a mumbled, "Sire." Skye could perfectly envision the way the noblewoman bowed her head. Not in deference, just… resignation. Because even if they could cut a hole to the south, the odds that they would be able to clear the roadways enough for a retreat…

No. He couldn't think like that. Not as another explosion cracked the air, this time to the north as one of those already-crumbling walls of earth collapsed. The shades immediately swarmed the hole in the barricade, breaking through and ripping into the line of shadow mages that threw themselves in front of the civilians.

Skye took a shaky breath. He had been trained to fight. He had been taught to lead. And he would. Even if he didn't feel ready—he would. His stomach lurched as he loosened his grip and let his body drop. Catching himself at the last moment, he began propelling himself forward, barking orders on the comm, watching as the shadow mages on the north side shakily fell into formation.

Metal clanged, and boots shuffled. As the shadow mages began to push, Harin took a step back and started pulling civilians from the huddled crowd. Anyone that looked like they might have a whisper of magic got shoved into line.

Skye dropped to the ground, pulling his staff from his coat as he moved to the front. Another block in the barricade began to fall, and a great keening wail went up as more shades flowed through the opening.

Skye ran, infusing aether into his legs and barely feeling the crack of bone as he slammed into the enemy wave. The ground trembled underfoot as the fallen earth mage tried to summon another barrier, but the shades were already clawing their way forward, barely stumbling as rippling streams of water flew past. Skye spared a glance back at Harin and the lowborn rank, his stomach sinking as the realization set in. They didn't have enough magic to form ice.

The comm squealed, and then, "Shadow mages dropping in 30 seconds. Clear the forward bridge."

Skye jolted at the familiar voice, and that slight blip in his attention cost him. A blade embedded in his shoulder, and he snarled, slamming his fist into the shade's cheek. Blood spurted as he yanked the dagger from his arm, the pain so hot it made the rest of him feel cold.

"Ten seconds. Air mages—be ready to provide aerial support."

Skye looked to the sky, still searching for the source of that voice and nearly stumbling from the shock of relief that shot through him. It was subtle, barely more than a glimmer, a slight bend in the light that didn't quite seem natural. But he saw it—saw the glamour just seconds before the veil of water magic dissolved, revealing the monster of wood and metal swimming through the clouds.

"Five seconds."

Skye couldn't stop the laugh that bubbled up. That was Ivain's voice. That was Ivain standing above the gunport. That was Ivain's crest—the Fairmont fox—flying at the mast of the massive airship.

A rusted sunburst swirled across the bow, sweeping along the sides in whorls of burnished red, and great wings of tattered canvas propelled it forward on a howling river of wind and rain. A line of air mages stood along the main deck, their bodies consumed by light as they raised their hands to the sky, summoning the squall.

"Lyric—take command of the deck," Ivain said, curt. "I'm going groundside."

With renewed vigor, Skye plunged into the rank of shades that pressed through the gap in the barricade as fully armored men and women dropped from the sky. Each one wore leather and steel, and they carried magical hammers and staves, each one glowing with magic.

Bursts of fire and ice and electricity hailed from the sky as the contingent of shadow mages split the air, striking the ground with explosive thuds that cracked the pavement. Shades flew back, knocked off their feet in waves, and the shadow mages cut their way forward. Each man and woman looked hale and rested, and Skye could scent the tang of aether over the stench of rot. The enemy flank was already starting to fall as the airship continued its assault.

And through the clash of steel and the sting of smoke, Skye kept his eyes trained on that familiar figure in black armor that was already cutting his way forward with lethal precision.

The other shadow mages flanked him, but it was Ivain that led the charge. The man was a storm, a raging tempest of fury and death. He carried a massive hammer, and among the lines of blue and red that pulsed beneath the polished granite, electricity crackled. A touch followed by a brief flare of shadow magic was all it took to send the shades sprawling. Wave after wave, until the road was laden with pieces of bone and bits of gore, stained black with rotted blood.

The roar of battle began to wane as Ivain's mages whittled down the enemy force, and the airship continued to circle overhead. And when Skye swung his staff for the last time, crushing it into a body so far gone he could no longer tell if it had been a man or a woman, fey or something else entirely—he simply stood there for a moment, almost bewildered to be standing still again as he watched a troop of mages disappear into the trees, no doubt looking for stragglers.

A bright flare streaked the sky to the south, followed by a rippling cheer that rose above the screams of the people still trapped on the bridge.

Skye could only stare as the flash began to fade, like a dying star.

He felt numb—numb to the pain of his wounds that had yet to heal, numb to the burn that had settled in his lungs, numb to everything except the overwhelming fatigue that rushed in to fill every empty space.

Because the fighting... the fighting had stopped. The shades were gone, and the healers were rushing onto the field, looking for wounded.

Somehow, by some miracle... they had won.

CHAPTER 7

- *An excerpt from On Time: Unraveling the Mystery*

The time mage is an inherent contradiction. They exist both within and outside the natural order; they are both the weavers and the thread. Objectively weaker than any other class of mage with seemingly no offensive capabilities—a single time mage can shape a nation.

Taly leaned farther back in her chair, watching the slow creep of dawn edge across the floor. Rows upon rows of books lined the walls of the small tower library, and every so often, a gust of wind would rattle the strips of leaded windows set into the walls high above. In the next room, the terrace door stood open, letting in the scent of rain.

It rained every morning before dawn for approximately seven minutes—a typical summer storm that rolled in without warning and disappeared just as suddenly. Taly knew this because after spending two weeks in a place doomed to replay the same day over and over again, she'd cataloged every sunrise and sunset, every drop of rain. She'd even timed the explosions that would start at the end of every day, using what she knew of the island to match them to the individual gates.

An ambitious undertaking, but there hadn't been much else to do. Taly hadn't seen or spoken to the Queen since that day in the Water Maze, and the fairies kept their distance. She might've thought she'd been forgotten entirely if it weren't for the *assignments* Leto delivered every morning with breakfast—books and papers that Taly was to have read and analyzed before her first lesson.

Not that anyone had told her just when that was going to be. That would've required talking to her, maybe answering a question or two. And really, the not knowing was the point, she had decided. It wouldn't be proper psychological warfare if the prisoner knew when their purgatory would end.

Biting back a yawn, Taly swung her bare feet off the surface of the heavy oaken desk. Her nightgown twisted between her legs, and she tugged at the fabric as she gracelessly lurched out of her seat and began to pace. The white marble tile was comfortably warm beneath her feet—heated by magic, no doubt—and as she finished the familiar circuit only to begin again, she eyed the bed peeking through the arched doorway longingly, sighing at the mess of blankets piled on the floor.

She'd had another nightmare. Just one of many since she'd come to the palace. Sometimes she woke up sobbing, sometimes screaming, usually both. Every night, she watched Skye die in some new horrible way, and every night, there was nothing she could do to save him.

The dreams were so real, so full of blood and rot and death.

Last night, she'd barely made it to the washroom before she began to retch. There had been no going back to sleep after that.

Taly drew in a long breath, then released it as she circled back around to her desk, picking a random book from the stack sitting on the corner. Her latest assignment, delivered by Leto the previous day.

"Aether Mechanics," Taly read aloud, running a finger across the silvered letters stamped into the spine. Snorting, she tossed it aside. She'd read all three volumes before she turned ten.

Selecting another book, she flipped through the pages, and then tossed it back onto the pile. She picked another, scowling when she saw the title.

Every book she'd been given so far was part of the first seal curriculum, and that made sense, she supposed. The study of magic required a basic understanding of aether, and the first seal examination was little more than a demonstration of that knowledge. Every magical guild was structured this way, and they all used the same standardized testing format to initiate new mages.

Still, Taly couldn't help her frustration when Leto kept delivering books like *Introduction to*

Aether along with silly little block games that were obviously meant for children. She'd grown up with shadow mages for Shards' sake, and taken the same courses as Skye, who was already a solid decade ahead of his peers. She knew more about aether than most highborn mages would learn in a lifetime and had told Leto as much, though it never seemed to do any good. Leto arrived with the same books and papers and stupid games every morning, and absolutely no word from the Queen.

At this rate, Taly would be old and gray before she ever got to go home. Although, as a fey, she supposed she would neither look old nor gray even when she was thousands of years old. This new body would never age, never change despite a countless number of mortal lifetimes passing.

Considering the circumstances, that didn't make her feel better.

A door groaned and snicked shut.

Metal clinked, and Taly's stomach gave an embarrassingly loud growl as the scent of food drifted into the darkened study.

"Mistress?"

"I'm up," Taly called, already moving from her study to the library and through the bedroom, towards the dining room on the other side. Her prison cell was spacious. At least she had that going for her. "And for the last time, Leto—it's not My Lady, or Madam, or even Mistress. It's Taly. *Just* Taly."

Leto hovered in front of a small round table already laden with food. Eggs, bacon, batter cakes, even porridge—it would all be delicious and perfectly prepared by the fairies that haunted the kitchen. Since spirits didn't eat, Taly wondered just how they still managed to get the taste right.

"Of course," Leto conceded, ripples of star-kissed mist swirling around her ethereal form. She pulled out a chair. "If it pleases you—*Ma'am.*"

Taly sighed and dropped into the chair, not sure why she still bothered. There were more books and more papers stacked beside her plate—all first seal literature. Some of them repeats of things she'd already received. It seemed the Queen couldn't even bother now to check the things she was sending. "Is this how it's going to be, Leto?" she asked, picking up a paperback journal from the top of the stack. There were two identical copies sitting on her study desk. "I get shoved into a room with no one to talk to and a bunch of books I've already read—is that really the Queen's idea of training?"

"Everyone starts with the basics, Ma'am."

"I know my basics. Something I would gladly tell Her Royal Pain-in-my-ass if she ever deigned to talk to me. Why is she wasting my time, Leto?"

"All initiates—" Leto began.

"*Don't,*" Taly snapped. "Don't give me another bullshit excuse. I've known enough fey to understand just how much they like fucking with those they see as smaller and weaker, so for the love of the Shards, just tell me what the hell is going on. What kind of game is she playing? Why keep me here under the guise of training if she's not going to *train* me?"

"I cannot say, Ma'am." She never could. Leto did work for the Queen, after all.

With a sigh, Taly reached for the cup of coffee steaming beside her plate. It was bitter and strong, too harsh for a fey palate. But she drank it anyway. There were some things from her human life she simply wasn't willing to give up.

Leto was already preparing to go. She never stayed for very long. "Is there anything you would like me to tell the Queen today? I would be happy to relay another message."

Taly took the smallest sip of coffee she could manage, wincing at the taste. "No," she said after a moment. She'd already tried sending messages and notes. They never did a damned thing.

Two more days passed.

Taly ate her meals alone.

She went to sleep alone.

She woke up screaming and sobbing Skye's name in the dark alone.

Leto continued to deliver the same books and papers with every meal.

On and on, each day was exactly the same, until one morning, Leto arrived with no more books and no more papers.

But instead a formal summons from the Queen.

Taly huffed as she paced around the spacious study for what seemed like the hundredth time. After Leto had shown her to the room where her lessons were to be held, she'd been left to wait.

And wait.

And wait.

With nothing else to do, she'd already completed the test booklet she'd found on a long table. What she assumed was her first seal examination.

She'd even had time to go back and check her answers.

Twice.

And after another hour of waiting and pacing and flipping through the various stacks of paper and discarded books decorating the many shelves and tabletops scattered about the room, any anticipation she might have felt about finally meeting with the Queen a second time had given way to frustration.

It was a power play. Taly knew it, though it did little to calm her rising anger. The Queen wanted her to know just how small and insignificant she really was. That was no doubt why she had waited more than two weeks to call for her. Why she still continued to keep her waiting.

Hands clasped behind her back, Taly wove between the now intimately familiar stone columns and dark leather and mahogany furniture, the silk rugs muffling the sound of her footsteps. The long coattails swishing around her knees caught on the edge of a table for not the first time, and she growled as she tugged them free.

An Initiate's uniform, Leto had said. Every mage guild had some sort of regalia it used to distinguish its members, and as Taly had been informed earlier that morning as Leto draped her body in silk and braided her hair with ribbons to match, the Queen had requested that she appear for her first official day of training in formal dress.

The beryl-blue robe was long and loose with whorls of gilded thread that swam across the whole of it. A red sash cinched her waist, draped and pinned so that it wouldn't bunch the fabric of her white silk tunic, and a single time crystal, gold and glittering with aether, had been fastened in the center—a perfect match to the crystals that decorated her ears and wrists and fingers. Tailored gray leggings and soft kidskin boots tied just below the knee completed the ensemble.

Could be worse, Taly thought, smoothing a hand over the braids that had been coiled around her head like a crown. When Skye had started his training, his uniform had looked far more ridiculous. He'd been so adorably gangly as a youth, and the closely fit layers of violet and black that heralded his discipline had only served to emphasize his teenage awkwardness.

He had, of course, eventually grown into his looks. And the uniform. Filled it out quite well actually.

"Good morning!"

Taly jumped at the sound of the voice, whirling just in time to find herself crushed against the Queen.

"I always forget just how tiny you are!" Azura exclaimed, giggling at the squeal Taly let out when her feet abruptly left the ground. "Skylen's right—you're like an angry kitten. All you need is a fuzzy set of ears."

"Put me down!" Taly snapped, wriggling like her life depended on it. The moment her feet found solid ground, she stumbled back, desperate for space. She hated when people picked her up. And from the way Azura smiled serenely, pressing a finger to her lips as she struggled to keep in her laughter—she knew it.

Shards, this woman—she was poking at Taly like an animal in a cage.

Azura was dressed similarly to Taly. She wore the same white tunic, and her robe had long, bell-shaped sleeves that nearly touched the ground. But instead of a single golden crystal, the Time Shard's crest hung from her neck.

"I always did like this uniform," Azura said, brushing an invisible speck of dust from Taly's shoulder. "Of course, you should've seen the regalia when Graysen still held the throne. Anything would've been an improvement over that man's horrendous sense of style."

Chuckling at the memory, Azura turned and strode across the room to the table with the exam booklet—

"I finished already," Taly said a bit testily, watching as Azura laid a hand on the completed exam. "I've been waiting for three hours. I'm not sure what else you expected me to do."

Azura paused a moment. Then straightened. "Well… there goes my entire lesson plan for the day," she said, turning on her heel as she strode for a small sitting area in front of the window.

The test booklet remained unopened.

"Aren't you going to grade it?" Taly asked.

"No, dear. I trust you."

Taly shoved down her frustration. After ignoring her for two weeks, the least this infuriating woman could do was look at the damned thing. "I don't think that's how tests are supposed to work."

"I'm a queen," Azura replied, gracelessly falling into an overstuffed red velvet chair next to the window. "They work the way I say they work, and I always did hate grading papers. As far as I'm concerned, you're an Initiate, and we can begin the second seal." Azura waved a hand towards a small dagger sitting on a nearby table. "Now—throw."

Taly paused, confused. "What?"

Azura just snapped her fingers. "*Throw - it.* The second seal requires combat training, and I need to assess your strength."

Taly tentatively reached for the knife. "Where should I—"

"I don't care. Just throw the damned knife."

Taly hesitated only a moment, and then flicked her wrist.

A new body. That's what it felt like sometimes. One that was faster, *stronger,* and still not quite her own. Her washroom door—a great massive slab of sturdy oak—had cracked down the middle the first time she shut it too hard, and she'd broken so many wine glasses at this point, Leto had started bringing extra.

And her poor piano… Taly sighed. She'd only tried to play it once, giving up after she'd cracked half the keys.

So, it was no surprise that the dagger flew across the room fast as a shooting star, embedding itself down to the hilt in the nearest bookshelf.

"Again," Azura commanded.

Stepping across the room, Taly yanked the dagger from the wood, and then aimed for the door, managing to catch the center of an elegantly carved knot of wood. She used less force this time, but it didn't matter.

The dagger stopped with a solid thud, embedded down to the hilt, the blade no doubt protruding from the opposite side.

"You're strong," Azura commented, running a thoughtful finger across her chin. "And you seem to have some fighting skill. Do you know how to use a sword?"

Taly shrugged. "I manage."

"What do you mean by that?"

"I prefer guns," Taly answered simply. "Or bows. Any ranged weapon, actually. Ivain always told me to avoid getting too close."

"Smart man," Azura mused. "I've never seen a human win a fight against a fey. And I've been alive a long time." A snap of her fingers had the dagger shuddering, and Taly ducked as it yanked itself out of the wood, flying across the room to land back on the table like it had never left. "Leto says you were unhappy with your reading assignments."

Taly bristled. It seemed the Queen had been getting her messages—and just hadn't cared enough to do anything about it. "I have a solid background in aether mechanics," she said. "Something you would've known if you'd taken just a few moments to speak with me. But since you didn't, these past two weeks have been a waste."

Azura chuckled softly, clasping her hands in front of her as she settled back in her chair. "Already concerned about time, I see."

Taly's heart pounded out her frustration. "Of course, I'm concerned. I don't want to be here, remember?"

"And just where do you want to be?"

"Home," Taly bit out. "I want to go home."

"Back to Skye, I imagine."

Taly remained silent, refusing to look away from those strange, golden eyes.

"Funny," Azura said, the edges of her mouth lifting into a mocking smile. "You were so eager to leave him at Ebondrift. I wonder what changed."

She had survived, that's what had changed. The more Taly thought about it, the more she came to realize that she had never expected to come out of the Vale relay. She had left Ebondrift fully expecting to die, but now that she hadn't—she wanted to go back. She wanted her family.

Azura rested her head on a fist. "I've already told you—you're here until I say you can leave."

"Actually, you said I'm here until I can earn my third seal."

"And I suppose you're looking to hurry that up?" Azura arched an amused brow. "As if running back to the man you abandoned will change the fact that you ripped his heart out when you left? Or did you not think of that? I've always wondered—does Talya Caro ever think of the people who get hurt when she decides her life isn't worth as much as theirs?"

Taly's temper finally snapped, and the air in the room began to spark as she snarled—actually *snarled*—in a way that was more beast than woman.

"*Tem-per*," Azura crooned.

Taly followed her gaze, sucking in a gasp at the wisps of golden aether that snaked around her arms. She shook her hands, and the fog immediately dissipated.

"Good," Azura muttered, letting her head fall back. "I rather like this room. It would be a shame if you reduced it to dust on your first day." Before Taly could ask what she meant, Azura continued, "Now then—for the second seal, we'll be covering basic spellcasting and aether management, so from now on, I want you to spend at least an hour each morning meditating."

Taly resisted the urge to roll her eyes, muttering under her breath, "Shards, I knew that was coming." Every mage learned how to meditate, to inwardly manipulate the rate at which their bodies absorbed aether from the air. "Look," she said, putting her temper on a tight leash, "are you sure meditation is the best use of my time? Surely there's something else I could be doing, like casting or crystal inscription. You know—useful things."

Things she would need for her third seal.

Azura fixed her with a stare. "Meditation is a necessary skill. Every mage has a pool of magic—a set maximum concentration of aether that can be dissolved in their bloodstream at any one time."

"I know."

"No, child—I'm not sure you do. Knowing a thing is not the same as doing it, and while the size of your aether pool is immutable, the rate at which your body replenishes itself can be trained. Your magic is a muscle, and though you may have potential, make no mistake—right now, you are *weak.*"

"Fine," Taly sighed, and sat down in a chair opposite Azura. "If it's so important to you, I'll meditate." *Maybe*, she added silently. If there was time.

"Good," Azura said with a slight nod of her head. "Now then—aether manifestation will also be important. Your magic has been suppressed for so long, you've more than likely lost any instinctual ability to manipulate your magic. So, in addition to meditation training, I want you to practice summoning. Every night—summon and dismiss your aether until it becomes second nature. No casting—not yet."

"Why not?" Taly asked, trying to keep the sharpness from her tone. They were never going to get anywhere at this rate. "I'm hardly a child, and I would appreciate it if you stopped treating me like one."

Azura refocused her attention, giving her a calculated look. One that was cold and cutting, ancient and shrewd and—

Gone. In an instant. Replaced with a smile so sweet, it had Taly inching back in her chair.

"I can clearly see that you disagree with my methods," Azura said, each word oozing honey. "And I'll take partial blame for that. Obviously, I've made a miscalculation on just how to approach your training, and since careful planning and moderation seem to offend you so deeply—well, I suppose I'll have to think of something different."

The Queen's smile continued to widen. And despite the tremor of doubt that scuttled down her spine, Taly lifted her chin, refusing to be cowed.

"Cast something," was all Azura said.

Taly sat up a little straighter. Was this another trick? The Queen was smiling, and she was pretty sure that meant this was a trick.

"What's wrong?" Azura pressed. "You've made it very clear that you believe I've underestimated your abilities. Show me that you can cast a spell. Prove me wrong, and perhaps I'll even consider letting you send a message to your precious Skye."

Taly schooled her expression into something that she hoped resembled cool indifference. "Do… do you really mean that?"

"Cross my heart."

Taly frowned, hissing out a strangled "*fine*" if only because she couldn't find it in herself to admit that she didn't know the first thing about casting.

That she had been hoping to figure it out as she went along.

And so, not quite knowing what she was going to do, Taly took a shaky breath and closed her eyes, ignoring that smile and that gaze that still assessed and studied as she held out her hands, palms facing up the same way she had seen other mages do. It took a moment, a few seconds of searching, but eventually, she found it: that simmering buzz that had flared with her anger, a kind of effervescence that made her skin prickle. She gave a gentle nudge, a single thought directed at that place deep down that was already perking awake, and a golden cloud of aether immediately snapped into focus.

"I did it!" Taly exclaimed, waggling her fingers and watching the aether dance and sway. She looked to the Queen, grinning widely.

"Congratulations, dear. You managed to summon your aether—something a five-year-old can do instinctively." Azura gave an impatient wave. "Spell. Now."

Taly's palms began to sweat, but the smile on her face never wavered. True, she didn't know any spells. But the harpy, the shades—she had made them stop. That had been a spell of sorts, and she still remembered what it had felt like. Remembered that rush of magic. That wave of sizzling heat that pushed against her skin as it released. Maybe she could do it again.

Her thoughts turned inward, and she forgot about the Queen, stopped hearing the soft patter of summer rain that had started to streak the windows. It wasn't hard to find that vast well of power simmering just beneath the surface.

Hello, it whispered, so eager, so excited—an old friend that had somehow been there all along, waiting to be remembered. It was like standing before an ocean, and when she gently brushed a hand along the surface, it surged. A wave of pure energy swept across her skin.

The air around her began to stir, and she dipped back down, gathering just a little more, imagining that golden power slipping through her fingers like water.

"So, tell me—have you let Skye take a turn around the bush?"

Taly's eyes popped open, and the aether she had manifested hissed and sputtered as the spell promptly died. "What?"

The Queen had sprawled her body across the chair, letting one foot dangle over the side. She gave Taly a feline grin. "*Skye*, dear. If I recall, it's still early in that little tryst, yes? I imagine not then."

"I'm not going to discuss my love life with you," Taly replied curtly. Closing her eyes and ignoring the heat warming her cheeks, she turned her attention back to the spell.

"That bad, huh?" Azura ran a finger along her pendant, feeling the sharp point of the crescent moon. "If it makes you feel any better, your love life is about to really pick up."

"Stop trying to distract me."

Azura pulled a face, muttering, "Alright, alright—I can clearly see that you don't want to talk about Skye." Another grin. "Tell me—have you met Kato yet?"

Taly bit back a curse, diving back into that well of power. A shimmer of light manifested in the air around her.

A pulse. *Now?* her magic seemed to say, coiling beneath her skin, straining to get free as Taly began to wave her hands, shaping the spell. The cloud of aether sparked, responding easily.

She rolled her shoulders, breathing just a little bit easier. *Good.* Now if she could just—

A wad of paper bounced off her head, and Taly sighed, the spell fizzling. Her eyes flicked to Azura. The woman had abandoned her seat and now paced around the small sitting area, hands clasped behind her head.

"What was that for?" Taly asked.

"You didn't answer my question," Azura replied as though it should've been obvious. "Have you met Kato yet?"

"You mean Skye's asshole of an older brother?" The same one that had discovered her magic and threatened to give her over to the enemy. "Yes, we've met."

Azura sighed, and her eyes took on a faraway look. "I know he's a little grumpy right now," she said, "but once he lets go of all that anger, he's not so bad. And I know, I know, you and Skye have history. But just wait. Just wait until you see Kato's *abs* before you make any life-altering decisions."

"I have no interest in Kato," Taly said, hoping that would buy her a few moments of silence. "Or his abs."

"That's too bad," Azura replied sadly, "because you two definitely have chemistry."

"Shut up." Taly turned, facing the opposite direction. She tugged on her aether, harder than she intended, but it was no matter. The spell began to form, and she imagined a bubble. When she had been attacked by shades in the streets of Ebondrift, the spell had looked like a bubble.

"Aiden's not too bad either," Azura went on. "In fact, your boys are in a three-way tie as far as I'm concerned. I'm still not sure which I'd choose if I had the option."

Ignore, ignore, ignore, Taly chanted silently, even as the edges of the spell stuttered.

Azura was still talking—something about Aiden and transmutation charms.

And now just earth mages in general—how they had an almost *primal*—

"I don't want to talk about Aiden either," Taly snapped, pulling out a little more aether and testing the barriers of the enchantment.

Azura rolled her eyes. "Let me guess—because of *Skye*?" A snort. "Shards, and we're already back to Skye, Skye, Skye! Can you never talk about anything else?"

"You brought him up," Taly pointed out, taking several long breaths. Too fast—the spell was progressing too fast.

The shimmering film of golden energy surrounding her began to ripple.

"He's never far from your mind, dear." Azura stopped in front of a gilded mirror, preening. "And I suppose I can understand your infatuation. After all, the boy *is* handsome. A little lean, but I know you like your men lanky."

Taly hissed. She could feel time beginning to unwind, but it was twisting and tangling, and she didn't know how to reel it back in. She reached out a hand, plucking at the translucent web and trying to pick out the snarls.

Azura completed her circuit of the room, coming to stand behind Taly's chair. "I know you're listening," she said, eyeing the spell with a slight frown, "so don't even try to pretend otherwise. The only thing about Skye—and don't ever tell him I said this..." A pause. She drummed her fingers against the back of the chair. "Well, it's that *wife* of his—so possessive."

Taly's breath caught in her throat, and she lost her grip on the spell just as the web coiling around her tightened and snapped into place.

Her aether extinguished, and she scanned the surrounding room. There was no flicker of magic, no remnants of the spell she'd been trying to cast.

Overall, nothing seemed out of place. The room looked about as normal as a room in a magical palace could look.

So why did she feel so nauseous? Why wouldn't her hands stop shaking? Had she failed?

No. At least, she didn't think so. She'd felt... *something*. A tug. A release. So where had the magic gone? What had she done?

"It's that *wife* of his—so possessive."

Slowly, Taly turned to look up at the Queen. The woman still stood behind her chair, fingers drumming against the frame.

"It's that *wife* of his—so possessive," she repeated.

"Stop it," Taly hissed as something in her chest tightened to the point of pain. "I don't know what kind of game you're playing now, but that's not funny."

Azura was still unmoving, still just... *standing* there. Ignoring her. Not even looking at her. "It's that *wife* of his—so possessive."

Taly shot to her feet. "I said stop it! I'm tired of your fucking bullshit!"

"It's that *wife* of his—so possessive."

Shards, that word—*wife*... Why did that word hurt so much? Why did it make her stomach turn? She had always known that Skye would eventually take a wife—a proper lady that would make a proper Duchess. That was a certainty. That was his duty.

"It's that *wife* of his—so possessive."

Taly hugged her arms around her body, swallowing past the painful lump that had lodged itself in her throat. They had only kissed a handful of times over the course of a single day, and he had thought her human at the time. There could never have been anything between them. Was never going to be anything between them, though she realized now that a part of her had begun to hope. Now that she was fey, like him...

"It's that *wife* of his—so possessive."

Apparently not.

Someone began to clap, slow and mocking. "Well, well, well..."

Taly whirled around at the sound of the voice, only to find—*Azura*. She leaned against the windowsill, smiling and looking entirely too pleased. "This is a nice little hole in the fabric of the cosmos you've managed to carve out for yourself."

"What the hell?" Taly breathed. Her head whipped back-and-forth between the two women.

One unmoving, still repeating that cursed phrase. The other had begun to pace around the room, occasionally stopping to inspect something of interest.

Taly stabbed a finger at what she could only assume was a fake—an echo. "Did you do this?" she said to the woman who had stooped to peer underneath a table. At what—Taly had no idea. "Is this a trick?"

"No, my dear. This was all you." Azura moved to inspect her double, picking at the duplicate's clothing, then her hair. "It seems you created a time loop *inside* a pocket universe. And if you consider that you were already inside a time loop inside a pocket universe..." She chuckled and shook her head. "Well, it truly boggles the mind."

The image of the duplicate Queen stuttered, and for a moment, Taly thought this hellish torture was finally over. Either the spell had exhausted itself or maybe Azura had taken pity on her and intervened.

But then the echo began to flash, and all hope died as its words slowed, the syllables becoming long and drawn out.

"I think," Azura began, "that you were attempting to cast a snaring spell—to slow time." She glanced at Taly, who simply nodded in reply. "If that's the case, then I'm almost impressed by how badly you messed this up. It took me a moment to figure out just where you'd popped off to."

Another flicker of magic rippled through the air. "It's that *wife* of his—so possessive." Faster now, and the woman's voice was starting to turn shrill. "It's that *wife* of his—so possessive." The words repeated before the sentence was through, blurring together into a high-pitched whine.

Taly winced at the sound. "Would you just shut her up already?"

Azura pointed to her second self, and her grin widened. "This really bothers you, doesn't it?"

"Yes." Taly threw her hands up. "Yes, it does." It more than bothered her. It made her heart hurt, and her eyes sting with tears. Shards, a few kisses, and apparently, that was enough to turn her into some pathetic, love-sick fool who completely lost her shit over a predetermined inevitability.

"It's th-that w-w-wife of his—so p-p-possessive," the duplicate began to stutter.

"This is marvelous!" Azura waved a hand in front of her double's face. "What else does she do?"

Taly's fists clenched at her sides. "Please, just help me," she growled, trying to muster anger because anything would feel better than this empty, hollow feeling that was ripping a hole in her chest. "I don't know how I did this. I don't know how to undo it."

Azura looked up from where she had been picking lint off her double's coat sleeve. "Oh. *Now* you need my help? Now that you've trapped yourself in this lovely little pocket universe?"

"Well, maybe I wouldn't have messed this up so badly if you hadn't been distracting me?"

Azura rolled her eyes. "I'm sorry, but do you really expect your enemies to give you complete silence while you're trying to cast a spell? If this is what happens when you're confronted with a little friendly gossip, I shudder to think of just what you'll do when you have an army of shades at your door. Create a black hole? Rip open space and time itself and end all life as we know it? Should be interesting, to say the least. If only there was something that could help you improve your concentration and focus. Something like, oh I don't know… *meditation*?"

"I said I would meditate!" Taly nearly shouted. "I already agreed to meditate!"

Azura tsked her tongue. "Come now, my dear—do you really think I can't tell when you're lying? You were never going to meditate. You were going to go digging through libraries and practicing spells. You were going to do everything you thought was more important than the things I told you to do, never considering that *I know you*, Talya Caro. I know that you were educated by one of the greatest living shadow mages of his generation, and I know how much you hate being ignored because it reminds you of all the times during your life when you felt mortal and small and utterly invisible. I know that you let your emotions cloud your judgment, and I know *exactly* how difficult it's going to be retraining you to think with your head rather than your heart."

Reaching over, Azura thumped her on the forehead, making Taly jump. "We're time mages. We're offensively weaker than every other class of mage, which means we have to fight with our brains. We have to be smart, able to manipulate our battlefield, our enemy, but all you showed me today was how easy *you* are to manipulate. A few weeks of isolation, and you lose all control of your temper. One mention of Skye and a woman I could've made up, and you would've been stuck here without me to come find you."

The image stuttered again, and Azura glanced over her shoulder. "Now she's getting on my nerves too." Holding up a hand, the Queen's aether flared, plunging the room into blessed silence. Her eyes found Taly's. "Well, dear? What will it be? Will you do everything that I say—without question? Or should I leave you here to think about it?"

Taly stared at the double that now stood frozen. "Fine," she sighed, because what else could she do? "I'll study. I'll train. I'll be a model student.

But in return, I want your word. No more disappearing for weeks at a time. No more ignoring me. If you're going to teach me, then teach me. No more games."

Azura arched a brow. "You're not really in a position to bargain," she said, clearly amused.

Taly lifted her chin. "If you want me to follow you without question, then be someone worth following."

Azura's eyes narrowed—just slightly, as though she were considering the proposal. "Is that all?"

"Yes," Taly said. "I might not know you as well as you claim to know me, but I have a feeling there's nothing else I could ask for that you would consider giving."

Azura huffed out a laugh that turned into a long tapering chuckle. Taly got the distinct feeling that she'd just been backed into a corner. "Agreed," she chirped, clapping her hands twice.

Taly's ears popped, her vision blurred. It was as if all the air in the room got sucked out at once. The lights flashed, plunging the room into darkness—

And then it was over.

The double was gone. The room was silent save for the *tick tock* of the clock on the wall.

Groaning loudly, Taly fell back into a chair. Her heart beat out an unyielding rhythm, and she pressed a hand to her chest, desperate for air.

Azura claimed the seat across from her, smoothing out the fabric of her robe. "Well, I think that's enough spellcasting for today," she said, reaching for a small bell that rested on a low-lying wooden table. "Tea?"

Without waiting for a response, she rang the bell. A moment later, a door creaked open, and Leto entered the room, pushing a cart laden with tea and sweets.

"Now then," Azura said, replacing the bell on the table, "let's talk about meditation."

Taly leaned her head back as the Queen began to speak, noting with some relief that instead of tea, Leto handed her a cup filled with brandy.

CHAPTER 8

-An excerpt from the Essential Fey Survival Guide

Rule #127: Water mages are tricky bastards.

A high-level glamour can fool the senses, imitating flesh and blood, light and color, warmth and scent. It can build palaces out of mist and conjure spirits from fog. It can conceal nightmares just beyond the veil of perception.

If you find yourself the unfortunate victim of a water mage's illusions and wish to escape, you will need to do one or more of the following:

1. *Find the water mage;*
2. *Find the anchor for the spell;*
3. *Set yourself on fire;*

4. *Set your surroundings on fire and hope the rapidly evaporating water aether doesn't boil you alive;*
5. *Pray that the water mage grows tired of your screams for help and lets you go;*
6. *Accept the inevitability of death.*

By the time the Ebondrift refugees arrived in Della, the sky had long ago gone dark, painted velvet black and crowded with stars.

For as long as Skye could remember, the tiny village at the center of the island had always been grim and ordinary, reflecting more than any other area just how far Tempris had fallen after the Schism. A few rows of gray stone houses, a public stable, and a moss-covered inn—that was all there had been when he passed through last week.

There was even less now.

The cottages had been burned, and the inn's characteristic marble columns had been reduced to rubble. The smell of blood and smoke and unwashed bodies filled the air.

Ivain and his forces had been stationed in Della for nearly three days, using the abandoned village as a waypoint while they searched the rest of the island for survivors. A wall of rock and dirt had been erected around the perimeter of the village square, and the earth mages were already using their magic to carve small keyholes in the battlement, placing the flash cannons from Ebondrift at strategic points around the camp. The airship hovered over the eastern wall, a smudge of blackness against the starry night sky.

An airship, Skye thought with a slight shake of his head. He still wasn't entirely sure he hadn't hallucinated that part of the battle. For as long as he could remember, Ivain had been trying to get that rust bucket up in the air. Who knew all it would take was an entire city of mages at the old man's beck and call?

Skye sighed and readjusted his pack, weaving his way through the milling crowd. The village square was clogged from end-to-end with tents bunched around flickering campfires.

They'd had little time to celebrate their victory at the canyon. Ivain had given Skye a hearty pat on the back by way of greeting, and then it had been back to work. They'd counted the dead and burned the bodies, and when the sun had started to sink beneath the horizon, they'd finally begun the long process of loading the caravan onto the airship, saying a silent prayer that their wounded survived the trip to Della.

Hungry and tired, every muscle barking as new aches and pains began to make themselves known, Skye slipped inside Ivain's war-tent and slumped onto a bench. The interior was plain, unadorned except for a few benches and chairs and a large table spread with maps and papers. Fire lamps in each corner of the tent provided warmth and light, and silencing wards—just strong enough to dull the sounds of the camp outside—shimmered across the white canvas walls. A low wooden platform kept the mud and rain from seeping in, and a curtain separated what Skye could only assume was the sleeping and living area.

Skye grimaced as he reached for the buckles on his armor, letting the scaled pieces of leather fall to the ground. He was still covered in grit and gore, and the entire right side of his shirt was soaked through with blood. He had used far too much aether both during the battle and after as they loaded the flash cannons onto the ship, and it was taking longer than it should have for his wounds to mend.

The tent flaps pushed to the side, and Skye rose to his feet as Ivain ducked inside. His white-blonde hair was speckled with blood, and there were lines around his eyes that hadn't been there before. He had already discarded his armor, revealing a plain shirt that, once finely made, was now stained and tattered.

"Boy," Ivain said in greeting, clapping a hand to Skye's shoulder and pulling him into a tight hug. One that Skye readily returned, indifferent to the blood and dirt that coated them both. "I can't tell you how relieved I was to see you out there today."

"The feeling is mutual." Skye was nearly limp with fatigue, and he sagged a bit when Ivain released him and took a step back. "What about Sarina?" he asked. Without the relays, there had been no news from the rest of the island, and no way to know if the people he called family had made it through. "Is she—"

"Fine." Ivain gave him a tight smile. "Just fine. As are Aimee and Aiden and the rest of the household staff. The manor, amazingly enough, was untouched. Those wards you and I installed around the main property last year did their job, and they did it well."

Skye shifted his weight, noting the name Ivain had left out. "And Taly?" he asked. Ivain had sent scouts to every nearby village, looking for survivors. It was possible he could've found her. "We got... separated."

Ivain's face fell, and he opened his mouth to answer... only to shut it.

Skye's heart sank as a little bit more of the hope he'd been clinging to slipped away. *No.* The answer was no. She wasn't here.

Voices approached from outside, and moments later, Eula, Kato, and Harin trudged into the tent.

"We'll speak when this is done," Ivain said, giving Skye's shoulder one more squeeze before moving to the massive table that ran the length of the tent. Planting his feet firmly, he straightened his shoulders and stood a bit taller, and suddenly there was no more Ivain. Standing in his place was the Marquess Castaro, High Commander of the Gate Watchers.

"As I'm sure you all know," Ivain said, addressing the people as they gathered around the table, "approximately five days ago, Tempris came under attack from an unknown enemy. Every major city on the island has been invaded by shades, and many high-ranking officials in the Gate Watchers have gone missing in what is likely an attempt to disrupt our chain-of-command. We do not yet know how many lives have been lost. We do not know who we're fighting or why. All we know is that our enemy has stooped low enough to weaponize the dead. They've arrested the souls of those trying to pass through the veil and trapped them in a house of decay. They've committed one of the few crimes the Genesis Council has deemed an act of true evil, and that makes them capable of anything."

Ivain paused, meeting the eyes of every person in turn. "I applaud you all for the bravery you showed today. I commend you for the courage you've demonstrated in leading these people and keeping them united. I thank you for the service I know each one of you will continue to give. It is not an easy thing that we have been called upon to do, and there will be worse days ahead. Days that are harder, bloodier—that will steal away your resolve. But take heart. Find hope in the knowledge that we are stronger together. That our enemy tried to break us and failed, and that today's battle, despite our losses, was a victory. We are still here, and we will keep fighting, until the war is finished."

Ivain turned to the man standing at the farthest end of the table. "Marshal Harin," he said, expression stern. "Report."

Harin began to give his statement, clasping his scarred hands behind his back as he accounted for the number of wounded, the duty roster, and other details about the refugee integration.

Skye tried to listen, but his attention kept slipping to the calculated gaze he could feel boring into him from across the table. Kato had fought valiantly that afternoon, but there was still the issue of Taly. Kato believed her to be a traitor, and he *would* bring the issue before Ivain. The only question was when and how big a spectacle he intended to make.

Eula stood beside Kato. Her face was clean, but flecks of gore still clung to her dark hair. There was a cut on her cheek that was struggling to close, and she wiped at it occasionally, frowning at the blood that streaked the back of her hand.

"Thank you, Harin," Ivain said, making a quick note on a scrap of paper. "With those numbers, that makes the final count… 142 dead, four times as many injured."

And the largest documented loss of fey life since the Schism.

Ivain didn't say the words, but Skye heard them anyway, each one cutting sharp as a blade. He'd failed these people. They'd chosen him to lead, and he'd taken them to their deaths.

"I take full responsibility," Skye said as hollow guilt caved his chest. He was unfit to be standing at this table, and everyone knew it. They were thinking it. They had to be. "The shades—they surprised us. We scouted every inch of the forest. I… I think they were using water magic. I felt it when I was scouting the area around the canyon, but I didn't realize what it was until we were already on the bridge."

Ivain gave him a quiet, steady look, as if he could see the inadequacy. "You're right," he said, reaching into his pocket. He produced a small drawstring bag and dumped out its contents. A handful of blue stones caked with gravel and dirt spilled onto the cluttered tabletop. "My men found water crystals buried just behind the highway wardline. These were discovered on the north side of the canyon, but there were twice as many on the south side, some as far as the turnpike. The enchantments were complex and expertly woven; I'm surprised you noticed anything at all. My guess is our enemy glamoured their forces and waited until you were crossing the bridge to launch their attack."

Kato's eyes cut to Skye. "Which would mean they knew where and when we planned to move. Almost like someone told them."

The sudden pulse of strained silence that passed between the two brothers wasn't lost on the rest of the group.

"Sire," Eula interjected, turning to Ivain. "On the subject of security—"

Ivain held up a hand, and Eula ducked her head. Even Kato's mouth clicked closed. "I'm already well aware of your troubles with foreign agents."

The room stilled, the low din of the camp outside trickling into the tent as every eye settled on Ivain.

"How?" Harin asked in that low, gruff way of his.

"The same way I knew to come to your aid." Ivain hesitated a moment. "I think it would be easier to hear for yourselves."

The group glanced at each other apprehensively, trying to anticipate what Ivain was about to reveal.

His expression was stoic as he reached beneath a stack of papers and produced a fogged sheet of glass rimmed with alternating rows of shadow and water crystals. It was a glamour interface, the kind typically used in scrying relays.

Keying in a command that had the water and shadow crystals blinking to life, Ivain said, "We received this transmission from Vale five days ago."

The picture on the interface remained stubbornly blank, but Ivain's voice came through: *"This is Relay 12-001—Ryme. Identify yourself."*

"Ivain?" came a breathless, feminine voice.

Eula gasped, and Skye flinched. Kato's eyes went impossibly wide, and even Harin looked a bit more interested.

Because that voice—that was *Taly*, and Skye wasn't sure if he wanted to laugh or cry. She had made it to the relay. She had actually gone for the relay. She hadn't betrayed them.

Her voice was grainy through the playback, and Skye listened greedily, irritated when she would fade away, nearly snarling every time someone spoke over her. Her image flashed in his mind—dirty, flushed, hair a mess and falling out of its braid.

Beautiful. So beautiful. So *alive.*

Taly started speaking faster, her words rushed and panicked. *"I don't know how much time I have. Um… Plum was burned, Vale is overrun, and someone here was talking to Strio. They said something about what sounded like a leader of some sort, and they have a list of people that they're trying to recruit. That's all I was able to overhear before they cut the connection."*

Something groaned in the background, and Taly muttered a quiet curse. *"I need to go. Just to be safe, I wouldn't trust any more transmissions from this relay or Strio."*

The message clicked, the lights along the interface flickering and finally fading. The room went silent.

Several long moments passed, and, surprisingly, Kato was the first to ask, "Where is she?" with what appeared to be genuine concern. Because even he couldn't refute this evidence. No matter what kind of foreign magic he'd discovered penned onto her skin, Taly had done exactly what she said she'd do. She had made her way to the relay. She had sent out a distress signal and gathered valuable intel. She had secured the backup they so desperately needed and saved the life of every man, woman, and child on that bridge.

She wasn't a traitor. Or a spy.

She was a hero.

"We don't know where she is," Ivain said softly. "This transmission came in just after the attacks began, and we haven't heard anything since."

"Shit," Harin quietly cursed, turning his face away. The fire mage had always had a soft spot for Taly.

"Who was in the room?" Eula asked, mirroring Skye's own concern.

"And did she get away?" Kato again.

Skye shifted, inching towards the entrance of the tent, but Ivain's eyes locked with his, anchoring him in place.

"Vale is only a few hours on foot," Skye said, clinging precariously to what was left of his composure. He could make it there before dawn, have the entire area scouted and surveyed before even the earliest of early risers began to stir.

"I'm aware," Ivain said, never letting Skye out from underneath that icy blue stare. "And I've already sent Aiden to search the area. He left shortly after we made camp in Della."

Skye's brows rose. "Aiden?" he asked. That didn't make any sense. True, he and Taly were friends, had grown even closer after the incident with the harpy. But Aiden was an earth mage. Why would Ivain risk a healer when there were so many wounded?

Sensing the question, Ivain said, "He insisted. Quite vehemently." Sadness tempered with guilt flickered in his eyes, as if to say, *I couldn't say no.*

Healers were precious, but Taly was as much a daughter to Ivain as if she'd been born of his own flesh. If she was in danger, he couldn't stand by and do nothing. Not when someone was volunteering to go where he couldn't because the situation demanded he prioritize the lives of the many over the lives of those he never wanted to live without.

"Now then," Ivain said, and Skye breathed out a slow sigh when those eyes finally slid away. "Harin, Eula, you're dismissed. Skye and Kato—you stay."

Harin made a hasty exit, shoulders straight and head held high. Eula lingered, accepting a firm clap on the shoulder from Ivain as well as a few words of encouragement. She gave Skye a tight smile before she too exited the tent.

When they were alone, Ivain turned to Kato, who—to Skye's surprise—had the good sense to hang his head.

"Kato Emrys," Ivain drawled with something that almost sounded like amusement. "To say that you were the last person I expected to see today would be quite the understatement. Would you mind telling me just what you're doing on my island?"

"I'm a Marshal in the Gate Watchers, Sire." Kato's answer was easy and swift, said with a hint of a smile—so at odds with the tense set of his shoulders and the way he shifted from foot-to-foot.

"So I've gathered," Ivain said. "However, I'm curious to know why I was unaware of your enrollment until just a few hours ago. The Gate

Watchers are an elite group, and I take pride in cultivating the men and women in our ranks. I can't review every new application, but I still should have been made aware when you began to advance. Especially considering how quickly. Why have I never seen your name, Marshal?"

Kato's throat bobbed. "A little bit of persuasion and a sizeable donation," he answered, then hastily added, "I'm not here to cause trouble, Sire. I just wasn't willing to risk having my relationship with my brother be the reason for having my application rejected. I have legitimate business to attend to in the mortal realm, and I wanted to be close by when the Aion Gate opened. That's all."

"The Aion Gate won't be opening for a few months yet," Ivain countered. "Eula tells me you've been here for almost a year."

"True," Kato conceded. "But the bridging connections have been less and less stable, the last one only lasting a week. I needed more time than that, so I decided to come to Tempris to see the gates for myself. I've been working on the Mechanica for almost two decades, and there's so much proprietary technology tied up in those suits of armor. I thought there might be something that could stabilize the connection, keep the gates open longer. Turns out I was right. That new tuning harmonic you're using this year? That was me. It was part of the comm system for a prototype suit I was helping to develop."

Ivain almost looked impressed as he slipped his hands into his pockets. "I require loyalty from my recruits. Loyalty and honesty and honor—all things you have yet to demonstrate."

"Sire," was all Kato said in reply. Not arguing for once.

Ivain looked to Skye. "Is this going to be a problem?"

Skye heard Kato's heart fumble. He waited just a beat longer than necessary before saying, "No. My brother fought well today, and I have no doubt that he will commit himself to this cause and these people. He has shown himself to be a man willing to make difficult decisions in the pursuit of what he believes to be right."

Kato's face went slack with surprise, but Skye just shrugged. He'd meant every word.

Ivain's lips thinned as he glanced between the two men, his attention finally settling on Kato. "A ringing endorsement, your history considered. You'll be on guard duty every night until I say otherwise, and if I were you, I'd use those hours to consider the role of subterfuge and just how far it *won't* get you within this organization. Prove to me that you're worthy of my trust. You won't be getting a second chance. Dismissed."

Skye watched his brother slink through the break in the canvas, waiting for the flicker of the air wards as they reengaged. When he turned, Ivain was already staring at him expectantly.

"Well?" he asked.

Skye schooled his expression. "Well what?"

"*Skylen*," Ivain warned. "Do not test my patience. Word around camp is that you sent Taly to the relay as your scout, but I sincerely hope you're not dumb enough to try to pass that off on me. You'd sooner throw yourself in front of a sword than put that girl in harm's way. Why was she in Vale? Explain."

Skye ran a nervous hand through his hair, eyeing the break in the canvas and the shadows that flickered just outside. "You're right," he whispered, quiet enough to confuse any listening ears. "And for what's it's worth, I had my reasons for lying."

Reasons he explained as calmly and succinctly as possible. He told him about the traitor, about the missing crystals in the Seren Gate. He explained the spells that Kato had uncovered and the glamour concealing the underlying web of magic. He even showed him the note she'd left behind—the few lines of scribbled text that had knocked the world out from underneath him and sent him spinning through space.

And when Skye was done, the older man stared at him for a long moment, eyes wide and skin too pale, as though the weight of all his many years had crashed into him at once. "Oh, my little one..." He blinked, and a tear slipped free. "What did you do?"

Skye glanced at the darkened interface that lay discarded on the table. "The spells—what do you make of them?"

Ivain shook his head. "I wouldn't know without inspecting her myself. It could be some kind of concealment magic like your brother believed. I've heard of rival families trying to infiltrate their enemy's stronghold with glamours and tricks, disguising one of their own to look like someone else. It could also be something innocuous. Something she, perhaps, did to herself. There are mages that prey on humans, charging them exorbitant amounts for spells and charms they claim can extend their lifespans."

"Taly wouldn't fall for something like that." Life-extension magic was dangerous and highly regulated, and she was too smart to get pulled into some back-alley enchanter's shop.

"Probably not," Ivain conceded. "Though it would make sense. She's been grappling with her mortality this past year, and I think I would prefer that explanation to any of the alternatives."

Ivain turned and leaned against the table, looking tired and worn in the dim light of the tent. He dragged a hand across his face, wiping the moisture from his eyes. "I'm sure I don't have to tell you the risk you took when you lied. Kato had a valid concern, and if Taly really had been working with the enemy, as the evidence at the time suggested… You can't let personal feelings get in the way when the consequence could be someone else's life."

"I followed my instincts," Skye insisted, placing a hand on the darkened glamour interface. "Just like you taught me to do. Taly didn't betray us. I don't know why she left. Maybe she was running from something. Maybe I was just being a blind fool, and she saved me from myself, but… she didn't betray us. She did the exact opposite. We would've died on that bridge if you hadn't known to watch the southern roads. Lying was the right choice, and you would've done the same."

Ivain said nothing. It was answer enough.

"Let me look for her," Skye said softly. "We won't be leaving here for several days yet. Let me go to Vale."

"I'm sorry, Skye. No."

"Please, Ivain. I stayed when every instinct screamed at me to go. I stayed, and I did my duty, but these people are safe now. Safer with you than they ever were with me, so please—let me go. *Now*, while there still might be a chance of finding her."

Ivain crossed his arms. "I've already sent Aiden."

"I could help him. I could find him and send him back here. A healer is no use in a forest, miles away from the people that need him."

"Earth mages can do more than heal," Ivain countered. "They have tracking magic."

True. It was true. Aiden probably still had samples of Taly's blood from when she was recovering from the harpy, enough to cast a locator spell. He would be able to find her so long as her feet remained firmly rooted to the ground.

Still, the thought of being here when she was out there, when she could be hurt, maybe dead or dying…

"You know I'm right, Skylen."

Skye hated that his first instinct was to obey. To accept that the choice wasn't his to make. All his life, none of the choices that mattered had ever been his to make.

He sunk down on a nearby bench. "Please," he said again, broken. "Please, Ivain, I… I love her." And she would be furious if she knew just how much he was willing to throw away to find her, but he didn't care. "I love her, so please... let me go. I can't just stay here and do nothing."

Ivain gave him an unreadable look, quiet for a long moment. Long enough that Skye began to worry that he'd made a mistake. Ivain wasn't a hateful man—he'd raised a human as his own. But he was rational. And loving a human was *not* a rational thing to pursue. Not for a man who would be duke, whose birth demanded that he ascend the throne to the most powerful dominion in the Fey

Imperium, whose family would demand he leave her behind.

Finally, Ivain gave a weary sigh. "I know," he said with something like sympathy in his eyes. "I know exactly how you feel about that girl. Sarina and I both have watched the two of you growing closer for years, and I'm sorry you only discovered it for yourself now. That neither of you got the time you deserved. But that doesn't change my decision. Part of the burden of leadership is having to stay behind. It's having to assess people's strengths and weaknesses and knowing when someone else is more suited to the task. Aiden can track her, he can heal her, he can move through the forest undetected, and he has already been sent."

Fair points. Well made. Though it was little comfort.

He still looked pale, but Ivain straightened his shoulders and pushed away from the table, slowly pulling himself together. "You made a mistake today. I won't deny it. But everyone that has ever been forced into a position of leadership has made mistakes. I know you want to find Taly. I do too. But these people are still looking to you. You still have a duty to them. One that is not yet fulfilled."

That word—*duty*. Skye felt the weight of that word settle into his bones.

Ivain was right. Staying was the *sane* decision. It was the *right* choice.

Even if he hated it.

Skye gave a shaky nod of his head. "Sir."

Ivain breathed out a sigh. He looked relieved. "I sent Aiden with a comm," he said a bit more gently. "He's due to check in tonight."

"Okay," Skye said, and Ivain gave his shoulder a squeeze before retreating to the back of the tent.

Okay, he would wait. Okay, he would stay behind.

A crystal on the glamour interface flashed, indicating that the memory chit was full.

Skye pulled it closer, tapping a finger against the glass.

"Ivain?"

Taly's voice was like a balm, and when the message was done, he replayed it again.

And again.

And again.

CHAPTER 9

-A letter from Sarah Dixon to Kato Emrys, former heir to House Ghislain

Dearest Kit,

I still don't agree with your decision to send me away, and I hate that you made that choice for the both of us. I hate that I'm the one that has to leave our home, and I hate that you turned your back on the life that we made here. But I don't hate you. I don't, and I'm sorry that those will likely be the last words I ever get to say to you in person. I've had some time to think, and I understand now why you did what you did. Your duty is to your family, and I know that I will never fit into the future they have planned.

You'll find enclosed with this letter the sum of gold you left in my purse the last time you visited. Even if I wanted your coin, Kit, fey gold won't do me much good where I'm going. Without you, there's nothing keeping me here anymore, so I've decided to go home—back to New York. When my sister last wrote to me, she said exciting things were happening in the human realm. They'd put a man in space, and they were already talking about going to the moon. It seems so hard to believe, but if it's true, I want to see it. Science is a kind of magic, after all, though I imagine most fey would disagree.

For what it's worth, I don't regret a single moment of the time we spent together. For the rest of my life, I'll always be glad that I was able to know you.

With all my love, because it has and always will be yours,

Sarah

Kato sighed as he shouldered his pack, mumbling a tired apology to the mortal woman that stumbled into him.

The night had quickly turned cold, but the fires that dotted the camp warmed the air. Fey and mortal alike huddled together, stretching their hands towards the flames, desperate for any meager trace of heat they could find. There were tarps to ward off the rain, and a few places where water mages had laid down enchantments to wick away moisture. Many of the refugees had bound themselves in rough blankets that were already damp with mist.

Funeral pyres burned at the far edge of the camp, close to the healing tent where the menders were busy sorting the living from the dead. They'd lost even more men and women on the trip from the canyon, those whose wounds were too severe to warrant saving.

Kato paused, watching as one of the earth mages ducked out of the healing tent carrying a body far too small to be covered in a death shroud. A tuft of blond hair peeked from beneath the black linen. In the dark, he could just make out the delicate arch of a fey ear.

Kato swallowed back bile. *The priestesses lied,* he thought. Death was rare among the fey, but during the few times he'd heard the Faerasanna speak on the subject, they had described a journey. They had spoken about a boat and a peaceful homecoming. They'd told stories about tall, shining gates waiting to welcome the world-weary traveler into the rolling green hills of Moriah.

But none of that was true. Not unless that boat was made of bone, those hills blanketed with corpses. Not unless the rivers of that rotting kingdom ran red with blood.

A keening wail sounded over the din of the camp as a woman tried to claw the child's body from the healer's hands.

Kato wanted to blame his brother for this. The battle at the canyon was a massacre—an outright slaughter. They had walked straight into a trap, and Shards, he'd felt so vindicated as he watched those people dying. Now though, facing the realization that Skye's "scout" had saved them all… all he felt was remorse, guilt, and just a touch of shame.

All week, he'd been *sure* that Taly was the traitor. He'd convinced himself that Skye had known, had let her escape with all their secrets.

So, instead of preparing these people, instead of using his skills and talents to repair weapons or even learn about those damned guns, he'd wasted his time trying to pin guilt on an innocent woman.

So really, today was as much his fault as anyone else's. He'd been more focused on seeing his brother fail than helping him succeed.

"Hey, hold up there!"

Kato started, turning just in time to see a man weaving through the crowd. His hair was bone-white, and his eyes were a bright highborn blue. His face was narrow, his jaw artfully shaved. Instead of armor, he wore a stained frock coat and scuffed riding boots.

Quickly falling to one knee, Kato winced when his pack tweaked an injury that was still trying to heal. He recognized the man as Lord Kalahad Brenin, the High Lord of Earth's younger brother, and although Kato possessed a higher standing among the nobility, he was no fool. He had learned early on that bad things happened to those stupid enough to piss off a Genesis Lord's favorite.

"Sire," Kato said as the man came close enough to hear. A contingent of guards followed close behind, each one adorned with the High Lord of Earth's crest—Yggdrasil, the tree of life.

"None of that," the man said, laughing. He pulled Kato's pack from his shoulders, pulled him straight to his feet. "Call me Kalahad. And you're Kato, yes? Kato Emrys?" When Kato nodded, Kalahad said, "Come. Sit with me."

Not knowing what else to do—and too tired to put up a fuss—Kato allowed himself to be led over to a large grouping of tents near the edge of the camp. A massive bonfire crackled in the misty haze, and more guards milled around, cleaning weapons and charging crystals. They dispersed as soon as they saw Kalahad and Kato approaching, sketching out hasty bows as they backed away.

Beneath the main pavilion, there was a scattering of mismatched chairs and couches, even a rug spread over a few pieces of planked wood. Old sheets had been hung around the sides of the tent to keep out the moisture, and there was a serving bar set against the back "wall" where women in smocks and aprons were spooning stew into real china.

"Sorry about the mess," Kalahad said as he dumped Kato's pack and bedroll next to the fire. Throwing himself onto a large leather-bound chair, he leaned back, lounging in a way that reminded Kato of a king on his throne. "I had my men scour the village for anything still intact, and this is what they came up with. I don't mind, but some of the other nobility took great offense at the prospect of sleeping outside." Kalahad held up a hand, and the serving ladies began to flutter with activity, reaching inside boxes and crates. "I hear that Lord Achard and his wife-to-be have taken shelter on the main floor of the inn. You're welcome to take advantage of my hospitality, but I have no doubt they're more comfortable. If that's where you choose to make your bed, no hard feelings."

"I... thank you." Kato blinked at the cup of wine that was suddenly thrust into his hands. "I appreciate the offer, but that's probably a non-issue." A woman with a bowl of stew approached him, but he waved her off. He was still covered in blood—his and others—and he didn't think he could stomach anything just yet. Even if it did smell delicious. "I'll likely be on guard duty most of the night."

Kalahad nodded, accepting his own cup of wine. "That's right. I remember now. You joined the Gate Watchers last year. In fact, I hear you were leading the party sent out to find me."

"Uh... yes." Kato claimed a seat—a scuffed wooden affair with a ripped blue cushion. It was true. Lord Brenin—or rather *Kalahad*—had come to Tempris only a handful of weeks ago, claiming an interest in the island's economic rehabilitation. Instead of going to see Marquess Castaro, however, the noble had set off on his own, intent on inspecting the farmland on the southeastern edge of the island. The Gate Watchers had lost track of him after the attacks began.

Kato hung his head. "We didn't do a very good job, I'm afraid, and for that, I apologize."

Kalahad smiled, holding out his glass. A servant immediately rushed to refill it. "Not to worry—I have a tendency to wander off. I got separated from my group, and Lord Castaro and his scouts found me two days ago—dazed, confused, and covered in mud, blood, and my own filth."

"And the rest of your party?" Kato asked, sipping from his cup. The wine was remarkably smooth, and he savored it. It was likely the last good wine he'd have for a while.

"Fine, all fine. My brother made sure that I had only the purest of the purebloods on my protection detail. Mages with long illustrious backgrounds that loudly resented being sent here to babysit a half-breed like myself."

Kato looked up. "You'll have to forgive me. I was unaware you had human blood."

Kalahad shrugged. "On my mother's side. You're a demi-fey as well, yes? Your father was a Feseraa?"

Kato nodded, but before he could open his mouth to respond, Kalahad signaled for the servant to refill both of their cups. "Nice to know I have a friend in this place," he muttered. "Us half-breeds—we have to stick together. We're not highborn enough for the highborn, but the lowborn are still too scared to even look us in the eye."

Kato snorted. "A High Lord's younger brother? I'm sure there's no shortage of nobles wanting to kiss your ass."

"And you can say differently?" Kalahad grinned. "You used to be heir to the most powerful household in the Imperium."

" '*Used to*' being the operative phrase there," Kato shot back, trying to keep the sharpness from his tone and only half succeeding. His disinheritance was common knowledge among the nobility, but that didn't mean it was a pleasant topic. "Like most households, my family still prioritizes purebloods in the line of succession. My brother—Skylen. He's the heir now."

"Passed over for the younger brother," Kalahad drawled. "A common tale. Not particularly fair, if you ask me, but then again, few things are. I must say—I've always been quite happy to be so far removed from my family's primary bloodline. Far fewer consequences when I make an ass of myself."

Kato huffed out a laugh. "That's one way of looking at it, I suppose."

"There's freedom in being unimportant," Kalahad said with a wink. "I'll never have power, and that suits me just fine. I'm content draining my brother's coffers and leaving the business of ruling to my betters. Though I get the feeling you don't feel the same. It couldn't have been easy losing your family's favor for something so far outside your control."

It was Kato's turn to shrug. "I never cared much for power, but for a very long time, I was the Duchess' only son. Taking her place seemed inevitable."

"Good you have your brother then. Now you're free to live the life you want."

Kato grimaced. *True.* Or it would be if he hadn't already made so many sacrifices in the name of duty and family. He'd given up the life he wanted a long time ago, and there would be no getting it back. Those decisions couldn't be undone.

"Say now..." Kalahad mused, swirling his wine. "If I recall, you had that little human tryst a few centuries back. What was her name again? Sylvia? Sabrina?"

Sarah, a small voice immediately supplied. *Her name was Sarah.*

Kato silenced the voice, forcing a smile and making sure his eyes crinkled just so. The smile was the hardest part to fake, but he had gotten good at it over the years. Good at convincing people that he'd forgotten about the woman he loved. Good at pretending he didn't care that he had been ordered to send her away. The heir to Ghislain couldn't take a human lover. That would have been too much of a scandal.

Not that it mattered anymore. That sacrifice had become gut-wrenchingly irrelevant the moment his baby brother took his first breath.

"Is that why you're on the island?" Kalahad prodded. "Is the black sheep of Ghislain finally going to claim his bride? Rumor says she relocated to the human realm, and with the time differential—she might still be alive."

Kato drained his cup, forcing that smile to spread just a little wider. "You know," he said, "I'm starting to think you're a bit of a gossip."

"Yes," Kalahad answered easily. "Yes, I am, and since I've now been discovered, I feel no shame in saying that the word around camp is that your brother finds himself in a similar situation. Is it true he's taken a human mate?"

"I'm not sure." Not a lie, though Kato did wonder why he hadn't just said "yes." The golden boy was clearly infatuated with Taly, and that relationship would surely bring shame to both him and their family. If this were any other time, any other situation, he'd have no problem sowing a few seeds of dissent just to see how far people were willing to go to kiss his brother's ass—but not about this. This would affect Taly too, and if she ever found her way back, he didn't want to hurt her more than he already had.

The same way he had never wanted to hurt Sarah.

"Would you like to talk about it?"

Kato's brows rose in question. "I'm not sure I follow."

Kalahad just shrugged. "I know that look. It's been a shitty day, but that look… There's a woman involved." At Kato's answering sigh, he let out a loud bark of laughter. "I knew it. It's true, isn't it? Skylen Emrys took a human mate, and judging from that look, she must be something special. I suppose she would have to be to make it to the Vale relay with undead monsters roaming the forests."

Kato frowned. "And how would you know about Vale?" Surely, Ivain had kept that information restricted.

Kalahad gave him a flat stare. "All I've heard since I got here is *'Talya Caro this'* and *'Talya Caro that.'* Apparently, someone snuck into the Marquess's tent and made a copy of the relay transmission. Everyone's heard it by now. She's the hero of the hour, and I'm sure you can see now that if you tell me anything less than both of the Emrys brothers have fallen head over heels for our young heroine, I'll be sorely disappointed. Anything less, and it just won't be worth the retelling."

Kato snorted. "Sorry to disappoint, but I harbor no such feelings. All I can say is that I found her refreshingly tolerable."

"Are you sure that's all?"

"Yes."

"I don't believe you. There's something about this girl that's gotten underneath your skin. I can tell these things."

Kato dragged a hand through his hair. Was he that transparent? "I made a miscalculation. That's all."

"And was this miscalculation the subject of your and Skylen's quarrel on the road?"

Kato looked up. He thought he'd been careful when he confronted his brother, making sure there was no one close enough to overhear.

"Gossip," was all Kalahad offered in explanation. "Rumor is the two of you had a bit of a tiff."

Not careful enough, it seemed.

Kato drained what was left in his glass. "Yes. That's what we were arguing about. I jumped to conclusions, and I doubted one of the few people I've actually liked in a long time—present company excluded, of course," he added quickly, earning him a bemused grin in return.

Kato leaned back in his chair, staring up through a rip in the canvas. "I've been thinking quite a lot lately about making amends," he found himself saying. "With mortals—there's never enough time. They die, and we're left here still shouldering the weight of everything that never got said. And now with these attacks with the..."

"Shades," Kalahad supplied. "Horrible business. I take it this *Taly* is still out there?"

"Yes." Kato swallowed and held out his cup, grateful when a serving woman immediately refilled it. He probably shouldn't. This was fey wine, and he was already feeling woozy. But when he considered what had likely happened to Taly, when he wondered if his actions had perhaps been a catalyst... He took another long draw. "I love my people and my family, and I've made decisions over the course of my life that I've had to live with. But this time—I went looking for answers in the wrong places. I thought I knew something, and I accused someone of something that I now know was wrong."

And Shards, why did that bother him so much? He had been wrong before. Hell. He was over two centuries old. He'd been wrong lots of times, and while yes, Taly reminded him of Sarah—they both had that same fire, the same undeniable intelligence—she was just a human. Transient. Little more than a blip of light in the darkness, snuffed out by the slightest breath of circumstance.

So why then? Why was it eating at him? Why did he keep trying to imagine what Sarah would've said or done if she could see the man he had let himself become?

"Sorry," Kato said after a moment, realizing he'd let the conversation lapse. "You probably have no idea what I'm talking about."

"Does it matter?" Kalahad asked. "I find that sometimes just saying a thing is all a person really needs."

Kato couldn't argue with the logic, even if finding that level of empathy in another highborn was a bit of a shock.

And suddenly he began to wonder if accepting the wine had been a mistake. Had he said too much? Given away—

"I know that look too," Kalahad said. "Fey do not come by trust naturally, and you've just made yourself vulnerable. So, in exchange, I will give you one piece of information about me. Ask me a question, and I'll answer."

Kato blinked. An unusual offer. Among the fey, information was currency. This was the highest sign of trust one highborn could offer another. He would be a fool not to take it.

"You're notoriously anti-human," Kato said. "So much so that there are rumors that you steal them away from their conclaves."

Kalahad's lips twitched. "I see I'm not the only gossip."

Kato asked simply, "Is it true?"

To which Kalahad replied, just as easily, "All rumors have some truth."

Kato's stomach clenched. "So, you steal humans?"

"Yes." Once more, Kato was surprised at this man's candor. "However, what most people fail to ask is *'what do I do with them?'* I've worked hard to cultivate my reputation, because when people make assumptions, it makes them easy to manipulate."

Kalahad sat up, setting his cup to the side. "I steal humans, but because I'm rumored to hate them, people assume I must be doing something nefarious. But what if I was simply giving them a different life? I've visited the free cities, spoken with Feseraa once they've been relieved of their contracts. They live in squalor. They sacrificed to attain immortality, and now that they have it..." A soft, derisive chuckle. "It's a great cosmic joke. They discovered the secret to eternal life, only to discover that it wasn't worth living."

Kato stared at the man. "And how do I know you're telling me the truth right now?"

"You don't. But I just confirmed a rumor my brother has been working very hard to quell. Good or bad intent, it wouldn't look good for someone of my station to be seen fraternizing with the lower classes. I've given you a certain amount of power over me. Consider that a token of good faith."

A flicker of movement at the northern end of the camp drew his attention, and Kato saw a familiar shock of dark hair weaving through the crowd. His brother was still covered in blood, and his face looked haggard and worn. It was the look of a man that had been hollowed out, that only continued to move forward out of necessity.

Kato pushed himself to his feet. "Thank you for your hospitality, but I really should go." After all, he still needed to check the new duty roster. His guard rotation could've already started, and he wouldn't even know it.

"I understand," Kalahad said, rising from his chair. "It was good to meet you. If you ever need anything at all—even if it's just a drink—don't hesitate to bend my ear. I don't have as much sway here on Tempris as I would back home, but I'll try my best."

Kato took the man's hand and gave it a firm shake. "Thank you," he said earnestly, for the first time noticing the serving ladies behind them as they still ladled soup. They passed the bowls through a break in the tent—to humans. Even with the meager resources available to them in camp, he had his people feeding the shardless.

Maybe Kalahad wasn't just blowing hot air.

"I don't know if I trust you yet," Kato said, meeting the man's eyes, "but I'm glad we met."

Kalahad's smile widened, and he laughed, clapping a hand to Kato's shoulder. "Us half-breeds have to stick together."

CHAPTER 10

-An excerpt from the ABCs of Time Magic

M is for mimic.

The mimic is a Class VII multidimensional eldritch beast that feeds off anomalies and aberrations in the timelines. During periods of overpopulation or famine, they can be drawn to our world to feed, often lured by the imprecise nature of a young time mage's magic. For this reason, the mimic is considered one of the greatest risks for untrained time mages. Adult mimics are highly aggressive and predatory and will suck their victims down to the marrow, sometimes continuing to feed on a time mage's anima once their bloodborne aether is spent.

"Time is a tapestry," Azura said one morning over breakfast.

Taly was seated on a low garden wall, idly chewing on a piece of toast while she scribbled notes. They didn't usually take their morning meal together, but when they did, Azura insisted they start their day in the solarium. With its glass ceiling and glass walls all covered with creeping vines dotted with clusters of fat red berries, it made dealing with the Queen almost tolerable. Especially considering the early hour.

"Not literally, of course," Azura went on, carefully trimming a handful of berries from a nearby bush. "But that is, perhaps, the easiest way to visualize it. If you look at a tapestry on a loom, the threads all interlock, weaving together into something larger; something more than its individual parts. And then if you begin to think of those threads as people, animals, places, each one forging its own path through the weft, all feeding into the greater design—it's like a tapestry.

"All of creation is bound by time, every one of us—our lives, the decisions we make—merely threads on a loom. That is why we call the picture it creates the Weave. It's simpler, that way."

"So then where do time mages fit in?" Taly asked, checking over her notes before looking up from her journal.

Azura arched a brow—a signal to continue.

"If you cut a thread in a tapestry," Taly said, "it begins to fray. Loosen or pull that thread, and the image distorts. A time mage's spells inherently alter time, which means that if time really is a tapestry, they would change the structure of the Weave—loosening, pulling, cutting. Why doesn't the whole thing unravel?"

Azura moved to the next plant, rearranging the smock she wore over her sunshine yellow gown as she said, "Can a tapestry not be repaired? If a thread is cut, can it not be rewoven so that the greater work of art remains unbroken? Our magic alters time—that is true. But if a spell is cast correctly, it will stabilize the surrounding threads."

"And if a spell *isn't* cast correctly?"

"It depends." Azura clipped off another cluster of berries, adding them to the basket hanging from the crook of her arm. "Sometimes nothing. Time does have some ability to self-repair." She shot meaningful glance at Taly. "In other cases, you'll see a mage that manages to remove herself from the Weave entirely, creating her own little time loop outside the fabric of reality." Taly blushed, ducking her head and pretending to write something very important. "That is why untrained time mages are so dangerous. Their magic is unpredictable and can have far-reaching consequences."

Moving to a nearby table, Azura set down her garden shears and her basket, then pulled the floppy brimmed hat from her head. She picked up a cluster of berries, smiling as she held them up to the light. "Have you ever seen a more perfect sugarberry?" she asked. "It took me 400 years to refine the growing process. They need full sun in the morning, but also protection from the afternoon heat. If the soil goes dry at any point during the growing cycle, the crop suffers."

There was a small control interface resting on the edge of the table, and Azura touched a finger to a water crystal set into the surface, releasing a flurry of liquid butterflies that flitted through the air. They alighted on leaves and berries before dissolving into a rain of mist that began to trickle down. "I never had time for such things when I was serving as queen, but now... well, I've become something of an amateur horticulturalist. I've set up several solariums inside the protection of the palace, where time still moves linearly. Tomorrow, I'll take you to see my orchids. They started blooming last night."

Taly let out a soft sigh, licked butter and jam off her fingers, and reached for a cup of coffee sitting beside her. Turning a page, she skimmed her notes from the previous day. The Queen was always going off on tangents. Eventually, she would find her way back to the lesson, and until then, all Taly had to do was nod at the appropriate times and give the occasional "uh-huh."

Which she did as she turned another page, only half-listening as the Queen droned on about soil acidity, pH balance, and other things that weren't time magic.

After two months, life at the palace had fallen into a relentless rhythm, sliding by in a blur of hard work and constant toil. Meditation before breakfast, then she'd spend the rest of the morning studying chronal theory in either her room or the library. Afternoons, she worked one-on-one with the Queen, and if their lesson released on time, she would be sent to the training yard for conditioning exercises and weapons training. Otherwise, Leto would pick her up straight from the study room, rushing her off to be primped and plucked and stuffed into a frothy creampuff of a dress for a formal dinner with the Queen.

Every day followed the same pattern, the same endless cycle, right down to the nightmares that chased her from sleep every night. Most mornings, she woke up feeling worse than she had when she'd collapsed into bed, although sometimes, if she was lucky, she managed to push herself past the point of exhaustion. That was the only way to stop the dreams.

Tonight would be one of those nights. She could feel it—even her bones ached, and the skin beneath her eyes had turned a lovely shade of purple.

A sugarberry bounced off Taly's head.

"I don't feel like you're listening to me," Azura said a bit sharply.

"That's because I'm not." The sugarberry landed beside her, and Taly reached for it, popping it into her mouth. Living up to its name, sweetness burst onto her tongue. "Unless you grew these plants with time magic, this has nothing to do with, well, anything. I'd also venture to say that this is hardly the perfect sugarberry. It's a touch bitter." Though a part of her wondered if she ever would've noticed the difference as a human. Maybe it was the perfect sugarberry. Maybe this was the way sugarberries were supposed to taste, in which case…

Shards, first coffee, and now being fey had even ruined sugarberries.

Azura frowned as she tossed her shears onto the table. "I see there's no accounting for taste," she said, holding up her hands in what looked like surrender. "Fine. I thought that for one moment we might… but never mind. Lady Fun-Killer demands that we work, so that is exactly what we shall do."

Taly felt a small pang of guilt as Azura removed her smock and began folding it. She wasn't sure yet if she believed that there was some future version of her that became this woman's friend, but if there was, that Taly probably would've gladly listened to her ramble on about sugarberries.

Azura asked, "How are your individual studies progressing? Are you still meditating?"

Taly nodded. "Every morning."

"And your aether? How are you at controlling it?"

Taly held out a hand and nudged the magic she could now feel sparking in her veins. A golden haze began to crackle the air. She snapped her fingers, and the manifestation immediately extinguished.

"Good," was all Azura said as she laid the smock next to the shears and the basket. "That means we can move onto casting."

Taly sat up a little straighter at that. *Finally*. There was a long list of spells she needed to master before she could pass her third seal and be called an Acolyte, and up until now, she'd been forbidden from casting anything at all.

"The second seal requires only a basic understanding of spellcasting," Azura explained. "You'll need to demonstrate how to slow, accelerate, and stop time within a limited area of effect. These three spells form the foundation of all time magic. Entire wars have been won using only the fundamentals."

Taly began jotting down notes. She'd have to transfer them later to the journal she kept in her room—the one that had been transcribed, organized, and supplemented with annotations from her readings. If this had been five years ago, Skye would've come begging for a copy later that night. She never thought there would be a day when she missed that inevitable knock on her door.

"For most fey," Azura said, leaning back against the table and reaching for a cup of tea, "casting is a reflex. It's not something that's taught; it's just something that you *do*. Many children begin using their magic mere moments after their Attunement Ceremonies. Even you—before your mother made you human—were no doubt performing basic spells. However, after observing you these months, I think it's safe to say that as an adult, you've lost the ability to consciously manipulate your magic. My normal teaching methods won't work, I'm afraid. You'd likely just end up dead. Or stuck in another pocket universe. Neither are ideal."

Taly couldn't help the way her expression fell. "What do I do then?"

Azura shrugged. "You're just going to have to work at it. Bash your head against the problem until you rediscover your instincts." She took a sip of tea before setting the cup aside. "When you were being attacked by the harpy, by the shades, by Vaughn—your magic instinctively rose up to protect you, which means that somewhere deep down, the ability is still there. You just need to remember that feeling, to learn to summon it at will." Snapping her fingers, a large drawstring pouch appeared out of nothing and dropped into her hand. Taly jumped—she'd never seen magic like that—but the Queen didn't explain, just continued on. "I don't usually endorse the use of crystals for casting—they can quickly become a crutch. In this case, however, I don't see any other way forward."

The contents clacked together as she placed the pouch in Taly's hand. "These crystals have been enchanted to freeze time," Azura said, straightening. "All you need to do is feed a small amount of your aether into the crystal, and it will cast the spell for you. Your new assignment is to use these crystals to stop time on an object of your choosing, memorize the feel of the spell, then do it again. Over and over until you can replicate that feeling unaided.

"Think of them like magical training wheels," Azura said with a wave of her hand. Then, smiling: "That's a human expression, by the way. The mortals do love their turns of phrase. They have one for almost everything."

"Fantastic," Taly grumbled under her breath. She'd upgraded from grade school lessons to magical handholding. She wouldn't be surprised if Azura had her working with finger paints next.

The Queen clucked her tongue at Taly's tone, then leaned forward, her eyes awash with a golden glow and the air thrumming with aether. "Make no mistake, while crystals can be a crutch, they are not mere playthings. They are dangerous weapons in the hands of a skilled mage."

In a flash, Azura's magic dissipated, and she turned toward the exit. "Wait," Taly called after her. "That's it? That was the lesson? You dragged me down here at six bells just to hand me a bunch of crystals I don't know how to use?"

Azura paused in the open doorway of the solarium, sunlight streaming in behind her. "You're making progress," she said with none of her usual flippancy. "You've found your aether now, figured out how to make it respond, but casting—that's like giving your magic shape. It should be instinct—as natural as breathing. While I can eventually teach you how to wield your magic with efficiency and intent, this first step can't be trained—only done. You're going to have to figure this one out on your own."

Six days passed, and Taly threw herself into her lessons—flipping coins into the air only to stop them mid-spin, suspended at the apex of their fall.

That was the object she had chosen to practice on. A coin. She had found a bag of them in a dresser drawer one evening, and since money had no value here, she figured nobody would mind if she accidentally disappeared the entire purse into another pocket universe. It seemed… safe.

Flip.

Suspend.

Fall.

Every day, coin after coin, she used the enchanted crystals to make them hover. She watched her aether carefully. She even tried closing her eyes to get a sense of how the flow of energy *felt* as it swept through the crystal and then into the air, bending and twisting into something new. And when she thought she had figured out the shape of the spell in her mind, she tried casting it unaided.

Only to fail.

So, she moved back to the crystals.

Then tried to cast the spell herself.

Back and forth until she was gasping for breath and sweat coated her body, her very blood aching as her aether began to drain.

It was hard work, and it certainly didn't feel like instinct. But she kept at it, coming to the solarium every evening with a coin purse and her bag of crystals.

Overhead, the sky was dark, and ash pelted the glass, almost like snow. The air was humid but cool, scented heavily with the smell of mist and freshly packed earth. Taly was sitting at her usual spot at the little round worktable beneath the center of the largest of three glass domes when the leaves began to rustle.

She dismissed it at first, moving back to the task at hand. It wasn't even 21 bells yet, and she was already exhausted.

Taly flipped the coin and watched it hover.

One second. Two seconds. It was motionless, stopped mid-spin.

The crystal felt warm in her hand as she reached out with her magic, tracing the now familiar shape of the enchantment.

After a moment, she released the spell and let the coin drop.

Setting the crystal aside, Taly teased out the tiniest thread of aether, letting it curl through her fingers, pushing back when it began to rise up. Precision was also important, the Queen had told her. Too much aether could ruin a spell just as easily as too little.

So, she forced her mind to clear, forced down that restless impatience, and flicked the coin into the air. Half a heartbeat later, threads spindled from her fingers, forming a web that crisscrossed the space in front of her and caught the coin mid-spin—

Only to let it fall through.

It hit the table with a spiraling clatter, and Taly slammed a hand down on top of it. It was progress. Not instinct, but… progress. Very slow, very frustrating, *it-was-starting-to-feel-like-she-might-just-be-a-really-shitty-time-mage* progress.

Something was rustling again. Turning around in her chair, Taly peered into the darkness. The only light came from rows of water crystals set into the glass overhead, and they cast a soft glow. The solarium was at least three times as long as it was wide, and leaves were shaking on the far side.

She rose from her seat at the table and followed the noise. It was probably just one of the fairies. They were always hanging around, chirping and whispering, sometimes playing pranks.

The leaves began to shake more violently as Taly crept closer. A few berries dropped to the ground. There was a low hiss, and then two beady blue eyes peered at her from between the branches.

The creature was small, not much larger than a walnut, and vaguely feline in appearance. It had large bat-like ears that were at least twice the size of its head, a long whip-like tail that sliced through the air, and a thin layer of black fuzz coating the entirety of its body. When it opened its mouth, growling and revealing a set of fangs that were quite remarkable given its size…

Taly melted.

It. Was. Adorable.

And when it squeaked… Oh Shards. Her insides turned to jelly.

It was even cute as it snapped at her, snarling with all its tiny might—though it lost a bit of its charm when it launched itself out of the bush, lunging straight at her face.

Taly yelped, narrowly ducking out the way. She groped for the little beast as it dropped to the floor, but it was across the solarium before she had time to blink.

"Shit," she muttered. It was small, but fast—unbelievably strong for its size, darting from the floor to the table to the branches and leaving a truly impressive trail of devastation in its wake. Ceramic pots shattered, and bags of dirt toppled over. The Queen's berries got trampled as Taly reached for it and missed.

"How in the nine hells?!" she barked, barely managing to catch a trellis before it toppled over. The creature was no more than a black streak, ricocheting across the room like a bullet.

Glass cracked, and vines groaned overhead. It was heading for the door. The door that led outside. The same one that she'd stupidly left open because she liked to watch the way the ash piled up against the barrier surrounding the palace.

Another trellis snapped and nearly fell on top of her.

"Stop!" she pleaded with the creature. It hissed back at her as it leapt from branch to branch. "You can't go outside!" If it didn't get killed by the blasts, it might get swept away when the day reset. She wasn't sure if a living thing could come back from that.

The little beast bounced as it hit the floor, its claws scraping against the bare stone as it skidded and weaved its way forward. The way was clear. There was nothing stopping it now, and panic slammed into her—panic for this tiny terrified creature that had no way of knowing the danger that awaited it just outside that set of doors.

She chased after it, reaching for that pressure that was pushing against her now. Straining beneath her skin.

It was a familiar feeling. She recognized the shape it began to take.

The creature hit the threshold, but the power was spiraling out from her, like threads from a spindle. Threads that glittered in the air like some great golden web as she held out a hand...

And time in the solarium suddenly stopped.

Taly stood there for a moment with a hand still outstretched, panting.

She'd cast. She'd actually done it. Threads of magic ensnared the little beast, now motionless and hovering just off the ground in a leap for freedom. But she didn't have room in her brain to care about that right now. Not as she rushed to the creature and gently plucked it from the web.

She kept her grip on the spell, loosening it just enough that time began to trickle by. The creature's movements were slow, and its eyes blinked open, staring up at her with an emotion she instantly recognized.

Fear. But not just that. It was the feeling of being small and weak, helpless against those that were bigger and stronger. Who were *always* going to be bigger and stronger. Those who allowed you to live by their grace alone.

She remembered that feeling. She had felt it every day of her life as a human.

"It's alright," she cooed softly, and the creature gave a little squeak. It moved like it had been dunked in molasses, every twitch of its legs exaggerated and slow. "I'm not going to hurt you." She gave its ears a gentle scratch, and it blinked. It seemed to like that, so she did it again.

Moving away from the door and back to the table, she cleared the debris and set it down, still gentle, still keeping a hold on the spell in case it tried to run. When it didn't, she released the spell entirely, watching as it gracelessly rolled back to its feet.

It stared at her.

She stared at it.

"Hello," she said.

It gave a soft, trilling mew in return.

And just like that, she'd made a new friend.

Taly didn't let herself worry about the solarium. The damage was done, and if Azura killed her, she figured that death was also an escape. One that seemed more likely, not to mention quicker, than earning her third seal.

What she worried about instead was bathing all the berry juice and soil from Calcifer and then fixing him up with a bed that she'd made out of a teacup filled with fire crystals for warmth.

Calcifer—that's what she had named the little creature. She'd also decided that it was a *he*. She didn't know why. Wasn't even sure what the beast was or if it had a sex. But there was something about him that was distinctly goofy, something good-natured that reminded her of Skye, so she went with it.

"Hey now," she chided gently, laughing when he swiped at her fingers. His claws clacked delicately against the wood of her dining room table. "I am not food. This—" She pushed a piece of ham in front of him. "This is food."

But just like everything else she'd tried to feed him so far, he turned up his nose and went back to trying to gnaw on her fingers. She gave him the end of her braid instead, and he climbed up her hair like a rope, perching on top of her head.

She popped the ham in her mouth. "Not a carnivore then." Or an anything else for that matter. She'd tried meat, vegetables, fish, fruit—he didn't want any of it. "I hate to say it," she said, shivering as Calcifer crawled down her neck to her shoulder, his needle-like claws scraping against her skin, "but I think I'm going to have to ask the Queen just what you are. Eventually, you're going to get hungry."

Calcifer's ears twitched—his only reply as the main door to her tower apartment opened and closed.

"Taly," Azura called. "Now, I'm not angry." Funny, she sounded angry. "But the fairies said there was some kind of commotion, and then..." She stopped in the doorway to the dining room, face going pale.

Taly eyed the broken sugarberry branch clutched in the Queen's hand. "I suppose it's a bit cliché to say that it wasn't me."

Azura didn't laugh, didn't smile, didn't frown. She just stood there, so deathly still. "Don't move," she breathed.

Taly immediately froze, though it was hard to keep from laughing as Calcifer's tail began to tickle her ear. "Why?"

Like a beast freed from its leash, Azura snapped into action. She dropped the sugarberry branch, and her entire body began to glow. The air grew heavy, even the palace seemed to shake as she summoned her aether—summoned the power of the Time Shard in all its devastating glory.

Golden tendrils of magic began snaking forward, creeping across the marble like liquid vines, lifting up, rising from the floor and moving towards—

Taly jumped from the table, grabbing Calcifer and holding him protectively to her chest. "What are you doing?"

"Taly, don't move!" the Queen snarled, and Taly backed up another step. "Just put the mimic down," she said a bit more gently, like she was negotiating. "Put it down and move away. For once in your life, please don't question me, child."

"A mimic?" Taly looked down at Calcifer. "Is that what you are?"

Azura held out a hand. "Give it to me, Taly. That is a direct order from your High Lady."

Taly clutched Calcifer closer to her chest. The Queen had told her to start training her instincts, and right now, her instincts were telling her that her new friend was in danger. "I don't understand."

"And that is my fault, I suppose. I didn't think their kind would be able to find their way into this world." Azura took a cautious step forward. Her aether dimmed but didn't extinguish. "That is a mimic. It's an eldritch beast, a creature that lives alongside the Weave. They only ever come to our world to feed."

"On what?" Taly watched as the Queen edged closer. "I've tried everything, but he won't eat."

"That's because it doesn't want food. It wants time aether."

Taly blinked. "What?"

"You heard me." Azura's eyes never left the mimic. "It feeds on time aether—*us*. That one is small right now, but when it's older, it will be impossible to track and even harder to kill, and believe me, girl, it will drain you without remorse."

Taly held up her hand, letting Calcifer climb onto her upturned palm. His hind legs splayed out to the sides as he tilted his head. "He doesn't look dangerous."

"Because it's young—newly hatched. This is the only point in their life cycle when they're vulnerable. I don't know what drew this one here, but we need to kill it. *Now.* While there's still time."

Azura was almost close enough to grab him, so Taly plucked Calcifer up by the scruff of his neck, placing him back on the table. Reaching for the plate she'd brought up from the kitchen, she overturned its contents as she bit down on her thumb.

The Queen's power guttered, and she looked on in mute horror as Taly smeared a trail of blood across the white porcelain.

Calcifer immediately pounced, making the strangest little purring sound as he began to lap at the plate. Azura had been right. He wanted time aether.

At least, that would make feeding him easy.

"His name is Calcifer," Taly said. "And I don't care if he is dangerous. The Sanctorum judges people based on the things they *could* do rather than what they've done. I won't be the same."

Azura stumbled back a step. "You're insane," she murmured. Then, louder: "Do you not understand? That thing will *eat* you when it's grown. Do you have no sense of self-preservation whatsoever?"

"If I did, I probably wouldn't have ended up here."

Azura only frowned.

Point. Set. Match.

Before the Queen could lodge another complaint, Leto drifted into the room, pausing in the doorway. The set of her shoulders immediately stiffened; her glow slightly dimmed. The tea service she held in her ghostly hands began to rattle.

"Leto," Azura hissed. "Please talk some sense into her."

Leto looked from the Queen to Taly to Calcifer and back again. "I believe," she said after what seemed like an eternity, voice soft and careful, "that the Lady Caro has often spoken of a pet named Calcifer."

"That's a housecat," Azura whispered harshly, as if Taly wasn't right there.

"We *assumed* it was a housecat," Leto corrected just as quietly, drifting to Azura's side. "It was never explicitly stated."

"No," Azura said to Leto. "No, no, no. It's too dangerous—"

"Consider the timeline, Majesty."

Azura hesitated at that, a frown creasing her brow. She and Leto exchanged a glance, something unspoken passing between them.

"Fine," Azura finally relented. Turning back to Taly, she said, "If you're intent on gambling with your life, there's not much I can do. But I don't want to see that thing outside of this tower. You keep it away from me, away from the fairies, away from… everything."

And with that, Azura turned on her heel and swept out of the room. A moment later, the door to the apartment slammed.

Taly looked to Leto. "I think Azura might need something a little stronger than tea tonight."

Leto made a sound that sounded suspiciously like a sigh as she placed the tea service, originally meant for the Queen, on the dining table. "I suspect you are right," was all she said as she drifted out of the room.

Taly watched her go, then turned back to Calcifer, who was now curled up in his teacup bed, snoring contentedly. "I've never had a pet," she said, resting her chin on her folded arms. A slight smile curved her lips. "Let's just hope you don't eat me in my sleep."

CHAPTER II

-The following is an interview with three-time Arcana laureate Juniper Pots.

Azura Raine was the most recalcitrant, unruly mage I have ever had the misfortune of teaching. I still have nightmares about the stunts she pulled, but her second seal assessment... Shards, I'll never forget it.

I gave her a standard trial. She was to stop, slow, and accelerate time on a falling boulder while reciting a poem. I began administering the test, and everything was proceeding according to plan. That is until I dropped my quill.

I bent to retrieve it—it couldn't have taken more than a few seconds—and when I stood back up... it was snowing. In the middle of summer. She'd accelerated us six months into the future, and at first, I thought it a mistake. Students make mistakes during exams all the time, though never on this scale.

I was confused, close to panicking, but I set to work, checking the integrity of the Weave, trying to ensure the safety of my charge. Azura, though... she was so calm. Just staring at me with her arms wrapped around her body, shivering in the snow. And then in the most pitiful voice I'd ever heard, she said, "Please, Professor Pots, may we stop the test. I've been holding this boulder for so long."

I still remember my answer. I was only able to stammer out, "I'm not sure this counts."

Needless to say, a full meeting of the academic faculty was called to oversee the disciplinary hearing, and when asked why she did it—why she damn near broke the Weave all for a silly stunt—she simply said, "If you're going to give me a test, at least respect me enough to make it a challenge."

Once Taly figured out that first spell, the rest came easily. She began to experiment with slowing and accelerating time inside little pockets of warped reality, flipping coins into the air and tinkering with the flow of aether. And when she got tired of coins, she moved her spellcasting practice outside, often going on walks through the woods that surrounded the palace complex.

She froze swarms of insects midair and slowed the fall of leaves. There was a pond right on the edge of this world, where the land abruptly fell away, and sometimes she would skip rocks beyond that line dividing the green of the forest and the darkness of nothing, speeding them up faster than her eyes could follow.

It was equal parts wondrous and odd to be the source of such strange magic, and it seemed like she never really got the chance to catch her breath. In addition to her other studies, Azura had begun teaching her to enchant crystals, linking them to the same spells she'd been practicing for weeks on end. It was dull and monotonous work, endlessly inscribing runes on time crystals and then testing the magic by flipping coins into the air.

After only a few days of this, she'd been ready to brave the Schism; ready to find out if a living person could survive the day's reset. She figured dead people didn't have to enchant crystals, though with her luck, hell would probably be a classroom with Azura standing at the front of it.

So, in the name of survival and her rapidly deteriorating mental health, Taly had decided it was time to do some independent study.

"What do you think?" Taly asked, taking a step back to admire her work.

Perched on top of a stack of books on her study desk, Calcifer gave a mewl of approval. He was the size of a small kitten now and growing larger with each passing day. He'd outgrown his teacup in a matter of weeks, and while he was more than welcome to any one of the many pillows on her mountain of a bed, he always insisted on following her when the nightmares struck, curling up on the cold tile of her library floor as she paced until dawn.

Which is what had given her the idea for her current project. It had started as a simple tower made of coins and then expanded into what she thought was a recognizable imitation of Infinity's Edge. Situated in an empty corner of her study, she'd stacked coin after coin, each one frozen in place with a spell tethered to one of the many time crystals that formed the "moat" circling the structure. Various bridges and walkways connected the outer towers to the main building, the tallest of which came up to her shoulders and even bore a little red flag. Inside, she'd built platforms and tunnels and ramps for Calcifer to play on while she was away during the day.

Holding out an arm, Taly gave a whistle, and Calcifer glided across the room, alighting on her upturned palm. His wings had come in yesterday. True to their name, mimics impersonated the world around them, the older ones able to change their form at will. He'd been watching the birds outside the window, and suddenly two scrawny black wings had sprouted from his back. Ever since, he'd been flying around the apartment, making the oddest little chirping sounds.

"Do you think the Queen has noticed I'm not downstairs yet?" she asked, lifting a hand and letting Calcifer step onto the large platform at the top of the tallest tower. The afternoon lecture was supposed to have started two hours ago, but of course, *Her Most Supreme Imperial Majesty* had been late.

More than three months now—going on four—and it felt like half her time had been spent waiting on that woman, the other half wasted on *tea*.

There was midmorning tea and afternoon tea, and then they would stop whatever they were doing for royal tea just after the explosions began. Taly had complained once about how many times per day they had to break for tea, and the Queen had proceeded to give her a full day lecture on the beverage's origin—how it was grown, how it was harvested, how it was dried, how it was brewed.

The next day, instead of picking up where they'd left off on Afroditi's *Theory of Time,* Azura had launched into a lesson on the different kinds of pastries that were to be served with tea. Then the rules and proper etiquette depending on where one was in the Fey Imperium as well as the political goal.

Taly had come out of that lecture with two conclusions.

The first: she hated tea. Black tea, green tea, even reysang tea—it didn't matter how divine it tasted to this stupid new body where every damned thing had to be so jarringly different. As far as she was concerned, *tea* was just another word for dirty water.

And the second: even though she had been at the palace three months already, waiting and biding her time, the Queen had been here much, much, *much* longer. Time moved differently inside the loop—faster compared to normal reality, though she had no way of knowing just how much. She supposed if she'd been alone for hundreds, maybe *thousands* of years, she'd probably look forward to little things like teatime just as much as the Queen. Anything to give the days structure and meaning.

I wonder how long it'll be before I'm that nutty?

It seemed like a valid concern, which is why she refused to find any enjoyment in teatime. It was a gateway to madness, she had decided. Not the isolation, or the boredom, or the way each day blurred into the next, becoming one big blob of stagnated time—it was the damn tea's fault.

"Oh my Shards, she built the mage-eating monster a house," a new voice murmured, and Taly turned to find Azura standing in the open doorway. She was dressed all in white, and a frown tugged at the corners of her mouth as she took in the house of coins and the moat of crystals surrounding it. "This explains why my treasury looked so empty."

Taly shrugged. "You told me to practice my crystal inscription," she said, watching as Calcifer wriggled his tail, preparing to make a jump. "So, I did."

"I can see that," Azura said a little too carefully. Stepping further into the room, she began to circle the miniature palace, stepping over the piles of leftover coins dotting the area around it. "You were supposed to be waiting for me downstairs."

"You were late."

"A queen is never late, my dear." Azura crouched and began picking through the crystal moat. "Did you enchant all of these?" She looked over, and Taly nodded. "You're still using too much aether."

Taly sighed and fell back against the edge of the desk. While summoning and shaping her aether had become second nature to her now, her magic lacked precision. She was always using too much aether, even for the simplest enchantments, but no matter how hard she tried, how long she meditated, how many times she crooked a finger at that inner well of power and begged it to behave—the moment she would start to cast, her aether would rise up, like it had been contained for so long beneath her mother's spells that it simply refused to be held back any longer.

If she tried to freeze a coin, she ended up canvasing an area the size of her desk. Slowing spells were glacial, accelerations faster than the eye could see.

There was no in between.

Remember, Azura was always saying, *your aether is a part of you, linked to both your conscious and subconscious desires. You control it, not the other way around.*

But most mages began taming their aether when they were still children, and as Azura had told her many times, a child's mind was malleable, whereas Taly's was "stubborn," "bullheaded," and "needlessly contrary." According to the Queen, she would need to work twice as hard to control her power, to push past habits that had ingrained themselves over the course of a lifetime.

Which was just peachy. And unhelpful. And more than a little disheartening. She was no stranger to hard work, but at some point, there just wasn't anything left to give.

The Queen dropped the crystal she'd been inspecting and rose to her feet. "Still," she said, pulling Taly from her thoughts. "Your spells are consistent from crystal to crystal, and the penmanship is good. The enchantment is robust despite the oversaturation of magic. Overall, I'd say not bad."

For reasons she couldn't begin to fathom, Taly found herself smiling at the praise—but then quickly cut off the expression mid-way. She didn't want this woman's approval. It was just... nice to do something right for once. Azura was always finding her lacking in one way or the other. It was almost laughable. In a very depressing sort of way.

Azura gave the coin palace one more look, throwing a pointed glare at Calcifer lounging in the courtyard, then snapped, "Well, come on," as she turned and exited the room. "We haven't got all day."

Taly cursed under her breath—the Queen had left her waiting for two hours, after all.

She was still cursing as she ducked to retrieve her boots from underneath the desk and slipped on a blue brocade vest over her tunic before following Azura out of the apartment and down the stairs. She was wearing far too many layers for the weather, and the fabrics made her skin itch, but Leto... Well, the fairy had an eye for fashion, and Taly had learned to pick her battles when it came to the wisp and clothing.

Taly jogged to keep up with Azura's brisk pace as they passed from hall to hall, each one draped with silks and hung with paintings and decorated with those same rich furnishings that seemed so commonplace to her now.

"Where are we going?" she asked when they came to an unfamiliar part of the palace. The windows and doors were all closed tight, and the air was near sweltering. She was suddenly very glad she had let Leto fuss over her hair while she yawned into her coffee that morning. The coiled braids kept her hair from sticking to her neck.

Azura clicked open a fan. "I thought we could both use a change of scenery this afternoon. Classrooms have their place, but for this lesson, I have something special in mind."

"What about my weapons training?" Taly asked. She actually enjoyed that part of her day.

"Canceled."

"And my—"

"Also canceled."

They approached a wide set of double doors at the end of the hallway. The wood was nearly black, and the crests for each of the Shards were carved in even intervals. Crystals of every shape, size, and color flickered, flanked by circles and runes that had been etched into a delicate geometric pattern.

Azura raised a hand, and the fairies that had been bouncing along behind them rushed forward, pushing against the wood. The doors slid open on silent hinges.

From stifling heat to open air, the room beyond was breathtakingly large, big enough to fit an airship and still have space left over, and Taly gasped, looking around with wide eyes. There were no windows or walls, just staggered rows of ivory columns holding up a gray ring of stone. Set around a central altar were pews carved from ivory and inlaid with long strips of that same black wood. They fanned out to the far reaches of the room in ever-widening circles, the aisles like the spokes of a wagon wheel.

Taly grinned, craning her head to stare up through the wide wooden rafters at the clear blue sky. The ceiling had been left open to the elements, protected by a dome of air magic that shimmered if the light caught it just right. "You brought me to temple."

"Obviously," Azura muttered as she strode down the main aisle. "Close your mouth, dear. You look like a fish." Avoiding the row of golden thrones off to the side—one for each of the Genesis Lords—Azura took a seat in a pew near the altar.

"Come now. Hurry up. I was hoping to get an earlier start than this."

Resisting the urge to roll her eyes, Taly made her way to the front of the temple, smiling at the fairies that bounced off the dome, seeming to make a game of it.

But wait… No. They weren't bouncing off the dome. They were ping ponging through the rafters, throwing down dust and splinters and—

There was a loud *crack*. Then another as one of those long beams buckled in the middle. It was solid wood, at least three feet thick, and there were countless others like it all stemming from a massive marble column at the center of the room and terminating in that gray ring of stone. All of them cracking and bowing as the fairies ricocheted back and forth.

Mortar and stone ripped free.

"Catch, dear."

And then every single one of those dark wooden beams came crashing down.

Instinct kicked in, and Taly fell to the floor as splinters and dust and debris rained from up above. She raised her hands, the gesture futile against the hundreds of pounds of broken wood that were hurtling toward her.

But then somehow—from somewhere—there was another instinct. A reflex that hadn't been there before. Her aether exploded out of her, flickering threads of golden magic spindling the air and shooting towards the sky.

The world went quiet. Still. And for a moment, it was all Taly could do to lie there, listening to the thunderous beat of her heart and the fairies' giggling overhead.

"Not bad," the Queen remarked, almost bored. She hadn't moved from her seat at the pew, and she stared up at the cloud of chaos overhead, frozen midway down. Covering the whole of the temple, it was like a nebula interspersed with scores of jagged beams and pieces of stone and crystal. Sunlight glinted off each suspended mote of dust, casting strange unmoving shadows. "Finally, a situation suited to just how much aether you like to throw around."

"What the hell?" Taly panted, still crouched defensively on the ground.

But Azura just continued to look up. "A bit sloppy, though." Her fan flicked closed, and she gestured to the web of threads crisscrossing the temple. "I shouldn't be able to *see* the spell. You're still using too much aether. Fix it."

Sweat beaded on her brow as Taly fought to keep the spell steady. Her magic simmered beneath the surface, restless. "Are you joking?" she said through gritted teeth. "I'm holding up the damn ceiling."

"Fix it. Believe me—you'll thank me later."

Taly exhaled through her nose and pushed against her power, shuddering when it tried to snap back at her, like a child that had just been told it couldn't go outside to play.

Slowly, the flickering threads began to dim until the air was clear.

"Better?" she asked breathlessly.

Azura eyed the cloud of splinters and shattered beams, then looked to Taly, pursing her lips at the dull glow that still surrounded her fingertips. She gave a slow nod. "Much." She patted the pew beside her. "Come. Sit."

No way. Taly didn't trust herself to breathe, much less move.

"My dear," Azura said, twisting in the pew, "are you in any danger of losing the spell?"

Taly looked up, then back to Azura. She tentatively prodded at the spell. "No," she said after a moment. Her aether was bucking at the reins, still wanting to fan out. But her grip on the spell was surprisingly steady.

"Then sit down."

A command from her High Lady, and Taly obeyed, slowly, carefully, easing herself off the ground. Even though she tried not to, she kept glancing up as she slid into the pew beside the Queen.

Azura said, "I want you to hold the spell until I say stop." That fan flicked back open. "This afternoon's lecture—"

Oh, you've got to be kidding me, Taly thought, eyeing a portion of the spell that was beginning to warp, allowing a few splinters to trickle down.

"—will focus on crystals. Every facet of our lives involves crystals in one way or another. They're in our homes, our businesses. They're used to grow food and power our plumbing. Even the fabrics we use to clothe ourselves were likely woven on crystal-powered looms. Crystals form the cornerstone of our very way of life, and yet, very few take the time to understand just what they are. Tell me, dear—do you know where they come from?"

"They're mined," Taly replied automatically.

"True. But I didn't ask you where we find them. I asked you to tell me where they come from? How are they formed?"

"I..." Taly hesitated. "I don't know."

"And what is it that allows them to focus and refine aether."

"Um..." Taly frowned. "I'm not sure."

"What is it that makes them go dark?"

Ah! That one she knew. "The Genesis Shards. Crystals need their respective Shards to function, so if the Shard suffers, so do the crystals."

"But why is that?"

Taly felt herself deflate slightly. "I don't know."

"And this is precisely why I always like to devote at least one lecture to this particular topic," Azura said, giving Taly a knowing look. They always did this. The Queen would start each new subject by proving to Taly just how little she knew before finally making her point. It was like she took some sort of sadistic pleasure out of making her feel stupid.

"Now then." Azura settled back in the pew. "What do you know about the Genesis Lords?"

"I know that one of them is one Shard short of a full Council." Taly flinched when that fan whacked her on the back of the head.

Wood groaned overhead.

"Answer the question," Azura said, frowning.

"The Genesis Lords are the six men and women chosen to wield the Genesis Shards," Taly answered mechanically. "Together, they form the Council—the highest governing body in the Fey Imperium."

"And the Sacred Six?"

Taly turned to study the central altar. The Sacred Six stood in a perfect semi-circle, their bodies lithe and nimble and draped with wings that, even carved in stone, looked to be made of gossamer. They were beautiful—familiar and yet so utterly *other* that no one could mistake them for anything but what they were: gods—beings of supreme and absolute power and grace.

"I don't know much," Taly admitted. "Ivain only took us to temple on the high holidays, but I do know the standard story. Before the Fall, there were six great kings and queens sent by the Magnus, blessed father of all, to rule over all that is, all that was, and all that ever would be."

Fingers still glowing with magic, she pointed to each of the statues in turn, reciting the stories she had learned as a child: "Fire, Water, Earth, Air, Shadow, and Time—the Magnus gave each of his children a kernel of divine power and commanded them to go out into the cosmos and multiply, to spread and fill all of the worlds with life. They fashioned creatures great and small, each of a single divine element, but to the fey, their most beloved creation, their *true* children, they each gave a piece of themselves."

Azura nodded. "And what of the central figure?"

Taly looked at the seventh statue that stood in the center of the semi-circle beneath a shroud of velvet black. "He is the Judge, the Magnus' eldest son, the god of Death."

"His face shall never be seen," Azura said softly, quoting a passage from the Book of the Faera so well-known that even Taly recognized it, "and his name shall never be uttered. For his betrayal, he shall sleep until the stars fall and the heavens shudder."

Taly took a breath when she felt her aether begin to dip, and she closed her eyes, teasing out a bit more power. To her great relief, the spell never wavered. "What does this have to do with crystal-based magic? If I wanted to learn about religion, I'd go to temple."

"You're in temple, dear."

This time, Taly did roll her eyes. "You know what I mean."

"Religion is history," Azura replied simply. "Not always accurate, but history, nonetheless. And since crystals derive their functionality from the Shards, it's directly relevant to today's lesson."

Azura sighed, fluttering her fan against the summer heat. "No matter the realm, no matter the species, the Sacred Six are there, hidden in myth, their stories twisted by the passage of time. We know that ancient race of gods as the Faera, but to the Nephilim, they are the Aerin; to the Draegon, the Xolos. Humans simply called them Titans. Every story has its distinctions—none of them get it completely right. Nevertheless, one thing rings true: the Sacred Six were very real, as tangible as you and me."

Taly's brows rose. Though she had never considered herself religious, she did believe that the Genesis Shards held power, even if she wasn't sure that power heralded from the soul of a slumbering god. But to hear that the Sacred Six had been real—actual people that lived and breathed, ate and slept… She wasn't sure why that surprised her.

"Spell, dear."

Taly yelped when a broken piece of beam crashed into a row of pews across the room, and she pulled on the spell, tightened the web before anything else could drop. She looked to the Queen, and her heart gave a tiny skip when Azura nodded her head, not quite pleased but, at the very least, not dissatisfied.

"The priestesses of the Faerasanna," Azura continued, "have made the Sacred Six out to be these all-knowing, all-powerful beings of good and light, but it's all superstitious nonsense. Yes, they wielded power that we'll never begin to be able to fathom, and yes, they could be kind, but they were also capricious, self-serving, and, at times, foolish. They were, in many ways, just like the creatures they created. Imperfect and subject to the whims of folly and chance. They had an entire universe of possibility at their feet, and yet they still squabbled like children."

"You're talking about the war."

"Yes."

"So, the Judge and his Sickness—was that real as well?"

"Also, yes." Azura let her eyes drift to the veiled figure. "The Judge was sent down to watch over his brothers and sisters, and when he saw that they were growing too powerful, he created an equalizer—a balancing force to their divine gifts. He created death and unleashed it upon all of creation."

Azura paused momentarily, pressing her fan to her lips. Then, Taly felt it. A sharp tug on the spell, as though the Queen were trying to wrestle pieces of the wreckage away from her and speed them along their path toward the ground. The attacks came from all around, like a million tiny taps on the inside of her mind.

Gripping the edge of the pew, Taly shoved at the presence. Shoved and pushed until her body began to ache and sweat soaked her collar. Seconds passed, or maybe it was minutes—she couldn't be sure. But eventually, bit by bit, thread by thread, she picked her way along the web of magic and regained her grip on the spell. There was another sharp snap of magic, but Taly held onto every piece of damned debris. Held them and *yanked*, shaking off that invisible hand.

Azura gave a satisfied nod. "The Judge's plague," she continued, "planted within us a seed of mortality. It gave us the ability to die, and for that, the Sacred Six went to war, or so the priestesses would have you believe."

"You don't think it's true?" Taly asked, her eyes flicking from the Queen to the cloud and back again.

"Oh, it's true." A pause. The Queen amended, "In a way. You see, like most fables, the truth of the war that heralded the Fall of the Faera is distorted. History is shaped by those that live to tell it, and once you've been around long enough, you'll see that the victors always find a way to absolve themselves of any true blame."

"I don't understand. Are you saying the Judge didn't create death?"

"I'm saying that nothing is ever black-and-white, and there are very few things about the Faera that anyone can say with any certainty. What we do know is that they quarreled with their elder brother, and as a result, all of creation began to die."

"Because of the Sickness," Taly said softly. Even those that debated the origin of the Shards' power agreed that the Sickness had been real—some unknown plague that had crossed worlds and species, eradicating everything in its path before disappearing back into the pages of history.

"Yes." Azura fanned herself, considering her next words. "The Sickness spread from person to person, race to race. The Six tried to combat its effects. When they failed... well, there are some stories that say they went to their brother and begged for mercy, others that say they threatened him. Either way, the gods went to war, and the Age of the Faera came to an end."

Taly shivered despite the warmth of the sun streaming down through the wreckage above. "Why didn't they kill the Judge?" she asked. "The stories say that he was never going to give up until every living thing had been snuffed out, so why didn't the Six just kill him when they had the chance?"

"Because they couldn't. After so many centuries of fighting, it took all their remaining power to banish him and his plague to the dark pits of Maluum, and without magic to sustain them, their bodies turned to stone. Which, in case you were beginning to wonder, is how we come back to the subject of crystals."

Taly's brow furrowed. "I'm not sure I follow."

Azura reached into her pocket and produced a time crystal as big as her palm. "Whether you choose to believe that the Magnus, in his great mercy, took his children's remains and spread them to all corners of the world or that they were dispersed by more scientific means—one thing stands true. The bodies of the Sacred Six broke apart and were eventually scattered to all corners of the universe. They were buried and overlooked, regarded as little more than pretty pieces of stone until a man named Jyn Frano discovered that these crystal remains could focus and refine aether."

Taly blinked. *But that would mean...* "No."

Azura chuckled softly. "Yes."

Taly touched a tentative finger to the surface of the crystal. "You're telling me that's a dead god?"

"A piece of one."

"I feel like you're lying to me."

"What would I gain from that, dear?"

Taly pulled her hand away, wiping her fingers on her trousers. "I don't know. Just to mess with me? I wouldn't put it past you."

"As much fun as that sounds, I'm telling the truth. This time," she added, laughing at Taly's answering grimace.

"Even with their bodies shattered and dispersed," Azura continued, not even trying to hide her smile, "the souls of the old gods still lingered, tethered to the bit of rock that used to be their hearts. The day the war ended—that was the day the first Council was formed. The six fey generals that fought side-by-side with their gods made one final sacrifice. They joined their souls with the Sacred Six, giving their creators the ability to watch the world through the eyes of their most beloved creation."

"So, wait…" Taly hesitated, trying to piece together the bits of information. "If you're a Genesis Lord—"

"One day you're going to stop stating the obvious, and oh what a day that will be. I think we'll throw a party."

"If you're a Genesis Lord," Taly repeated, purposely ignoring the Queen, "and you bonded your soul to the Time Shard…" Taly's eyes went wide. "Are you telling me that in all the time that I've known you, you've been carrying around the calcified heart of a god in your pocket?"

Azura gave her a flat stare. "Don't be silly. I don't carry the Time Shard in my pocket. That would be terribly inconvenient. The humans weren't exaggerating when they called them *Titans*. It's very large."

Taly slouched down in the seat, leaning her head back and closing her eyes. Her head was starting to hurt. "Why is this the first time I'm hearing about this? If we were truly using our fossilized gods to power our technology, surely, that would be public knowledge."

Azura gave a noncommittal hum. "The *'shattered god'* theory isn't widely accepted. And even though the members of the Genesis Council are in a unique position to set the record straight, we decided as a group that it was better not to endorse an official theory."

"Why?"

Azura shrugged. "Many reasons, the primary being that we need crystal-based technology to sustain our way of life. Can you imagine the backlash if the Faerasanna discovered that the remains of their gods were being used to power an oven, or an aircar, or, Shards forbid, a tavern toilet? It would be far more trouble than it's worth."

That's fair, Taly thought. The Faerasanna had become more political in recent centuries. Their influence was far from absolute, but if they challenged the orthodoxy of crystal-based technologies, it would be a difficult battle, even with the support of the full Council.

"And so, the time crystals going dark…?" Taly looked to Azura. That was one thing that still didn't make sense. If the Queen was here, and if the Shard was still bonded to her—

"*Spell.*"

Taly's heart lurched. The spell. She'd forgotten about the spell, and now it was unravelling, allowing beams and other debris to come crashing down. She managed to grab some of the wreckage, slowing the descent of some of the larger pieces directly overhead, but splinters and chunks of stone still bombarded her.

"Azura," she pleaded, trying to reshape the spell, throwing more aether into it as the it continued to fray. "Help. I need help!"

The altar toppled, the statues shattering as one of the largest beams hit the ground with a mighty *boom*.

There was a loud sigh as the Queen held up a hand, and Taly felt the enchantment rushing past her. But not to stop time.

Instead, the debris began to lift into the air, spiraling and spinning as pieces came together and beams reformed. Cracks melted and dissolved into nothing, and stones fitted themselves back into walls.

A moment later, the beams were once again crisscrossing overhead. The altar had been righted. The temple was pristine, the same as when they had first walked in.

Azura leaned back, rubbing at the bridge of her nose as though she were trying to ward off a headache. "That's good enough, I suppose. You pass."

Taly was still gaping at the scaffolding above, trying to figure out the magic the Queen had used. The fairies were once again bouncing off the shimmer of air magic just beyond. "What?"

"*You - pass*," Azura repeated, enunciating each word as though she were speaking to a small child.

Taly finally managed to pull her eyes away. She stared at the Queen, confused.

"Daft girl," Azura muttered. "Your exam. This was your second seal assessment, and you passed. You're a Neophyte now."

Taly went still. It was as if a hand had reached up inside her, slowly squeezing her heart as the realization began to sink in.

A test.

This had been a *test*?

"But..." Taly rasped. "But you didn't tell me this was an exam."

She hadn't studied, hadn't prepared. What if... what if she had failed? How long would that have set her back? How much longer would she have been stuck here?

"Oh, don't give me that look," Azura said. "You either know a thing, or you don't. And true, you likely would've failed if I had held you to Guild standards, but we're on a schedule, and I figure you can sharpen up your skills during the next seal. It's more hands-on, and we're far past the point of you accidentally getting yourself locked away in your own little loop."

Leaning forward, Taly placed her head against the back of the pew in front of them and resisted the urge to scream.

She hated time magic. She hated the Queen. She hated feeling so horribly out of her depth, and she absolutely *loathed* that part of her that was starting to crave this woman's approval.

"Come along." Azura rose from the pew. "It's almost time for tea."

Of course, it was. It was always time for *tea*, and Taly—well, if she was being honest, that didn't sound all that bad right now.

CHAPTER 12

-An excerpt from Pointless Battles in History

"To the fey, family is everything, though I wish a few members of mine would have the decency to die."

Eyewitness accounts report that this phrase was first uttered by a patron in a bar of no renown. Relatively benign in isolation, it was followed by so many rounds of toasting, a drunken mob formed in the hours before dawn.

This, of course, led to the burning of Emir. The blaze was so impressive, the Fire Guild funded the reconstruction, and then promptly relocated their guild.

"Taly?" Skye's eyes stared at the sky, pain-addled and blank. "Taly, are you there?"

Taly was sobbing as she crawled through the mud, her nightgown soaked and transparent. All around, people were lying on the ground, screaming out their pain as the camp burned. Tents had been reduced to ashes, and the trees of the surrounding forest were still burning. The sky had turned black with smoke as rain pelted down.

Della. They were in Della. The inn was gone, but she could still see the columns standing through the smoke.

"I'm here, Skye," Taly choked as she took his face in her hands, turning his head to look at her. "Just stay with me. *Please.*"

"Taly?" he murmured again. His chest had been split open, and a sword pinned him to the ground. She could see his lungs, his heart. All struggling to hang onto the rhythm like a winding-down clock.

"Em." His eyes drooped, and Shards, why wouldn't he look at her? It's like she wasn't even there. "Em—Em, I'm here. I'm right here, so—"

"You left."

He may as well have turned that sword on her.

"You're gone."

Taly closed her eyes, pressing a hand to her heart. A dream. The rain was cold, and his blood was warm, but this was just a dream. It had to be.

"Taly?" It wouldn't be much longer now. Already his breathing was growing weak, rasping out of his chest. His heart struggled to beat.

"I'm here," she whispered and took his hand. "I know it doesn't seem like it, but I'm here, Em. I won't leave again."

"Taly?" he murmured again.

She lay down on the ground beside him in a puddle of muddy rainwater streaked with blood, surrounded by the screams of the dying. "I'm so sorry, Em. I promise—I'll never leave again."

Taly dropped the stack of books on the long library table, tugging her robe more firmly around her body as she took a seat. It was late—late enough that some might consider it early—and like so many nights before, she had lurched awake, sweating and shaking and still screaming Skye's name.

Some nights were easier than others. A few generous pours of brandy and Calcifer's soft purring were generally all it took to banish the nightmares back to the darkest recesses of her mind.

But other nights—nights like tonight when she had woken up with the scent of blood still in her nose and Skye's voice in her head, when she couldn't quite tell what was real and what wasn't... she couldn't stay in her tower.

So, she had come here. There were countless libraries in the palace, and this one was cramped and shabby with threadbare carpets and cracked firelamps. The light was dim, the chairs uncomfortable, but she still found herself drawn here night after night for the sole reason that this room housed the largest collection of birth records in the Fey Imperium.

Taly pulled the first book from the stack, an accounting of every birth in House Glimmerwood up until the Schism. Even with her mother's spells gone, she didn't remember much from before the fire. A few faces, snippets of songs, the smell of burnt stew—the few flashes of memory she had managed to recover in the past months were disjointed and scattered.

But she did have a name—Breena. And she knew that her mother had been a member of the Crystal Guard. The enrollment rosters had given her a good place to start, though it was possible her mother had enrolled after the Schism. If that was the case, she would eventually have to expand her search.

"What do you think?" Taly asked the fairy that had been shadowing her since she left her tower. She held out her hand, smiling when a flickering blue orb alighted on her outstretched palm. "Do you think my mother was from House Glimmerwood?"

"I would look farther south," a soft, feminine voice suggested.

Taly jumped at the sound, turning to find Azura standing in the open doorway. Her hair was unbound and fell to her waist, and she wore a pale ivory dressing gown that shimmered in the dim light. Though she smiled, it didn't quite reach her eyes.

"House Glimmerwood," Azura continued, coming closer, "does not allow their women to be trained in the martial arts, and I'm pretty sure your mother was born with a sword in her hand."

Taly sighed and closed the book, setting it back on the stack. That left 182 more options spread across all major families.

Breena was a common name among the fey.

Taly looked to the Queen. She had the answer. She knew exactly which book contained her mother's name, but she wouldn't tell her. Taly already knew that much, which is why she'd never asked.

"It bothers you," Azura said after a moment's pause. "Not knowing about your family."

"Is that surprising?"

"A little," Azura admitted. "As a time mage, you get used to seeing people out of order, but it never takes away the strangeness of encountering someone when they're younger than you know them to be. Still grappling with issues you know they'll eventually overcome. It's like seeing a painting that's not quite finished."

It was an honest answer. One that caught Taly off guard.

"I have a family," she said, because an honest answer deserved honesty in return. "Ivain, Sarina, Skye—because of them, I never felt deprived or alone or unloved. But there were times when I still wondered where I came from, who I would've been if Vale had never burned. There are so many things that get taken for granted: birthdays, number of siblings, which parent you take after…"

Taly shrugged, not sure how to explain the feeling of loss. "Everyone I ever met knew those things about themselves, but I didn't. It was like there was this entire part of my life that had been excised, and no matter what I did, I was never going to get it back. Of course, it bothers me."

Azura considered her for a long moment, her expression carefully blank. "Yule," she finally said.

Taly looked up.

"You were born in the month of Yule," Azura clarified softly. "You were, and still are, an only child. You look like your mother, though you inherited many of your most prominent personality traits from your father."

You inherited your father's recklessness.

Her mother's words. Something warm settled in Taly's chest, glowing inside her like an ignited ember as a few more pieces of who she was and who she had been settled into place.

"Walk with me," Azura said, and Taly rose from her chair, following her out of the library and into the hallway beyond.

"I prefer the art galleries on nights when I can't sleep," Azura said as they turned down a corridor that stretched away to the right. "The palace's collection of Draegon art cannot be rivaled."

"Sarina used to say that Draegon art was incomprehensible."

Azura snorted. "I think the more political term would be *'modern,'* but yes... she makes a valid point."

More orbs of fairy fire trailed behind them now, drifting on an invisible breeze. Taly held out a hand, and the same fairy that had taken to following her landed gently on her palm.

"Who were they?" Taly asked, gesturing to the ball of light. It wasn't the first time she'd asked the question, nor would it be the last. Azura and Leto were very good at giving answers that revealed nothing.

"They were friends." Azura said. It was a dull, hollow answer, filled with quiet misery.

And... a kernel of truth.

Taly tucked it away with the other bits and pieces of information she'd collected over the weeks. She opened her mouth, another question already poised, but Azura held up a hand.

"Let us not speak of such things," she said. And though her tone was mild, almost pleasant, Taly knew an order when she heard one. "Tell me, dear—what has you out of bed at such a dark hour?"

"I could ask you the same question."

Azura smiled at the obvious deflection. "I often find myself awake until it's over." She glanced at one of the windows they passed, the rain of ash still pelting the glass. "This was the worst day of my life, after all. You try sleeping through that."

Another honest answer. Taly eyed the woman. She had given up asking "why." Why shut down the gates? Why kill millions of people? Why topple an empire?

Those were questions the Queen was never going to answer, so she tucked away that piece of information, and answered with a simple, "Dreams," as they rounded another corner. "I keep dreaming about Skye. Almost every night now."

"Judging from your expression, I take it these aren't the good sorts of dreams."

Taly almost laughed. "Not unless seeing the people you care about get ripped apart by shades counts as *good*."

Azura grabbed her arm, bringing them to a stop. "How long has this been going on? How long have you been dreaming about your island?"

"Since I got here."

"And why is this the first I've heard of it?"

Taly shrugged half-heartedly. "Because they're just dreams."

"Perhaps." A pause. And a grimace, hastily concealed. "Perhaps not. Your premonitions, the visions you used to see—that was your Sight manifesting itself, but the Sight's true power lies in dreams."

Taly's heart stuttered. "They aren't real," she insisted, as though saying it out loud could somehow make it true.

Azura gestured for them to continue forward. "The Sight is a very curious gift," she began, patting Taly's shoulder when she no doubt saw the rising panic leech the color from her cheeks, "and one that is sorely misunderstood. As time mages, we cannot *see* the future because the future is inherently malleable. Each moment has an infinite number of variations, each one based on the decisions of an infinite number of players. The *Sight* allows us to see each of those variations and the key decisions that led to that outcome."

Taly forced herself to breathe. "So… what you're saying is that I'm seeing possibilities? Possible futures where Skye dies?"

"I believe so."

"That doesn't make me feel better." At all. Because even one future without him in it was too many.

"This is my fault," Azura muttered to herself. "I thought it was still too early to begin training your Sight, but it seems I forgot to consider the variables."

Taly frowned. "I'm not sure I follow."

Azura hesitated, considering her words. "*Normally*, you would find it exceptionally difficult to focus on a single person's future. Even during times of peace, when you don't have so many players on the board making pivotal decisions, if you don't take measures to keep yourself centered, dream divination can be a bit like groping around in the dark."

"How do you stay centered?" Taly asked as they began ascending a wide staircase.

"There are a few ways," Azura said. "The most common is to meditate with a personal item. Something the person carried with them. Something they valued. Blood would also work. Hair too. Essentially, anything that could connect you to the person whose future you wish to see."

Taly's frown deepened. As far as she knew, she didn't have anything of Skye's. She had lost her pack when Byron got spooked and ran off, and Azura still hadn't returned her dagger and pistols, both of which Skye had placed his mark upon in some way.

Which then begged the question: "Why am I able to focus on Skye's future?"

Azura waved her off. "I'm sure it's nothing to worry about. For now, it's just important to understand that these visions aren't necessarily real. Although," she added with a sympathetic glance, "I understand that this will be little solace while you are experiencing them."

Taly bobbed her head. That made sense. Sort of. "So... he's not dead?"

"Probably not."

"You're not sure?"

"Anything is *possible*," Azura said as she led them up yet another staircase, "but not all things are likely. For example, it's possible that elephants could learn how to fly, but that doesn't mean I'm going to build a net to keep them out of the gardens."

Oh. That made Taly feel marginally better. Except— "What's an elephant?" Other than something that couldn't fly.

Supposedly.

Azura smiled—a real smile this time, free of that strange melancholy that had been hanging around her like a cloud all evening. "It's an animal from the mortal realm. Magnificent creatures. Ugly, but... in a regal sort of way."

"That makes no sense." Taly swayed a bit on the final stair. Shards, she was exhausted. Even her bones felt tired.

"You really should rest," Azura said, something like worry dimming her eyes.

Taly shook her head. "I'm—"

"Don't say fine. Not when it's such an obvious lie." Azura stopped in front of a door. Taly's door. The Queen had somehow led them back to her tower without her realizing. "My advice to you right now would be that if you find yourself in a dream from which you'd like to wake up, find a ledge and jump. A good fall is generally all it takes to snap you right back into the waking world."

No teasing, no disparagement. Not for the first time, Taly realized that she knew nothing about this woman—and likely understood even less. "Can I ask you one more question?"

"You can ask," Azura said with a hint of a smile, "but I can't promise that I'll answer."

Taly pulled her robe against the chill of the night. "That first day, you said there had been other time mages born since the Schism, but all the Sanctorum has ever found are suspects. What happened to them?"

Azura's eyes shuttered. "They're dead," she murmured. Her fists clenched and unclenched at her sides. "All taken by the Sanctorum at their Attunement Ceremonies, and later killed. Their mothers were not as resourceful as yours. Or as willing to remove a Sanctifier's head."

Taly's brows rose. "My mother killed a Sanctifier?"

Azura snorted, giving a little half-smile. "Three of them, actually. The more powerful the mage, the more Sanctifiers they assign to their Attunement Ceremony. Their deaths were, of course, covered up. The Sanctorum's war is as much psychological as it is physical. They don't want the public knowing that time mages are still being born, and they've worked with the noble houses to make sure that information stays buried."

Taly opened her mouth to ask why, but Azura fixed her with a look. "That was two questions." Reaching past her, Azura turned the handle, opening the door. "Which tells me that you need to go to bed. Shards know you'll be useless tomorrow if you're too tired to even count."

Taly didn't put up a fight as Azura ushered her inside, and the door softly closed behind her. She was already half-asleep by the time she fell into bed, barely noticing Calcifer as he curled up beside her.

Moments later, her aether flashed as she was sucked into another dream.

"All time mages keep a journal," Azura said, pacing the length of the study room, speaking to Taly in her usual seat at a long wooden table. "Meeting people out of order, seeing futures that may never come true, walking through the past—it wears on a person, and reality starts to get muddy. The best way to keep your thoughts in order is to write them down. Shards know I would've lost my mind nine times over without a journal to keep me straight."

Azura placed a book on the table, and Taly resisted the urge to point out that the Queen's grip on reality was, at best, tenuous, as she reached across, pulling the book closer. It was plain, wrapped in soft brown leather with a blue-ribbon marker stuffed beneath the pages. Ordinary enough, except—

"Where did you get this?" Taly asked.

Because that wasn't just a book. It was a diary. *Her* diary—one that had long since been filled and abandoned back in Ryme, hidden where nobody but her knew to look.

"You gave it to me, of course," was all the Queen offered in explanation, and Taly had no choice but to believe her.

For indeed, there was no mistaking it. Like all her diaries, the letters *TC* were stamped into the bottom right corner, and the dates were written along the spine in red ink. This one read: *Anon 244*
–

The rest had been rubbed out.

Running her fingers along the soft leather, she traced her initials, felt the fraying ribbon, the ends knotted and re-knotted as the braided threads came undone. As soon as she lifted the cover, she was met with her own familiar handwriting.

From the personal diary of Talya Caro

That phrase marked every page as Taly began leafing through the entries. She had been fourteen when she started this diary, what became the first of many, and she cringed at the crude drawings of Skye lying dead on the ground with swords sticking out of his back. Needless to say, she hadn't been happy when he was introduced at the Dawn Court, nearly doubling the time he spent away each year. Ivain had suggested journaling to help her sort out her thoughts.

And now the Queen was doing the same.

Azura said, "I want you to spend the afternoon writing down your dreams. All of them. Anything and everything you can remember since you came to the palace. Sometimes the tiniest, most forgettable details are the key to avoiding catastrophe."

"But it's full," Taly pointed out, still flipping through the pages. She'd filled this book from cover to cover.

"A time mage's journal is never full." Azura leaned against a nearby desk, arms crossed. "Look."

Turning to the last page, Taly watched with detached fascination as the letters began to blur, dissolving until there was nothing but a blank white space, waiting to be filled.

A time mage's journal indeed.

"The entries aren't gone," Azura said. "Only hidden. The pages are enchanted to phase in and out of the present reality."

"Like a pocket universe?"

"Like a thousand pocket universes, all layered on top of each other."

Taly frowned. The pages were in fact blank now, and if she focused, she could feel magic woven into the paper itself. "Ivain keeps a journal. He said his eldest sister was the one that got him started."

"Well, his eldest sister was one of us, so that comes as no surprise. Time magic runs strong in the Castaro line."

"Did you know her?" Taly looked up. "Ivain hardly ever speaks about her."

Azura nodded, something sad creeping into her expression. "I did. She was a very dear friend, even after she had the gall to take the Bryer name." Her lip curled. "I'm sure I don't need to tell you that the Raines and Bryers are sworn enemies."

Taly shook her head. She didn't. It was common knowledge that the Raine bloodline founded House Thanos, only to be usurped by one of their vassals. Azura had lived long enough to see both families rise to power, and had used her influence as Queen to protect her bloodline from extinction. The Bryer Matriarch was not known for mercy. If she'd had her way, the entire Raine family would be nothing but a memory, even the children executed.

"You never wanted to rule," Taly said. She wasn't sure how she knew it, but she did. "House Thanos changed leadership just after you took the throne, which means that you would've had to take the Rites to inherit the Shard while there was still fighting going on. You were pushed into it, weren't you? To save your family?"

Azura's frown deepened. It was all the confirmation she needed.

Azura pushed herself off the desk. "*Write.*" A pointed glance at the journal. "And every time you complete an entry, I want you to practice summoning and dismissing your Sight. If I'm not mistaken, that is something you already know how to do?"

Taly nodded. She had figured out how to summon her premonitions when she was still mortal. It wasn't exactly second nature, but she remembered the feeling. Enough to do it again.

"Good," Azura said. "I'll be back in an hour. If you have any questions, Leto can help you."

Chin resting on her hand, Taly watched as the Queen exited the room. Leto was waiting in the hallway.

Interesting, she thought. Not because the Queen had given anything away. She'd already had the information, simply needed to see the connections. But it was still interesting in that way that Taly found all things the Queen didn't want her knowing interesting. Maybe one day the dots would connect, and the things that woman said and did would start to make sense.

With a sigh, Taly turned to a blank page. There would be hell if she didn't do as she was told. So, reaching for a nearby quill, she began to write.

Closing the door behind her, Azura leaned against it. Sometimes, it amazed her that she was still capable of feeling guilt over things that happened so long ago. But there it was. A familiar sickness hollowing out her chest.

War was never easy, and no one came out the same as they were before.

"Majesty?"

Azura turned to the haze of soft blue in her peripheral vision. "I don't like how perceptive she's becoming," she said to the woman. "We will have to be more careful with our words. All knowledge has its time, and I'm only now just getting her to trust me. We can't let that be undone."

Leto's light pulsed softly. An affirmation. "I have the names you asked for."

Azura pushed herself to stand. "Good," she said. She hated sending the fairies outside of this place. It degraded their sense of self, ate away at what was left of their anima. But sometimes—like now—it was necessary. "And they're aware of the potential cruelty of this task?"

Leto nodded. "Yes."

"Good," she said again. "Let's go speak with them then. Certain events have already been set in motion, and we must make sure that all the essential players find their proper places."

CHAPTER 13

-*From the personal notes of Ivain Castaro, Marquess of Tempris*

The 2nd day of the month Litha, during the 235th year of the Empty Throne

Today, I did the thing I swore I'd never do again. After three years of letters and calls and thinly veiled bribes, I finally agreed to take on Adriana Emrys' youngest son as my live-in student. I'm not sure how she knew that Sarina and I would be touring the Ghislain countryside, but she did, cornering us in a tavern in Eroun with her son in tow—a shy, quiet boy named Skylen.

Sarina fell in love immediately, and even I must admit he was not what I was expecting. Barely nine years old, but he's powerful, smart, though it was plain to see that his tutors have been mishandling his education. Mages with that much aether—it's always a balancing act of keeping them challenged without needlessly endangering their lives, and in the right hands, this boy could be molded into something special.

After Breena, I never thought I would take on another student. I regret that we never settled our differences before her death, but perhaps my sister is right. Teaching has been one of the greatest joys of my life, and maybe it's time to stop punishing myself for that failure and start looking to the future.

Skye turned in a circle, taking in the scattering of fire lamps, the sprawling marble dance hall, the soaring towers of champagne flutes brimming with sparkling wine.

"I'm... home?" he murmured, his voice lost amid the crowd of highborn fey that surrounded him on all sides.

Or rather... he was back in Ghislain, at his family's mountain estate overlooking the Bay of Margo. Not home. No, this place hadn't been home for a long time—not since he'd been sent to live and train with Ivain nearly sixteen years ago.

He searched his memory. The last thing he could remember was being in Della. It was cold and wet; the temperature had dropped that day, and even the wards on Ivain's tent hadn't been able to completely ward off the chill of night. He had been huddled inside his bedroll, shivering so hard his teeth chattered, and—

"I'm dreaming," he concluded, eyeing the draped garlands and evergreen wreaths above the doors and archways, the tiny sprigs of holly that decorated every dress and lapel, even his. He had to be. That was the only reasonable explanation for why he would suddenly find himself back in Ghislain for his family's Yulemas celebration.

Skye began weaving through the crowd, flurries of magical snow dusting his shoulders and catching in his hair. The faces blurred together, and the walls seemed to shimmer as the dream warped around the outer edges of the room, almost like a bubble. There was music in the background, a combination of strings and flutes, but every time he tried to focus, attempting to pick out a tune or melody, the song would shift into something else equally unrecognizable.

"Excuse me," he said, sidestepping a woman in a vibrant blue dress that nearly twirled into him as she exited the dancefloor.

He blinked, and her dress was suddenly crimson. The woman gave him a smile, her eyes hungry as she surveyed him from head to foot, taking in his black dress suit and white tie.

A heartbeat later, her dress had turned from red to lavender.

"Excuse me," he said again, ignoring the pout that pulled at the corners of her gold-painted lips.

Skye felt a tug, gentle but insistent. Almost like there was a string attached to one of his ribs. It tugged again, and he froze, craning his neck to see over the milling crowd of nobles as he tried to pinpoint its source.

There.

A pair of wide, double doors marked the center of the back wall, leading to what memory told him was a balcony.

Another tug and Skye began to move. He carefully pushed his way through the crowd, but time seemed to stretch in this strange half-world. No matter how far or how long he walked, the entrance to the balcony was always just a few steps out of reach.

That thread continued to pull him forward, and he imagined himself grabbing it, twisting it between his fingers and wrenching whatever it was on the other side towards him.

The dream abruptly shifted. One step—he was still inside the ballroom, muttering apologies as he was being pushed and jostled. The next, he found himself standing outside on a balcony that jutted into the open air, blissfully alone.

Skye stood there for a moment, relishing the cool night air and taking in his surroundings. In the distance, the sea glittered in the moonlight, smooth as glass, and the lights of the surrounding city were so bright, he could barely make out the stars that shivered high overhead in the dry winter night. Despite the chill, flowers curled along the stone railing, filling the air with the scent of jasmine.

There was a soft sigh from somewhere in the shadows, and—

Skye jolted.

A woman sat on the far side of the balcony, perched on the wide stone railing despite the sheer drop that opened up below. Her dress was a soft pink, pinned and tucked and draped so effortlessly, it seemed to have been sewn from a single length of silk. Her shoulders and arms were bare, and the bodice molded to her body before seamlessly flowing into a voluminous mass of skirts and petticoats that fluttered in the breeze.

Wisps of pale blonde hair framed her face, and strands of jewels had been woven into the intricate braid that draped across her shoulder, each one glistening in the moonlight.

The look was elegant, if understated, especially compared to the elaborate styles that were currently in fashion. She would've looked out of place compared to the ladies inside, but this woman—even without the trappings of court, the rich fabrics and extravagant hairstyles; even though her ears were round instead of arched, her eyes lacking that inherent glow of magic that marked his species; even though she was human, mortal—she was more beautiful than any fey woman could ever aspire to be.

"Taly," he breathed, smiling so wide it hurt. Even knowing this wasn't real, he couldn't help but feel overwhelmed by the sight of her.

He rushed forward, needing to have her in his arms—desperate to feel her warmth, her heartbeat, and praying that the dream would allow such small mercies.

But since this was Taly, and since she never did what he expected—even in his dreams—that's not what happened.

Slowly, her head turned, and those gray eyes went comically wide as her face contorted into what could only be described as horror.

"No." She began to shake her head, pressing her back against the wall of the estate. The sheer panic in her voice had Skye stumbling to a stop. "No, no, no."

"Tink." Skye reached out a hand, but she continued to inch away. "It's alright. It's just—"

"You can't be here." She tried to untuck her feet from beneath the puff of her skirts, but the fabric twisted between her legs, and she began to fall backward.

Skye cursed, surging forward and just managing to loop an arm around her waist before she tipped over the edge of the railing.

She struggled against him, slapping her hands against his face and chest, all the while shrieking at him to *let me go, let me go, let me go!*

"Shards, woman..." Grunting, he finally managed to pull her back onto the patio, but it was like trying to hold onto a thrashing hellcat. "Would you please just calm—"

Her skirts pooled beneath his feet, and he tripped, sending them tumbling to the ground in a heap. Their heads smacked together, and they both let out twin groans of pain.

"No, no, no, no, no..." she was still moaning, hands covering her face. "I thought this was just going to be a normal dream. Why do you always have to ruin everything?"

"It's good to see you too," Skye grumbled, rubbing his head as he rolled off her. This dream was quickly turning into a nightmare. He'd tripped, made a fool of himself in front of the woman he loved, and nearly given them both concussions.

Maybe he was the one that needed to take a dive off the balcony.

"So, what's it going to be tonight?" Taly pushed herself up on her elbows, glaring at him. "Are you going to fall into a canyon? Maybe get eaten by shades? That happens a lot, you know. Just last night, I had to watch you drunkenly stumble into the old airtram station outside the Swap. I thought we were good when you didn't immediately fall down the stairs and break your neck, but then when you saw that there were no guards, guess what your dumb ass decided to do."

She was on her knees, leaning over him, and yes, this really was a nightmare because now she was berating him and not in the fun way that made her look like an angry kitten.

"You decided to investigate the tunnels—the ones that lead outside the city where there are *shades*—by your-Shards-damned-self!" She flicked his forehead. "Alone." Then his ear. "And unarmed." A punch to his shoulder. "And did I mention drunk?" She sighed, deflating slightly as she ran a finger across the satin lapel of his dress coat. "Jerk. What kind of idiot bumbles into an abandoned airtram station that's been left unguarded and unlocked during the middle of the apocalypse, and then decides to investigate it by himself?"

"Taly, I—"

"You need to *stop dying*." That caught him off guard. As did the pleading look she gave him as she said, "Do you have any idea how many times I've had to watch you die? You're a shadow mage—you're supposed to be indestructible, but every night..." She lifted her hand as if to give him another solid punch on the shoulder, then let it drop. "Why did you go in the tunnels, Em? There are so many terrible things in the tunnels."

Skye dragged a finger across her cheek, then down the line of her jaw. She looked just the way he remembered. So beautiful—every feature so infinitely dear. "This is absurd," he whispered. He'd never had a dream this vivid before, one where he felt so... *present*. If it weren't for the way the ballroom still shifted and swayed behind them, shimmering like a film of soap, he might've been able to convince himself it was real.

"I'm aware," she said with a snort. "Believe me—I know how crazy I sound. Which is why I need to jump off the balcony now."

Pushing herself to her feet, she began climbing over the railing, but Skye was at her side in an instant.

"*Stop it*," she barked, trying to shake him off.

"No, you stop it." Placing both hands on her shoulders, Skye twisted them around so that he was standing between her and the balcony ledge. "This is my dream, and I'm not going to watch you fling yourself into an early grave."

But in typical Taly fashion, she just huffed. Then chuckled. Then rolled her eyes, muttering a "Nice try," as she cut a glance to the balcony railing behind him. "Move," she said. "I need to wake up now. I refuse to watch you die again."

He held out an arm when she took a step. "What does jumping off a balcony have to do with waking up?"

Taly shrugged. "Someone told me that if you fall in a dream, you wake up. That's why I came out here. I wanted a quick exit."

"Well…" Skye glanced behind him, beyond the railing at the hundreds of ships lining the shore. "I'm not dead. *Yet*," he quickly added when it looked like she was going to say something. "See?" He reached for her, pressing her hand to his heart. That brief touch, along with the soft sigh that slipped out of her as she leaned into him, made his knees go weak. "So… what's the rush?"

She looked up at him through a thick veil of lashes, and for a moment, he could've sworn that her eyes seemed to shine with an inhuman light. She blinked, and it was gone.

"I suppose that's true," she said, flexing her fingers in the fabric of his coat. "But if a group of shades suddenly burst through that door—"

"I'll push you off the side of the estate myself." Skye grinned when she seemed to relax, a small smile tugging at the corners of her lips. He held out a hand. "In the meantime—dance with me?"

Taly stared at his outstretched hand like it might bite her. "What?"

Skye laughed as he stepped closer, placing a hand at her waist. Even through the dream, she felt warm. "If, as you say, I'm just biding my time until I inevitably die—can't I at least spend my last few moments dancing with a beautiful woman?"

The scowl she gave him was one of her best—truly well done—but he didn't miss the way her lips twitched. Just at the corners. A faint blush stained her cheeks, and when she finally huffed, refusing to meet his eyes, he knew he'd won.

The music started up, trickling out from the ballroom. Skye took her other hand in his, waiting for her to gather her skirts before he took a step, then another. She followed his rhythm effortlessly.

"You're a better dancer than I remember," Taly said a bit airily as he spun her around.

"Well, it's easier to lead when your partner isn't purposefully trying to step on your feet."

A light snow had begun to fall around them, but Taly's sharp bark of laughter as he continued to steer her into the dance chased away any cold he might have felt.

The music quickened, but the steps were familiar. They'd learned this dance together, back when they were still children. And even though they were older now, and she was wearing a dress instead of trousers and heels instead of boots, the press of her body against his as they eased into the next dance was as comfortable as it was new.

Like coming home, he thought as he pressed his nose to her hair. That was why he had dreamed of this place, this house that he went out of his way to avoid. Anywhere that Taly was… that would be his home.

It could've been minutes, hours, *days* since the dance began. And still, they continued to waltz around the small patio, spinning, never faltering, each step perfectly in sync.

The music finally began to fade, and as Skye spun her into the final step of the dance, he dipped her low and pressed a gentle kiss to the hollow of her throat.

Taly's answering gasp had him smiling against her skin as he slowly dragged his lips along the column of her neck. When he reached her mouth, even though it pained him, he pulled back just enough to find her staring up at him, her eyes soft, the look on her face a mix of breathless desire and gentle affection.

In that moment, it frightened him the things he would do to make sure she always looked at him that way.

"Back in Ebondrift," he said, and then let his eyes drop to her mouth, "you said I had to ask for permission to kiss you? Does that rule apply in dreams?"

Taly smiled, so warm and lovely, it made everything around them seem just a little bit brighter. "Why? Are you getting tired of asking?"

Skye pulled her out of the dip, snapping her into his arms. "You know I would never ruin your fun. Although, I was thinking that if you intend on enforcing this rule, I'm going to need to come up with a form. It might save me some time."

Taly angled her head, her hands sliding up his chest to circle his neck. "It sounds like this is something you plan to be doing a lot."

"Yes," Skye said, nodding. He still felt the pull of that phantom thread, tugging just a little tighter as he began to lean forward. "In fact, when you come back, I plan to never stop kissing you."

"Well, that's just impractical," she whispered, her lips nearly grazing his. "You'd have to stop some time. To eat. To sleep. And considering how much you love the sound of your own voice, I don't see you taking a vow of silence."

"You know you're not as funny as you think you are."

"I am exactly as funny as I think I am."

Her eyes drifted closed. His lips had just barely touched hers when he felt something snap, fluttering just out of reach as the world went dark.

Skye had never seen the streets of Ryme packed so full of people.

Mortals and fey alike crammed between the rows of market stalls and street vendors, and merchants rushed about, bickering and bartering as the villagers and refugees frantically bought up what little food was left at the end of the day. Stray dogs hovered around the edges, no doubt waiting for whatever scraps might come their way, and several earth mages pushed their way through the crowd, leading milk cows and carrying crates of chickens and other fowl as they made their way to the areas that had been set aside for livestock. Mud and hay and Shards only knew what else coated the broken cobbled pavement underfoot, and as Skye passed by yet another darkened alleyway, he grimaced as the stench of the street mixed with the scent of spices and roasting meat that lingered on the air.

After the battle at Crescent Canyon, they had stayed in Della only a handful of days, waiting, searching, and allowing the earth mages to stabilize as many of the wounded as they could with so few resources. They kept in touch with Aiden via the comms, and when he sent word that he had found a lead on Taly's whereabouts and would meet back up with them in Ryme, Ivain made the decision to start moving the refugees.

It had taken four trips to load up every man, woman, and child onto the airship and transport them back to the village at the northern end of the island, and then one more to go back for their supplies. Sarina had cried, and cried, and cried when Skye and Ivain finally stepped off the airship as it was docking for the night. Even now, almost two days later, the woman was still fussing.

Skye breathed a sigh of relief as he turned onto a quieter street, grateful to be free of the crowds. The houses were larger and more evenly spaced in this section of town, each one made of sturdy stone and trimmed with little patios circled with painted iron. The Castaros' townhouse—a five-story, gray-bricked manor that sat on a parcel of land larger than any of the rest—perched at the very top of the hill.

Since the attacks began, Ryme had been transformed. The slums had been repurposed, every inch of underused space converted into gardens and farmland, and food production had moved inside the walls. Their supplies were holding, as were their walls and fortifications, and thanks to the preparations the Gate Watchers had begun months ago in anticipation of the Aion Gate opening, the repairs on the Swap as well as other key structures were nearly completed. Soon, if their luck held out, every refugee would be afforded the luxury of a warm bed and a roof that didn't leak.

They could hold the city for months, long enough to escape through the Aion Gate and into the mortal cities. It was the best scenario they could've hoped for, even if there were too many missing faces to make that victory seem anything but hollow.

Finally making his way to the top of the hill, Skye placed a hand against the lock that sat in the center of a set of wrought-iron gates. There was a click, and the gates swung open on creaking hinges.

Ivain had bolstered security on the townhouse since the attacks began. There was still a traitor in their midst, and even with Taly's warning, they still hadn't been able to narrow in on just who might be working against them. More than ever, they had to be vigilant, and since Ivain's office now harbored information and orders that may very well spell the difference between life and death for an entire city, countless layers of steel, iron, and magic now separated the lavish house from the rest of the village. Only family and a few of the more trusted members of the serving staff could unlock the wards. Everyone else had to be vetted.

Skye made his way inside the house, only stopping to drop his pack in the outdoor workroom before entering through the kitchen. He was still scraping mud off his boots when Sarina found him.

She had changed clothes since he'd seen her that morning—removing the dirt-stained tunic she wore to work outside in favor of a pale blue gown. The scent of smoke and aether clung to her, indicating that she'd most likely spent her day helping Ivain burn away the rubble and wreckage that had collected at the northern edge of the city. Very few fire mages had the skill to produce flames hot enough to melt stone, and Sarina, even if she didn't like to flaunt her abilities, was no ordinary fire mage.

"Where have you been?!" she hissed, pulling him inside. Skye grimaced at the muddy boot prints that trailed behind him as she ushered him forward.

"I was helping the Gate Watchers set up the monitoring station," he said as she pushed him down the hall and up the stairs. Though it wasn't a perfect solution, they did have equipment that would allow them to track the status of the Aion Gate remotely—let them know when it was time to move closer. "Sarina, what's—"

"Aiden's back."

Skye stopped abruptly, turning on his heels. He barely caught Sarina before she ran into him.

They shared a look.

And then he was running, up a second set of stairs, following the familiar path to the study on the third floor, Sarina close behind.

The door at the end of the hall stood open, the light spilling out onto the plush carpets that blanketed the dark hardwood. Just beyond, Aimee was crying into her brother's stained overcoat, pulling back occasionally to make sure that he was, indeed, still there, alive and unharmed.

Ivain leaned against a massive desk stacked with papers and books, his grim expression at odds with the cheery fire that roared away inside the carved marble hearth.

Skye slowed his pace, stepping inside the study and scanning the room. The hope that had flared to life so suddenly flickered and died.

Because Taly… wasn't there.

Which meant that Aiden hadn't been able to find her.

Which meant—

Skye took a breath. It meant nothing. Only that Aiden hadn't had any luck and that Taly was still out there, waiting to be found.

"Aimee." Ivain turned to his niece. "Would you go find Eliza and ask her to prepare something for Aiden? I'm sure the boy is famished after such a long journey."

Aimee bobbed out a curtsey, wiping her eyes as she reluctantly stepped away from her brother. So far, the siege had taken little effect on the water mage's sense of style. Her dark hair was immaculately curled, and the teal gown she wore was pressed and pinned to flatter her slim waist and full bust. The only change Skye could see was that she had taken to wearing a jeweled belt with a red velvet bag attached.

Skye's nostrils flared. It wasn't a scent. Not really. More a sense, an awareness that thrummed just beneath his skin. *Water crystals.* He knew it instinctively. Those were water crystals clicking together in that bag. It seemed that after the incident with the harpy, Aimee had finally started taking her magic seriously.

She gave him a teary smile. "I hope it's good news," she whispered. Somehow, Skye knew that she meant it, despite her and Taly's mutual animosity.

Sarina placed a hand on the girl's shoulder as she passed by, closing the door after her.

"Sister." Ivain gave Sarina a pointed look.

"If you tell me to leave," Sarina said, sinking down onto a green velvet couch that sat opposite the desk, "I'll gut you where you stand." The smile she gave her older brother was sweet—and lethal. "You don't need to spare me, Ivain. Taly is just as much mine as she is yours, and if something's happened, I want to know about it."

Ivain sighed, smart enough to recognize when he'd already lost. He turned to Aiden. "Maybe we should back up a bit for Skye and Sarina. You were saying you started in Vale?"

Aiden gave a shallow nod. The earth mage looked exhausted. His face was drawn and pale, his lips nearly bloodless. His red hair was longer than it had been less than two weeks ago—no longer shaved but curling around his ears. That meant he'd been injured, seriously enough to need healing magic.

"I couldn't get a good read on her with the locator spell, so I thought it was as good a place as any to start." Aiden's voice was hoarse, and he swayed on his feet, favoring his left side. Sarina gestured for him to sit, but he refused. "To put it mildly, Vale was destroyed."

"What do you mean?" Sarina pressed. "Was it abandoned, attacked...?" Her eyes cut to her brother and then back to Aiden. "Were there bodies?"

"There was nothing," Aiden whispered. "No bodies, no buildings; even the relay was in pieces."

Ivain stiffened at that. The relays were made of hyaline, and even a fully trained shadow mage would have trouble shattering a piece that large.

Aiden went on, "I was able to get a read on her there. Even though it looked like a bomb had gone off in the middle of town, I can say with complete certainty that she walked out of there—*alive*."

Sarina took a sharp breath, and even Ivain looked hopeful before he carefully schooled his expression.

Skye waited patiently, soaking up every scrap of information. If Aiden hadn't been able to find her, that meant it was his turn. He'd leave tonight if he had to.

Aiden pulled a vial from his pocket. There was less than a few thimblefuls of blood left at the bottom. "I followed the trail east, through the forest. That's where I found her horse—Byron. He was injured, and it looked like he had been wandering the woods for several days. Taly's pack was still strapped to the saddle, and when I went into the horse's memory—I was only able to get a few flashes, and I'm not a beast master, so it was muddy. But I think she was thrown."

Ivain took a breath, ready to speak, but one look from Sarina silenced him. Skye already knew what the man wanted to say: Taly was too good a rider to get thrown, especially from a horse she had helped train.

Still, even Elvethan spooked. And if she'd been injured—

"I went through her pack," Aiden rasped, mumbling out a quick thanks when Ivain handed him a glass of amber liquid. The healer knocked back the glass, and his voice was a little steadier as he said, "There wasn't much besides some clothes and papers, but I was able to salvage a few strands of hair for a second locator spell. It led me to Infinity's Edge."

"The old palace?" Ivain's eyes widened, and Skye could already see the man running through the variables. Why had she fled to a place that was abandoned? Had she been seeking shelter or... what? Why the palace? Why not Della?

Aiden nodded. "That's where the trail ended, but..." He shook his head, dragging a finger along the rim of the glass. "I've never seen anything quite like it."

"What do you mean?" Skye asked.

Aiden's eyes found his. "I spent two days investigating the area. I circled the palace grounds so many times I lost count, but the locator spell kept leading me in circles. One moment, she would be there, and the next, the spell would just die."

"But that doesn't necessarily mean anything," Sarina said, her voice soft—hopeful. "Locator spells aren't perfect. All she would need to do is climb a tree or go inside a building to sever her connection to the earth, and—"

"I checked the palace, Sarina," Aiden interrupted, his lips a thin line. "Believe me, I'm aware of the limitations on my own magic, and I checked every building and every tree in the area.

I even tamed a wolf to see if he could sense something that I couldn't, but the only thing I found was…" His eyes fell to the floor.

"*What*," Ivain growled. A demand, not a question. He still gripped the edge of the desk. The wood began to groan.

Aiden sighed, glancing at Sarina and then Skye as he shoved a hand into his pocket. Silver flashed, and when Aiden uncurled his palm, Skye had the distinct feeling that the world had somehow slipped out from underneath him when he wasn't looking.

Even caked with mud, and gravel, and blood that had already dried to black, he recognized the tiny, teardrop pendant. Taly had worn it every day of her life, not even taking it off to bathe after a much younger version of himself had gotten it into his head that it would be a funny prank to take the necklace and hide it from her while she was in the bath.

Skye wasn't sure how he managed to stay on his feet as he watched Aiden place the necklace in Sarina's outstretched palm. He wasn't sure what it was that kept him from vomiting all over the carpet when Ivain asked, "Were there shades?" in a voice that was far too steady given the quiet devastation that dimmed those stark blue eyes.

Aiden nodded. "There was a small group patrolling the palace gates."

"Fresh?" Ivain asked.

Another nod.

"And the species?"

"Human."

Sarina let out a broken sob and clutched the necklace to her chest.

"No." Skye shook his head, refusing to even entertain the idea, the possibility that Taly could… that she was… might've been turned…

"They've been using humans to bolster their numbers," Ivain said softly. "Humans breed faster; they die faster. Even in the larger cities, no one bats an eye when a human passes. Whoever planned this attack has been preparing for a very long time, and if I had to guess, I would say that they've been harvesting areas with little in the way of defense in order to mount an attack on fortified strongholds. After all, we're more likely to let in a familiar face than we are—"

Sarina let out another sob as the implication began to settle over the group.

"No," Skye said again.

"Skylen." Ivain's voice held a hidden edge. "I don't like it either, but we have to be realistic."

"Taly's not dead." And Shards, it hurt. It hurt just to say that word. "She's not." Because he wouldn't accept it.

Aiden piped up, "I didn't see Taly among the shades I killed."

"I'm not surprised," Ivain said. "Whoever's doing this—if they have any inkling of what she is to me" —his eyes cut to Skye— "or to you, they'll save her. They'll use her against us. And considering the way that Aiden's spell reacted, I suspect—"

"*Don't say it!*" Even Skye was surprised by how vicious the words sounded.

The room went silent, save for Sarina's quiet sobbing.

Skye turned to Aiden. "I'm going to need the rest of her blood, her pack… anything you have of hers."

"*Skylen.*" Again, that sharp, lethal edge. Ivain finally let go of the desk, standing to his full height. And despite every instinct that told him to back down, to shut his mouth and obey—Skye met the old man's stare. "We are in a difficult position right now, and we do not have the luxury of entertaining folly."

"Brother," Sarina rasped, but Ivain held up a hand, shushing her.

Aiden turned away, staring out the window through red-rimmed eyes.

"Taly is dead." Ivain's voice cracked on that last word.

Dead.

Dead, dead, dead…

Until now, Skye hadn't even allowed himself to think the word. That horrible, horrible word that now clanged through him.

Something inside him began to scream as that hole that used to be his heart grew wider, and wider, and wider.

"She's gone, boy." Ivain again. He said something else, but Skye had already turned.

Someone called his name, but he was already out the door and down the stairs.

It was late when Skye finally stumbled out of the tavern. He wasn't sure how he had ended up there. And after a few dozen drinks, he didn't care. All he knew was that everything had become comfortably numb, that pain that threatened to cleave him in two temporarily muted.

The streets were far emptier now that the vendors had packed up their shops for the night, and the sounds of chatter and drunken laughter began to fade as he staggered down the street, somehow managing to stay on his feet.

He wasn't ready to go home yet. Sarina would likely be waiting. Ivain too. But Skye couldn't face that. Face them. Face that empty room across from his that still smelled like *her* or the reality that it was going to stay empty.

Not yet.

Skye turned down a random alleyway.

Taly was dead, and it hadn't really settled into him yet. He felt pain, but not enough. Yes, there was a hole that had been punched straight through him. And yes, he marveled at the fact that his heart could keep beating when hers didn't. But it didn't feel real. He was walking around in a fog, and when he finally forced himself to face that reality head-on, he would undoubtedly be inconsolable. He would fly into a rage, curse Aiden, curse the gods, curse any reality that didn't have her in it.

Dead.

And surprisingly, it didn't seem so hard to think the word now because it seemed so positively ludicrous.

Dead, dead, dead…

Because surely, he would know if she were gone. Some part of him would've surely felt that life extinguish, would instinctively know that the world had become just a little darker.

Do you have any idea how many times I've had to watch you die?

The words came unbidden to his mind. That dream had seemed so real, so tangible that even now, days later, the memory still refused to fade in that way that dreams were supposed to fade.

Stop dying, she had said to him as only Taly could. As though it were an imposition to *her*.

And if he could go back to that dream, he would scream, *"You first!"*

Stop dying. Stop being dead.

Come home.

Please just... come home.

Skye stumbled to a stop, catching himself on a rusty piece of railing that jutted up from the ground, just barely avoiding a nasty fall down the darkened stairwell.

The airtram station, he thought, peering into the shadows. In his wanderings, his feet had brought him to the old airtram station just outside the Swap.

Just last night, I had to watch you drunkenly stumble into the old airtram station outside the Swap.

Even through the fog of alcohol that his damned aether was already working to burn away, he could hear her voice clear as day.

You decided to investigate the tunnels...

Such a strange dream. The stairs stretched into the darkness, beckoning.

There are so many terrible things in the tunnels.

You need to stop dying.

But she wasn't here to tell him what to do. Not anymore. So, throwing an obscene hand gesture toward the darkened night sky, Skye began stumbling down the stairs. If there was an afterlife, he hoped she was watching—and that she was pissed.

Before the Schism, Tempris had one of the most advanced fast transit systems in the Fey Imperium. There were hundreds of airtram tunnels crisscrossing the island, and though some of them had caved in when the gates were shut down, many, like the tunnels that ran beneath Ryme, were still in working condition.

It was wet, and the smell of mildew permeated the air. There were old firelamps jutting from the walls, each one flickering as water dripped from overhead. The light was scant and patchy, devoid of warmth and failing to ward off the chill of the underground station.

Skye emerged from the stairwell and came to a halt. The large antechamber was dank and humid, and a heavy steel door had been dragged across the tunnel entrance. Securing the airtram stations had been a priority when Ivain and the other Gate Watchers locked down Ryme and the surrounding area. Countless stations peppered the island, each one a possible access point into the city, and while some of the sites had been filled with rubble, others caved in—a select few had been left open as a possible means of escape should the city ever be taken.

"Hello?" Skye called, channeling just a bit more aether and sharpening his eyesight. In addition to the reinforced steel door and magical wards lining the stairwell, this tunnel was supposed to be kept under constant guard.

... there were no guards...

Skye's heart began to pound as those words trickled through his thoughts.

Because the guards...

He had to force himself to breathe.

The guards were gone. And that heavy steel door had been dragged open.

CHAPTER 14

-The following is an interview with Arcana laureate Savannah Selket

What was Azura like as a teacher? Well, she was tough, stern—unconventional. You never quite knew where you stood with her, though it was easy to see exactly which students she thought were special. She pushed them harder than the rest, purposefully breaking them down so she could build them up stronger. Not all of them made it. Most of them didn't, in fact.

Me personally—I quit the day of my seal three examination.

The sun had barely begun to rise as Taly surveyed the arena. It was a large, circular space, blanketed with red dirt and surrounded by a ring of crumbling stone arches. A row of training dummies lined one side, each decorated with scatterings of water and shadow crystals. The dummy on the far right was malfunctioning, flickering through a series of combat presets—first a wyvern, then a basilisk, then a mountain of a man with eyes that burned like fire.

Taly pulled her eyes away. She still had a bruise from where the mannequin had knocked her on her ass the previous day. She'd been stupid enough to think she could spar with the shadow-mage-preset at full strength, and one swing of the man's staff had thrown her to the ground so hard, she'd dislocated a shoulder.

She was stronger now—but not that strong. Next time she would listen to Azura's advice: *get away, get distance, assess*. The only thing a time mage needed to know about close combat was how to get out of it.

Taly stood beneath one of the arches, wrapping both hands with long strips of linen. Leto had dressed her in plain, sturdy clothes that morning: trousers that were easy to move in, a tunic light enough to ward off the heat, and leather vambraces that covered her arms from wrist to elbow. Her boots were old and worn—comfortable.

They were the kind of clothes she might have worn to spar with Skye or Ivain, and that thought immediately put her on edge. After five months at the palace—five *long* months spent with the Queen—Taly had learned to hate surprises, especially ones that involved armor.

"Are you sure you can't tell me what she's planning?" Taly asked, leaning back against the curved wall of the gray stone arch. Leto crouched beside her, tightening the buckles on a pair of greaves that matched the other few pieces of armor she'd been given over the past few weeks as her training intensified.

"No, Ma'am," the woman said, rising to her full height. Her form shivered in the dim morning light. It was a struggle for some of the fairies to change their appearance, and no one except Leto was able to mimic the fey form so effortlessly. *She gets help from the Queen*, one of the fairies had whispered to her one evening when she'd found her way down to the kitchens. *Leto was always Her Majesty's favorite.*

Now that they were starting to warm to her, the fairies really were hopeless gossips. And even though she still couldn't say for sure just who they'd been in life, she had her theories. They had been fey—she was sure of that. They knew far too much about magic to be anything but. And judging from the few mannerisms some still clung to, many had been part of the noble class.

"Are you positive?" Taly asked, even if she knew Leto wouldn't budge. "You're absolutely certain you can't tell me anything?"

"You seem concerned, Ma'am."

"Usually, the Queen's *'surprises'* don't involve armor."

Leto selected a long wooden staff from a nearby rack.

"Or weapons," Taly added, her heart sinking, not quite to the floor, but definitely somewhere around her knees. She took the staff, inspecting the alternating rows of air and shadow crystals before giving it a few experimental swings. Heavy, but balanced. Likely reinforced with a core of pure viridian.

This was not going to be a good day.

"Good morning!" Azura's voice carried across the yard, far too bright and chipper given the early hour. She was dressed in a dove-gray morning coat that flowed down to her knees, and the sleeves had been rolled up to reveal several long, coiling chains of silver and gold threaded with time crystals. Her riding boots were polished to a mirror-like shine, and her hair was so tightly coiled, the ends brushed her shoulders rather than her waist.

She looked like she would be more at home on a courtly ride through the forest than in a dusty sparring ring. Clearly, she didn't plan to get her own hands dirty.

"Is it?" Taly sighed. "Good, that is."

Azura stepped into the shade of the stone arch, pouting. She looked to Leto. "Someone's already surly, I see."

"It's dawn," Taly grumbled. "Of course, I'm surly. I barely had enough time for a few sips of coffee, much less breakfast."

"I didn't say anything regarding your plans, Majesty." Leto bobbed her head. "Although, she did ask."

"Of course, she did," Azura said with a knowing smile. "I'd be disappointed otherwise."

"Can we get on with this?" Taly twirled her staff. "I'm tired, I'm hungry, and I'm not in the mood to play '*Let's guess the Queen's newest plan to torture her prisoner and make her wish she'd never been born*'."

Azura crinkled her nose. "Prisoner feels a little kitschy. I prefer, *reluctant student*. Has a much nicer ring, I think."

Taly frowned. "No matter what you choose to call it, I'm still being held here against my will."

Azura and Leto shared a look. "Surly *and* dramatic," the Queen drawled with an exaggerated roll of her eyes. Then, chuckling softly, she turned and strode back into the arena, gesturing for Taly to follow. "It's been two months since you earned your second seal, and you now have a working knowledge of every spell and enchantment required to pass the third seal examination. Granted, you have yet to fully master many of the concepts, but I personally believe there are some things that one must learn by doing."

The Queen came to an abrupt stop in the center of the ring, turning on her heel. Taly barely managed to stop herself from barreling into her.

"After all," Azura said, stabbing a finger in Taly's face and forcing her to back up a few steps, "time mages need to be able to anticipate any obstacle, outthink any foe. No matter the terrain, even if their aether is nearly gone, they must be able to cast instinctively. For someone like you—a young woman who has spent most of her life without any magic of her own—the reflexive use of aether in a combat situation isn't something that can be taught. It must be trained. Which is why we're here."

Azura spread her arms and took a deep breath. "From now on," she announced, smiling in a way that made Taly nervous, "you're going to play…" A dramatic pause. "*Tag*."

Taly's brows rose. "Come again?"

"*Tag*, dear. You've done well, make no mistake, but your theoretical knowledge is starting to outpace your applied proficiency. That's not uncommon, and if we were still living in a world where my fellow Council members didn't seem so intent on hunting my mages to extinction, we would have more than enough time to make up for your deficiencies during a later seal. However, we don't have that luxury. You will be hunted from the moment you set foot back on your island, and it really would be a bother if you went and got yourself killed after I've put in so much effort to train you."

Despite the warmth of the rising sun, Taly felt a chill cut straight through her. The Sanctorum, the shades, Vaughn, and his so-called *master*—she certainly had accrued an impressive list of enemies in a very short period of time.

"And how," she asked, "is a game of tag supposed to help me stay alive?"

Azura tilted her head, a small smirk curling her lips. "Tag is a ruthless, petty game, my dear." She took a step forward, and those eyes—those strange, golden eyes—began to burn. "It is a test of spirit. Of valor and determination. It is a dance between predator and prey—a push for survival that even children can understand. Stalking one's opponent, laying traps, doing whatever it takes to vanquish and conquer and slay until only *one* remains. A champion, gazing out over the field of battle, standing victor over the corpses of the fallen."

The Queen's voice had continued to rise in pitch, and she stared down at Taly, still smiling that small, horrible smile.

Taly took a step back, clearing her throat nervously. "I think one of us has been playing tag wrong," she rasped, worried that after only five months in this place, she couldn't exactly say which.

"You need to learn to think on your feet," Azura said, holding up a hand and signaling a small group of fairies that bobbed just outside the perimeter of the training yard. "And since there are no other mages for you to practice sparring with, this is the next best thing."

"I thought you said to avoid close combat."

"And how do you think one does that?" Azura waited, then said, "A shadow mage is deadly in close range, which means they will always try to pull you in. The only way to survive is to get very good at running away."

"But—" Taly tried.

"No *buts*." Azura waved a dismissive hand. "It is my wish that you play tag, and you will comply. Now then—the rules are simple. Freeze the fairies in place. Once you've captured all of them, the game is over."

Taly gripped her staff. "That's it?"

A vague nod. "You're not to use time crystals during the match, and since I know you feel more comfortable with a weapon in your hand, I've instructed the fairies to respond to air attacks." A glance at the staff in Taly's hands. "Not that it will do you any good," the Queen added as she moved to rejoin Leto underneath the stone arch.

Leto leaned in to whisper in Azura's ear.

"Oh, that's right," Azura said and snapped her fingers. A massive silverleaf oak flickered into existence in the center of the ring. The bark was red like blood, and clusters of pearl-shaped flowers speckled a dense canopy of leaves that shone like burnished silver. "What game of tag would be complete without a place for your enemies to hide?"

Taly blinked, but the tree was still there, taking up space that had only moments ago stood empty. "How...?"

"Pocket universes," Azura said simply. "They make wonderful storage. Now then—"

She clapped her hands twice, and Taly raised her staff, eyeing the fairies still hovering around the periphery. There were ten in total, and their forms began to shiver, churning the air around them with a near-electric spark. Their light began to deepen, going from a gentle blue to something more fierce, something that made Taly think of cold and ice, winter and snow. They were already moving to surround her when Azura shouted, "Begin!"

There was a beat of hesitation, and then the fairies were moving, hurtling through the air, little more than streaks of blue light painted against the brightening horizon. Taly dipped into her aether, already weaving the spell, but they crossed the wide expanse of the training arena faster than her eyes could track.

Instinct had her dancing back, and a swing of her staff sent out a shrieking gale of wind. The swipe was erratic, kicking up a cloud of red dust, but three of the fairies got caught in the blast, and they immediately pivoted, veering off to the left at a sharp angle.

Two more fairies converged on the right, but she waited.

Her aether shuddered, pulsing with each breath.

The air split behind her, and Taly dropped to the ground, releasing the spell as the fairies sailed overhead.

Gossamer threads of golden magic flickered and then faded.

The fairies abruptly halted, suspended and frozen as her web began to tighten. Even their light seemed to dim, and when they stopped moving altogether, Taly couldn't help but let out a crow of victory.

Two down, she thought as she regained her feet. Maybe this wouldn't be so—

Something slammed into her knee, throwing her to the ground. The pain was electric, like grabbing a live wire, and maybe she screamed. Maybe she was still screaming as the agony reverberated up and down her spine, singeing every nerve. She wasn't sure. She wasn't sure about anything as she spat out a mouthful of dirt and groped for her staff.

There was another crackle of pain at her shoulder, her wrist, then her other knee. The fairies were converging on her, barely grazing her skin, but each touch, each kiss of aether, made her body jolt. She only vaguely registered the veins of blue energy that spread along her arms and legs, down the length of her spine, as a voice announced, "Game!"

Azura waved a hand, and a rush of gold swept across the training arena, washing away the blue glow but only a fraction of the pain.

Still, she could move again, and Taly immediately flung herself to her feet, snarling as the Queen entered the ring. It was a vicious sound, and even after months of adjusting to this new immortal body, the instinctive reaction still surprised her.

"Oh dear," Azura muttered. "Dear, dear, dear..." She picked a piece of gravel from Taly's braid, and it was a struggle to plant her feet, to stop herself from reaching for her staff and knocking that smug grin off the woman's face. "Did I forget to mention that the fairies can hit back?"

"What the hell was that?" Taly hissed.

But the Queen just tsked her tongue and looked to the fairies who were regrouping just outside the edge of the arena. "Again."

"No." Taly backed up a step. "I'm not doing that again." Just the memory of that sizzling pain was enough to make her wince.

The Queen turned to exit the arena. "That's too bad," she said over her shoulder. "I was going to send you home after you won."

Taly's heart leapt into her throat. "You don't mean that."

"Oh, but I do," Azura said. Behind her, Leto's light looked uncharacteristically dim in the shadow of the arch. "Our agreement was that I would send you back when you earned your third seal. You have the knowledge. Now all that's left is to show me you know how to apply it."

"You give me your word?" Taly stooped, picking up her staff. "If I win a game, then I get to go home?"

"That's what I said, isn't it?" Azura smiled, but it was far from comforting. "Consider this a part of your final examination."

Taly swore under her breath. She was missing something. She knew it. Nothing with the Queen was ever so cut and dry. But right now, she had no other choice. It was never her choice. Not anymore. It was a pretty cage, no doubt—with soft beds and good food. But at the end of the day, she couldn't leave.

Not until the Queen said so.

The fairies were already lining up—ten dots of blue energy that circled the arena.

Taly fell into a defensive position. *This is going to hurt,* she thought, adjusting her grip on the staff. *Oh Shards, is this going to hurt.*

The Queen signaled the start of the next game, and Taly let out a sharp bark of pain as a blast of crackling energy immediately crashed into her shoulder.

Taly doubled over.

The pain was a living thing, clawing at her chest, crawling beneath her skin. It knocked the breath out of her lungs and brought her to her knees. Even after six hours of this nightmare, the intensity of each blow hadn't waned. Her sense of pain hadn't dulled. If anything, she had just grown more sensitive to each strike.

Another fairy crashed into her shoulder, and her arm went limp. *Shit.* She needed to focus. She raised her staff with her off-hand, flicking the switch embedded in the grip and barely managing to deflect another bright-blue ball of energy hurtling towards her with a gust of wind.

Grunting, Taly lurched to her feet and hobbled across the open area of the training yard. Her left leg was almost useless at this point, and she had to lean on her staff, dragging her leg behind her.

One hit stunned. Two hits paralyzed. Thankfully, the effect was transient and didn't radiate beyond the point of impact. A few more minutes, and she'd get her leg back thanks to the miracle of fey healing. The blow on her arm had only been glancing, leaving her a small amount of movement. If she could keep from getting hit again, she just might be able to win this thing.

Her breath came in ragged gasps, and her boots slid on the damp, red dirt. Her vision was a cloud of gold, but the premonitions were erratic—unreliable.

Taly hated her Sight. Maybe one day, when she learned how to use those visions that had signaled the initial manifestation of her power, it would be useful to her. But right now, amid this bizarre fairy war game, trying to glean anything valuable from the flickering afterimages that danced across her field of vision was a near impossibility.

There was a flash of movement, but it skittered away. Taking a breath, Taly grasped at her aether and tugged.

The arena exploded in a wash of gold, gilded in a fog only she could see.

Three seconds. Since she had started training her Sight, she could only see three seconds ahead.

How disappointing, the Queen had said. *Your grandmother could see 10 seconds backward and forward when she was your age. I expected more.*

It had been an effort not to rip her face off.

A tinny buzz sounded from her left, and the hazy wash of magic surrounding her rippled. A small mental tug laced with a sliver of carefully honed intent was all it took to summon more aether.

Three seconds. She saw the fairy's afterimage zip past her three seconds before she dropped to the ground and rolled, just managing to dodge the shrieking blue orb that careened through the air. Another tug on her magic and her net tightened, freezing it in mid-air.

Six down.

Panting, Taly scanned the yard and the six dots of blue fairy fire that hung suspended. Their ghostly forms shivered despite the spell that held them in place. This was another rule of the game Azura hadn't explained until it became necessary. It wasn't as simple as just tagging the fairies out. No. She had to keep them contained until she had managed to stop time for every fairy in play.

Even now, Taly could feel the fairies struggling. If they managed to break free, they could rejoin the game.

She had learned that rule the hard way.

Just four more, she thought, trying to push past the pain. She was exhausted, her aether nearly gone. But if she could just tag out four more of these little bastards, she'd be done.

Taly moved to take a step, and the pain almost had her crying out. But she didn't stop. She took another hobbled step forward, towards the tree in the center of the arena. She needed something solid at her back—just until her leg recovered.

Navigating the group of suspended fairies that peppered the arena, she scanned the branches overhead. Early on, the fairies had taken to hiding in the foliage, darting in and out of the spindling limbs in a way that made it almost impossible to predict their next attack. Even if she used her Sight, trying to trace the chaotic pattern of her premonitions through the leaves, she was still left scrambling.

As though her thoughts had summoned them, one of the fairies chose that moment to dive towards her. Acting on instinct, she immediately lifted her staff and fired off a column of condensed air. The wind threw the fairy back through the branches, shaking loose a rain of leaves and petals that fluttered to the ground like snow.

Taly struggled to see through the flurry, scanning the branches and tracing each chirp and rustle. She could just barely make out the faint golden afterimages as they moved through the branches, each following the threads of their individual decisions. Right or left. Down or up.

The threads shifted.

Taly began weaving the spell. *Four more.* They were all overhead, bunched together and about to descend.

A hiss of wind was her only warning before pain exploded at the base of her neck. Taly let out a scream as her back arched and her body jolted. Her staff fell from nerveless fingers, rolling away as she slumped to the ground.

A fairy—one she had thought frozen—floated just inches above her face, giggling merrily.

"Game!" Azura called from the sidelines.

Taly groaned, trying to move her arms first, then her legs, both unsuccessfully. Her head lolled to the side, but the movement triggered some other injury. Her body twitched violently, drawing a whimpered gasp from her lungs.

"What the hell?" she moaned. Even talking *hurt*.

Azura leaned back in the tall green velvet chair Leto had brought down shortly after lunch.

"You forgot to guard your back. A well-placed blow to the neck can incapacitate a fey. If this battle had been real, you would be dead by now."

"Good to know," Taly bit out. The words burned her throat. She could barely breathe.

The Queen waved a hand, sending out a tendril of magic that snaked across the yard. The spell licked at her skin, and Taly nearly sobbed in relief when the pain began to ebb.

A simple reversal spell, one Taly could have cast on herself.

If she could just figure out how to think around the pain.

"Again," Azura barked.

Taly decided she hated that word.

Taly yelped as the ground flew up to meet her. Every nerve ending crackled with heat as a thousand needles pricked her skin, and even though a wave of numbness followed close behind, her body began to spasm uncontrollably. The manic cackle of the two fairies that bobbed overhead only served to complete yet another humiliating defeat.

Sadists. All of them. The palace was full of fucking sadists.

Dirt crunched, and a polished boot prodded at Taly's shoulder, kicking her with what felt like an unnecessary amount of force. She groaned as she was rolled over onto her back.

"You're still allowing yourself to get hit," Azura said. The woman stood over her, her body blotting out the sun as she crossed her arms imperiously. Even though the details of her face were lost to the shadows, Taly somehow knew that the woman was frowning. "I keep telling you to guard your back, but do you listen? Of course not. Because Talya Caro knows everything. Everything except how to guard her back."

Taly grumbled a curse and wriggled feebly. Her body was still completely paralyzed—she couldn't even manage a crude gesture. "I hate you," she muttered, her scowl deepening when Azura grinned. "I hate you so much, you crazy bitch."

"That's sweet." Azura chuckled as she poked Taly in the stomach with the tip of a folded parasol. "But flattery will get you nowhere. You know what will get you somewhere, more specifically out of here and back where you belong? Guarding your back."

"You're such a bitch," Taly groaned as the Queen sent out a small wave of magic. Something crunched as it moved back into place.

"You said that already," Azura chirped, ignoring the poisonous glare that Taly sent her way. She reached down and hauled the smaller woman to her feet, grabbing her by the waist when her knees immediately buckled. "Anyways, my dear" –Azura waited for Taly to find her footing before releasing her— "I think we should call it a day. The gates will be closing soon, and I have a feeling you're going to want a bath before dinner."

Taly would've rolled her eyes, but the pain that movement would inevitably trigger wasn't worth it. Yes, she needed a bath. She was filthy.

But she didn't need the woman that had been sitting in the shade drinking tea all afternoon pointing that out.

Taly swayed on her feet, panting. She leaned against the tree when the world began to tilt. Her heart was still beating too fast, and there was a slight haze creeping in at the edges of her vision. Her stomach turned, but she waited until both the Queen and Leto had disappeared behind one of the stone arches before sinking back down to her knees and vomiting.

She heaved until there was nothing left inside of her—until she was crying not only from the bile that stung her nose and throat but the lingering pain that tightened like a vice around every cell and muscle and nerve.

After so many weeks spent in the palace, she had never felt the urge to give up quite so violently as she did right then. Through every bullshit test and trial, every random whim the Queen decided to throw at her, she had managed to grit her teeth and bear it.

But those had been mere annoyances; nothing compared to this new hell.

A manic laugh bubbled up and out, scraping against her throat like a knife. It really was funny in the worst possible way. After everything she had endured—harpies and magic spells and undead monsters—a simple game of tag would be her downfall. *You'll play until you win,* the Queen had said. But she was never going to win. It was too much—stalking and hunting, fighting and casting, all while managing more pain than she ever thought possible. Just the idea of coming back here tomorrow, of going through this again and again and again—

Taly doubled over as her stomach gave another heave.

It all seemed so pointless. There were some days she wondered why she even bothered to get up at all. Because even if she did win, somehow managing to eke out a victory and earn her freedom, what would she be going back to? Would her family accept her now that she was fey? What would they say when they found out she was a time mage? That just knowing her could put their lives at risk?

And that, of course, assumed they were even still alive to be angry at her. Tempris was under attack when she left, and she had no idea how much time had actually passed. Time moved differently inside the loop, but what the hell did that even mean? What if her family was already dead? Or worse, what if they had been turned into shades? What would she do if she ever came across Skye, rotting and dead, staring back at her through milky eyes?

Oh Shards, what if her dreams came true and Skye—

Taly twisted her fingers in the red dirt, forcing herself to breathe. *Skye*. Just his name was enough to give her pause. She missed him. It snuck up on her sometimes just how much, pulling her from whatever she was doing and making it hard to think. The few nights she was able to take control of her dreams, somehow escaping those blood-filled visions of a future she prayed never came to pass, she would sometimes find him, alive and whole and waiting for her.

Those dreams were the only thing that still had her going to sleep at night.

Taking another deep breath, she closed her eyes. *Get up.* She could practically hear the words, as clearly as if he were whispering in her ear. *Stop feeling sorry for yourself and get up. Get up and do it again. Come home to me.*

Skye wouldn't give up. Arrogant highborn bastard that he was—he wouldn't give up. And he wouldn't let her give up either.

Taly gritted her teeth, swallowing back the next wave of nausea. It wouldn't end like this. Not here. Not today.

Get up. And that's exactly what she did. Slowly, aware of each lingering ache and pain, she staggered to her feet.

Do it again. And she would. Again and again. Until she won. Because she was stronger now, as strong as Skye. Because she was Talya Caro, and that bitch didn't give up.

The first explosion crashed in the distance, and the ground began to tremble. Holding her head high, Taly wiped her mouth on the back of her sleeve and began making her way back to the palace.

Azura hid in the shadow of the wide stone arch. "I can feel your judgment," she said, glancing at the woman that had drifted a few paces ahead. More than a friend—a sister, even if there was no shared blood between them.

Leto floated back down the darkened tunnel to where the Queen had stopped to watch as the girl began retching in the training arena down below. "Permission to speak freely, Majesty?"

"Of course. You are always free to speak your mind. You know that."

"You're too hard on her," Leto said after a beat of hesitation, never taking her eyes off the girl.

"I knew you were going to say that."

"I'm not the only one that has raised concerns."

"I'm aware." She had ears, after all, and the fairies were hardly circumspect when it came to their whispering.

"She has passed her seal examinations in a fraction of the time than any other student you or I ever trained."

Azura picked at one of the chains coiling around her wrist. "I know all of this, Leto."

But her friend went on. "She told me what you had her do for the second seal assessment. Most mages would not have been able to hold up a simple coin so soon into their training, much less an entire temple ceiling. Under any other circumstances, she would be considered a prodigy, and yet you still belittled her."

True. All true.

Azura said, "You know as well as I that the Lady Caro was prone to arrogance when she was younger. She said so herself."

Leto gave her a sidelong glance. "Even so—this new trial is unorthodox."

Azura kept her chin high. "I know."

"Even at the highest levels of training, this would be considered needlessly vicious."

"She needs to get stronger."

"At what cost?" A gentle question, laced with quiet fierceness. A wolf defending a cub. "You made me your advisor for a reason, Majesty, so listen to me now. I know you have plans for the girl. I know that some things have already been set in motion. That certain events would've played out even if we hadn't chosen to intervene. But this trial, this *game*—she is no good to us if she breaks."

Azura's lips pressed into a thin line. "We both know what's coming for her. We both traveled through the Weave, and we saw that future." A nod. Leto's shoulders slumped forward. "If she is to break, I would rather it be now—rather it be *here*, where we can still pick up the pieces."

Leto shifted her gaze back to the girl heaving in the center of the arena. "I still think about that day."

Azura placed a hand to her chest, as if she could force down the hollow ache that had settled there. The Schism—it was such an appropriate name for the thing she had done. She had torn the world apart and then scattered the pieces.

"As do I," Azura said softly. "I want her to live, Leto. I set her down this path, but that doesn't mean I can't try to mitigate the damage. When this war finally finds its conclusion, I want that girl to have a life. I know you question my methods, but everything I have done so far has been towards that end. Towards that chance, slim as it might be."

Leto went quiet for several long moments as they both watched the girl still kneeling in the mud. Taly's retching had finally subsided, and she seemed to be having some sort of internal debate.

"She did well today," Leto said as she turned to go. "She would've won if someone wasn't cheating."

Azura barked out a laugh. "Time mages *always* cheat," she called over her shoulder to the surly fairy. "You know that as well as I."

"But she doesn't," came Leto's reply as she disappeared down the long tunnel, moving back towards the palace.

No, Azura conceded silently. *Not yet, at least.* That was always a difficult lesson to teach. And just one of the reasons why she had decided to go with a more unorthodox approach when it came to this final phase of Taly's training.

Azura looked back to the yard as Taly began to pull herself up, barely managing to stagger to her feet and swaying slightly. Her hair was falling out of its braid, and mud stained her clothing and streaked every visible inch of skin. She was in pain, but that didn't stop her from taking one lurching step forward, then another, straightening her shoulders and holding her head high.

"Good girl," Azura whispered, guilt shifting into pride.

Leto was wrong. The girl wouldn't break. Not when it mattered.

Smiling, Azura called after Leto, "Tell the kitchen to make veal and truffle risotto tonight—the human recipe you and I picked up the last time we were on Earth. Taly doesn't know it yet, but it's her favorite."

CHAPTER 15

-An excerpt from the imperial scrivener's collection of medical records, housed at the Arylaan Archive

Hundreds of shades remain now that the fighting is done. We continue to experiment, doing our best to make them comfortable, but all they ever utter now that they are free of their masters' control are two words:

Kill me.

Kill me.

Over and over.

It has led me to a single conclusion. For the shade, death is a door that remains locked. The kindest thing we can do for them now is to open it.

It had been three days since Skye entered the tunnels that ran beneath Ryme. At least, that's what the mages that came bringing food, water, and medical supplies had told him what might've been an hour ago. Time lost all meaning in the dark.

Skye swung his sword, feeling the crunch of bone.

Another shade fell at his feet. One of many.

After stumbling down that stairwell drunk and alone—and then stumbling back out—Skye had rushed to the townhouse, thankfully sober enough that Ivain hadn't taken his words as the ramblings of a mad man.

The tunnels were unlocked. The guards were gone. He had heard a low growl shuddering through the dark.

Within the hour, Ivain had mages down in those tunnels, working to repair the locks and fighting off the first wave of shades that had already found their way into Ryme. No one was hurt, though a few traders lingering at the entrance of the Swap after closing may have soiled themselves when a shade poked its head out of the station entrance, only to be immediately cut down.

An attack had been imminent. One more hour and they might've lost Ryme.

Something rattled up ahead, and he burned more aether, letting his pupils go wide. The only light this far inside the airtram tunnels came from algae that grew on the brick arching overhead, feeding off the groundwater seeping through the cracks. Even with its soft blue glow and his enhanced senses, he could barely see more than a few yards ahead.

He stepped carefully over the airtram rails, gripping his sword and resisting the urge to let his aether flare. The light would give his position away. It was the same reason he hadn't been given a torch.

Another step—he was aware of every muscle, every nerve, as he moved with the kind of preternatural quiet that only a shadow mage could manage. Ivain had taught him well, though Skye couldn't help but wonder if Ivain would have allowed him to do something as dangerous as scouting an abandoned airtram tunnel if he knew that it was a dream that had led him down here in the first place.

Skye still had no explanation for the dream—couldn't be sure if it was coincidence or if Taly really had found a way to warn him. But there would be time for those questions later. Right now, the only thing that kept him moving forward was just not thinking about it.

About Taly and if she was alive or dead. If it was possible for a human to walk through dreams. He wanted to hope, but... something held him back. His own fears, perhaps. If he allowed himself to hope, his rational mind said, it would be that much more painful when those hopes were crushed.

A shadow lurched toward him, and Skye dodged. Adjusting his grip, he flicked the switch beneath the hilt of his sword. Flames danced along the blade, releasing a gust of smoke as he sliced along the creature's groin. It shrieked, the sound echoing through the tunnel. Two more swipes—one at its belly, the other its neck. The creature fell, and he used the heel of his boot to crush the shadow crystal sputtering in its chest.

Skye stood there for a moment, working to slow his breathing. Listening for any other movements in the dark.

All he heard was a faint scurrying—rats. Nothing larger.

"This area is clear," he called back. Up ahead, he could see the iron grating that had been lowered to block off the tunnel. It was still intact, which meant the shades weren't coming in through this line. The ones he'd spent the last hour cutting down had been nothing but wandering stragglers, not the main force.

Footsteps approached, accompanied by the flicker of torchlight. Moments later, Ivain and a small contingent of mages emerged from the darkness, all looking as haggard and tired as Skye felt.

Ivain gave him a nod as he passed, crouching to inspect the shades Skye had found lurking in this section of the tunnels. After securing the entrance, they had methodically worked their way through the subterranean network, trying to find which tunnel was allowing the shades entrance into the city. It was slow work. The airtram system had been built in layers, some of the tunnels almost 300 feet underground, and they were having to clear out the shades one area at a time.

From what they had been able to gather so far, several stations just outside the city had been excavated after the Gate Watchers sealed them off, the shades allowed to enter and roam aimlessly underground. When it was time for the attack, bait had been set to lure them into the city.

And the guards… Skye still shuddered at the memory. They had found the guards that had been stationed in the tunnels a few nights ago scattered along the airtram tracks in pieces, a trail of freshly slaughtered breadcrumbs.

"More light," Ivain said. He gingerly gripped what was left of the shade's jaw, turning its head this way and that. Another mage held up a torch, a single fire crystal flickering at the heart of the flame. "Human. Female."

Brown eyes. Not Taly.

The comparison was instinctual, though Skye knew it was unlikely that Taly would be down here, even if she had been… turned.

Ivain prodded at the waxy skin, slightly bloated with a sickly green tint. "I'd say she's been dead a month. The magic used to reanimate them slows the decay, but it can't stop it."

"Look at this." Kneeling, Skye used the tip of a dagger to prod at the shade's hip. There were the cuts he had made to fell her, each one oozing rotted blood. Countless other gashes peppered the whole of her body. But the cuts on her hip, visible beneath what was left of her clothing—they were clean and neat, sutured shut.

Ivain looked to where he was pointing. "Her legs were removed."

"And then reattached?" Skye asked. "Why? I thought shades could reform themselves."

"They can," Ivain said. "You experienced this with the abomination in Ebondrift, and that's what seems to have happened *here*." Grabbing the woman by the shoulder, Ivain turned her over. Skye had to swallow back bile at the row of bones protruding from her back like spikes.

Shades needed aether to thrive, and the more they decayed, the stronger their thirst became. It drove them to hunt anything they could find so long as it contained aether, consuming blood and flesh and scavenging parts to augment and reform their own decomposing bodies.

One of those spikes still had feathers, another looked like a child's arm, and still others were unrecognizable in their decay.

Demons fashioned from rot and pain. That's what these things were. That's what would have come surging up from beneath the city, pouring into the streets, if the tunnel gates had been left unlocked and unguarded.

"This, however," Ivain said and turned the woman back over. He gestured to the hip bone and the neat row of sutures. "This was done purposefully. See how the bone has been fit back into the socket? If I had to guess, I'd say that this woman's legs were not serviceable, even for a creature that cares nothing for pain or balance. She was pieced back together by a surgeon, likely with parts taken from another specimen. Then, she was released and allowed to scavenge."

Ivain spoke with clinical detachment. He had served during the Shade Rebellion. He had seen these tactics before.

Skye wished he could be so unaffected. The smell alone made him want to retch.

"Take this one back to the city." Ivain rose, gesturing to one of the three mages standing around him. A lowborn woman with dark hair and light eyes stepped forward. She held a rag dipped in perfume over her nose and mouth. "I want her dissected and studied. See if there were any more modifications made, and, if so, compare them to the other bodies we've taken. Also, there's still enough of her face intact—we might be able to identify her. If she has family, let the healers decide on how to inform them."

The woman nodded, gesturing for the men behind her to get to work.

"Those spikes," Skye said, watching as the mages began laying out a tarp, rolling the shade on top of it. "The placement seems too even, almost..."

"Intentional?" Ivain offered. Skye nodded. "That's because it likely is. The first step in creating a shade is procuring a soul, one that's been harvested at the moment of death. During the Rebellion, we often observed shades ornamenting themselves. We don't know how much of the individual remains, but there is evidence to suggest that they retain a portion of their mental faculties, even pieces of their personality."

Skye's stomach turned. That meant they were still in there, whoever these men and women had been. He'd known, of course. The Shade Rebellion was as much a stain on the fey psyche as the Schism, but to hear it confirmed... to see the evidence... "Could it be reversed? If one were to procure a living body, could the soul be reinserted?"

"In theory. There was some experimentation after the Rebellion, but the souls recovered..." Ivain shook his head, expression grim. "They'd all gone mad. It was kinder just to let them pass than to attempt revival."

"Sire," a woman called from behind them. "We found another breach."

"I'll be right there," Ivain replied. Then, to Skye, "I heard Sarina was at the Swap with food and water. Go back, tell her we're both still alive, and get some fresh air. You've been down here longer than anyone else. I don't want you burning out."

Ivain didn't wait to hear his answer, already barking orders at the line of mages waiting in the shadows, but Skye didn't need to be told twice. He wanted to see the sun, smell something besides rot.

So, he made his way back through the tunnels that had already been deemed *"safe,"* the ground wet but clear of debris as he walked beside the long metal tracks that once guided the trams. Men and women milled about, some carrying supplies, others bodies. A line of torches marked the way home, each one a pocket of light and warmth amidst the gloom.

Hello?

Skye stopped in the middle of an intersection where two tunnels crossed, turning towards the sound of the voice. It was faint. For a moment, he thought he'd imagined it but—

Somebody, please...

There it was again, coming from one of the tunnels that had already been searched. The voice drifted from the inky black, and he strained his aether trying to see, to hear. He couldn't tell if it was a man or a woman, an adult or a child. It was just a whisper, easy to dismiss. He could've just kept walking, but—

Anybody...

Other mages passed him by, none of them reacting.

Please, I'm hurt.

Skye grabbed the arm of a nearby woman. Another shadow mage. "Did you hear that?" he asked.

She looked to where he pointed. Over the arch of the tunnel was a small brass sign that read Infinity's Edge. This line used to lead to the palace.

The voice still whispered— *please, please, please...* —but the woman just shook her head. "It's probably the wind. It comes in through the aboveground stations, plays tricks with your head. Jorgie thought he heard his mother calling to him, only his mother's been dead for nearly a century."

Help!

That time, there was no mistaking it. The voice echoed from the dark.

But the woman readjusted her grip on the crate she carried, saying, "It's just the wind," as she turned to leave.

Skye stood there for a moment, listening to the whimpering cries as they drifted in and out. Maybe she was right. Maybe it was a trick. Just the long hours and lack of food finally getting into his head, but then again... the tunnel had been deemed safe. It would be irresponsible not to look, just to see if they'd missed something.

He felt a tug. That thread from the ballroom had followed him into his waking hours, though he had never felt it as strongly as he did now, like a string pulling him forward.

His feet began to move, away from the mages carrying supplies in and out. The light of the torches faded, and then there was only the algae above and its faint blue glow. If he burned more aether, he could make out the arch of the tunnel as it curved away into the dark.

Skye blinked. There was a flash of blue up ahead, brighter than the rest.

He took a step, squinting.

There it was again. Three flashes that flickered—then faded. Like fireflies.

"Hello?" Skye called. His voice echoed, as did his footsteps as he stepped carefully along the rails. He drew his sword, flicking the switch and letting the flames chase away the shadows. "Answer if you can hear me."

Something giggled—the sound like windchimes—and Skye's heart began to pound.

"Who are you?" Wielding his sword like a torch, he peered into a darkened doorway set into the side of the tunnel. An old supply closet. The door had rotted away to nothing. "*Where* are you?"

I'm here.

The voice was at his ear, and Skye whirled—

Only to find empty air.

What's wrong?

Behind him this time. The voice was morphing, changing into something far, *far* too familiar.

Skye?

Taly's voice. That was Taly's voice, calling to him now.

Where are you, Skye? There was a soft whimper, as though she were crying. *Please…*

His mind raced. Could she really be here? Aiden had found her horse and her necklace, followed a trail of her blood to the palace, but what if… what if she had found her way into the tunnels? There was a station beneath the palace that used to be a private platform for the queen and her guests. What if that was the reason Aiden's locator spell had led him in a circle? Not because she was dead but because she had gone down below.

Injured and bleeding—what if Taly had crawled her way back home?

Skye?

"I'm here!" He ran towards the sound.

Where are you, Skye?

Behind him again. He abruptly turned, but a flash of that same blue light came shrieking towards him.

Find me! it urged as it streaked past him, leaving a long ribbon of light trailing in its wake as it disappeared around a corner.

Skye made to follow, but another blue wisp zipped around the curve. He backpedaled, stumbling over the tracks along the floor. Somehow, he caught himself, swinging his sword as he adjusted his footing. But the phantom twisted midair, swooping for his hand.

CRACK.

The shock ricocheted up his arm. His entire body jerked as the pain blasted through him. There was a clatter, and he realized his sword had dropped from the hand he could no longer feel, still flaming on the ground.

Another shock hit him square in the chest, and he crumpled.

Why aren't you trying to find me?

Another flare of blue light joined the first.

Because he's a coward.

A third now.

Because he can't.

They were all using her voice, buzzing around him like gnats.

Or maybe…

What?

Say it.

They giggled softly, like it was some grand secret to share.

Maybe he just doesn't care enough.

Skye dropped to his knees, pressing his hands to his ears. "Not real," he murmured. "This is just in my head." It was just the dark and the lack of sleep, the guilt and the grief finally getting to him.

It's your fault, you know.

Oh Shards, he could still hear them. Hear *her.*

I left because of you.

Because you weren't strong enough.

"I know," he whispered. Shards, he knew. He knew he had failed her just as much as he had failed those people at the canyon. He hadn't listened when she needed him. He hadn't realized she was saying goodbye.

What will you do, Skye?

The voices hissed at him. He thought he felt tiny shocks against his skin.

Are you listening?

What are you going to do?

Hey, Skye?

What are you going to do?

Are you going to let me die?

"Enough!" A fourth voice—still the same, but far more real. Skye cracked open his eyes to find a woman standing over him.

But not just any woman. No. This was the owner of that voice—Taly. He wasn't sure if he wanted to laugh or cry… or whether he had finally lost his Shards-damned mind.

She shooed away those vicious blue lights, not backing down when they let out a chimelike snarl. She seemed to repel the darkness itself as she pointed towards the ceiling, towards the world above, and barked, "Go! I shouldn't have to tell you this is wrong."

To his surprise, the lights obeyed. They chittered as they rose, hissing their displeasure. One took a swipe at her outstretched hand, only to skitter away when she didn't yield, didn't even flinch at the electric shock that crackled the air. "Go," she said again, and they disappeared into the ceiling like wisps of blue smoke, leaving only the faraway drip of water and the rasp of Skye's own ragged breathing.

There was a rustle of silk as she knelt on the ground beside him, and for a moment, Skye could only stare, greedily taking in every detail. Marveling at the impossibility.

Her skirts pooled around her, a mass of soft peach tulle that spilled across the debris-littered ground. Leaves embroidered in gold peeked from underneath, creeping across her waist and up her torso. They thickened across her body, tangling together to form the bodice. The neckline may have been considered modest if not for the way it clung to her, showing off every dip and curve. Her hair hung around her shoulders in golden waves, decorated only by a twisting crown of diamond roses.

She watched him carefully, her appearance so at odds with this dark and dirty place. The fire from his sword made the jewels in her hair, the gold of her dress, shimmer—like his own personal sun.

He mouthed her name. *Taly.*

Still not quite believing.

There was something strange about her features. She looked the same as he remembered, but also... older. Ageless in that way that all mature fey seemed ageless, despite the human roundness of her ears.

"Hello," she said, smiling softly. "Sorry it took me so long to get here. You weren't where you said you'd be."

Skye straightened, slowly letting his hands drop from his ears. He reached out to touch her, then hesitated, not sure his heart could take it if he didn't find flesh and bone. "You can't be real," he murmured.

"I assure you I can," she answered, eyeing his hand, still hanging in the air between them. "Though you're correct in assuming I'm not. The variables could still change."

Skye frowned in confusion.

"For now, let's just go with *maybe*. If we get this right."

She rose then, and Skye followed suit, his mind still grappling with the impossibility of what he was seeing. He could hear a heartbeat, yes. He could detect her scent over the reek of mildew and rot.

But it was off. Not quite the way he remembered, though he couldn't say why.

The way she moved, the way she spoke, even the clothes she wore—it was all wrong. Like his perception of reality had been skewed half a degree.

Like he had wandered into a dream.

"I don't understand," he said.

"That's not surprising," she replied, stepping away from him. He heard the click of her heels as she moved farther down the tunnel. Her skirts trailed behind her, more of those shimmering golden leaves embroidered along the train. The delicate fabric remained clean despite the pools of blood she stepped over. "But unfortunately, I can't say more. You see, I'm already breaking a lot of plates just to be here. It's important to make sure they're all the right ones."

Skye's chest felt too tight. He couldn't breathe. "That doesn't make any sense."

"That's the point." The words weren't flippant. They were solemn, said with more sincerity than he had ever heard her use.

But something inside him still cracked.

"*Don't*." The word was clipped. Ragged.

Taly stopped, glancing back.

"Don't do that," he rasped. "Don't toy with me. Not after I followed a fucking *dream* down into these Shards-damned tunnels where I've spent the last three days covered in blood and rot and constantly looking over my shoulder."

She turned to face him as he closed the space between them. "In the past two weeks," he said, voice shaking as he stood over her, "my entire life has gone to shit. My home was attacked, and then you left me right after I got you back. And then after five days of worrying about you and trying to unite a group of people that I was in no way fit to lead, I steered those same people to their deaths. I got them trapped on a bridge with shades closing in from both sides because I didn't anticipate that our enemy would use something as basic as *water magic*."

Taly was silent, her back too straight. This was usually the time she would've told him to stop feeling sorry for himself, but she didn't. She just waited, listening with something like sadness in her eyes.

"We still have traitors in our midst," he said, because now that he had started, he couldn't stop.

"And I'm pretty sure that's because of me too. Because I couldn't find them back in Ebondrift, and now they're here in Ryme, using the same tactics and trying to bring us down from the inside. That's why they killed those guards, and that's why these tunnels are infested, and… I should've seen it sooner. Everything I do, it just feels like I'm never fast enough. Like I keep getting it *wrong*. I can't remember the last time I actually felt like I knew what I was doing, and I'm starting to wonder…" He trailed off, reluctant to finish that sentence.

Reluctant to look up and see the pity in her eyes.

Skye took a deep breath, not caring that his eyes were wet. "And now *this*…" His voice cracked. "I know you aren't really here. I know that I'm hallucinating and that you left, and I want to hate you for that…" Wiping at his eyes, he stumbled back. "I want to hate you so badly, Tink, because if I hated you, then I wouldn't miss you. I wouldn't feel like my heart was being ripped in two every time someone mentions your name, and I would stop asking myself what I could've done differently to make you stay. I'd stop trying to figure out where I messed up, and it wouldn't feel like it was my fault that you're not coming back."

A pause, the silence heavy as the darkness that encroached in upon them.

"My fault," he murmured, gripping his hair hard enough to hurt. "It's my fucking fault, and I… I can't do this."

His back hit the tunnel wall, and he slid to the ground, sinking in on himself as he tried to find his grip on reality.

He could still feel her there.

Silent.

Staring.

He heard the click of her heels and the swish of her skirts. He didn't look up when he sensed her kneeling beside him.

"Look at me," she said.

But he shook his head. He didn't want her pity. She was nothing but a ghost. An illusion. The thing his mind wanted most desperately to see.

Not *real.*

"Look at me," she said again, and though her voice was soft, the sheer *command* in those three words—

He lifted his eyes.

Only to close them as she cupped his cheek. *Warm.* She was warm and solid, and even though his rational mind was screaming not to give in to the delusion, he gripped her hand, squeezing it like a lifeline.

"You *can* do this," she said, gentle but firm. So unlike the woman he knew and yet somehow the same. "There is a reason you are the light of Ghislain. There is a reason people follow you, and it's not because of some title. It's not because your blood is bluer than all the rest. It's because you're *you.* No one else but Skylen Emrys, one of the few men I've ever known that deserves the power that came with his position. You're intelligent, and courageous, and loyal. You protect the things that you care about, and you don't give up. No matter how hard it gets."

That faint hint of hope... it hurt. More than any blow.

He felt a tear slip free, and she caught it with her thumb.

"You're not real," he said, rejecting her words, that hope.

Letting go of her hand, he nearly flung it away from him.

"Aiden said that I might start seeing things if I didn't pull back." Skye squeezed his eyes shut, pressing a hand against the ache in his chest. "The battle at the canyon, the stress of losing you, the lack of sleep—that's what this is. It's just my mind trying to cope, making up stories more palatable than the truth. I probably heard something when I was drunk and passing by the Swap that night. The dream was just a coincidence. The blue lights were just a hallucination, the dark finally getting to me, and then *you*..." The laugh that came out of him sounded hysterical, even to his own ears. "I mean... look at you. Look at that dress!"

Taly glanced down, picking at her skirts. "What's wrong with my dress?"

"You'd never wear it. That's what's wrong with it. That dress is a product of my own imagination. I had a dream where we were dancing, and this entire conversation..." He shook his head, taking a shuddering breath. "This is just me torturing myself."

Skye let his head hit the wall, half tempted to give in to the insanity. There were more shades and more fighting waiting for him, more decisions to be made. But maybe... maybe this was where he stopped. Maybe this was where his story ended, alone and in the dark with the ghost of a woman he had failed to save.

"I know it's hard." Her throat bobbed. Her own eyes glistened. "And I'm sorry to say that things are going to get a lot worse before they begin to get better. The problem you're facing..."

She paused, letting out a soft sound of frustration as she considered her words.

"All your life," she said carefully, "everything has followed a logical path. The next step was clear, the answers were easy, and when they weren't, you had someone telling you what to do. This time, though—what seems right will be wrong, what's wrong will be right, and you're going to have to decide for yourself which is which. You're going to have to evolve. You have to start seeing the world in intersects and angles instead of just straight lines."

Standing, Taly offered him a hand.

But he just stared blankly, unable to muster the energy to take it, to make himself stand. She offered him hope, but... Taly would never say these things. She was more likely to kick him than offer him words of encouragement. This was just his subconscious telling him what he wanted to hear.

With a sigh, she let her hand drop. "If what you need is proof, I can offer that."

Skye's eyes snapped to hers. His heart began to pound, even if he was still reluctant to seize that spark of hope.

"Back at my room at the tavern," she said, "there's a loose board underneath the bed. Go there and take what's inside. Tell me then if you think I'm real or not."

Taly dipped down so that their eyes were at the same level—him kneeling on the ground, back against the wall, and her leaning over him.

"Don't give up, Em. This is not our last chapter. You will see me again."

And then she kissed him—soft as a whisper. His eyes drifted closed.

When he opened them, she was gone.

CHAPTER 16

-An excerpt from the Essential Fey Survival Guide

Rule #2: If you happen upon a time mage's journal, do not retrieve it. It has not been misplaced.

There was a black suit spread out on the bed, freshly pressed and waiting.

Skye wasn't sure how long he had been staring at it.

They had finally cleared out the tunnels, and the first thing he had done when he had been released was shower. The water had been hot and strong, and he had stood there in a daze, watching as the grime of the past week spiraled down the drain, streaks of black against the white porcelain.

But now that he was clean, standing with a towel around his waist in his darkened bedroom on the top floor of the Castaros' townhouse, there was that suit to deal with. Sarina must have laid it out while he was in the washroom. Or maybe he just hadn't noticed it when he trudged past the first time, peeling off his armor as he went.

It was black. The shirt, the pants, the coat... Mourning colors.

Because Taly was gone. Dead.

And even though they were living in a world gone mad, fighting an enemy that had no name and no face, there were still customs that needed to be observed. The family would dress in black, and the curtains would remain drawn—not because the dead demanded it but because the living needed something to give order to their pain. Some sort of structure on which to mount their suffering so that they could move forward.

So that they could forget.

Skye let the towel drop. He almost reached for the shirt—then stopped.

If what you need is proof, I can offer that.

He shook his head at the memory. He hadn't gone to the tavern, if only because going would feed into the illusion. Everything he had seen and heard down in those tunnels—it wasn't real. He knew that. Just like he knew that if he put on those clothes, those colors, it would be admitting an end. It would be the start of a goodbye he'd never wanted to say, and was he really ready for that? If there was even a whisper of a chance, no matter how impossible it might seem, why wouldn't he grab it?

Turning to the dresser set against the far wall, Skye pulled out a white shirt and navy slacks. He found an overcoat in the closet—gray, not black; anything but black—and after splashing some cold water on his face he decided that, yes, he was really going to do this.

He was going to follow a hallucination to an empty room at a tavern the same way he had followed a dream into an airtram tunnel. He needed to because if he didn't, he would always wonder. He would never be able to move on.

And so, Skye slipped down the stairs and through the darkened house, avoiding the pockets of light and the sound of voices as he went to confirm his madness.

It was easy to find, even in the dark.

The tavern was in the worst part of town, made more terrible by recent events. There were two stories, the first a shitty bar that served equally shitty ale. Skye dodged a few patrons that came lurching through the main doors, stepping over piles of vomit and Shards knew what else. He was headed for the second story, to a curved walkway with three doors that led to single-room apartments. At the end of the row was a door that had been painted blue and padlocked shut, though the lock came away easily when Skye channeled his aether and gave a tug.

The floor creaked as he entered the drafty little room, cramped despite the lack of furniture. He'd never been inside, though he'd always known exactly how to find it. Ivain and Sarina had kept close tabs on Taly after she left the manor, even going so far as to secure her with permanent lodging when she couldn't find anyone willing to rent to a human.

Indirectly, of course. Skye doubted that Taly knew that her room had been bought and paid for with Castaro gold, only that Sarina had gotten word of a tavern in Ryme that had recently relaxed their policy on mortals for unknown reasons.

Skye took another step, closing the door behind him. There were stacks of old books scattered about, all stained and waterlogged; the only real piece of furniture was an old wooden bed stuffed into the corner. The windows and doors had been covered with threadbare sheets, and when he flicked the switch for the overhead fire lamp, it sputtered, giving barely any light.

Still, despite the ramshackle appearance, the space was immaculately clean, the blankets all folded neatly on the end of the bed. Every stack of books he passed had been arranged in alphabetical order, and there were snowdrops drying by the window.

Skye almost smiled. Taly had lived here. Even though Sarina had cleared out nearly all her possessions, even though her scent had faded, he knew it to be true.

He resisted the urge to poke around, to see which books had been read and dogeared, her favorite passages noted in the margins, aiming for the bed. That's where his hallucination had told him to look, so, grabbing the bed by the frame, he lifted it easily, pulling it away from the wall.

The floor was, unsurprisingly, free of dust. Leave it to Taly to clean beneath the bed. It was probably how she had figured out there was a loose board to begin with.

"Well," he said to the silence, "you're here now. Let's get this over with."

Skye's stomach was in knots as he fell to his knees and began testing each board, starting from the corner and working his way out.

Halfway down the length of where the bed had stood, he began to feel sick. He really had been hallucinating. The woman in the tunnels, the dream—none of it was real, and he'd just broken into an apartment in the middle of the night, following his grief and that stupid thread that was still tugging at him incessantly—

A board lifted.

Holding his breath, he gave the end another tap, ratcheting it up far enough to slip his fingers underneath. The space below was less than a handspan deep, three times as wide, and inside he found—

"Diaries."

Taly's diaries. Ten in total. The dates were all marked with red ink on the spines.

Hands shaking, Skye pulled each book from the hidden cache, stacking them on the floor beside where he knelt. There were bits of ribbon and old glamographs stuffed between the pages, and beneath the row of books, he found a small bag of gold as well a wooden box filled with more pictures, ticket stubs, and other seemingly inconsequential trinkets and mementos he hadn't known she'd kept.

It was everything she hadn't wanted anyone to find. The things she would've been most devastated to lose if someone had forced their way in and stolen what few possessions she had to call her own.

Skye closed the box with the reverence it deserved, running a hand over the lid. He had a choice to make now. He could figure out a way to explain this, come up with something sane and rational, or… he could just believe. He could take the evidence at face value, accept that the world was full of impossible things, and allow himself to trust in the one person he should've known never to doubt.

Skye found his feet.

A choice. That's all it was.

So, aiming for the door, he chose.

He chose to go downstairs and buy an old canvas bag from the kitchen. He chose to go back to that room and pack up the diaries, the box, and that little bag of gold.

The dream had been real. He chose to believe that.

He chose to accept the impossibility of that woman and the hope she had given him.

He wasn't going to give up. Not yet. Not ever.

That's the choice he made.

Skye pulled the door shut as he left, attempting to fix the lock as best he could. But he didn't turn towards the townhouse. There was still one more thing he needed to find before he was done with this place.

Beneath the stairs, there was a gap between the ground and the building's foundation. Pulling a mealy carrot he'd bought along with the canvas sack, he crouched, holding it towards the gap.

Moments later, a quivering pink nose emerged, followed by a mangy ball of white fluff speckled with bits of tan. A rabbit. Its eyes were ringed with black, and it limped slightly. There was a scar on its back leg devoid of fur.

Skye sighed as the rabbit began to nibble on the end of the carrot. It was obviously used to being fed. "Marshmallow, I presume." The prize from Taly's first and only attempt at hunting. She had always had a soft spot for animals, so it came as no surprise that she hadn't been able to kill a rabbit, not even when she was starving.

With a sigh, he grabbed the rabbit by the scruff. It struggled and squealed, calming slightly when he pressed it close to his body.

"C'mon," he said as he turned for home. "Taly will have a fit if she comes back only to find out you got turned into stew."

The rabbit looked up at him, wriggling its nose. He could only assume that meant *"thank you."*

CHAPTER 17

-An excerpt from Of Tyranny and Time Mages

We already bow down to our noble houses. We give our allegiance to the Shards. But there is a great distinction that no natural or religious reason can account for, and that is the distinction between fey and time. We all have our allotments of aether, the good or bad fortune we are born with, but why do we also bow down to the time mages? Why are they exalted above all others, and why do we continue to give them our allegiance when they have yet to earn it?

Only the time mages are able to see the Weave, and yet they expect us to believe in their good intentions? They shape time, determine the fate of nations, but they go unchecked. They ask for trust, but do nothing to earn it. They have proven themselves to be tricksters and cheats, and I will no longer bend the knee to a false Queen, whose only power derives from tradition and fear.

Taly took her time in the bath. Even with the gift of immortal healing, there were still bruises on her arms, her knees, up and down the length of her spine, and even a black eye that still felt swollen and hot to the touch. After so many weeks of playing *"tag"* day after day, every part of her ached, and she could've spent all night soaking in the scalding heat. Maybe part of the next morning as well.

The Queen's magic was good for some injuries—like burns and broken bones—but in order to reverse time on a wound and make it so that it had never been, the pain had to be re-experienced. Considering the beatings she took most days, Taly had come to prefer traditional healing methods and very, very hot baths.

The tower washroom was massive, with gold-veined marble and gilded fixtures. The back wall had been left open to the elements, and wind and ash pelted at a veil of protective magic that muffled the sounds of the explosions in the distance. Fire crystals heated the air, the floors, and kept the water from going cold. The ceiling was glamoured, and the nighttime sky stretched out above her, slowly cycling through the heavens.

She wasn't sure which sky she was looking at tonight—none of the constellations looked familiar. But judging from the twin red moons that were drifting across the vast, starry expanse, she figured it must be some forgotten gate world.

The view was lovely. Undeniably so. But also, off in a way. Too flat to be anything more than an illusion.

There was a knock at the door, but Taly ignored it, sliding down even further in the bath. A tiny horse made entirely of water galloped across the surface, climbing the raised dome of her knee like it would a mountain ridge. It was a simple enchantment, one intended to lure reluctant children into the bath, but even as an adult, she had never tired of playing with water clones.

The miniature horse reared back, and Taly tapped a finger to its nose, watching as it morphed into a sparrow that began to flutter about the room. Skye was always complaining about how long she took in the bath, and yet he never failed to bring her back a new water clone when he visited the mainland. Dragons, and lions, and bears. Even a giant sea serpent.

She hadn't really liked that last one, and when she'd told him so, he'd had the brilliant idea to install the clone inside the pond that bordered the main highway. It had given everyone that passed by a good scare, rising out of the water when anyone got too close to the fence. They had even figured out a way to make it roar a few years later—this horrible, screeching sound so grating it frightened away the local wildlife.

With a sigh, Taly sunk down even further into the fragrant water. As usual, Skye was never far from her thoughts. She wondered what he was doing, if he was safe. Every time she looked in a mirror or felt the tips of her ears, she imagined what he might say when she finally found her way home and he saw that she was… changed.

Would he still find her beautiful? Would he still want her the same way he had in Ebondrift? After all, she was no longer human. She was like him now. Fey. Highborn. A time mage, but maybe he wouldn't mind that so much. And if he did... well, she couldn't really blame him. He would have to give up everything to stand beside her. His family, his home, any hope for a normal life free from the Sanctorum.

Everything was a lot to ask of a person.

A vision of a Yulemas ball flashed through her mind's eye.

Most of her dreams were filled with blood and death, but that one... that one she had liked.

So much that she often found herself revisiting the dream, fantasizing about what might've happened if she had let the vision play out rather than trying to dive off the side of the balcony.

He would've slowly closed the doors behind him, glancing at the footman that stood just off to the side in a way that said there would be a generous tip coming his way so long as they remained undisturbed. And then, he would've slowly sauntered towards her, hands in his pockets, looking utterly breathtaking in his black dress suit and white tie.

She would've stared at him the entire time, trying not to fidget with the bracelets at her wrists, but he would have known exactly the effect he was having on her. He was a shadow mage, after all. He would've sensed the frantic beat of her heart and known that the flush on her cheeks wasn't just from the cold.

But she wouldn't care. Because his eyes would reflect the same hunger that had haunted her ever since he'd pressed her up against that library bookshelf and kissed her.

Closing her eyes, Taly sighed as she let her fingers drag along the inside of her thigh.

And then, when he got close enough, she would've reached for him. Just a hand, outstretched and trembling. Because even though they had kissed and teased and flirted… this line they were about to cross—that wasn't something that could be undone.

A friend and a lover.

Her first.

Her only.

Taly's stomach clenched as her fingers continued their exploration. How many times had she imagined this scenario? How many different ways? One kiss and that arrogant bastard had managed to turn her into a raging mess of hormones and lust and… somehow, she didn't really mind.

He would've drawn her into the dance, gently placing his lips to her neck, then her jaw, her mouth. Slow and soft at first but gaining in intensity. Until her lips felt bruised. Until she was aching with a need that was all for him. He would press her against the wall, his hand slipping beneath her skirts—

Taly finally let a finger dip between her thighs, wishing it was Skye's hand that was touching her, teasing her.

And then—

There was another knock at the door, and Taly started, snatching her hand away. She blinked a few times as the fantasy began to clear and—

Damn, Taly thought, kicking at the edge of the tub. A heady ache still pounded between her thighs, but it would have to wait until later, when she was alone.

Except…

She was never really alone now, was she? Leto was always within earshot, and the fairies, the Queen, Calcifer…

Shards, had she really been here so long now that she had started to miss the solitude of those first few weeks?

Growling softly, Taly fiddled with the controls on the bath until the water turned icy.

By the time Taly dragged herself from the bath, a jeweled blue gown was already laid out on the couch in her dressing room. She could only muster a half-hearted protest as Leto began helping her with the various layers, thankful that the fabric fit her loosely and didn't require a corset.

Instead of heels, the fairy produced a soft pair of satin slippers, the color a perfect match to the red velvet ribbons woven through her hair. It seemed that since the Queen had begun enforcing daily games of fairy tag, Leto had taken pity on her, dressing her for dinner in clothing that wouldn't restrict her movement or aggravate any slow-to-heal injuries.

Thank the Shards for small mercies. And Leto.

"You did well today," Leto said as she finished pinning the folds of the skirt.

"It doesn't feel like it," Taly mumbled, staring at her reflection in the mirror. She looked pale, and several blood vessels had burst in her right eye. Coupled with the bruises on her face, the effect was decidedly gruesome. "In fact, Azura said that the only thing I'm getting better at is *not* bleeding."

Leto straightened, eyeing Taly from head to toe and tugging at the fabric. "Her Majesty jests, I'm sure."

"I'm not."

Leto hesitated for a moment, considering her words. "You do still struggle with your Sight, but that's not unusual for young mages. It is a difficult ability to master. It took Her Majesty nearly three centuries to be considered truly proficient."

"Thank you, Leto." Taly gave a wan smile before turning to leave the dressing room. Down the hall and into her parlor—her body barked in agony, protesting every step.

"The Queen," Leto said, following her, "has requested that dinner be served in her private dining room this evening."

"That's nice for her." Taly grabbed a book from a nearby table and carefully eased herself down into an overstuffed chair next to the window. Calcifer jumped up beside her. He had grown considerably, enough that it was getting hard to remember him in his little teacup bed. He was as large as a housecat now, if still a bit gaunt and spindly, and two tufts of vibrant gold fur had sprouted around his still too-large ears and on the tip of his tail. A match to the golden rings that were beginning to develop around his icy blue eyes. "You can tell the Queen that I'm not going."

"But you need to eat, Ma'am. Your aether cannot efficiently recover without adequate nutrition."

Taly cracked open her book—something about physical time travel and why it was a bad idea. "I don't care," she lied, praying that her stomach didn't growl and give her away. She'd almost depleted her aether that afternoon, and she was well and truly starving.

Taly fidgeted in the chair, trying to get comfortable. Calcifer gave her an irritated mewl. Leto didn't deserve her moodiness—she knew that. But she was sore and tired, and if the Queen said one more time that she needed to learn to faceplant with a *"little more grace,"* she might burn the palace to the ground.

Leto dipped her head. "And what would you have me tell Her Majesty?"

"Tell her..." Taly turned the page, scratching behind Calcifer's ears. "Tell her that I'm protesting stairs."

It wasn't exactly a lie. There were far too many sets of stairs between her tower and the West Wing. Maybe if she was lucky, she would muster up the energy to crawl down to the kitchen later that night—after the Queen had retired.

"Of course, Ma'am," was all Leto said.

Taly didn't look up as the door to her apartment closed.

Azura held up a plate. “Again.”

Slumping forward, Taly glared at her over the small dining table. “No, Az,” she pleaded, not caring that it came out as more of a whine. “Just… no. I’m done for today.”

After she had refused to come down to dinner, the Queen had come to her—along with Leto and a formal seven-course meal that could have easily fed ten people.

Or rather, should have. Taly stared at the empty salad bowl, wondering if it would be bad form to lick the dressing out of the bottom. The bowl was accompanied by many other empty dishes and platters, but she had difficulty feeling any embarrassment.

She had once watched Skye devour two whole casseroles, a plate of eggs, several loaves of bread, and an entire tin of ice cream after a particularly brutal day of training. Granted, he had been young and still growing into his long legs and gangly body, but it hadn’t stopped her from teasing him. Mercilessly.

That memory made her sad now. If she had it to do over, she might not tease him quite so much. Not when she finally understood that gnawing hunger, the need to be full, if only because she instinctively knew that the more she ate, the quicker the burning sensation in her lungs, the weakness in her limbs, would finally begin to fade.

What had once seemed so alien to her was now a way of life.

In short, she was beginning to realize what it meant to be fey, and it was still awful. Eating never used to be such a chore.

Leto removed her empty plate, replacing it with another filled with chicken and potatoes and some sort of sausage mixture that Khanna—the fairy that ruled over the kitchen with an iron spatula—claimed was an old family recipe. Wasting no time, Taly dug in, ignoring the sigh of exasperation from across the table.

"Your manners are atrocious," Azura commented.

"I'm hungry," Taly said around a mouthful of food. "And injured, and tired, and…" The Queen looked unmoved. "Shut up. You're the one that didn't listen to me when I said my aether was depleted."

"Your aether wasn't depleted." Azura finally set down the plate, and Taly let out a sigh of relief. "You merely thought it was."

"I couldn't move, and it felt like someone had set my lungs on fire." Taly took another bite of chicken. "That's textbook aether depletion."

"My dear, considering your pedigree, you should've had enough aether to cast three times as many spells as I saw you throw around today. You could go for days without ever needing to stop if you just learned to stop wasting so much magic. Which is why—"

Azura picked up the plate once more and this time let it drop from her fingers. The porcelain shattered as it hit the marble, and Calcifer, who had been sniffing around beneath the table, scattered. "*Again.*"

Grumbling out a curse, Taly set down her fork and held out a hand, wincing at the pain the movement elicited. She tapped that well of power and felt it instantly recoil, like a wounded animal.

Just a little more, she begged, but it was like trying to squeeze water from stone.

So, she gripped it.

And pulled.

And dragged.

Until finally, golden pinpricks of light sparked around her fingers. Until every breath felt like fire, and that ache that had settled so deep and so fierce began to blaze and twist and scream.

But then she felt the spell catch. She heard the porcelain clink as the fragments were pulled through the air by an unseen hand and carefully knitted back together. The cracks blurred and faded, and the plate continued to rise, until it finally reappeared over the edge of the table and placed itself back into the Queen's waiting hand, whole and unmarred.

Taly gasped for air, reaching for her glass of wine. She was surprised the syrupy sweet liquid didn't turn to steam when it hit the column of fire that had ignited in her throat. Draining the glass in a few gulps, she barely tasted the alcohol.

Taly slammed the glass back down on the table, barely managing to choke out, "Why is going backward in time so much harder than going forward?"

Azura eyed the plate in her hand. "The future has a certain momentum. It twists and turns with every decision that gets made, but it's moving inexorably *forward.* If you can see the variables, then you merely need to nudge the timeline one way or the other.

"But the past..." She waggled the plate for emphasis. "The past is rigid. It has a set path, and though the more powerful members of our order can pull elements from unrealized timelines and blend them into the Weave, perhaps even travel physically through time and try to push a set of events in a different direction, that's not something I would recommend doing."

"You're talking about changing the past," Taly said, picking up her fork and diving back into her food.

"Yes," Azura said with a nod. She placed the plate back on the table. "Changes are cumulative. A hundred years from now, something as inconsequential as fixing a previously broken plate can spiral into chaos. Which is why we, as time mages, must strike a delicate balance. Part of our ability to do what we do stems from our magic's inherent ability to stabilize these changes, to keep them from rippling out through time and having untoward effects."

Taly eyed the plate. "So how do you know which future is best then? How do you make sure all the right plates get broken?"

Azura shrugged. "You don't. It's not your job to go around breaking plates." Her lips twitched. "It's *mine*." A nudge of her fingers was all it took to send the plate clattering to the floor.

Taly took a breath, wincing as she once again tugged on her aether. The plate landed back on the table with a soft thud—whole.

"You're still using too much aether for simple spells," Azura remarked.

Taly ignored her. "So, is that why they're afraid of us?"

"What do you mean?"

"Well..." Taly snatched the plate when Azura began to reach for it again. "We don't have the strength of a shadow mage or the offensive abilities of a fire mage; we can't conjure water, air, or earth to shield ourselves, and our ability to heal our own injuries is limited."

Taly paused, reaching down to absently pet Calcifer as he curled between her legs. "Yet despite our inherent weaknesses," she went on, "people fear us. The Dawn Court and the Sanctorum were able to paint all time mages as evil and vicious based on the actions of a single individual. That makes me wonder if they were preying on a fear that already existed."

"And why do you think they would fear us?" Azura asked, uncharacteristically serious.

"Because..." Taly tilted her head, considering the question—then shrugged. "Because if we can use our magic to save lives, do good, what's to stop us from using it to cause harm as well? If we can sift through the timelines and break all the right plates, what's to stop someone from going back and breaking the wrong ones?"

Something finally clicked in Taly's mind. "I suppose we could accomplish frightening things if we had the power and ability." Like the Schism. Maybe worse. "And nobody would really be able to stop us. Not if we can see them coming."

The Queen gave her a sad smile and finished off her glass of wine. "And maybe she's not so daft after all." She turned to Leto. "Be a dear and bring us some champagne. The Lady Caro finally said something intelligent, and I think that's cause for celebration."

She turned back to Taly and leaned forward. "Besides," she said, a small, strange smile curling her lips, "I suspect you might need another drink."

"Why is that?" Taly asked, confused.

"Because you haven't considered the next question. From an outside perspective, how would you know that a time mage was acting for the greater good?"

Taly hesitated. "I'm not sure I follow."

Azura leaned back in her chair, turning to look out the window and the ash tapping against the glass. "Let's use an example then, shall we? If you had the ability, would you go back in time and kill the man that invaded your island before he had the chance to do any harm?"

"Of course," Taly answered immediately.

"Even if he was innocent?"

"But he's not innocent. He's killed thousands of people. Maybe more."

"Yes, *now* he has." Azura gave her a pointed look. "In order to stop him, however, you'd need to go back to before he began turning men and women into shades. Before he'd even conceived of the idea. You'd have to find him when he was still blameless, and then you'd have to kill an innocent man."

"It would still be for the greater good," Taly insisted. "Especially considering what he's done."

"I agree," Azura conceded. "But you and I are both time mages, and we can see exactly how many lives a single man's death might spare. What I'm asking you to do is to think about those that can't see through the Weave, the people that will *never* see that future if we do our jobs correctly. If we go back in time and kill a man *before* he's committed a crime, how are those around us supposed to know that we were acting in their best interests? That we were trying to minimize the amount of harm done to society by killing one man before he could kill millions?"

Taly's stomach turned as the realization began to sink in. "They would have to take us at our word. To them, our actions would look unprovoked, perhaps even malicious. It's easy to say you're acting in good faith, but proving it..."

"Is another matter entirely," Azura finished.

"So, what is it you were trying to avoid?"

Azura merely arched a brow.

"When you shut down the gates," Taly clarified. "What is it you were trying to avoid? What was it that made that many lives worth that kind of sacrifice?"

Azura drummed her fingers on the arm of her chair, shooting Calcifer a deadly glare when he jumped in Taly's lap. "How do you know I had a reason? Maybe I was just tired of ruling over the gates. Maintaining them had become such a bother, and the other Genesis Lords were always pushing me to build more. As if we already didn't have enough power and influence..."

"No," Taly said with a shake of her head. "I don't buy it. You might be crazy, but you're not cruel, and everything I've ever read about you leading up to the Schism painted you as a wise and fair ruler. No matter what you say, you're not going to convince me that you didn't have a reason."

Azura gave a polite smile. "Today is not the day for answers, my dear."

"It never is," Taly muttered.

Azura glanced at her in warning—though the rebuke was mild at best—rising as Leto entered the room. "Today," she said, wiggling her fingers for one of the champagne bottles the fairy carried in her arms, "is the day we're going to get rip-roaringly drunk and try to find an appreciation for Draegonian art."

Taly winced, opening her mouth to object.

"No *buts.*" Azura popped the cork and took a swig directly from the bottle. "We're going to go look at art, dear. You need a little culture in your life. I'll even let you bring that… *thing.*" She waved a hand at Calcifer, crinkling her nose. "So long as it's on a leash. A very sturdy one."

Taly took the second champagne bottle from Leto, holding it just a little bit tighter when she saw the label. This particular vintage cost more than an entire month's rent back at Jay and Laurel's tavern. Feeling slightly nauseous, she popped the cork. "Fine," she said. "I know better than to argue with you at this point."

"Finally, she's learning!" Azura exclaimed. She clapped a hand to Taly's shoulder, loosening her grip when Taly winced. Food had helped lessen the pain of her injuries, but she was still bruised. "Now then, my dear—the first thing you need to know about Draegonian art is that it is delightfully vulgar. Once you figure it out, that is."

CHAPTER 18

-From the personal notes of Ivain Castaro, Marquess of Tempris

Breena is angry with me again. She's so talented, so smart, which unfortunately means she grows bored easily. I've tried to keep her challenged, but I still caught her dabbling in forbidden magic two nights ago. She hasn't spoken to me since, and I'm afraid I may have punished her too severely.

The spells contained within the Vetiri are forbidden for a reason, but as someone who began his study in bloodcraft, I can see how those restrictions might feel limiting. No other class of mage is regulated as heavily as we are, and for the gifted, nothing is as devastating as the knowledge that you've been confined. That you could go farther, that you could reach for the heavens and pluck the stars from the sky if it weren't for an arbitrary set of rules chaining you to the ground.

Skye's heart beat out a nervous rhythm as he strode down the familiar hallway. The Castaros' townhome was more of an estate than a house, sprawling up instead of out in the way that Harbor Manor did. Eight stories—three of them underground—it was a marvel of white marble and dark mahogany, so elegant and new it was sometimes easy to forget the horrors that lay in wait just outside the city.

Skye hadn't been able to eat after he returned from the tavern. He'd barely been able to sleep. The knowledge that Taly was alive sparked inside him, and he'd spent most of the night glancing at the stack of diaries sitting on his bedside table, afraid they might disappear.

He still didn't have a plan for how to bring her home. After all, Aiden had tried and failed, and Skye didn't have anything that could compare to an earth mage's locator spell. But he knew her scent, and he had Aiden's maps and notes. That was enough to get him started, so long as he succeeded in getting outside the city. Ivain was monitoring everyone that came and went, and without special permission, he'd never get past the gates.

Skye sighed. He had considered telling Ivain about the dreams, the woman in the tunnels, the diaries—all of it. But then he'd actually imagined how that conversation might go.

So... I've been having dreams. About Taly. And even though she's human with absolutely no magic, I think they might be real. You see, she told me about the tunnels, and that's actually why I was down there that night. And then after spending three days cutting down shades in the dark, I followed these little blue lights off by myself where

I actually saw *her. Or a version of her. She didn't really act or look like herself, and she was wearing a dress. Which, granted, seems unlikely considering Taly only ever consented to wearing a dress on pain of death, and no—no one else saw her but me, but just go with me here because she gave me proof that she's not just some figment of my grief-stricken imagination. She sent me to her old apartment. Where I broke in. And then I found some diaries underneath an old floorboard, so yeah, I think the evidence should really speak for itself.*

In conclusion, not crazy, and please let me leave the city to go look for her.

He was pretty sure any version of that would end with him restrained and heavily sedated, waiting for a healer to come poke around in his head to see which wires had gotten crossed.

Which meant he was going to have to lie.

Too soon, Skye found himself standing in front of Ivain's office door. Voices filtered from inside, and he steeled himself, raising his hand to knock.

Breathe, he thought as he rapped on the door. His heart was pounding. *You're a shadow mage for Shards' sake. You know how to lie.*

Just never to Ivain. Never anything more than a few childhood stories, trying to avoid getting in trouble for some terrible idea Taly had dragged him into.

The door swung open, and Skye was greeted by a pretty lowborn girl with freckled cheeks and dark hair that had been pinned and tucked beneath a white maid's cap. Most of the serving staff had decided to stay on after they'd found their way to Ryme, some having nowhere else to go. She bobbed out a nervous courtesy as he stepped past her.

Ivain was already at his desk, a half-eaten breakfast tray pushed to the side, and Sarina stood by the window, sipping a steaming cup of tea. They were both dressed in black, a stark contrast to the plain white shirt and gray slacks Skye had chosen to wear instead.

Sarina took in his appearance, pursing her lips but choosing to say nothing. It was his choice if he wanted to go into mourning. Taly wasn't related to him by blood, so she couldn't force the issue.

"Ryanne." Sarina looked to the maid. "Have Eliza prepare a breakfast tray for Skye."

"I'm fine," Skye said, holding up a hand.

Sarina gave him a pointed look. "Eliza tells me you haven't been eating."

Skye opened his mouth… and then shut it. She wasn't wrong. He'd missed dinner last night, and when he was down in the airtram tunnels, most of the meals Sarina had sent had gone untouched. "It's hard to have an appetite when you've been dealing with corpses all day."

"Bring him a tray," Sarina repeated in a tone that brooked no argument.

Before he could lodge a second complaint, the maid had already sketched out another nervous curtsey and scuttled out the door.

"I thought you'd be downstairs already." Ivain's voice was gruff, and he didn't look up from the stack of paperwork in front of him—the inventory for the food supply, from what Skye could tell. "Did you finish the repairs on that Mechanica armor the ensigns pulled out of storage? Now that we have the tunnels sorted, that's your priority."

Skye approached the desk. "Uh... no. There was..." He shifted his weight from side-to-side, fumbling for words. "There was something I was hoping to speak to you about."

Ivain still didn't look up. "I'm listening. What is it you need?"

Skye took a breath, thankful that his voice sounded steady as he said, "Now that the Ebondrift refugees have gotten settled and the tunnels have been secured, my role here inside the city has become redundant. My brother is better suited to repairing the Mechanica, and Eula is overseeing the Gate Watchers and monitoring data collection for Aion. Going forward, I'd like to be reassigned to the search-and-rescue effort. I think I could do some good there."

Ivain finally looked up. "You want to look for survivors?" he asked, frowning.

Skye nodded. "The preliminary census data indicates that 75% of the island population is still unaccounted for. And while I understand that we're fighting an enemy capable of turning our own against us, I believe we owe it to the people of Tempris to try to recover as many individuals as possible."

Ivain and Sarina shared a glance.

Ivain said, "Why do I get the feeling you're only concerned about one individual in particular?"

Skye's throat bobbed. "I won't deny that I still hope to find Taly. Without a body, we can't know anything for sure. However, I don't believe that diminishes the validity of my overall goal."

"Skye," Sarina interjected softly. Her skirts hissed as she moved to refill her cup from a small tea service that had been left beside the desk. "We've already talked about this. As much we all want to believe that Taly is still out there, the overwhelming amount of evidence points to the contrary. Aiden's locator spell—"

"Was inconclusive," Skye said as calmly as he could manage. "It led him to Infinity's Edge."

"It led him to the place where Taly likely died," Ivain said. Sarina's breath hitched. His expression softened as though to say, *I'm sorry.*

"You don't know that she's dead," Skye insisted.

"I do know," Ivain said as he pushed himself to stand. He looked tired, worn around the edges, but his expression was stern. "I know because I've seen what shades are—what they can do. Taly was strong. Her actions at the relay proved that, and now thousands of people owe her their lives. But it's been two weeks since that transmission, and during that time, not only was Aiden unable to find her, but he found her horse and her personal effects, all of which were covered in blood—fey, human, and shade alike."

"The evidence is overwhelming." Sarina took a sip of tea, the cup rattling as she placed it back in the saucer. "I know we used to joke that Taly was too stubborn to die, but a human in a forest full of dead men and magical beasts, all alone with no supplies… It really is an impossible situation."

Skye made a small, disgusted noise in the back of his throat. "You've already given up," he said lowly. "You've both given up on her, and you're just going to leave her out there to *die* based on an assumption."

Ivain let out an uncharacteristic growl, but Sarina's answering hiss had the old man backing down.

She turned. "Hold your tongue, *Skylen*." And just that tone was enough to make him feel like a child again. "You're not the only one grieving."

But he couldn't back down. He needed out of this city, and if subterfuge didn't work, he'd use force instead. "You're grieving someone that's still alive."

"And you know that how?" Ivain snapped.

Because I've seen her, Skye wanted to say, even if he knew he couldn't. What he had witnessed down in those tunnels—it was too absurd, and they were already looking at him with concern.

"I just do," he said, willing them to believe him. "She's out there. I can feel it."

A pause. Sarina and Ivain shared another glance.

"I know it's a difficult reality to face," Ivain said. The pity in his eyes made Skye want to hit something. "I really do. But my answer is no. If you're unhappy with your duties, then I will reassign you, but I won't let you throw your life away trying to find a corpse."

Skye's fists clenched at his sides. "With all due respect, I didn't come here to ask for your permission. I'm going with the search-and-rescue parties. Telling you was merely a courtesy."

"Please, Skye." Sarina's voice was soft and sad. "Don't make this harder than it has to be. Be reasonable."

"I *am* being reasonable," Skye insisted, even if it felt like a lie. The resolve he'd felt so strongly the night before began to waver, so he clung to stubbornness and anger instead. "And I'm leaving first thing tomorrow with or without your blessing."

"You know I can't let you leave," Ivain said far too calmly.

"Then you're going to have to stake me to the ground," Skye growled. "Unlike some, I still give a shit about the people I claim to care about."

Skye turned to leave, but there was a sharp gust of wind accompanied by a spark of aether. Ivain was standing in front of him faster than he could blink, one hand gripped around his bicep.

"You think your pain means more?!" Ivain barked in his face. The grip on his arm was almost painful, but Skye returned the old man's snarl with one of his own. Sarina shouted something in the background, but it was just noise.

"You lost a friend, but I lost a *child,"* Ivain continued, his eyes hard as ice. "One I have already risked more to recover than I can justify. I sent Aiden. I jeopardized a *healer* during a time of crisis to hunt for a single human girl. What if he had died? Or been captured? How many more would have been lost to that single act of selfishness?"

Skye clenched his jaw until it hurt. "You don't need me here. You have others that could take my place."

"You're either stupid or willfully ignorant if you believe that." Ivain gave him a shake. "Think it through. Please, just stop to think for one moment. What happens if I send you away and we're attacked? What's the result, the consequence of that action? Will it be Sarina's life? Aiden's? Someone else that we care about? You're my best fighter and my Precept, and during a time when we have spies in our midst—unlocking our tunnels and leaving us vulnerable—I need people I can trust. I *need* you, Skylen. The same way I needed you back in Della. Surely, you can understand that."

A heavy quiet settled over the room, broken only by the steady *tick-tock* of the clock on the wall.

"Taly is dead," Ivain said, soft and quiet and lethal. But that word didn't hurt so much now. Not when Skye knew otherwise.

"Brother," Sarina warned. She took a step forward, smoke curling around her body as her own temper began to burn. "You've made your point."

But Ivain said again, "Taly is dead. She is gone, she left, and the sooner you accept it, the better off we all will be."

"I told you to stop," Sarina said, louder this time.

"You're wrong." Skye shook his head, and the laugh that slipped out of him was reckless, edging towards hysteria. "And if she dies" —he wrenched his arm away— "it really will be your fault, old man. And I hope you never forget that you're the reason why she never came back."

Skye only had a moment to process the utter devastation that flashed across Ivain's face before Sarina screamed, "*I said that's enough!*"

The fire inside the mantle flared, scorching the ceiling and sending the papers littering the desktop flying as a wave of heat swept through the room. Marching forward, she shoved the two shadow mages apart.

"This is no one's fault." Her eyes darted between the two men. Skye: panting and glowing with ire. Ivain: broken, all traces of anger gone, replaced with sorrow.

"Taly chose to go," she went on. "She *chose* this, and all we can do now is try to live with the consequences of that choice. She wouldn't want you two ripping each other apart!"

Ivain opened his mouth to speak, but a sharp knock interrupted him. He turned, placing both hands on the desk and seeming to cave in on himself as Sarina moved to answer the door.

The same maid from before stood timidly in the hallway beyond. She said, "The Lady Eula Valdaerys for the Marquess Castaro." She bobbed a curtsey, keeping her eyes securely fixed on her feet. "She's here to receive her orders."

"Ivain?" Sarina asked, turning. "Are you—"

"I'm fine." Ivain straightened, smoothing his hands down the front of his black waistcoat. "Skylen, I want that Mechanica armor down in the workshop fixed." He ducked his head as he went to follow the maid. "That is your only task."

"Go easy on him," Sarina said once the door had snicked shut. "Ivain has lost too much, even for someone as old as he is. His wife, his daughter, our sister, Breena, even my husband, who, despite their differences, he considered a very dear friend. But Taly..."

Sarina stopped and took a long, shuddering breath, pressing a hand to her chest. "I think Taly's loss is harder for him in a way. She was the daughter he never got to raise, and unlike you and me, he doesn't have the luxury of showing his grief. Too many people are looking to him for strength. They're counting on him to keep them safe, to keep this village united, and that is a heavy burden."

Skye immediately felt shame. He knew the weight of that burden. He'd experienced it in Ebondrift, and then he'd pushed it onto Ivain the first chance he got.

Something tugged at him—that thread. He turned back to the door, staring as if Taly might walk through at any moment, laughing and vibrant, ready to tell them all how stupid they were being. "I have to do this, Sarina. If there's even the slightest chance that she's still out there… Can't you see that I have to do this?"

Sarina gave a bitter laugh. "You don't have to do anything," she said. "You're choosing to. The same way Taly chose to go. The only difference is that she left because she wanted to save you." Sarina pressed a finger to his chest, smoke leaking from the corners of her eyes. "Just you, Skye. That girl would've tried to move the stars if you only asked, and I know it's hard for you to see right now, but that's exactly what she did. Against all odds, she brought you home, and if you leave now, you'll be throwing that sacrifice away. You'll be spitting on her name and her memory, and I won't stand for it."

Skye winced as the tears began to flow freely down Sarina's cheeks, each drip hissing and fizzing and turning to vapor.

"Don't throw your life away," she said as she moved towards the door. "If not for yourself, then for me. I'm not sure my heart could take losing both of you."

The door opened and shut, but Skye couldn't find it in himself to say anything as she quietly left the room.

CHAPTER 19

-From the personal notes of Ivain Castaro, Marquess of Tempris

Breena is gone.

She left last night through her window, and though Sarina is begging me to forgive the child, I cannot. I warned Breena time and time again of the dangers of bloodcraft, but she's always been a curious one. Ever since she was a girl, she's insisted on pushing boundaries, and for the most part, I've allowed it. However, her most recent stunt was seen by the entirety of the Genesis Council, and I fear there's little I can do now. If I speak out, it will draw too many eyes to my own household, and Sarina and Madoc have finally found a little bit of peace. I will not risk drawing them into the public eye—not after everything they had to sacrifice just to find each other.

Still, Breena has been my student for nearly five centuries now, and I will not leave her to the wolves. I am considering writing to Atlas. He's new to the Council, and he's always liked Breena, ever since I introduced them in Arendryl.

Perhaps he will be able to protect her where I cannot.

Skye had barely closed his eyes when he found himself pulled into the dream.

A snow-veiled forest surrounded him on all sides, quiet save for the howling gust of wind that rattled the branches, shaking loose a rain of ice and sleet.

His breath hung in the air, and his boots crunched as he turned in a circle. Thankfully, he was dressed for the cold in heavy, fur-lined wool, a long cloak, and—

Wait.

Skye turned again, taking in the long, even rows of trees, the half-buried basket in the middle of the aisle, the snow-covered barn just visible through the grove. This wasn't a forest, he realized. It was an orchard. Full of apple, sweetpear, and even a few sickly lemon trees that Sarina had always insisted would eventually take root and grow.

Looking to the west, he smiled when he saw smoke curling above the trees. Harbor Manor. He was back at Harbor Manor. This time, he really was dreaming of home.

Something tugged at him—that same thread from the ballroom—and he began to move.

Walking, then running as the pull became stronger.

The rows of trees began to stretch and repeat.

The world turned on its side—twisting and whirling and bending reality in the way that only dreams could. He grabbed at branches, lunging from trunk to trunk.

Abruptly, the world righted itself, and he fell to the ground with a thud and a groan. Rolling, he was back on his feet again, following the tug of that thread once more.

He ran and ran for what could've been minutes or hours, reaching for his aether only to find it faraway and sluggish. Sleeping.

Panting, he tried to go faster. Towards that thread and the girl he knew would be on the other end.

The trees flew by, throwing down more snow and ice. And when the lanes began to twist, circling back around, in and over in ways that didn't make sense, he imagined that thread. Saw it in his mind's eye and reached for it. Reeled it in before giving a vicious *yank.*

The world blurred and then snapped into focus as he hit something solid.

Or rather, someone. A very startled human woman that gave a sharp cry as they both went tumbling down the hill in a tangle of limbs and into a bank of freshly fallen snow.

For a few, breathless moments, all Skye could do was stare at the woman that had landed on top of him. She was pink-cheeked and bright-eyed, bundled against the cold in white and blue wool. She'd lost her hat halfway up the hill, and her golden hair spilled around her shoulders, already damp from the snow.

Alive. Taly was alive and whole and… staring at him like she wanted to hit him.

He should probably say something. Not just to escape the beating he knew was coming, but to get as much information as possible before one of them woke up.

Questions raced through his mind, blurring together, each little more than a half-formed thought.

Where are you?

Are you safe?

How are you here?

How did you know about the tunnels?

Why did you leave?

Why haven't you come back?

They all seemed critical, all a good place to start.

She saved him the trouble of having to decide.

"What fresh hell did you wander in from this time?" she asked, placing a hand on each of his cheeks. He felt the faint tickle of aether, just at the edge of his senses—most likely a part of whatever spell she was using to pull him into this shared dream.

When he didn't answer, just continued to stare up at her wide-eyed and panting, she gave a low huff.

"Never mind." She rolled away, and he immediately missed her warmth. "I don't care where you came from, but if you sit down and don't touch anything, I'll let you stay."

She was on her feet now, looking out across a large frozen pond. Skye moved to follow, but her eyes snapped to his, pinning him in place.

"I mean it." She stabbed a finger at him. "I don't know how you're here or why, but I'm not watching you die tonight. Your only job is to sit there and keep yourself alive. Think you can handle that?"

Skye held up his hands in surrender, almost laughing when Taly gave a suspicious yet satisfied nod. "You said that last time too."

"Said what?" she asked, dusting the snow from her clothes.

"That I always die." He waited for her to turn. "Why do you keep saying that?"

"Because you always die." The *idiot* was implied. "Every night, I dream about you dying. So far, you've been eaten by shades, killed by mages, ripped apart by beasts. I even saw Sarina set you on fire in a fit of temper once. Granted, it wasn't the fire that killed you. But you were still just as dead after you fell off the city wall and into that swarm of shades."

Skye swallowed. "It sounds like you really want me dead."

"The exact opposite actually," she said as she sat on the ground beside him. "Leto says that my subconscious is instinctively seeking out the things I'm most afraid of and... running the variables. Trying to find a way around it. Which is why" —she glared at the pond— "I can't figure out why I keep ending up here night after night. This is the past. The past doesn't change."

Groaning, she fell back into the snow. "It's so cold. And wet. And cold. And why couldn't I dream of someplace warmer? If I'm going to be stuck in the past, I'd rather be at that beach in Faro we went to the last time the Aion Gate opened. It was so nice and sunny, and they had those fruity drinks with little umbrellas. The humans really struck gold on that one—all drinks should come with little umbrellas."

"Taly?" Skye said, leaning over her. When she didn't open her eyes, he flicked her nose. "I don't understand *any* of that."

"That's not surprising." She reached up, blindly patting him on the head. "But you're not real, so it would be a waste of time and energy to try to explain."

Skye's stomach clenched. *She thinks this is just a dream.* And that meant she wasn't the one doing this. She hadn't used some kind of spell or device to signal him. Not intentionally, at least.

He shook his head. *Later.* They could figure out the how later. Right now, he just needed to know one thing.

"Where are you?" he asked. "Just tell me where you are, and I'll come find you."

A snort. "Don't be ridiculous."

Skye bit back a growl. They didn't have time for this. "Where are you?" he asked again, almost succeeding at keeping his tone even.

"You know," Taly said, turning her face towards the sun, "I'm pretty sure I told you not to come looking for me."

Oh, she had. In that damned note he was still carrying around in his pocket two weeks later.

"That was a really shitty thing to do, by the way." He didn't try to hide the hurt in his voice. Because surely—surely, she had to know she had ripped his heart out and taken it with her when she left. "What did you expect me to do when I found that note? Huh? *'I'm sorry, but I have to make this right. Don't come looking for me.'* What kind of bullshit was that?"

Taly finally cracked open an eye.

"You promised me you weren't going to lie anymore." He ran a finger along the downy line of white fur on her collar. "You promised, and you did it anyway, and that's not fair, Tink. It's not fair that I'm always the one that gets left behind."

Taly sat up, and he'd never seen her eyes so sad.

"Where are you?" He was begging now, but he didn't care. "I know you think this is just a dream, but for one minute, pretend it's not. Pretend that's it's real, that *I'm* real, and tell me how to find you. Please, Tink. Just tell me how to find you."

"You can't."

"Please, this isn't—"

"I mean it." Her hand came up to cup his face, and he leaned into the touch, reaching up to thread his fingers through hers. "Even if you looked, you wouldn't be able to find me. It's not as simple as *where* I am. If it was, I'd already be home."

"Explain," he demanded. "If it's not about *where*, then what is it?"

Taly sighed. "We live on an island where the veil between worlds is naturally porous. An island that's been ruled by time mages ever since it was discovered eons and eons ago. And even though they're gone now, that doesn't mean their magic no longer exists. The gates alone are proof of that. Which means that on Tempris, the question of *where* starts to get complicated. It gets all tangled up with *when,* and that's why no matter what you do, no matter what kind of magic you wield, you're never going to find me. I'm not there for you to find."

Skye wasn't sure if he was breathing anymore. "So, are you saying... If it's a matter of where *and* when..." He closed his eyes, trying to collect his scattered thoughts. "How long have you been gone?" It seemed like a silly question, but important, nonetheless.

Taly turned to gaze across the pond. "Six months."

Skye's heart may have stopped then. *Six months?* How was that possible? It had only been two weeks since Ebondrift.

He opened his mouth, a million more questions already forming on his tongue, but then she was shushing him, looping an arm through his as she pulled his attention back to the pond.

"Taly, we need—"

"*Shhh.*" She pointed towards the pond. "Watch. *Listen.* This is the reason we're here, after all."

Skye followed her stare, straining his ears. He hated not having his magic—he felt blind and deaf, completely cut off. But eventually, slowly, voices trickled over the hill, along with the crunch of snow and the scrape of metal.

Two figures appeared, and Skye blinked, his heart giving a painful lurch. "Is that…"

"Yes." He could hear the smile in her voice. "That's us."

The boy, a gangly dark-haired fey no older than fourteen, was laughing, walking hand-in-hand with a gray-eyed human girl that smiled up at him from beneath a wild mop of golden hair. They were both dressed for the snow, carrying skates and rucksacks and dragging an old wooden sled.

"Is this a memory?" Skye asked, nearly choking on a laugh when his younger self slipped on the ice. He had been clumsy at that age, always tripping over his own feet. But in this case, that tiny version of Taly—far too small to already be ten—had *definitely* pushed him, even if she tried to play it off.

"Yes and no," Taly said from beside him. "It's the past."

"What's the difference?"

Taly smiled, but instead of answering, she said, "You were all legs."

Skye hated the heat he could feel creeping up his neck. She was right. He had grown five inches that year, and it was all in his legs. "I was awkward. And skinny."

"You were adorable."

Taly leaned her head against his shoulder, and for a little while, they simply watched. Occasionally making comments. Laughing when one of them would fall. When it came to ice skating—or anything really—Skye had always been fixated on speed, and unsurprisingly, his younger self was skating circles around the pond, trying to go faster with each successive loop.

Taly, however…

Well, Taly had always been good at anything that required rhythm, whether it be music, or dancing, or even singing. It was one of the reasons that after so many years, Sarina was still trying to turn her into a lady, despite a complete lack of enthusiasm for the feminine arts.

"Why did you stop skating?" Skye asked, watching as that ten-year-old girl executed some overly complicated series of jumps and twists that made his head spin.

"Do you really not remember?"

"No."

She winced. "You're about to."

There was a yelp, and Skye turned just in time to see that little girl trip over a crack in the ice.

He tried to scream—from surprise, to warn her, he didn't know—but she was already falling. Already skidding across rocks and twigs and ice.

She landed mere inches from their feet, face-down, panting and gasping for air as the snow around her began to turn red.

Skye was on his feet in an instant, but Taly grabbed him, pulling him back a step. "Just watch," she said. "They can't see or hear or feel us. This is the past. It's already happened. There's no point trying to intervene."

"Taly!" Fourteen-year-old Skye was half-skating, half-running across the ice. When he hit the edge, he scrambled through the snow, reaching for the girl.

Taly slowly curled in on herself, clutching her leg as blood welled between her fingers. The fabric of her trousers had been slashed from ankle to knee, and a long, angry gash ran the length of her calf.

"Shit." Skye gently removed her skate, then ripped away the ruined fabric. His hands were shaking as he prodded at the wound. The skin had been shredded, and beneath the smear of blood and mangled flesh—a flash of white. Bone. "Shit, shit, shit..."

"Em?" Taly said, her voice breathy and thin. Her face was streaked with dirt, wet with snow and tears. "I'm fine. It doesn't hurt that much." A lie. There was pain in her eyes. "Just take me home."

"No, this cut is too deep." Skye wiped at his eyes, smearing blood across his brow. "I... I don't know if I should move you."

"Em—"

"Just give me a minute," he snapped, his panic getting the better of him.

"Wait." Skye began to circle the scene. "I remember this."

Hands clasped behind her back, Taly leaned over, grimacing as she inspected the wound on her younger self's leg. "I'm surprised you forgot."

"I have an idea." Skye tore off his skates. "Stay here," he said as he began to run barefoot through the snow, back to where they'd left their packs on the other side of the pond. His aether flared, like violet mist in the cold winter air.

He was there and back in seconds, digging through his pack as he skidded to his knees beside her.

"What are you doing?" Taly's breath came in stuttered gasps, and she looked pale—far, far too pale beneath the dirt on her face.

Skye produced a silver dagger, and without bothering to explain, he sliced open his palm.

"How did you know to do this?" Taly asked.

Skye shrugged. "I just… I was panicking, and you were bleeding, and… I figured that if my aether healed me, it could also heal you."

Crouching, he peered into his younger's self's face, noting the intense look of concentration.

Blood dripped from his hand into the gash on Taly's leg, indistinguishable from her own human blood. And when the wound closed, he ran the dagger along his palm again, numb to the pain.

Again and again. More and more blood—aether. He needed to give her aether.

Taking a breath, he began to channel his magic, feeling for that little piece of himself that was slowly draining away, out of him and into her.

He felt it as it trickled between the dirt and pebbles embedded in her flesh.

As it bound to cell and sinew, nerve and bone.

He gave it a single command: heal.

Mend what was broken.

Make it new.

Skye remembered now—the strangeness of the thing he had cast that day. Not wrong, but... strange. So much of shadow magic was just pulling and pushing, moving aether from here to there. It didn't matter if it was something as subtle as sharpening his eyesight or commonplace as forcing aether through a crystal—it was all the same in the end.

But that day... that day he had felt something inside him begin to spark. Spark and transform and change into something new.

The edges of the gash began to reach for one another, the flesh threading back together. The bleeding slowly ebbed.

"It's working!" Skye exclaimed, grinning widely.

"Em, that hurts."

"Just a little bit more."

"Stop!" a new voice called. The tang of aether filled the air, and then Ivain was in front of them, a flurry of snow hanging in his wake. Those stark blue eyes were wide and filled with panic, and he

grabbed Skye's wrists, wrenching him away. "What were you doing, boy?"

When Skye only stared, too stunned to speak, Ivain gave him a rough shake. "Tell me!" he demanded. "Where did you learn that spell?"

Skye's mouth opened and closed. He looked to Taly, but her face was still scrunched up in pain. "She was hurt," he said feebly. "She's still *hurt."*

With a sigh, Ivain let him go, turning to Taly. "What happened?" he asked as he began to gently prod at the half-healed gash.

"I tripped," Taly sniffed.

"That must have been some fall," Ivain said gently. He shrugged out of his greatcoat and began ripping the fabric into strips. "We'll have to be more careful next time. Although" —he rotated her leg, wiping at the blood— "it looks like you may have also broken your ankle, so I don't think you'll be doing any more skating for a while. Not until a healer comes to the island."

"If you would just let me finish—" Skye's mouth clicked shut when Ivain shot him a look.

"Listen to me, boy," Ivain said, kind but firm. "I'm not sure how you did what you just did, but you're never to use that kind of magic again? Understand?"

"But—"

"Never again," Ivain snapped. "What you just did—it's a type of bloodcraft."

Skye's brows rose. "How was that bloodcraft? I was healing her."

"Bloodcraft," Ivain said, slipping into the role of teacher as he began binding Taly's leg, "covers a wide range of spells—anything from healing to aether contamination to ascendancy. More so than any other discipline of shadow magic, it is the most

intimately connected to aether, focusing not only on the way it moves through this world but the way it shapes it. Aether is everywhere and in everything, and our magic allows us to control it. To use it to transform ourselves and the world around us."

Ivain moved to Taly's ankle, pulling a dagger from his boot and using it to splint the broken bone. "Before we had so many regulations on shadow magic," he went on, "I could've taught you how to turn your skin to bone, your bones to metal. I could show you a spell that would track a person across space and time using only a few drops of blood. Now, however, with our numbers dwindling, I can't. The Dawn Court has decided that most forms of bloodcraft are too dangerous to be taught or practiced."

"It doesn't seem dangerous," Skye muttered, kicking at the snow.

It seemed powerful. Alluring. Years later, he could still feel the pull, the temptation to reach inside and find that feeling again.

"Could you teach me?" Skye asked, helping Ivain tie off the last of Taly's bandages. "The few spells that are still legal, I mean. It wouldn't interfere with my studies. I promise, I… I just want to learn."

Leaning down, Ivain let Taly wrap her arms around his neck and carefully lifted her from the ground. "Skylen, bloodcraft is dangerous." Skye opened his mouth to protest, swallowing back the words when Ivain gave him another look. "With bloodcraft, even something meant to heal can be deadly in the hands of an unskilled mage. What you just did—you're lucky you didn't cause lasting damage to one or both of you."

Skye paled.

"I know it's tempting." Ivain clapped a hand to the boy's shoulder, adjusting Taly in his arms. "Believe me, I know the draw that kind of power has. It's why I spent so much of my life studying it. But even if I could teach you, Skye—even if that doctrine hadn't been regulated into near-extinction—I wouldn't. That road leads to some very dark places, and let's not forget, your family sent you to me to become a crafter. If I do not uphold the promise I made, if they find out you're dabbling in bloodcraft under my watch, they'll take you away from me. From me and Sarina and Taly. Is that what you want?"

Skye shook his head, a stricken look on his face.

"Good." Ivain ruffled his hair before letting his hand drop. "Now then, go get your boots and your gear and let's get back to the manor so Sarina can tell me what a terrible idea it was to let you and Taly strap sharpened blades of metal to your feet."

Skye ran to the other side of the pond and back, falling in beside Ivain. He let out a yelp when Ivain immediately cuffed him on the back of the head.

Taly snickered, tightening her grip on Ivain's neck as he said, "And don't let Sarina hear you cursing. Either one of you. I'm sure I'll be blamed for that too."

Skye stood there for a good minute, staring at the trio as they disappeared over the hill.

A laugh bubbled up. Then another. Soon, he was doubled over, laughing long and loud and not caring that Taly was staring at him like he was crazy.

Which maybe he was.

No—no, he *definitely* was. Because the plan that was piecing itself together in his mind was crazy. No doubt about it. It was categorically mad. And if he could pull it off… Shards, if he could pull it off, it just might work.

"That's it," he crowed, punching the air.

"What the hell has gotten into you?" Taly asked, a wary smile curving her lips.

Skye grabbed her shoulders, still laughing. "A locator spell. Using bloodcraft, I can cast a locator spell that can track a person through space and time. It's both the where *and* the when. *That's* how I find you."

Taly began to shake her head. "But that spell is illegal."

"I don't give a shit."

"And dangerous."

"Well, you keep saying that I'm destined to die, so maybe this is how I go. Not in a fire. Not eaten by shades or trying to keep you from jumping over the side of a ballroom balcony. Not even drunk and stumbling through an abandoned airtram station, which thank you for the warning, by the way. Because of you, Ryme is still standing, and I'm still alive."

Taly hesitated. "I didn't warn you."

"Oh yes, you did." She took a step back, but he followed, grinning madly. "Well, you actually sort of yelled it at me, but that doesn't matter. I got the message."

Something like horror dawned in her eyes, and Skye nodded. She was finally catching on. This wasn't just a dream. It was so much more.

"Skylen Emrys," she said, soft and lethal, craning her head as he took her face in his hands, "don't you dare do what it is I think you're going to do. You stay right where you are. Stay where it's safe, you arrogant—"

Skye kissed her—hard. And Shards, he wanted more than the dream. He wanted to feel her warmth, to hear her heart beating. But this—this was enough. Right now, that sigh and that gasp and that tiny moan—it was enough.

"No," he said against her lips as the dream began to fall apart. The ground shook, cracks spiraling out around them, and through the wind and snow, the sparkling spindrifts of magic that whirled in the air, he said, "I'm going to find you. And now I know how."

They began to fall, and he held onto that final vision of her, eyes wide and lashes flaked with snow, as darkness swept in.

A moment later, he woke up, warm and safe in his bed. The glow of dawn had barely started to brighten the windows, but he didn't feel tired. The dream was still vivid in his mind, and for the first time, the way forward was clear. He finally had a plan, and the first step began three stories below ground on the basement floor of the townhouse.

The place where Ivain had locked away every book of forbidden magic that they'd brought with them from Ebondrift.

"What about this one?" Aimee asked, handing the glamograph to Sarina. They both sat at the long table in the formal dining room, combing through box after box of old pictures. In the weeks since the first attacks, Ivain had made several trips to Harbor Manor, rescuing the serving staff, emptying the vaults and armories, and, even though it was a luxury they could barely afford, salvaging personal items and family mementos.

Keepsakes that they were now sorting through.

Sarina wanted to hold a funeral for Talya, and Aimee had volunteered to help organize it. True, she and Talya had never gotten along, but now that the human was gone... well, Aimee wasn't sure how to describe her feelings. Not sadness. They hadn't been that close. But she did feel regret. And perhaps some grief by association. She didn't like seeing her aunt and uncle so devastated, and she felt helpless when she passed by her brother in the hall, the pain and regret dragging behind him like a physical weight.

And Skylen...

Aimee sighed. She was worried about him the most. She'd run into him that morning—literally. He'd nearly knocked her down the stairs, using one hand to keep her on her feet while the other clutched a large cloth-wrapped bundle to his chest. There had been something manic in his expression, and she got the distinct feeling that he had just come from a place he wasn't supposed to be.

"She looks very pretty in this one," Aimee added as Sarina took the glamograph from her hand, smiling sadly. It was an image of Talya, fifteen years old according to the scrawled handwriting on the back. She was standing next to a skinny brown foal.

"That's Byron," Sarina said. "No one thought that horse was going to survive, but Taly stayed with him all night, talking to him and trying to get him to take a bottle. Needless to say, we were all amazed the next morning when they were both still there, and she'd managed to get that foal to feed."

Sarina placed the glamograph off to the side, where there were two stacks, one slightly larger than the other. "That one will work for the service, I think." She wiped at her eyes with a handkerchief, then her nose. "Taly loved that horse. I'm glad Aiden was able to find him."

Aimee placed a hand on Sarina's shoulder as she rose, moving to the hearth to stoke the fire. The formal dining room was lovely, even with sheets still covering most of the furniture. A section of the table had been cleared, and pieces of jewelry, drawings, books, even hair ribbons were neatly organized in piles. Without a body, they had decided to place items representing Talya inside an urn that would be buried on the property.

"I remember hearing Talya practicing the piano," Aimee said, placing the iron poker back beside the mantle. "Perhaps we should include some sheet music."

Sarina gave a teary nod, staring at a glamograph of what appeared to be Skylen and Talya sitting on the front steps of the manor. They were both laughing, unaware of the person holding the glamera. "Look in that box over there." She waved a hand at a wooden chest halfway beneath the table. "I kept all of her old practice manuals."

Aimee nodded and heaved the box onto the table. She found the practice manuals easily, all scrawled with childish handwriting. Some had drawings in the margins. There were more glamographs too, from when Skylen and Talya were both very young.

Aimee picked up a faded stack of glamographs, pulling the fraying ribbon holding them together. There were pictures of them in the sparring ring and working with horses, and more still where they'd obviously been posed, their shoulders stiff and their clothes clean and pressed.

A perfect, happy childhood. A family formed despite a lack of shared blood.

Aimee couldn't help the small stab of jealousy. They were lucky. Even for the nobility, life was hardly ever that kind.

Younger and younger they became until Aimee pulled a faded glamograph from the stack. In this one, Talya was standing in a doorway alone, skinny and pale, dressed in an oversized shirt that dragged the ground. She hugged a stuffed bear close to her body. Her expression looked distinctly hollow.

"That was Taly's first night at the manor."

Aimee jumped, not realizing Sarina had risen from her chair and come to stand behind her.

"Skye was the one that found her," Sarina went on as she began gathering up the practice manuals. "Her house burned in the Vale fire, but she was hiding in the basement. She was covered in so much ash and soot—it wasn't until we got her bathed that we realized her hair was yellow."

Aimee only half-listened, still staring at that face. It tugged on a memory, something deep and buried. "Excuse me," she said abruptly. She didn't wait for Sarina to respond before striding from the room, the glamograph clutched in one hand.

Up the stairs and through the darkened hallways, she made her way back to her quarters on the third floor. Falling to her knees, she reached underneath the bed, pulling out a faded navy trunk.

Her uncle had found it during one of his trips to Harbor Manor, and she'd nearly cried when she saw it strapped to the back of the cart. Inside was everything she treasured. Pictures and trinkets and other things that reminded her of a time when her family had been whole and happy—when her father had still been alive.

It only took a few moments to find what she was searching for tucked away in an old cigar box that had been wrapped in one of her father's shirts.

Aimee's hands were shaking as she held up a glamograph of another little girl with yellow hair and a broad smile on her face.

One she'd long thought dead.

CHAPTER 20

-A letter from Lady Adriana Emrys, Duchess of Ghislain, to her son, Lord Kato Emrys

Kato,

Be glad it is me writing to you rather than your grandfather. We were unamused, to say the least, by your showing at the Arylaan Arms Convention. While you did technically showcase the remote capabilities of our new unmanned prototype, having the Mechanica do what you so eloquently called a "line dance" for the fully assembled Dawn Court and their generals was perhaps not the soundest decision.

The family elders want you punished—they have been pushing me for years to bring you to heel. For the time being, however, I've decided to do nothing. I'm not going to tell you that what you did was juvenile. I won't waste my time reiterating all the ways I see you wasting your life, your talents, or your family's good name on these adolescent pranks.

For now, all I will say is that I'm sorry about Sarah. I heard about the letter that came in the post, and considering the life expectancy of humans, I can guess at the subject.

With all my love,

Your Mother

Kato fell back against a stack of crates, panting. "Maybe we should just let the shades kill us."

Eula sighed and made a note as she continued her inventory. One of the flash cannons lay disassembled at her feet. "That's a bit dramatic."

"Says the woman who's been holding a clipboard all morning instead of helping me carry crates up and down and up and down and... You get the point."

Still trying to catch his breath, Kato took a swig from a canteen filled with water and faeflower, shuddering at the taste. It had been almost two weeks since the battle at Crescent Canyon, and the Marquess was still punishing him. He got the worst guard rotations, was always on duty to build funeral pyres and pile corpses. He was the best Shards-damned crafter in this entire city, and yet the only thing he'd been tasked to repair was toilets, which were somehow always covered in shit.

Two fucking weeks and he was sick of it. Sick of the shit jobs and long hours. Sick of feeling like he'd lost any amount of control over his life.

But most of all, he was sick of Eula Valdaerys.

He had never spent much time with her before the world had gone to hell, but he'd heard of her. According to the other Watchers, she'd been born with a stick so far up her ass, it was a wonder she'd survived to adulthood. She had a fair amount of aether, was a good fighter, but for reasons no one had been able to articulate, she'd never progressed past the rank of Acolyte. She was the Marquess' favorite, which was perhaps why his leash had suddenly been passed on that morning to *"the queen bitch."*

That's what the Ensigns called her. It lacked imagination, true. But it was accurate.

Especially as she marched up and down the length of the wall, barking orders at both him and the nearby earth mages as they tended to newly planted gardens. Kalahad was among them. Kato had taken the man up on his offer a few times since they'd returned, meeting up at one of the taverns for a drink—which is how he'd learned, among other things, that the High Lord of Earth's baby brother had a passion for farming. While this wasn't unusual for an earth mage, it was less common for a man of his standing to specialize in food production. But on more than one occasion now, Kato had listened as Kalahad waxed poetic about crop selection, and field rotation, and something called hydroponics, claiming that in a few days' time, the earth mages would be producing enough food to feed the whole of Ryme.

Which was great, since then there would probably be more toilets to fix.

"Is there a reason I don't see a crate in your hands?" Eula asked testily.

"Because these things are heavy." Kato kicked at a stack of metal sheeting with a mud-caked boot. Today, they were installing the flash cannons from Ebondrift onto the outer wall. The guns were massive, too large even for the cranes, so they were taking them up piece by piece.

Or rather, he was. Eula had done nothing but observe, clipboard in hand, while he lugged crates and materials up a series of dirt platforms the earth mages had installed when the ladders hadn't been able to hold the weight.

"Seriously," Kato said, wiping the sweat from his eyes. The wind was cold, but the sun was hot, and all he wanted to do right now was lie down and die. "This gun is made of viridian reinforced with star steel. I could use some help."

Eula never looked up from that damned clipboard. "All of my other shadow mages are spoken for," she said, because of course they were. It wouldn't be a proper punishment if he had help. "So get off your ass and pick up a crate."

"And if I don't?"

She shrugged. "Then I'll be forced to tell the Marquess that he was right. You're better suited to latrine duty, and I should've heeded his advice and asked for your brother's assistance instead. Skylen would have no problem moving my crates. In fact, we'd probably already be done."

Kato huffed. She was goading him. That much was obvious. But that particular barb stung, and he pushed himself to stand.

Half a heartbeat later, he was in front of her, wisps of aether curling off his skin and clothing like smoke. "Could Skye do this?" Fast as an adder, his hand shot out, and he grabbed her clipboard. By the time she noticed, he'd already scuttled out of her reach. "Probably not. While I might lack golden boy's brawn, I've learned to adapt in other ways. And what the hell is it with you and the Marquess anyway? Why do you spend so much time kissing his ass? Is it perfumed? Does he stick rose petals up there?"

Eula growled and reached for her clipboard, but he nudged his aether and pushed off with his legs. He was instantly standing a few yards away.

"Ivain Castaro is a better man than you could ever hope to be," she snapped.

"A good leader doesn't play favorites. He's only punishing me because of Skye."

"Skye hasn't said a single word against you."

"Bullshit. I'm the best crafter in this city, and Castaro has me doing menial labor."

"You want to prove yourself? How about you stop whining?" A flash of her aether and she was suddenly very close, her fist barreling for his face. Drawing on a tendril of his own aether, he immediately sidestepped, grabbing her fist and enjoying perhaps a little too much the way her eyes widened in surprise. He'd always preferred speed over strength.

Smirking, he harnessed her momentum, heaving her over his shoulder like he would a sack of grain.

But instead of going flying, Eula countered, twisting her body midair with cat-like grace. She landed in a crouch, her eyes never leaving his as she slowly rose to her full height.

Kato smiled. "I'm impressed."

"I'm not," Eula replied flatly. She held up the clipboard, and he refrained from telling her that he'd let her snatch it. That throw had won him a lot of coin back at the University, but she'd figured it out immediately.

This was an unexpected but not unwelcome turn of events, and he looked her up and down with new appreciation, noting that despite her words to the contrary, a glimmer of respect now shone in her eyes as well. "I suppose I'm glad to know that the woman holding my leash earned her position on the battlefield rather than the bedroom."

He'd been hoping for a reaction, but Eula merely arched a brow. "Trust me when I say I'm proficient at both." Kato made no effort to hide his smile at the implication. "Though regarding Ivain," she added, "you're underestimating him."

Kato snorted. "What did that man do to earn such loyalty?"

Eula looked back to her clipboard, and he got the feeling that she was stalling, searching for the right words.

"Ivain Castaro," she said carefully, "was the only one to give me a chance after my good for nothing grandfather gambled away my family's coin. He looked past these three measly lines on my arm and saw that I was capable of more, even if I didn't have the money or the connections to get a spot at the University. He gave me a future when I had none, and he'd do the same for you if you could just pull your head out of your ass long enough to show him that you're more than what the rumors say. There's no room in this organization for clowns."

Kato huffed, shaking his head as he looked away. Of course, his reputation would precede him—and immediately kill any chance of success he might've had otherwise. "A wise man doesn't base his opinion on assumptions."

"He does when those assumptions are confirmed by action." Throwing her clipboard on a nearby table, she grabbed his wrist, pushing up his sleeve. "You think I haven't seen these lines on your arm? You're barely 200, and you've already earned your seventh seal. It takes most mages centuries longer to get that far in their training, if they ever get there at all. That means you're smart, and at one point in your life, you actually gave a shit."

"And what makes you think that I don't now?"

"Because in the time that I've known you, all you've done is blame your problems on other people. You whine and complain about how life's not fair, but guess what? Everyone that lives long enough to get hurt figures that out. I figured it out when I was 32 and had to work as a sellsword to feed my baby sister because my parents still insisted on living like we had money. It wasn't fair. None of it. But when I got knocked on my ass because of someone else's selfish decisions, I made the choice to get back up. You have yet to show me that you're capable of doing the same."

Kato went quiet. Eula was direct—he'd give her that. The woman aimed to kill.

She took a breath. "The way I see it, you've got two choices," she said a little more gently this time. "Number one: you can play into every assumption Ivain has made about you and your character. You can go on as you are, complaining and refusing to take ownership of your life. You can keep fixing our toilets even though it's a waste of your talent and skill."

She still hadn't let go of his hand, and he watched as she traced the lines on his wrist with a featherlight touch. "I don't like that option," he said.

"Then I suggest you go with option two."

"Which is?"

Her fingers closed around his, and he was suddenly aware of just how close she was standing. She smelled like sweat and machine oil, but also—lilacs.

Her eyes lifted, finding his, and she whispered, "You can carry my crates."

Kato frowned, yanking his hand from hers. "You just ruined a really nice moment."

She shrugged. "Did you not hear what I said about the crates?"

"What is it with you and those crates?"

"They're down here when they should be up there."

They were still standing toe-to-toe, neither moving to give up any ground. He considered stealing her clipboard again, just to see what she'd do, when footsteps began to approach.

They both turned to find Skye weaving between the tables the earth mages had set up to organize their supplies. He looked unamused, to say the least.

Kato shared a look with Eula. He'd heard that Taly had been pronounced dead, and he'd known it would hit his brother hard. But the man making his way toward them looked like he'd tried to carve a piece out of himself to send with her.

"When was the last time you slept?" Kato asked with genuine concern. Indeed, there were shadows beneath his eyes, his skin was too pale, and his clothes were rumpled and speckled with what looked like blood.

Skye just shook his head as he came to stand in front of them, saying to Eula, "You sent for me?"

She cleared her throat, glancing at her clipboard in what, Kato guessed, was an attempt to mask her surprise. "Yes," she said, then at Kato's inquiring look, shrugged. "What? You were right. This is more work than one shadow mage can manage."

"And you couldn't have told me that earlier?"

Her lips twitched. "And deprive you of an opportunity to whine about the unfairness of life? I'm not a monster."

Kato threw her a crude gesture, and she laughed—a first for Eula Valdaerys, he was sure—as she began giving directions.

It took Kato all of five minutes to realize that bringing his brother in to help hadn't been an act of leniency on Eula's part. It was incentive. Even though the man looked like death, he moved like he was being chased by the Magnus himself, grabbing crates and darting up the earthen steps like they weighed next to nothing. It was 30 feet to the top, but he never stopped moving, not for a moment.

Kato, as much as he hated to admit it, struggled to keep up. Though he did. Barely. And only by using far more aether than seemed necessary for such a mundane task.

"Got somewhere to be?" Kato asked when Skye grabbed the last crate straight from his hands. He bounded back up to the top of the wall in a matter of seconds.

"I have my own duties," was all Skye said as he stepped off the side of the battlement. His aether flashed, and he landed easily in a crouch. "What about this?" he asked Eula, gesturing to the long metal barrel of the cannon. By far the heaviest part of the gun, it had been wrapped in cloth and strung with rope, which Skye was already wrapping around his hands.

"It goes up as well," Eula said. "But we're still waiting on the..." Her voice trailed off as he grunted and heaved. The ropes strained, but then Skye... he *lifted* the metal barrel over his head, resting it on his shoulders as he stood to his full height.

"...crane," she finished weakly. She looked at him, slack-jawed, and Kato was sure his expression matched hers.

Skye stepped onto the first platform. A violet shimmer was collecting on his skin, like he was leaking aether. But he kept going.

Up and up and up.

"Should we help?" Kato asked.

"I'm not sure we can," Eula answered. They had tried to lift the barrel that morning, but even between the two of them, they'd barely managed to get it off the ground. "Has Ivain had him doing special training?"

Kato shook his head. "Maybe? Golden boy always was an overachiever." Though to be fair, the same could've been said for him when he was younger.

Another step and Skye cleared the top of the wall, disappearing from sight.

"That's not emasculating. Not at all," Kato drawled unconvincingly. Eula took pity on him and snorted a laugh.

Skye stepped off the wall, landing with slightly less grace than before. His boots scraped against the dirt as he staggered to his feet. He gave them a wave and was already walking off, wiping sweat from his eyes, when Eula ran to catch up.

"Wait," she called.

He stopped, turning.

"Sarina said she was looking for things that represented Taly. For the funeral."

Skye looked for a moment like he'd been struck, but he quickly masked it. Kato felt a reluctant stab of pity.

Eula reached into her pocket, producing a folded piece of paper. "I taught Taly how to shoot," she said. The words were thick. "Eight years old, and the kid had better aim than some of my Ensigns." She held out the slip of paper. "It's a target. The same kind I used to teach her. I thought… it seemed fitting."

Skye gingerly took the paper, staring at it wordlessly for several long moments. "I'll give it to Sarina," he finally said. "I'm sure she'll be glad to have it."

He walked away, and Eula turned back, discreetly wiping her eyes. When she caught Kato staring, she frowned. "Why isn't there a crate in your hands?"

Kato pointed to the top of the wall. "Because they're all up there."

"Then why aren't you unpacking them?" she asked archly, marching past him.

Aiden leaned against the battlement, watching Skye as he retreated back to the townhouse.

He was worried. Skye had stopped sleeping—that much was obvious. And Sarina confirmed that he was barely eating, coming into the kitchen late at night and taking whatever scraps were left. He and Ivain were no longer speaking; he barely spoke to Sarina.

And then there was what Aiden had just witnessed down below. Skye shouldn't have been able to lift that cannon. Not on his own and not given his current physical state. But that then begged the question: how had he done it? What was he doing to himself behind closed doors? Aiden had heard of forbidden spells capable of altering a shadow mage's physiology, but even if he had access to that kind of magic, Skye had never been reckless.

But now with the specter of Taly's loss looming behind him like a shadow... well, Aiden was worried. Both as a healer and a friend.

"There you are."

Aiden turned his head. "Aimee?"

He was still surprised she had decided to go into mourning, but, indeed, as she poked her head around the darkened stairwell, her dress was black, as were her shoes, her gloves, her cape, even the combs pinning back her dark hair. She and Taly had never been close, but it seemed his sister wasn't completely unaffected by the loss.

Interesting.

"I thought you'd be working in the gardens," she said a bit out of breath, gathering up her skirts as she hopped over the final two stairs. They were broken, little more than rubble.

"I was," he said, holding out a hand and helping her step around several fallen sacks of sand. The little rundown alcove he'd found at the top of the wall was out of the way, mostly used for storage. "I just came up here to get some air. I don't think most people consider just how much manure it takes to grow food. I'm still not used to the smell."

Her lips pursed, nose crinkling. She looked around the small alcove, taking in the arched stone overhead, the crumbling battlement. On one side lay the city—this section of town had been devoted to food production. On the other, the forest spread into the distance.

"You get used to the screams," he said when he saw her flinch. There was a child crying from somewhere far away. He'd barely noticed. After spending so much time this close to the walls, the noise had faded into the background.

Aimee clutched her bag tighter, hugging it to her body. "Is it always like this?"

He nodded. "It gets louder at night. The shades—the fresh ones patrol the forest just outside the city. They're trying to lure people outside the walls."

A new voice joined in. A boy this time. He sounded young as he screamed for someone named "Sukie."

"Does it ever work?" she asked softly.

Aiden shrugged. "In the beginning, yes." He'd almost been fooled on more than one occasion. "But anyone stationed near the walls knows they're not real. Some have even started playing music to drown out the noise."

Aimee was quiet, growing paler with every moment she continued to listen. By some small mercy, music began to trickle up to them from somewhere in the fields, a lively fiddling tune that was soon joined by a flute and then a pack of wild drums.

"Did you need something?" Aiden prompted.

She jumped, shaking her head as though she'd just remembered. "Yes, I… Sarina asked me to bring you lunch."

On cue, Aiden's stomach gave a ferocious growl. He'd spent his morning in the gardens, and his afternoon had already been promised to the menders. Most nights he was so low on aether, he fell face-first into bed, only to blink and suddenly find that it was morning.

Aimee held out the bag, and he grabbed it, tearing it open. There were sandwiches, a few pieces of fruit, a jug of sour wine, some dried meat.

He took the dried meat first, savoring it. They wouldn't have meat for very much longer. Ivain had decided that livestock were too inefficient for the number of people they had to feed, which meant that when their current stores ran out, it would be grain and vegetables and little else.

Aimee chuckled softly as she took up a spot beside him on the wall, leaning out so she could see the mages working down below. "I suppose it wouldn't matter if I said you were pushing yourself too hard."

He gave her a playful roll of his eyes. Leave it to his sister to worry. "Once the food supply is stable, Ivain said I can focus on healing."

"And when will that be?"

"Soon." He took another bite, chewing. The meat was tough, but the spices were good. "It should get easier soon." He hoped. All their plans hinged on the Aion Gate opening. It was the only way off the island, and they just had to survive until then.

Aimee's aether sparked blue around her gloved fingers, and a ribbon of water swirled through the air. "So what were you thinking about when I got here?" she asked, idly playing with that bit of water magic like one might a piece of string. "You looked worried."

Aiden found his sister's eyes, the same jewel blue as his. As their mother's. "It's nothing," he lied.

Aimee's lips thinned. "You frown when you're worried, and it leaves these little marks between your eyes that look like italics."

He snorted, saying around a mouthful of food, "Are you telling me I have worry lines?"

She nodded sagely. "Big ones."

The ribbon of water formed itself into a hunched little man with a deeply lined face that he could only assume was meant to be him. Aimee had always loved molding water, creating little creatures to do her bidding. If their stepfather had allowed it, she could've done great things, maybe even surpassed their father. As it stood, she'd only ever been allowed to study ladylike pursuits. Glamours. And she'd never fought back.

A small part of him still resented her for that.

Reaching out, he waved a hand through the spirals of water magic as they began to reform, turning them to mist. "It's Skye."

As expected, Aimee perked up. She was always more than eager to talk about the heir to Ghislain, though Aiden doubted that she loved him as much as she claimed. They had nothing in common, other than their parents trying to push them together.

"He's not doing well," Aiden went on. "And there's a piece of information that I've been holding onto that I'm still not sure if I should tell him."

"Let me guess—about Talya?"

He nodded. "When I was treating her for the harpy venom, I found something. Something big. I… I know why she left home last year."

Aimee's brows rose. Their aunt and uncle had never spoken openly about Taly's departure, but it was clear to those that knew them just how devastating that loss had been.

"And you didn't tell anyone?" she asked. "Why?"

"Because Taly begged me not to, and I couldn't bring myself to betray her trust, even though I probably should have. For her own sake. Now that she's gone, though..."

It didn't matter. There was no trust to break. The information didn't hold the same weight as it had before. The Sanctorum couldn't hunt a dead time mage. They couldn't execute the people that protected her, if only because there was nothing left to protect.

"Taly was having visions." The words cracked out of him, and he hadn't realized just how hard it had been to keep that secret inside. "Of the future. Fractions of a second, but still..." He took a breath, the few bites of food in his stomach turning to lead. "She had time magic, Aimee."

Aimee's eyes went wide. "That's impossible," she breathed. "Humans don't have magic."

"This one did."

There was a pause as that information settled in, then she hissed, "And she told you?" The air around her sparked blue. "Why you? Why in Shards' name would she tell *you*?"

He wasn't sure when they had started speaking in whispers, but the accusation in her voice was evident. "I forced her to," he said. By telling him this secret, Taly had put his life at risk. She had made him a target of the Sanctorum, and that wasn't something Aimee would forgive easily. Besides their mother, they were all the other had. "I backed her into a corner, and I forced her to tell me. She didn't want to."

That placated his sister—somewhat. Her fingers gripped the side of the wall in what was no doubt a white-knuckled grip beneath her black gloves. "That's why you went to look for her. Because if she's a time mage..." She shook her head, sneering. "Shards, this was all because of your stupid duty to that stupid Crystal Guard."

True—to an extent. As a time mage, Taly had been the closest living link to the Time Shard. Which then made it his duty to protect her. But he'd also gone into that forest looking for a friend, and the way his sister was glaring at him, her careless words, the memory of past arguments, and all those underlying resentments…

"Watch your tongue," he snapped back. "The Crystal Guard was our father's legacy."

"And it got him killed!"

Aimee's expression was thunderous as she stared him down, and how she did that, how she managed to look so much like their mother when all hell was about to break loose…

He looked away. Needless to say, his sister hadn't been happy about his decision to join the Crystal Guard. She'd been even less happy when he'd signed away his claim to their father's lands in Picolo, in effect making her a future baroness. He'd had to do it, of course. It was the only way their stepfather was ever going to let him go.

Not that any of that mattered now that Picolo and the Crystal Guard were literal worlds away.

He sighed. "I just… I don't know if I should tell Skye. He's not okay, and I don't know if this information will bring him any comfort or if it will just make things worse."

Aimee pushed herself away from the wall, only to fall back against it when there was nowhere to pace. She jerked her head, as if coming to a decision. "There's something I need to show you."

Reaching into her cloak, she produced two glamographs that she laid out on the stone ledge side-by-side.

The first, he recognized. It was their baby cousin sitting on the front steps of their family home. She had died during her Attunement Ceremony when she was only five years old. This glamograph had been taken a week before what would become her final birthday.

In the other, the child looked remarkably similar. Blonde hair, gray eyes, similar features, similar build. But she was human where their cousin was fey.

"Well?" she said when he didn't say anything.

"Well what?" he asked, looking between the glamographs.

Aimee gave a soft growl. "Don't you see it?"

"I see two children that look remarkably similar considering they're two different species."

She pointed to the picture of the human girl. "This is Talya."

"I figured." That was Harbor Manor in the background.

"And this is—"

"I know who that is, Aimee."

"And?" Her voice became sharp, almost shrill.

Aiden sighed. This wasn't the first time something like this had happened. She was always searching for ghosts where there were none to be found, holding on to the hope that maybe one of the people they had loved and lost might not actually be gone. Their father, their aunt, their baby cousin—Aimee had been so young when they died. They had all left for Arylaan on the same day, all said their final goodbye as they boarded the same train. In her memory, the loss had become compounded, each death connected in a way that simply didn't exist.

All these years later, and she was still grasping at threads, hoping to find answers to questions that had already been settled.

"*And*," he said pointedly, "people change as they grow. You looked just like Father when you were small, but now you're the spitting image of Mother. I was born with blonde hair, and then it turned red. These two children look very much alike–I agree with you on that. But Taly was human. Our cousin was fey."

Aimee's hands clenched into fists. "But if Talya had—"

She slid her eyes to the ground below. There were only two shadow mages within earshot—Eula and Kato—but they were bickering, just like they had been all morning.

"*—time magic*," she mouthed; then continued out loud, "that would mean she wasn't completely human."

"Yes," he admitted. "Most humans wouldn't have that kind of reaction to harpy venom, and I've never heard of one surviving faeflower."

Aimee let out a muted squeal. "You gave her faeflower?"

Aiden winced, but nodded. He'd taken a huge risk when he'd given Taly what, at the time, he'd thought was poison. It had worked—thankfully—but he still shuddered at the thought of *what if it hadn't*.

"That means she was fey," Aimee insisted.

"Partly, yes. But she *looked* human."

Letting out a frustrated growl, she banged her fists on the battlement. "Why do you keep saying that? A glamour can easily make something look like a thing it isn't."

"Because it's relevant. Think about what kind of glamour it would take to pull off what you're suggesting. It would have to grow with her, change as she changed. I've never seen a glamour like that."

"Father could've done it. Easily."

And there it was. Aimee didn't care about Taly. She didn't care about their cousin. It always led back to their father, the only person capable of liberating their family from the man who had taken his place—Lord Aris Thorne.

"Father," Aiden said, "couldn't have put iron in her blood. That wasn't an illusion, else it would've snapped the moment I removed that blood from her body. Explain that to me. Explain why I could go right now and test one of Taly's blood samples, and it would show me iron instead of aether?"

"I… I don't know," Aimee replied, frustrated. He could already see the inevitable pain rushing in to fill the space where that momentary hope had been. "It's just…"

"I know." Sometimes, it was hard not to hope.

They were quiet for several long moments. Eventually, she gathered up the glamographs, tucking them back inside her cloak.

"For what it's worth," she said softly, not quite meeting his eyes, "I think you need to tell Skylen about Talya."

"I know," he said again. Because he did. "I'm just afraid of giving him false hope. He's grieving, and I don't want to be the reason he goes off and does something foolish."

"Then wait until after the funeral. Let them bury her, mourn her, but after that, you have to tell them. If not Skylen, then at least Uncle Ivain. It's going to hurt, but they deserve to know."

Aiden sighed and pulled the jug of wine from the sack. "I was afraid you were going to say that." He took a long draught. "On a scale of one to ten, how dead do you think I'm going to be when Aunt Sarina finds out?"

It was a feeble attempt at humor. Aimee took the wine from his hands. "An eight."

"Only an eight?"

She shrugged and took a sip of wine. "You saved Talya's life after the harpy, and then risked your own trying to find her. There's a decent chance she'll let you live. Though you're going to get a little singed."

CHAPTER 21

-The following is an interview with Miriam Fernlace

I still remember my seventh seal exam. Azura gave me a single task: she wanted me to break into a bakery and steal their recipe for sugarberry strudel.

Sounds simple, right? Except that this "bakery" she wanted me to break into—it wasn't just any local patisserie. It was Shadough Sweets, the bakery empire that services half of Lycia. As you would expect, they carefully guard their recipes. They're stored on a 300-acre compound surrounded by a 40-foot wall. The Mechanica patrolling their orchards, as well as their state-of-the-art surveillance system capable of detecting time anomalies, were both recent additions to their security detail. I'll give you one guess who was responsible for those generous "donations."

So, yeah—I failed the first time. And the second time, and the third, fourth, and fifth... I did everything I could think of, used every spell I knew and some I didn't. Hell, I even hired a professional thief at one point, but nothing worked. I was in and out of the local jail so much, the warden and I would sit and share a beer while we waited for the imperial pardon.

This went on for six months, until one day as I was preparing to add yet another criminal offense to my record, Azura just walked into my room and announced, "You pass!" around a mouthful of sugarberry fucking strudel. "Unbeatable games aren't meant to be won," she said. "They're meant to build character, and you've finally proven yours."

I checked myself into Calming Meadows that very night. I still have panic attacks when I smell baking bread.

A blast of energy slammed into the base of her neck, and pain exploded behind her eyes. Taly could vaguely sense herself hitting the ground, but the sensation was muted, momentarily dulled by the wave of mind-numbing agony that swept through her.

"Son of a Shard-sucker..." she groaned as she lay panting, sprawled across the red dirt of the training yard. Crackling electricity radiated down her spine, and she didn't even try to move her arms and legs. The hit had been mild compared to others, but experience told her she'd be paralyzed for several minutes at least.

Azura had added a new rule to the game last week. She could add more fairies, as many as she liked. Without warning.

Today's game had started out with ten. And when Taly had nine of them frozen, five more were added.

She had only managed to tag thirteen of those little bastards before she'd gotten herself completely paralyzed. Which meant she'd lost.

Again.

Lying flat on her back, she stared at the rapidly darkening sky. Rain began to drip into her eyes—just like it did every day at 12 minutes past the thirteenth bell—and *four* wisps of fairy fire lazily whirled above her. That meant the Queen had added two more during the final seconds of the match—bringing the final number to seventeen fairies in play.

That was a new record.

Their light had already turned from that cold, icy blue back to something soft and gentle. As they circled, golden duplicates trailed a few seconds ahead of each one, glowing and seeming to drag them along.

Taly blinked, dismissing her Sight. Their afterimages faded.

Azura clapped her hands, slow and mocking. "That was just short of nearly okay."

Taly groaned irritably, closing her eyes as the rain began to fall in earnest. "You could've at least told me that you'd added two more fairies."

Azura leaned back in her chair, sheltered from the rain by one of the gray stone arches that circled the arena as she sipped her tea. She was dressed in a pale golden gown, the color a perfect match to her eyes. The skirts pooled at her feet, a river of silk and lace.

"Where's the fun in that?" she chirped, setting her cup on a heavy marble tea table with a soft *clink*. "And really my dear, it's not as though your enemies are going to announce themselves before they take the field. You need to learn how to compensate for the unexpected—think on your feet and all that."

The Queen's viewing area had become quite grand. Plush rugs concealed the jagged flagstone underneath, and comfortable chairs and couches had been artfully arranged inside the cramped space, each one covered with jewel-colored suede and decorated with plush, silk pillows.

There was even a chandelier hanging overhead, and though Taly couldn't see the bejeweled monster from where she lay on the ground, she could hear the delicate chime-like tinkle of the crystals as they clinked together.

"You're a cheat," Taly huffed. "You just couldn't stand the fact that I was about to win."

"If you feel better believing that, then go right ahead."

Taly scowled, squinting against the rain that continued to drip into her eyes. It did make her feel better. Granted, she should've known about the additional fairies. The Queen wasn't exactly inconsistent in the way that she cheated. But it still felt good to believe that the unfairness of the situation was the reason she kept losing. Not her own recklessness. Or stupidity. Or pride—what little of that she had left.

Taly muttered a curse as the water began to pool beneath her.

Great—now she was paralyzed *and* wet.

Taly sighed when she felt the Queen's magic wash over her, wriggling her fingers, then her toes. Every part of her ached, but at least she could move again. "I still hate you, by the way."

"I'd be disappointed if you didn't." Azura held out her cup as Leto moved to refill it. "Do come in from the rain, dear. Your tea will get cold."

Pulling her legs to her chest, Taly kicked up to her feet. She peeled off her vambraces, then her tunic, revealing a soiled camisole and plain white undergarments, and began wiping at the sweat, mud, and rain streaking her skin. A small mental tug was all it took to release the suspended fairies, and Anka—one of the few fairies that seemed to have taken a genuine liking to her—chittered as she drifted across the training yard and rested on Taly's shoulder.

"I know you're sorry," Taly said to Anka, who seemed to shiver in relief. The orb of light pulsed before twirling back into the air, trilling out a chiming giggle as she rejoined the other fairies.

Taly frowned as she watched her go. As long as the fairies stayed inside the loop, they were safe, but if they ventured outside, back to where time followed its natural rhythm, they started to lose parts of themselves—pieces from when they had been alive. Leto had confided in her one evening that Anka had spent a considerable amount of time in the real world, and it showed. The poor fairy was barely capable of stringing together a few words, much less sentences, and most often communicated in chirps and flashes of light that the other fairies seemed to understand instinctively.

Leto was standing at the entrance to the Queen's viewing area, and Taly gave the ghostly woman a wan smile as she took her soiled clothing, handing her a fluffy white towel that smelled faintly of lavender.

Thank the Shards for Leto. Without her, Taly was pretty sure she'd have already lost every one of her marbles.

"You still fight like a shadow mage," Azura remarked, eyeing Taly from head to toe and frowning at the blood trickling down the side of her face.

"What is that supposed to mean?" Taly asked with a tired sigh, sinking down onto a green settee. Leto brought her a glass of water, and she gulped it down eagerly.

"You're a smart girl," Azura said with a dismissive wave. "Surely, you can figure it out on your own."

"That's not helpful."

Azura met Taly's glare with one of her own. "You're still allowing yourself to get hit," she said.

Taly couldn't help but laugh at that. "*Right*," she drawled, flexing her fingers. Her entire arm still tingled uncomfortably, and she was pretty sure there was going to be a sizable bruise right on her tailbone. "I'm *allowing* myself to get hit. Because this game is so much fun. I just love getting my ass kicked every day while some crazy lady sits on the sideline, commenting on my performance while taking her tea."

"Get up," Azura snapped, rising from her seat in a single, fluid motion, flicking her skirts behind her.

Setting her glass down with an audible *clink*, Taly rose to face the Queen. She had to crane her neck to look the woman in the eye.

"Good." Azura clasped her hands in front of her. "Now then—kill me."

"What the hell are you on about now?"

"Kill me," Azura repeated. "Using only your magic, I want you to try to kill me."

"But…" Taly hesitated, going through every spell she knew, both in practice and theory. There were very few offensive spells, and the ones that did exist were far beyond her current ability. It would take her centuries to learn the kind of magic that could accelerate a person's timeline to the point of decay. "I can't."

Azura's eyes went comically wide. "Wait, do you mean to tell me… Oh my—*what* a revelation! Here I am, the High Lady of Time, and I never once realized that time mages have so few offensive spells."

"You're mocking me." Resisting the urge to mutter a curse, Taly kicked at a fragment of a chipped cup that had rolled next to her foot, still there from earlier that morning when Azura had sent the entire tea service flying into the air just to prove a point.

"You're still not using your head," Azura said. "We've been at this for almost two months, and you still charge headlong into the fray without ever stopping to think if this is a battle you need to be fighting."

"But you told me I have to play," Taly pointed out. "Believe me, if I didn't have to play this stupid game, I wouldn't."

"Not all battles are won by fighting." Azura gave her a pointed look. "You're going to have to get more creative if you want to win. Part of being a time mage is knowing when to fight, when to run, and when neither one is necessary."

"That makes no sense." But then again, half the shit the Queen spouted ever did.

"You're also still using too much aether," Azura said, reclaiming her seat.

Something inside her caved at that. She thought she'd been doing better.

"How is your Sight?" Azura went on. "Have you had any luck increasing your range? I really would like you at five seconds before you return to your own timeline."

Taly sank back down into her chair. Leto tried to pick a few flecks of mud from her braid, but she waved the well-meaning fairy away. "No change. I can still only see three seconds ahead, but I'm getting better at summoning and dismissing the visions at-will. It's too much of a drain on my aether if I try to keep them active all the time."

"The Sight is a powerful tool, but also costly. Use it when you must, but use it sparingly."

"Why use it at all?" Taly asked. "Half the time, I get too much information to make sense of any of it before a fairy knocks me on my ass."

The Queen picked up her cup, taking a thoughtful sip as she stared out across the training yard. The rain had started to pick up, but a line of air crystals embedded in the stone archway kept the moisture and humidity at bay. "I've said it before, but I think it bears repeating. Time is an unfolding of moments, each one a single variant plucked from a limitless number of possibilities. The Sight allows us to see those possibilities, but intuition is what helps us make sense of what we see."

"Anything is possible, but not everything is probable," Taly recited. She had most of the Queen's favorite sayings memorized by now. "So how do I train my intuition then?"

"That's something that can't be trained, I'm afraid." Waggling her fingers, Azura picked a delicate teacake from the silver serving tray that Leto placed in the middle of the table. "Time and experience will help, but like the Sight, intuition is something you either have or you don't."

"I don't like that answer," Taly grumbled under her breath. In fact, she hated it. But, to be fair, she hated a lot of things these days: time magic, the Queen, fairy tag, as well as any and all things that were seemingly spinning out of her control.

That last item was going to need its own list soon, complete with sub-headings.

Feeling petulant, and tired, and so incredibly irritable, Taly picked up a cookie and tossed it straight at the Queen's head.

Unsurprisingly, the pastry stopped mid-air.

"I don't know why you look so morose." Azura picked the cookie from the air. "I've told you before—you have naturally high intuition. If you didn't, instead of three or four variations, you'd see hundreds. It's just going to take a few decades for you to learn how to read a situation. You're still young, after all. Little more than a babe in the woods."

"Hmm," was about all Taly could muster for a response. A *babe in the woods*—that was another one of Azura's favorite sayings. And just one more thing she had come to hate.

"You're frowning, dear."

Yes. Yes, she was.

"You're terribly unattractive when you frown."

Taly didn't even bother to glare. Just stared up at the stupid chandelier.

Azura set down her teacup. "How have you been sleeping?"

She really hated that chandelier.

"Answer me."

Taly let her head loll to the side so she could better frown at the Queen. "Better," she said truthfully. She was finally learning how to control her Sight while she slept, and most nights, her dreams were clear of those blood-filled visions of the future she could only pray never came true.

Sometimes she saw Skye; sometimes she didn't; sometimes the visions were so sweet, she had a hard time dragging herself from sleep.

Like last night—she had dreamed of a dingy little room with cracked windows and a thin wooden door. It had been cold, the fire in the stove having already gone out, but the man sleeping beside her had still managed to kick the blankets away during the night.

Even though there had been dark circles beneath his eyes and new scars on his chest, he was still the most beautiful man she had ever seen. Dark hair that perpetually fell into his eyes, lips that were more art than flesh, and muscle that flexed and shifted with every breath.

She had spent most of the dream merely staring at him, watching as his chest rose and fell in sleep and wondering how, after all the lies she had told, there was still a future where she would get to spend her nights beside him.

"Oh dear," Azura said, pulling a face. She turned to Leto. "She's thinking about Skye again."

"Am not," Taly muttered. But the blush that heated her cheeks said something entirely different.

"If you say so." Azura gave her a knowing smile but let the subject drop. "Still, shadow mages aside, you seem a bit out of sorts today. Anything you'd like to talk about?"

Taly considered saying *no*, just brushing the woman off and trying to fake a good mood until she could retire for the evening. But she knew the Queen would see right through that. The woman was irritatingly perceptive when she wanted to be.

"I'm scared," she said, surprising even herself. "All the time, I just feel so afraid. I'm worried about Skye, and Ivain, and Sarina, and every day, I find myself wondering if they're still alive, if they're safe, what they're going to say when I get back. I don't know if you noticed, but I'm a different species now. And a time mage. I've gone over that conversation at least a thousand times in my head, and I still have no idea what I'm going to say. What I *could* say. How am I supposed to tell the people that love me that I've been lying to them my entire life? That everything I ever told them, everything I ever knew about myself was a *lie*, and that sometimes, I still wish that the lie was true.

"And then..." Taly let out a mirthless laugh. "Even if they do decide to give me another chance, if they decide they want to protect a time mage... they're going to have questions. Questions that I can't answer. Like where I come from, or who my family is—because these glowey highborn eyes mean that I've probably got family somewhere. Family that I can't remember and whose surname certainly isn't Caro. That's just a made-up name to go with that made-up human."

Taly growled at the tears that threatened to fall, viciously wiping her eyes. "And then on top of all of that, I feel like I can't think straight most days. I'm so tired, and my head feels so *full,* like if I try to cram one more fact into my brain, the entire house of cards is going to all come tumbling down. I should've been able to figure out this match by now, but I've just hit a wall, and I don't know how to find my way over. I would usually talk to Skye, and he would help me figure it out. But he's not here. He's not here, and I don't know if—"

Taly let out a strangled scream of frustration, scrubbing at her face with her hands. Here she was—whining and on the verge of tears, in front of the bloody High Lady of Time, no less… How much more pathetic could she be?

"You know what I think you need?" Azura said after a moment. She waited for Taly's red-rimmed eyes to find hers. "Some fun. It occurs to me that there has been an alarming shortage of fun during your stay here, but thankfully, that is something easily rectified."

The Queen chuckled, then clapped her hands as she pushed herself to stand. "Come along."

Taly rose to follow. "I'm almost afraid to ask what you consider *fun.*"

"Don't worry about that," Azura said with an airy wave.

Taly had learned by now that meant she should probably be worried.

"Just step out," Azura called from where she stood in the middle of the Water Maze. The stone paths had been pushed to the side, and Taly was still gaping after watching the Queen stroll across the surface of the water like it was solid ground.

"I don't trust you," Taly shouted back.

"That's a fair assessment," Leto said from beside her.

"No one asked you, Leto." Azura began pacing back to them. The water didn't even ripple. "All liquids are made of particles," she said. "Each one with its own individual timeline. There are two ways to execute this spell. You can grab a cluster of particles, gripping their timelines like you would a rope, or you can manage each timeline individually. I shouldn't have to say which one is easier."

Taly peered into the water, plucking at the Weave with her aether. If she squinted, she could see faint threads crisscrossing the water, each one an individual strand of time.

"All you need to do is freeze time beneath your feet," Azura said, and then gave a little hop to emphasize her point. "The particles will remain stationary. Like ice, but more slippery."

Taly said, "You're not going to let me go until I do this, are you?"

Azura shook her head, smiling. "No."

"Okay then." Taly rolled her shoulders, reaching out with her aether and grabbing the threads she could see flickering across the surface of the water. Like a rope, the Queen had said, and that's what Taly imagined as she gripped it. Once she felt the spell catch, she took a step—

And the water held.

Taly began to laugh as she took another step, then another, groping for Azura's hand because it was, indeed, slippery.

"Holy shit!" Taly crowed as she watched a long silver fish drift beneath her feet. "I'm walking on water."

"You're still using too much aether," Azura said, smiling as she grabbed Taly's other arm, keeping her upright.

Taly's lips twitched at the corners. "Don't ruin this."

Azura looked unapologetic, but still she shrugged. "Sorry, dear."

And so, lurching like a toddler that had just found its legs, Taly allowed herself to be led farther out on the water, laughing for what felt like the first time in months.

The next morning, Taly dragged herself up the stairs to the arena, feeling just a little bit lighter than she had the day before. She had barely stepped foot inside the training yard when an arrow whizzed by, almost clipping her ear.

"What the hell!" Taly yelped as she rolled out of the way, barely dodging a second arrow that caught in the gray stone wall behind her, embedding itself down to the fletching.

The Queen was already nocking another arrow. "Shield yourself."

The bowstring snapped. The arrow flew. Taly dodged again, letting out a colorful string of curses when the point caught the side of her bicep.

"Oh, don't be so dramatic," the Queen called. "You'll heal."

Blood soaked the sleeve of her tunic, but when Taly checked the wound, the bleeding had already stopped.

Fey healing. She would've died several times over by now without it. Though something told her the Queen wouldn't be shooting arrows at her right now if she was perhaps a bit more fragile.

Gritting her teeth against the pain, Taly sprinted for cover. "What is this exercise supposed to accomplish?" she shouted, pressing her back against the smooth bark of the silverleaf oak in the center of the ring.

"Your magic lacks precision."

Taly had barely managed to take a breath before the tree at her back dissolved, collapsing in on itself in a sigh of dust. Tiny pinpricks of gold aether prickled in the air where the tree used to stand.

"How the—"

"Everything returns to dust in the end." Azura pulled back the string of her bow, taking aim. "I was just helping it along. Learn how to control your aether, and I might consider teaching you that spell—even if it is far beyond your current ability."

Azura let another arrow fly, and Taly barely managed to throw up a wall of frozen time, stopping it mid-flight.

"Effective, but crude," the Queen said. "Big spells mean more aether. You don't need to canvas an area to block a single attack."

Azura's magic flashed, and Taly felt her spell shatter. The arrow hurtled through the air, propelled along its original path but faster this time. Too fast for her eyes to track. She shoulder-rolled forward, barely managing to duck out of the way as it sailed overhead.

Another arrow, shot with lethal accuracy. Then another. Arrow after arrow until Taly was panting despite those new immortal reflexes that made every movement so effortless and easy. She dodged each one, occasionally managing to throw up a wall, but mostly relying on those fighting instincts Ivain had drilled into her as a child.

"Use magic!" the Queen barked.

Taly twisted as another arrow whizzed past, went to take a step and—

She screamed as an arrow embedded in her thigh. And then again when she gripped the shaft and pulled. If she didn't remove it now, every step would just aggravate the wound—keep it from healing.

Blood stained her trousers, almost invisible against the dark-blue fabric. The wound itched as it began to clot. The arrow wasn't poisoned, so she wouldn't have a scar. But Shards did it *hurt*. And she was losing aether with every drop of blood spilled.

She'd somehow managed to stay on her feet, but when she went to take a step, she let out an enraged scream.

Her legs had been frozen in place.

"What is this?" she snarled, something inside her coming dangerously close to snapping.

"Time mages don't get hit," was all Azura said before loosing another arrow. Taly threw up a wall, but it still managed to punch right through, grazing her cheek.

"Stop thinking about the individual spells. They're a crutch—a useful tool, but not a necessary one. Simply imagine what you want your magic to do, and then *make – it – obey*."

The arrows continued to fly, and Taly fumbled, legs still frozen in place, wincing at each new cut and scrape.

"This is insane!" she cried, desperately reaching for her aether.

"You were the one that said you'd hit a wall," Azura said. "All I'm asking you to do is to stop trying to go over it and just break through. Walls were made to be broken, my dear."

"That's actually the exact opposite of what walls are intended to do!"

An arrow grazed the side of her neck, quickly clotting, but not before a new spurt of blood soaked her collar.

More aether lost.

And she felt it. She was so tired. Tired and sore, and all she wanted was that human girl back. She wanted to go back to a time when she'd known exactly who she was and what her life was supposed to look like.

She probably would've started working in a shop when Skye was called back to the mainland for good. And maybe she would've married—a nice mortal man that wouldn't have minded that she had been given an education far above her station.

She would've visited the manor every week and let Sarina and Ivain fuss. She would've grown old, and eventually, she would've died.

She swore as another arrow grazed her brow, and the next was already on its way.

Getting closer.

Little more than a blur, a scream on the wind.

This wasn't supposed to be her life! Not this surreal parody with time magic and Queens and undead armies. She wanted that human life, transient as it was. She wanted the simplicity. She wanted Ivain and Sarina. She wanted Skye. She wanted...

She wanted...

Home.

She just wanted to go home.

The last part of her that had still been clinging to her old life, her old identity—the last part of her that may have actually been human—died as she finally reached inside, farther than she had ever dared to venture, and let out a guttural, fey *roar.*

Her magic balked, but Taly seized it, giving it a vicious shake when she felt it try to rebel. It was hers. This power belonged to her. Not the other way around.

The spell exploded out of her in a rush.

And the pain, the next nick or cut or scratch... never came.

Taly cracked open an eye. She let her upraised arms drop to her sides, taking a shaky step forward and only vaguely realizing that the Queen had released the spell holding her in place. Frowning in confusion, she circled the arrow that had stopped only a few feet away.

There was no wall of suspended time. Not even a localized shield. Her magic had covered the arrow like a veil, shimmering slightly in the early morning light.

She gave the spell a nudge, watching as the arrow reversed along its path, slow but… controlled. The pull on her aether was minimal.

"*Finally*—she learns." Azura handed her bow to Leto, who floated nearby. "See, I told you, Leto. She just needed the right motivation. Maybe now she won't be complaining about aether burnout at the end of every day."

Leto, to her credit, shook her head, looking to Taly and giving an apologetic shrug.

"Az," Taly said. She swayed slightly, probably from blood loss. "I really hate your teaching methods."

"You're not the first to say that." Azura was already signaling to the fairies that were lining up around the perimeter of the yard. "Now then, as they say—let the games begin. And this time," she added, patting Taly on the head as she passed by, aiming for her sitting area, "try not to let your feet flip over your head when the fairies tag you out. It's terribly unbecoming."

Taly frowned, pressing a finger to the tip of the arrow and rotating it slightly. She released the spell, and the arrow blinked out of existence, already halfway across the yard and heading straight for the Queen's back.

The arrow abruptly disintegrated in a puff of dust.

"Just for that," Azura said over her shoulder, "I'm adding five more fairies."

Taly snorted. And then laughed. A real laugh that had her smiling as she drawled, "Make it ten."

CHAPTER 22

-A letter from Lord Kato Emrys to his mother, Adriana Emrys, Duchess of Ghislain

Dearest mother,

Line dancing is a time-honored human tradition requiring coordination, grace, and complex motor skills, which is perhaps why we got three new contracts as a result of my "adolescent prank." Not in spite of, though I'm sure that's what Grandfather has already managed to convince himself to believe.

Also, do not ever mention Sarah's name to me again. Do not apologize. Do not give me false sympathy. I see you for what you are, so please kindly go fuck yourself.

With none of my love,

Kato

"Hello?"

Kato peered inside the darkened workroom. He could still feel Eula's eyes on him from where she stood just outside the front door to the townhouse, and he didn't dare look back. She had dragged him halfway across town that morning, insisting that he needed to go find his brother.

He's grieving, she had said, and since he and Skye happened to share a little bit of blood, that apparently made the passing of his brother's mate his problem as well.

That's what Eula had told him, at least. And since he had a feeling that she was likely behind the sudden change in his work schedule—he hadn't been asked to repair a single toilet since that day at the wall—he felt inclined to believe her.

It also helped that she had made her closing arguments that morning wearing nothing but a smile. The woman was direct, so it was unsurprising that she had invited him into her bed for the first time by pulling him into an empty room and ordering him to take off his pants.

He'd resisted the urge to tell her that she was abusing her power, feeling that, in that particular moment, it wouldn't have been in his best interest.

"Anyone here?" Kato stepped further inside the room, turning in a circle as he took in his surroundings.

The walls of the workroom were made of corroded metal, the ceiling sloped, ending in long rows of windows that spanned all four sides. There were worktables arranged in even intervals throughout the space, each one crammed with crystals and quills and other crafting supplies. An array of weapons, all expertly crafted and gleaming in the dim light, lined the opposite side of the room.

"Skye, I know you're here." Kato grinned, channeling the barest trace of aether. "I can hear you breathing. What's the matter? Shade got your tongue? They do that, you know. They'll take your tongue, your arm, your leg… anything really."

"I'm not in the mood, Kato." The words were rough. Raw. And coming from the far corner of the room from behind a tall, wooden partition.

"Someone sounds surly," Kato drawled, forcing a laugh and ignoring that strange pang in his stomach that most certainly wasn't concern or worry or any other equally useless emotion.

Kato's footsteps echoed as he made his way across the room, eyeing the suit of Mechanica armor that dangled from a mass of chains attached high overhead. At their core, these suits could give the strength and agility of a shadow mage to even a mortal man—there were prototypes that could even fly. This one was an older model, bulkier than anything he had seen in recent decades, with sharp lines of silver paint streaked across a faded coat of red enamel. The helmet was missing, and tangled knots of wiring gushed from the breastplate like innards.

"I was told the armor would be ready for pick-up," Kato said, "but it looks like I was told wrong."

"It's a work in progress," Skye grumbled as Kato poked his head around the corner. He was hunched over a workbench, mumbling to himself as he rifled through what looked like maps. Some were newer, with hand-drawn trails that cut through densely forested areas, and others must have been ancient—showing nothing but city overlaid with a neat grid-like pattern that was unlike anything Kato had ever known to exist on the island.

"*Hello*," Kato drawled. When Skye didn't respond, not even bothering to look up, he decided to poke a little harder.

"Why *hello!*" he said a little too brightly. "How are you, my *beloved* older brother? You are so wise and so handsome—I'm honored that you would see fit to visit *me,* your lowly younger brother, who is below you in both intelligence and charm."

He watched for a reaction—but Skye ignored him.

"Well, I'm just fine," Kato went on. "Thank you for asking. It humbles me that you can finally acknowledge my superiority in all things. Maybe there's hope for you yet."

When that still didn't get a reaction, Kato waved a hand in front of his brother's face. "Hey, you in there?"

Skye started, looking up at him. His clothes were wrinkled, his hair uncombed. If possible, he looked even worse than he had at the wall.

"You look like shit," Kato said bluntly.

Skye gave a disinterested snort, turning back to his maps. "Who asked you?"

"No one," Kato said with an affable shrug. "I've just always enjoyed giving my unsolicited opinion."

When Skye didn't answer, Kato peered over his brother's shoulder, curious to see what had captured his attention. In addition to the spread of notes and maps that covered the tabletop in haphazard piles, there was a vial of blood placed off to the side and a small pink quartz necklace resting in a blue ceramic dish. The way the silver chain had been so carefully coiled seemed almost reverent.

But that wasn't what caught his eye, even if he instinctively knew who that necklace might have belonged to. No, he was more interested in the stack of books that had been carefully hidden behind a set of empty glass vials—some bookmarked, others dogeared, and still more with notes stuffed between the pages. Though many of the subjects weren't immediately familiar, the few texts he did recognize made his stomach churn.

"Why are you researching bloodcraft?" he asked, reaching for an advanced text on aether contamination. He knew for a fact that several of the spells contained in this volume had been added to the list of forbidden rites almost a century ago when the process for turning humans into Feseraa had finally been regulated by the Genesis Council.

Skye snatched the book away, stuffing it between two unmarked lab journals. "It's unimportant."

Kato gave him an incredulous look. "Oh, this most definitely *is* important. You might be able to sell that argument to some lowborn fool, but I know exactly what *these* are."

And judging from the fact that Skye seemed to have chosen the darkest, most tucked-away corner of the townhouse he could find, Kato had a feeling Lord Castaro probably didn't know his ward was now in possession of forbidden magic.

Kato shifted uncomfortably. "I don't think I need to tell you just how dangerous some of these books can be. Or what Lord Castaro would do if he caught you with them."

He paused, letting the implication of his words hover in the air.

"Then don't," was all Skye offered in reply.

"I could also mention that you're breaking at least twelve laws just by having these in your possession."

Silence.

Kato sighed in frustration. This was worse than he'd expected, and he could only wonder if Eula had known just how far Skye was capable of falling when she insisted that he come by.

His eyes slid over a separate stack of papers and diagrams. "Is there a reason you're also studying human first aid?"

Again, no answer as Skye scrawled something in the margin of the map in front of him.

"I feel like I'm just talking to myself now." Kato reached for the necklace sitting off to the side, frowning when Skye immediately slapped his hand away. *Well then…* If his idiot brother was going to play this game, then he knew at least one way to get a rise of out him.

"You're going after her, aren't you? You're going to find your *mate*."

A pause.

Skye finally looked up. "Taly's not my mate," he said stiffly.

Kato huffed out a laugh. "I take it that's not by choice. She reject you, little brother?"

Skye ignored the barb, his expression giving away nothing. Save for concern. And grief. Even if they hadn't been lovers, Taly had still been dear in a way that many fey sought to avoid. Humans were so transient—their lives, even their loyalties. Loving one was always a risk.

"The armor's not ready," Skye said, going back to the mess of papers spread across the workshop table.

"Oh, I can see that," Kato drawled, glancing at the Mechanica suit still strung up on chains. "But I'm under orders to retrieve it, and some of us actually follow rules."

"Come back later tonight."

"Will it be ready then?" Kato watched as Skye produced a map of the palace. "Because I kind of have a feeling it won't be."

Skye made a sound that was somewhere between a grunt and a huff before lapsing back into silence.

"Didn't the Marquess give you a direct order? You were supposed to be working on the armor, Skye. Not... whatever the hell all *this* is."

Kato dragged a hand through his hair. The healing books were obvious. One nick in just the right place could kill a human in under a minute, and if Taly was still alive after so many days on her own, she was likely injured. Badly.

As for the bloodcraft... Kato sighed. He wasn't sure why Skye would need forbidden magic to rescue a human, but that was exactly the kind of stupid he would expect from a highborn grieving the loss of a mate. The fey were territorial by nature, and that instinct, that need to protect those things they held dear, could be overwhelming even at the best of times.

And this was most certainly not the best of times. The farthest thing from it, in fact. His brother had just had the thing he loved most ripped away, taken to a place beyond his ability to protect and defend, and Kato knew from experience that wasn't a wound that would heal easily. If it ever healed at all.

Over a century and he was still waiting to find out.

"Hey." Kato placed a hand on Skye's shoulder, backing up a step when he immediately flinched away. "Look, I know we're not what you might call close, but I heard that the earth mage found Taly's horse, and... well, I know that can't be easy. I'm here if you need to talk about it."

"No thanks."

"Are you sure?"

Skye rounded on him, coming toe-to-toe as his aether flared around him. "We might be stuck in this village together," he said, each word tight and clipped, "but don't think for one moment that means you get to come in here and start acting like the concerned big brother. You're no friend of mine—just some bastard I happen to share a little bit of blood with. Even if you've managed to convince Ivain that you're not as much of a prick as you come off as you're still the absolute last person I would ever want to talk to about anything."

Ouch. Granted, there was no love lost between them, but that one stung—just a little bit.

Although, he was glad to hear that his efforts to impress the Marquess hadn't gone unnoticed. He'd take that as a win.

When Skye once again turned away, his hands shaking as he began sketching out what looked like coordinates, Kato backed up another step, glancing around the corner at the suit of armor on the lift. There were two identical suits slumped on the floor, both in similar states of disrepair.

Another glance at Skye confirmed that his brother had already dismissed him.

Kato shifted his weight, glancing at the door. *Damn it all...* Skye was getting ready to do something stupid. He could sense it, even if the little shit wasn't willing to talk to him. A year ago he would've already been out the door, throwing his hands up and telling himself he had done all he could, but he had come to this island for a reason. And if he let his brother go off and get himself killed, if *she* ever found out...

Sarah...

Damn, damn, damn.

Coming to a decision, Kato grabbed a toolbelt from beneath the table, found a ladder, and set to work. If he was going to have to babysit his younger brother, he might as well make himself useful.

Only a few minutes had passed before Skye rounded the corner, drawn by the sound of clanking metal. "What are you doing?"

"What does it look like I'm doing?" Standing at the top of the ladder, Kato adjusted the overhead light. "Our family guards the secrets of this armor like a firedrake defending its nest—which means we're the only two people in this village that know how to fix these rust buckets. The guards on the wall are already scheduled to train with these suits first thing tomorrow morning, and since you've decided that your time is better spent pining after a woman who may or may not be dead, that leaves me on repair duty.

"Which," Kato added, digging in his toolbelt, "I don't really mind. This is far more interesting than a toilet."

Skye leaned against a nearby table, crossing his arms as he continued to watch. Several more minutes passed before he remarked, "You actually enjoy crafting."

It wasn't a question, but Kato still answered with a, "Yes," as he began stripping out the faulty wiring. "I've always liked building things—ever since I was small. Even if our family hadn't built their empire creating mechanized armies for hire, I think I still would've chosen crafting as my specialization."

Finding the crystal socket inside the breastplate, Kato pushed aether into the circuit, frowning when something began to grind.

"Why do you ask?" He looked to his brother, standing down below. "Don't tell me you're considering choosing something besides crafting. Grandfather will be crushed. He's been bragging about your metal sculpting skills for nigh on a decade."

"Does it matter what I want?" Skye asked a bit glumly. "I was told I was going to be a crafter the same way I was told I would be a duke. My decisions were made for me before I was born."

"A spoiled answer if I ever heard one," Kato mumbled, snapping a new aethostat into place.

Skye frowned. "What is that supposed to mean?"

"You think you have it bad?" Kato huffed out a laugh as he stuck his head inside the open breastplate, trying to get a look at the three shadow crystals set into the frame, each as big as his palm.

He pulled back, his eyes finding Skye's. "What have you ever had to give up?" he asked. "Mother calls you away from your perfect little life and your perfect little family two times a year and makes you go play the role of the dutiful son at court for a few months, but that's nothing compared to what she could do. What she *will* do if you don't fall into line when she finally calls you home. We're members of the most powerful family in all the known worlds, Skylen. We're afforded every luxury, granted access to the best of everything our society has to offer—but it all comes at a cost, one that you haven't yet been asked to pay.

"Your decisions were already made for you?" Kato rolled his eyes. "Well, boo fucking hoo. Welcome to the family, baby brother—where we all follow orders… or else."

Skye's jaw tightened. "I know what's expected of me."

Kato laughed at that. "Bullshit. If you did, you wouldn't have been trying to court a human."

"I've already told you, Taly's not my mate."

"For your sake *and* hers, I hope that's true." Slamming the breastplate closed, Kato gave a satisfied nod when a row of red and blue crystals began to flicker. "Relationships between humans and fey never end well. Especially among the nobility."

"And you would know that how?"

Kato's brows rose. "You seriously don't know the story?" He thought everybody knew.

"I know there used to be a rumor about you and a human woman named Sarah." Skye gave a half-hearted shrug. "That's about it, though. You've never told me any details, and I don't like listening to family gossip. It's all exaggeration and half-truths, and as little as I actually know about you, I doubt you'd ever try to force yourself on a woman—human or otherwise."

Kato grimaced. So that was where the rumor mill had landed. A hundred years ago, he might've cared enough to try to defend his honor, but now… well, he wasn't the heir. Not anymore. And if he continued to play the part of the snubbed elder sibling, nobody gave him a second look. He could have even taken a human lover—so long as he was discreet.

That part stung a little more than he was willing to admit.

Kato glanced at his brother still leaning against the table, thoughtfully running a hand over the heavy layer of stubble on his chin.

He didn't have anything against the kid—nothing personal, at least. It was more what he represented. Skye had been born. That was it. And as a result, everything that Kato had sacrificed had instantly become meaningless.

The decision he had made so many years ago to try and protect the woman he loved had immediately been forgotten. He had been stripped of his title, his duties—he had even been forced to move out of the main estate, as though his half-human heritage might somehow taint his new pureblooded brother.

The same brother that now, despite the different paths their lives had taken, was getting ready to make the same mistake he had made so many years ago.

"I met Sarah shortly after my 65th birthday," Kato said, tinkering with one of the gauntlets. Anything to keep his hands busy. "She was human, and she tried to sell me a rose one afternoon when I was visiting the Lyric flower market. At the time, I was young and stupid, and all I cared about was impressing the woman I was with—so, naturally, when a mortal approached me with some piss-poor excuse for a flower, I did the most prickish thing I could think of and crushed it beneath my boot."

Kato smiled at the memory. "Sarah insisted I pay for the rose—and pulled a dagger on me when I refused. I was so focused on trying not to draw blood in front of my lady friend that she managed to get me right in the gut. The lady—I honestly can't remember her name—screamed and disappeared into the crowd, and Sarah began to laugh and laugh and Shards, I thought she was insane. Here was this human girl—a hundred pounds soaking wet—trying to take on a highborn shadow mage with nothing more than a rusty dagger and a basket full of roses. And even when I turned to her, snarling, teeth bared, all she did was shrug and hold out a hand, telling me that now I owed her *four* silvers for bleeding on her shoes."

The air cannon finally slid back into the gauntlet. Kato jumped from the ladder, landing with a heavy thud. "Needless to say, I was smitten from that moment on. She was beautiful, smart, with a wicked sense of humor. After a single afternoon, I asked her to go to bed with me, and I think I fell even more in love with her when she nearly laughed herself silly.

"So, I showed up the next day at her stand and bought her entire inventory of flowers, and when she still refused to talk to me, I came back the next day and did it again. Day after day, I kept buying her flowers, until one afternoon she stuck around long enough to help me hand them out to children in the street. I let her believe I was being nice, but the truth was, I just didn't know what the hell to do with all those flowers, and the kids were the only ones that didn't think I was trying to sell them something.

"After that, she let me start following her to the tavern where she worked at night, and I would sit at the bar until she came to kick me out at closing. It took me a week to make her smile. Another two to make her laugh. By the end of the month, she let me buy her a meal, and when a year had passed, I finally convinced her to move back to Ghislain where we courted in secret for another five years."

"Is that when you sent her away?" Kato started at the question, looking to his brother. Skye just shrugged. "The rumor is that Mother gave you a choice—the heirship or your mistress. Since she's not here now, I'm assuming you chose to send her away."

Kato let out a low, joyless laugh. "I was never given a choice. Not really. When my *'affair'* was discovered, I was dragged before the family elders. They told me that it was a disgrace that I would choose to debase myself with a human, and if I chose to keep her, I would be forfeiting my right to the heirship. They said that they wouldn't stop me from living my life the way I saw fit, but that they would no longer support me or my choices if I decided to stay with Sarah."

Skye crouched, helping Kato lift an unwieldy length of metal meant to protect the spine. "That doesn't sound so bad," he said.

"Maybe on the surface," Kato conceded. On the surface, it sounded like freedom. "But think about it, Skye. The Genesis Council might be the highest ruling body in the Imperium, but our family isn't too far below their jurisdiction. If Mother and the rest of the elders decided they no longer wanted to support my *lifestyle*, as they so eloquently put it, where do you think that would've left Sarah and me?"

Kato paused for a moment, letting the realization sink in. "We would've been blacklisted. From restaurants, from stores, from inns and taverns, from entire cities. I wouldn't have been able to find work; we wouldn't have even been able to find a healer if Sarah got sick, much less if she ever got pregnant. The *choice* that Mother offered me wasn't a choice at all. It was a farce, little more than political theatre."

Skye's jaw had gone slack, but when Kato's eyes cut to his, he quickly shut his mouth, shaking his head. "I never knew."

"No. I suppose you wouldn't," Kato muttered, his grip on the wrench in his hand tightening until he felt the metal start to bend. This was a side of their family, of society in general, that his brother hadn't experienced yet, one the Castaros had shielded him from.

"Why are you telling me this?" Skye asked. Not suspicious, just… unsure.

"So you don't make the same mistake that I did," Kato said plainly. *And because Sarah would have my balls if I didn't,* he added silently. That little spitfire had always had a very black-and-white sense of justice, and Shards he'd loved her for it.

"I'm not going to try to talk you out of going to find Taly," Kato went on. "If you believe she's still out there, then I think you should go. But whatever you do, don't ever let our family find out about your feelings for her. Or what you're doing with those books. They'll use it against you—I guarantee it. And neither of you deserve that."

Kato threw the twisted bit of metal that used to be a wrench on a nearby table before grabbing an old cloth and wiping his hands.

It was a long moment before Skye finally said, “I’m going to find her.”

Kato snorted. “You don’t say.”

“Ivain doesn’t know I took the books on bloodcraft.”

“I know.”

“And he doesn’t know that I still plan to leave the city—even after he denied my request to go.”

Kato sighed, then said, “I figured.” He threw the cloth on top of the wrench. “Bloodcraft is dangerous. And illegal. You’re taking a huge risk.”

Skye turned, slowly, letting his eyes drift across the lights of the Mechanica armor as they flickered to life. “I’m not sure I see the danger.”

“Then you’re naïve.”

“Am I? What is bloodcraft other than learning how to master our own bodies? To use our ability to manipulate aether in order to alter our own biochemistry? Every shadow mage already uses bloodcraft to a certain extent. Every time we alter our perception, sharpen our senses, enhance our strength or speed. So what’s the difference between a basic aether augmentation spell and a spell that allows us to stop our heart or harden our skin or increase our cognitive efficiency?”

“Or bolster your strength?” Skye went quiet, and Kato had his answer. “You’ve already started experimenting on yourself, haven’t you? That’s how you were able to lift that cannon. It’s how you’ve kept yourself awake to do all of this in so short a period...”

Shit. *Shit*. This was worse than he thought.

"Look…" Kato pinched the bridge of his nose. How had they gotten here? "Bloodcrafters can alter their body chemistry—yes. Hell, they can even alter the body chemistry of anyone stupid or unlucky enough to ingest their blood. They can enact spells that can last for centuries given the right anchor; they can create undead minions; they can even invade the minds of their victims—but it's still a risk. Even if you were able to achieve a complete mastery of your aether and your blood—what happens if you mess up? The margin for error is microscopic when it comes to that sort of magic, and what happens if you stop your heart or your breathing or your brain and then can't start it back up?"

Skye's face paled. "If I can find Taly, it's worth it."

"Find Taly, find Taly, it's all about Taly. How do you even plan to find her?" Kato leveled him with a look. "Do you have a plan, or are you just grasping at straws?"

Skye's eyes cut to the door. "I figured out how to use a blood simulacrum. It's more accurate than an earth mage's locator spell, and it will work even if she's been turned into a shade. I've also been able to glean a few memories from the blood samples I lifted from her necklace. They're patchy, but… she was alive when she went through the palace gates. And if she's—" Skye stopped, seeming to think better of what he was about to say.

"If she's what?" Kato prompted, already knowing the answer. *Dead.*

But Skye shook his head. "Nothing. Just… she's alive. Taly's alive, and I'm going to find her. I won't leave her out there to die."

"If you leave the protection of the city walls," Kato said, not bothering to mince words, "you'll probably die."

"It's a risk I'm willing to take," Skye said just a little too quietly. His fists clenched at his side. "Do we have a problem?"

"No." Kato smiled, not in the mood to start a brawl. "I just figured if I didn't at least try to convince you to stay, Mother would kill me too. Likely throw my body into a grave alongside yours, and believe me, I don't plan to spend eternity next to you."

Skye's lips twitched, and he almost smiled.

"She'd probably also kill me," Kato went on, "if I didn't at least try to offer you some help. Lord Kalahad Brenin—I met him when we were camped in Della, and I've spoken with him a few more times since we've been back in Ryme. He seems honorable, despite his reputation, and he might have some resources at his disposal. Give me a day to talk to him, and I might be able to get you a contingent of men to guard your ass while you go rescue your damsel."

Skye gave Kato a long look, considering the offer, turning it over in his head. After a moment, he merely snorted and said, "Taly would kill you if she ever heard you call her a damsel."

"Oh, I don't doubt it." From the few days he'd known her, Kato had quickly learned that the little human was a hellion. "And if you manage to bring her back, I might even let her. After the way I confronted her, I think she's allowed to give me a good kick in the balls."

Setting himself down at a nearby table, Kato reached for a discarded helmet, frowning at the large dent that caved in one side. "In return," he said, sensing Skye come up behind him. "I want you to get out of this damned workshop. Take a shower, shave, comb your hair, maybe grab that earth mage I always see moping around here and go get a drink. You look so pitiful right now, I can't help but be nice to you, and that's not something I'm comfortable with. I'll fix the armor, even give you credit when the Marquess inevitably asks, if you just leave and don't come back."

"Why are you doing this?" Skye asked, a slight frown creasing his brow. "I mean really doing this?"

"Do I need a reason?"

A nod. "Most definitely. You're the biggest asshole I've ever met."

Kato laughed at that. He couldn't deny it. "I don't know," he said, shrugging. "Maybe I just know what it's like to send the woman you love away to die."

The words surprised even him, and he hunched, pretending he couldn't feel the pitying look boring into the back of his neck.

"You've changed," Skye murmured, and Kato paused, glancing over his shoulder. "Thank you. For this and... for not saying that she's dead."

"I hope you find her," Kato said and meant it. He pushed himself to his feet, grabbing the helmet and moving back to the armored suit still on the lift. "And if you want my help, then do what I say. Go out on the town, get a drink... enjoy yourself before you inevitably get yourself killed chasing after this woman that's definitely not your mate."

Skye turned to go, but Kato called after him, "And if you do manage to bring her back, don't be surprised when I take a pass at her. I have a weakness for beautiful women that know how to handle a dagger, and Taly did manage to stab me the first time we met. Given my history, that means I'm obligated to fall in love with her now."

Skye's answering growl had him laughing so hard he almost fell off the ladder.

CHAPTER 23

-From the personal notes of Ivain Castaro, Marquess of Tempris

Breena was married today.

Due to my position in the family, I was, of course, invited. However, since she hasn't spoken to me since the incident—ignored all my letters trying to explain my reasons for doing what I did—I thought it would be kinder to not attend. Breena always dreamed of her wedding day, and I did not want to spoil it with old grudges.

Sarina tells me that the ceremony was lovely, the bride more than radiant, and that the gift I sent was well received. I recognize Atlas' hand in this, but it still gives me hope that perhaps reconciliation may not be as impossible as it once seemed.

It was late afternoon, and Taly was sitting in the dappled shade of the great silverleaf oak that marked the center of the training arena. Her legs were crossed, her eyes closed. Bruises painted every inch of visible skin, and one of her wrists was broken, the bone already set but still mending. The pain, though excruciating, was a given at this point.

She'd taken a beating today. Worse than usual. And while she normally would've been sitting in the infirmary, guzzling faeflower and cursing Azura's name, time was of the essence. If she was going to try this, it had to be now. Before the explosions began and the world reset. Before the memory of what had transpired that day got erased.

Nothing can escape the influence of time; therefore, everything has memory.

She'd read that in a book last week, and it got her thinking. She would be making more progress with the fairies if she could watch replays of her matches. It was a common training technique. Skye used to spend hours watching and re-watching the playback from his sparring sessions with Ivain, trying to see where he went wrong, how he could improve. And while Azura hadn't been recording her matches, Taly had been toying with a new idea.

"Wake me up before the explosions begin," she called to the fairies that were likely nearby. She couldn't see any peeking out of the stone arches circling the arena, but they were there. They were always watching.

Leaning back against the smooth bark of the old oak, she closed her eyes, listening to the wind, the faint rustle of leaves. The Sight was a curious gift, and yes, she was still trying to condition herself to think of it as a gift rather than, at best, a nuisance. The past, the present, the future—they were all part of the Weave, all accessible to a time mage through dreams. And while one needed a tether to be able to focus the vision—to find the correct timeline, the correct person, the correct event—tethers could be anything. Pieces of hair, jewelry, well-loved books, even people.

Today, Taly wasn't using any of those things. Instead, she was using the ground itself. The training yard where she had spent all day getting her ass kicked by amorphous blobs of soul energy. Places could also retain memory, and if she managed to get this right, it would be better than any recording.

Taly evened out her breathing, feeling for the spark of her aether as she tied the final knot on the spell. Falling asleep with the intent to dream—she had never tried that before. Usually, she avoided her dreams. Skye was still finding new ways to die, to the point that the memory of him had become somewhat fragile in her mind. All her life, it had always been her death that everyone dreaded. She was mortal, and they were fey—the irony was not lost on her that so much of her mental energy was now consumed by the question *"is that stupid, indestructible bastard still alive?"*.

Deeper and deeper.

She cleared her thoughts.

Deeper and deeper.

The spell settled over her like a familiar weight.

Though she couldn't pinpoint the exact moment she drifted off, the next time she became *aware*, the light was softer, the air cooler. The sun had moved to the opposite horizon.

It was morning.

This past morning, to be precise. That was her standing beneath the gray stone arch, warming up and stretching and already dreading the day ahead.

Slowly, Taly stood, sighing at the blissful lack of pain. The edges of the dream were hazy, the vision seeming to curve around the area like a thin film of ice cracking under pressure. Since she was using the training arena as her tether, she couldn't see beyond it. There was just a cloud of rapidly fracturing light where the palace should've been.

A figure materialized through the haze, coming closer.

"Alright," Azura said as she strode into the arena, aiming for her usual place beneath the widest arch. She was dressed in red chiffon, and her chair was blue velvet as opposed to the wine-colored silk of yesterday. The fairies set up and tore down the Queen's viewing area every morning and night, making it more and more elaborate each time. One of these days, Taly was going to shatter that stupid chandelier that clinked, clinked, *clinked* all day long. The tinkle of its crystals had become the soundtrack to her humiliation.

"Not that it will do any good," Azura added as she took a seat, "but try not to disappoint me today. At this point, I'm as eager to get rid of you as you are of me."

That was usually how Azura started the day. With a call to arms that was anything but inspirational.

Taly looked to the memory of herself, watching as she grabbed her staff. Both women shared a sigh of resignation.

The first game began with very little fanfare, and Taly took a seat beside the Queen. There were 20 fairies, and she watched as her doppelganger tagged out fifteen before she got hit at the base of her spine, then both shins, then her neck.

She unconsciously rubbed the fading bruises.

The second game, she got to seventeen fairies.

The third, eighteen.

The fourth, eighteen again.

The fifth, twenty-two. The Queen had added five more.

Game after game, Taly watched herself cast and spin, dodge and roll. Her movements always came a fraction of a second too quick to be purely reactionary. She was using her Sight to predict the fairies' actions, countering before they had even made the decision to move. From this vantage point, it was hard not to feel just a little bit of awe, especially when that woman sprinted for the oak and jumped, planting a foot firmly on the bark before flipping and landing back on her feet.

She moved faster than a human, like she had born into that body. Like she had spent her entire life learning its balance and rhythms.

Taly didn't remember feeling like that at the time.

The three fairies that had been giving chase scattered in different directions, only to stop as the spell snapped shut around them.

That's nineteen, Taly thought. The other fairies hung suspended across the arena, dots of blue light that seemed to shiver their displeasure. There was just one more in play, and even though she knew how this was going to end, her heart began to beat just a little bit faster when that woman spun, already weaving a spell as she dodged the ball of blue energy that continued to lunge for her like an eagle without wings.

They got more aggressive when they were desperate.

Her second self swung her staff, using it more for balance as she executed a complex series of dodges. She used the tree to her advantage—the fairies weren't allowed to move *through* them—carefully navigating the sea of her suspended opponents and plucking at the strings of each spell.

A thread here, another there. It was easier to weave the spells together. Took less aether, and it allowed her to monitor a single enchantment rather than nineteen.

The spell executed, and the last fairy froze.

But as expected, more had already been added. The Queen always waited until the very last moment to add more fairies, though the wisps that entered the field…

From this vantage point, it almost seemed…

"They're moving too fast," she murmured. Like they were being propelled. *Sped up*.

And two of the fairies that had been frozen—they had somehow managed to force their way out of the spell holding them in place. She'd originally thought it was because of some weakness in the spell. That's what the Queen had made her believe. But if she stopped to think—now that she was outside the game and actually had time to *think*—stopping time was a basic spell, one she'd long ago mastered. There was no flaw in her casting, no chink for the fairies to exploit.

Which could only mean one thing.

Taly turned to stare at the Queen. Her eyes were slightly unfocused as she no doubt used her own magic to predict the outcome of the game.

And then alter it.

"You're cheating," she whispered. Sabotaging her spells, helping the fairies, and Shards knew what else. "You don't want me to win."

Even through the numbness of the dream, Taly felt her heart seize.

This was not a game she had ever been *meant* to win. It was just a farce, some impossible task to keep her reaching for some impossible goal.

Out in the arena, her other self slammed to her knees, the fairies converging on her in a flurry of shocks and blue sparks.

And Azura… smiled.

Confronting the Queen would get her nowhere. Taly had known the woman long enough to recognize that. Azura would just say something like, *"Leto, get the champagne. She finally discovered her real opponent."* Or: *"Do you really expect your enemy to fight fair?"*

Taly pushed herself to stand. "You're a…" She let out a frustrated scream, kicking a spray of pebbles onto Azura's skirts. It was petty and childish, but it also felt really good, so she did it again, sticking out her tongue for good measure.

Still grumbling a long stream of curses under her breath, she strode to the center of the arena, stepping over her dream self as she groaned in pain. It was the end of the day already, so she tugged at the spell holding the dream together.

The day began to rewind.

She was going to have to approach this differently. This wasn't just a straightforward game. One where she might eventually eke out a victory if she could just be faster and stronger than she had been the day before. It had been designed to be unbeatable, and while she couldn't cheat directly—Azura would see it coming—she might be able to find a weakness in the rules. Something she could exploit.

"I don't know why you're surprised," she muttered to herself, watching as the world whirled by in a blur of movement. In her frustration, she yanked on her aether, pulling that tether that would take her back to early morning. "This is Azura, after all. It's not like she's the patron saint of clear intentions."

The sky went dark.

"Shit." She'd gone too far.

Gripping the spell, she tried to pull it back, but time was still rewinding, day turning to night and back again. Even worse? The process was speeding up—days blinking by so quickly that the scene was now only flashes of black and white and red. A strobe light that signified the rapid passage of time.

Taly started getting nervous, images of that damn time loop returning to her. Except this time, there was no Queen to bail her out if she went too far.

It stopped. As abruptly as if she'd hit a wall.

Taly blinked. She was still in the training arena. There was the tree overhead, the red dirt underfoot, the cloud of splintered light where the palace should've been. She'd lost her grip on the tether, and that was a problem. A big one. She was dreaming, yes, but she'd entered this vision deliberately. A fall wouldn't pull her out of it like a natural dream. Without that tether, she had no way of waking herself up.

That was something she'd worry about later, though. Right now, she was more interested in the people that now stood around the base of the oak in groups of twos and threes. Some held staffs like hers, others held no weapons at all as they went through training exercises that were second nature to her now. Their hands glowed gold with magic, and in the center of them all stood—

"Azura."

Taly turned as two more figures walked into her field of vision. The man was tall and broadly built with sandy hair and eyes that glowed like molten blue metal. He was dressed in white robes of state with a crown upon his head. The gold swirled like the tentacles of a kraken, and a trident marked the apex.

Taly knew him instantly. Not because of any personal connection, but because she'd seen his image in books and newspapers. He was a very important man, but right now, that's not who she cared about. She only had eyes for the woman beside him, her face so familiar it caused her heart to clench.

Her mother.

Breena looked just as she had that night at the palace gates, in scaled black armor and coiled braids. The symbol for the Water Shard was stamped into her chest and emblazoned upon the sword at her side, and when she smiled, even though it was at the Queen—Taly was unprepared for the wave of emotion that slammed into her.

She had so few memories from before the fire, but that smile…

Taly remembered that smile.

“Atlas,” Azura greeted. She extended a hand to the man, as was the custom between Genesis Lords. Taly reluctantly forced her eyes away from her mother. For indeed, the man beside her was Atlas Venwraith of House Arendryl, the High Lord of Water.

And if he was on Tempris…

Shards, how far back did I go?

Arendryl used to be one of the most prosperous dominions in the Fey Imperium, but then one day, without explanation, they’d sold their lands and moved to the mortal realm, setting up a new nation.

The Shadow King had soon followed, bringing his entire household. Then the High Lady Cassi, the avatar for the Fire Shard.

And years later when Azura shut down the gates, when the remaining two Genesis Lords consolidated their power and formed the Dawn Court and the Sanctorum and began their centuries-long quest to eradicate time magic—the High Lords of Water, Shadow, and Fire vowed that they would not step a single foot back on fey lands until the bloodshed had ended.

It never did. And they never had. So if Atlas Venwraith was on Tempris, that meant that this was before the Schism. When Tempris had still been at the center of the Fey Imperium and the Council had still been in power.

It also meant that these people around her, the ones whose hands flashed with gold—they were time mages. The same ones that had disappeared along with their Queen. That the Sanctorum had spent over two centuries hunting.

Shards… maybe she had pulled on that spell just a little too hard.

"You're early," Azura said with a bland smile. By now, Taly knew her well enough to see the undercurrent of worry behind the expression. "First, you surprise me with a visit, and now you catch me completely unaware." She waved a hand at the dark leggings and loose silk shirt she wore. It was plainer than anything Taly had ever seen her wear, but still finely made. "Shame on you. Breena, isn't it your job to keep him in line?"

Breena bowed her head in deference, though there was a twinkle in her eye. "Name one Genesis Lord that's ever listened to the advice of their Crystal Guard?"

"I listen," Azura insisted. "Or I did. Once. For about five minutes. It was a terribly boring five minutes, so I decided not to do it again."

"Azura," Atlas said softly. His voice was mild and smooth, but still somehow carried the weight one would expect from a man of his station. "We need to speak privately."

Azura's eyes narrowed. "If that's the case, then I take it this talk must also be *urgent* since you came to interrupt me during a lesson as opposed to waiting for me in my tower—where there are fewer wandering eyes and attentive ears."

He nodded. "Auberin is also here."

"He heard of our visit," Breena added. "Nissa, of course, followed."

Auberin Brenin and Nissa Caeli—the High Lord and Lady of Earth and Air. They now reigned over the Dawn Court, though at this point in time, they were just members of the Council.

Azura closed her eyes and took a breath, as if she could will herself the patience to deal with whatever crisis this seemed to indicate. "I understand," she said. "Lady Graylin," she called over her shoulder.

A woman with sharp features and silver-white hair pulled away from where she had been instructing two other mages. "Majesty," she said. Taly jolted. She recognized that voice, even if she was used to hearing it from someone slightly more transparent. And blue.

"Take them inside." Azura glanced around the arena, and the other mages were already stopping their exercises and packing up. "Once they're settled, do a sweep. I'm sure Nissa already has ears in the palace."

The woman bowed. Her hair was loose, and it slipped across her shoulders, shining in the sun like frosted silver. "Of course, Majesty."

The arena began to clear, the mages talking in hushed whispers as they disappeared through the arches.

The Queen met the High Lord of Water's gaze, molten gold against molten blue. Taly wondered if that was some effect of the Shards, if bonding with a god was what made their eyes seem so strange and alien, even compared to the dream-like colors of the fey.

"Yes, I am aware that Nissa and Auberin are planning to move against me," Azura said when the arena had fully emptied. "That is what you were going to say, though for civility's sake you were going to stumble around the point for another few minutes in a way that I would've found wholly annoying. Yes, I know about the coup, and yes, I am aware they are already trying to paint me as unstable even though they heard that man's testimony the same as every other member of the Council. I will not be bullied, however. Auberin is not the first power-hungry High Lord I've had to put in his proper place, and I daresay not even the most cunning."

Atlas and Breena shared a look.

"We have no proof," Atlas said, "other than a madman's ravings."

"I checked the tomb myself," Breena added. "He sleeps. There is no evidence that he has awoken since—"

"I know." Azura closed her eyes, pinching the bridge of her nose. "I know, I know. But Aneirin is cunning, and Shards save us all if a human ever wandered near that tomb."

Taly's brows rose. Why did that name sound familiar? And why did the High Lord of Water and Azura both seem so… nervous?

"I'm not saying you should abandon your lands just yet, but be wary," Azura said, glancing at Atlas. "I know we've encountered false prophets before, but something about that man put me on edge. My dreams have been… unquiet ever since."

Breena visibly tensed. "Anything specific?"

"No," Azura said. "But…" The Queen's voice trailed off, and her head turned to the side as though she'd heard a sudden sound.

She looked straight at Taly, her brows nudging together in confusion.

"You're not supposed to be here yet," was all she said, and then Taly was falling as the world around her fractured.

As the dream was ripped apart.

Taly awoke with a gasp. Her heart was pounding, and her palms were sweaty. The pain of her injuries immediately rushed back in, and she welcomed it. Even welcomed the burn in her lungs as the last of her aether drained.

Azura had seen her.

How had Azura seen her?

That was the past. Just a memory. She couldn't have—

"Never eavesdrop on a Genesis Lord."

Taly looked up. Leto was drifting in front of her, nearly transparent in the late afternoon light. For a moment, she imagined that she could see a long straight nose, proud highborn eyes, and hollow cheeks beneath that smooth, featureless face—all framed by a shock of silver-white hair.

"They will know," she said in that calm, even way that had become so familiar to her now. She'd recognize it anywhere. Even inside a dream.

"Who is Aneirin?" Taly asked.

"No one of consequence."

Taly wondered if that was the first time Leto had ever lied to her. Something told her it wasn't.

"Come." Leto turned towards the palace. "What you just did was very dangerous. I have requested that Her Majesty speak to you about tethers during this evening's lecture. They are there to guide you into the dream and out, and you were allowing yours to fray. In the future, I do hope you dream more responsibly."

Taly was a little shaky as she pushed to her feet, and every step was agony as she made to follow. But still she smiled.

And decided not to tell the Lady Leto Graylin that she'd figured out what she was.

CHAPTER 24

-An excerpt from Shadow Mage Mixology

Shadow mages carry raw aether in their veins, a unique quirk in their physiology that allows them to augment their strength and speed, but can also make a night at the pub rather dull. Alcohol is metabolized and cleared almost immediately, which means that if inebriation is the goal, one must be fully dedicated to the task.

Arendryl's Rare Cask Crystal Brandywine is a good choice for the discerning palate. At 600 gold pieces per bottle, this honey-brown liquor is infused with hibiscus and water aether. The flavor has often been described as "warm and fuzzy, evoking the innocent joy of childhood... but with alcohol."

For those drinking on a budget, hydra choker is both cheap and effective. As the name suggests, this liquor does contain trace amounts of hydra venom, and it is usually reserved for the rowdiest of patrons, as it tends to put them to sleep almost instantly.

Skye slipped through the crush of people crowding the tavern, Aiden following close behind. It was busy that night, packed with highborn, lowborn, and mortal alike. Everyone was screaming and shouting, trying to be heard as they jostled inside the cramped space. The local taverns were the only businesses that hadn't taken a hit since the attacks began, and Skye could only wonder how they hadn't run out of liquor yet considering the rate some of the patrons around him were guzzling it down.

The earth mages probably had something to do with that. When they weren't healing, they were tending to the food supply, and keeping the people calm and happy was nearly as important as keeping them fed.

"Here." Skye jerked his head towards an empty booth in a dark corner of the bar. Shrugging out of his overcoat, he sat down, signaling to the barmaid who immediately brought over two mugs of ale, a couple of shot glasses, and a bottle of something that looked like whiskey.

Aiden slid in across the table, and Skye could feel that healer's gaze assessing him. He had taken his brother's advice and cleaned himself up—even going so far as to let Eliza cut his hair. The old cook had been hounding him for close to a month—telling him he looked like a vagrant—and she had been almost as delighted at the prospect of attacking him with a pair of shears as she had been when he managed to choke down a plate of food.

"I'm surprised you asked me out tonight," Aiden said, yelling to be heard over the other patrons.

Fishing inside his pocket, Skye pulled out a small slab of metal no larger than a playing card. It was plain, with a single air and shadow crystal set into the center. His thumb felt for the switch, and he tossed it on the table as a dome of air magic surrounded them and their booth.

The noise of the tavern immediately quieted.

"Better?" Skye asked, forcing a smile. At Aiden's answering nod, he poured two shots of the mystery liquor and shoved one across the table.

"As for why I invited you out..." Skye went on. "I guess I just needed some air."

And Kato had pushed him. But he decided to keep that to himself.

"I can understand that," Aiden said with a heavy sigh. Like the rest of the household, he had also chosen to wear black to honor Taly's *presumed* passing. The fine shirt, silk waistcoat, and slim-cut trousers were almost an exact match to the suit Skye had chosen for himself that evening—save for the color, of course. Though his suit was a dark enough blue it could've passed for black in the dim tavern light, his vest was a deep crimson red. When Sarina had seen him leave, she had pursed her lips in that way that told him she was displeased even as she remarked that it was good to see him "taking better care of himself."

"How is your sister adjusting?" Skye asked, finally taking a sip from his own glass. He winced at the taste. It was whiskey—or something like it.

Taking a breath, he downed the glass and then washed away the taste with a generous swig of ale.

Aiden knocked back his own glass, shuddering. Skye immediately refilled their glasses.

"Since when," Aiden said, eyeing the liquor like it might jump out of the glass and bite him, "do you have any interest in Aimee beyond where she is and how to make sure she stays as far away from you as possible?"

Skye snorted, clinking his glass to Aiden's as they both downed the contents. The liquor burned all the way down, and the taste was awful, but he could already feel its warmth spreading, forcing his shoulders to relax. "Believe me, that's still my goal. No offense, but your sister is intolerable." And fending off her advances was the absolute last thing he was equipped to handle right now.

"That's our stepfather's influence, I'm afraid." Aiden scowled into his glass. "Between you and me—I'll kill that bastard if I ever get the chance. Rip that rotten husk he calls a heart right out of his chest and feed it to him."

"I doubt anyone would mind. The few times I've met him, he seemed like a right prick."

They clinked glasses again and drank.

"At least, he mostly leaves our mother alone," Aiden said. "He thought it was beneath him to marry her—even if she was my father's widow. With a little luck, I'll find a place for her in the mortal cities once we figure out this mess with the shades, and so long as Aris hasn't managed to father a child by then, he'll be happy to see us go."

"You'd leave your sister behind?"

Aiden shrugged. "She's welcome to come with us—I've even encouraged her. But she won't sign over her claim to Picolo the same way that I did. She'd rather hold on to a bit of land and a house full of bad memories on the off chance that our father comes back to claim it one day."

Skye's brows rose. "Didn't the Crystal Guard confirm his death?"

"Yes," Aiden said. "But she still refuses to move on. Which I can understand, I suppose. She was so little, and we lost so many people all at once. Sometimes it feels like we're just waiting around for one of them to come back."

Aiden went quiet, staring into his glass. After a long moment, he said, "For what it's worth, I'm sorry. About Taly."

Just the mention of her name was enough to make Skye's heart lodge itself firmly in his throat.

Aiden shook his head, dragging a hand through his hair. "I tried to find her. I think… I think I almost did. I'm sorry I couldn't bring her back to you."

"There's nothing to be sorry for," Skye managed, though really he was thinking, *You never had a chance.* An earth mage's locator spell could only track a person so long as their feet remained rooted to the ground, and Taly wasn't on the island anymore. Not this version, at least.

He'd seen her almost every night since they'd sat together beside the ice pond, but only flashes. Like she was passing by too fast for him to catch up to. He was so tired and so tempted to sleep. He wanted to dream, to see her, but there was just too much to do and not enough time. The forbidden rites contained some of the most powerful shadow magic in the known worlds, and it was all far, *far* more complicated than anything he'd ever encountered. He'd had to break into the vault a second time just to find books to define the concepts.

But his hard work had paid off. So far, he'd found a way to track her, to heal her, to stabilize her in case she'd been turned into one of those *things*. He'd even found a way to make himself stronger to compensate for the lack of men and resources.

It still frightened him, this kind of magic. But there was always more to do, and it made those kinds of thoughts easy to ignore.

There was a commotion from somewhere across the bar, loud enough to break through the air ward, as a skinny lowborn boy climbed onto one of the tables. "To the woman that died so that we could live," he said in a loud, clear voice. He raised his glass, and Skye's stomach sank as every glass in the room rose in toast. "To the Savior of Ebondrift!"

Skye reached for his glass. "To Taly," he whispered and took a long drink. It had surprised him the first time he heard the name the villagers had given to the girl that risked her life to find the Vale relay. Hearing it now, knowing that they too thought she was dead...

Someone else climbed up onto the table, wrapping an arm around the boy as they began to teeter. "I was there when she fixed the tower gun," he began. "And I heard the message from Vale—"

Skye's grip on the edge of the table tightened, and Aiden glanced over at him when the wood began to groan in protest. He glanced from Skye to the two men standing on the table, still extolling the virtues of their "Savior," and back.

Aiden stood. "You know what I think we need?" he asked, grabbing the half-empty bottle. "More booze. *A lot* more booze."

He was on his feet before Skye could comment, and as he passed the table, he *"tripped,"* shoving the edge with his hip and sending the two drunken fools still wobbling on top flying off the side.

The only other toasts that night were to the floor—that benevolent lady that would always be there to catch you when you fall.

Aiden came back to the table with two more bottles, and when those were gone, two more. He went on and on, telling stories and jokes, and though Skye tried to laugh at those times when he thought it might be appropriate to laugh, the sound fell flat.

Eventually, Aiden ran out of distractions and looked content enough to sit back in the booth, nursing what was left of the bottle and watching as the patrons began to trickle out for the evening.

A young woman that Skye vaguely recognized from his time at court was still at the bar, sipping ale and leaning forward in a way that showed off the dangerously low cut of her dress. She had been trying to catch his attention for at least half an hour now, but he gave her yet another shake of his head, turning away and ignoring the mournful pout that pulled at her perfect features.

Aiden's eyes cut to the woman, then back to Skye. "Don't fall on your sword on my account," he said, resting his head on the back of the booth. "She's pretty. You should offer to take her home."

Skye gave him a tight smile. "I'm fine."

"Bullshit." Then, more gently: "You lost a friend."

"I've haven't lost anything," Skye insisted. "She's coming back."

"Skye—"

"*Don't* say it."

Aiden sighed, and they both lapsed back into silence. But the door had already been opened, and doubt began to creep back in.

What if Ivain and Sarina were right? What if he really was just out of his mind with grief? He kept trying to find meaning in his dreams—some sign that Taly was still alive. But what if the dreams, the tunnels, the beasts they'd found, the diaries, *her*... What if it was all just a series of coincidences? An illusion, a fantasy. His mind's way of trying to spare him from a kind of pain that he might not be able to find his way back from.

"Can I tell you something?" Skye asked. The buzz of alcohol was making his head swim, and the words were out before he'd even thought to ask the question.

"Sure," Aiden said, interest piqued.

Skye picked at a crack in the table. He probably shouldn't do this. He *knew* he shouldn't do this, but... he just needed to tell one person. A friend. Someone he could trust, who could tell him once and for all that he wasn't crazy.

He had almost told Kato earlier, but something had stopped him. Even if his brother's intentions had been noble, the trust between them was still too tenuous and new.

Aiden though... If there was anyone that could understand what he was about to do and why he had to do it, it would be Aiden.

Skye cleared his throat. "I-I've been having dreams."

Aiden arched a brow, sitting up slightly as he took in Skye's slightly hunched shoulders, the uncertainty in his eyes. "What kind of dreams?" he pressed.

And before he could think better of it, Skye began telling Aiden about the dreams. He told him about Taly, about the way she had warned him that the airtram station would be left unguarded. Everything—he told him about every dream, every detail he could recall. He even told him about the woman in the tunnels, and those damn blue lights, and the diaries he had found beneath the floor of her old room.

When he was done, Aiden simply stared at him, eyes wide. And that was fair. No cause for alarm. It was a lot to take in, after all.

"So..." Aiden finally said. He pushed his glass away, rubbing at the bridge of his nose like he could wipe away the haze of alcohol that still clouded his eyes. "Are you telling me you think your dreams are real?"

Skye nodded.

"And that Taly's real?"

Another nod.

"And you think that she... tells you to do things?"

When Skye gave another resigned nod, Aiden looked away, then back. His mouth open and shut, not unlike a fish.

"Grief... is a very strange thing, Skye." Every word was so careful—and slightly slurred. "And sometimes, it can play tricks, make us believe that—"

"She's real," Skye interjected. "I can feel it—in here." He placed a hand to his chest, and as if in response, that thread gave a tiny tug. It kept getting stronger, that tug. And that had to be a sign. Something to tell him that he was moving in the right direction.

"The only thing I can't figure out is how she's doing it," Skye went on, more to himself than the man across the table. "Maybe it has something to do with those spells my brother discovered or… something else."

"Spells?"

Skye slid down in the booth and let his head loll back over the back of the seat. *Damn it.* He shouldn't have said that. The dreams were one thing, but this… Ivain had decided that very few people needed to know about the spells and the lies he had told to conceal them. There were still too many unanswered questions, too many rumors of traitors lurking in the shadows.

But by the Shards, by the Magnus, by every supernatural deity that any member of any species had ever thought to entreat—the floodgates had been opened, and now the words seemed to spill out of him.

Skye began telling Aiden about the spells Kato had found inscribed on Taly's arm—a complex web of shadow magic concealed by a glamour so sophisticated, it was nearly imperceptible. His brother had taken it upon himself to interrogate her, forcing her to run, and although Skye had initially believed that she was being controlled by the individual responsible for the shades—that she might actually be the traitor, albeit unwillingly—he wasn't so sure about that now. She had found the relay, after all. She had sent out a warning message. But she hadn't come back.

"She tried to tell me something before she left," Skye said as his story began to wind down. Aiden still looked bewildered, but it was such a relief to get the words out, he barely noticed. "She tried to tell me why she left last year. I thought she was just nervous at the time, but now, I think she was scared of those spells, maybe of who put them there. I think she knew about them, and it terrified her."

Aiden had gone quiet, his eyes focused on some far-off sight. "Holy shit." The words were soft enough that Skye had to channel a bit more aether to untangle the sound of his voice from the low din of the tavern that still filtered through the air ward. "Aimee was right."

Skye sat up a little straighter. "About what?"

Aiden's eyes snapped to Skye's, wide and just a little frightened. "Nothing." He went to take another sip of ale, then thought better of it. "Absolutely nothing."

"Heartrate and breathing are both elevated," Skye murmured, tilting his head as he listened. He watched the healer tug at his ear. "Nervous tic." Aiden immediately dropped his hand, looking off to the side. "Won't make eye contact. You're lying," he concluded.

"It's nothing."

"Another lie."

Aiden tried to shove himself to his feet, but Skye grabbed the man by the arm and threw him back down.

"Tell me what you know," Skye demanded. He let his aether spark in warning, licking at his skin like violet flames. The fey were territorial by nature, and right now, this man knew something about the woman he loved. Something he wasn't saying.

That was a very dangerous line to toe.

Aiden held up his hands. "You need to calm down."

Skye gave him a calculated look. "If you won't talk, I suppose I could ask Aimee. Do you think she would tell me?" He smiled. "I think she would tell me."

That got Aiden's hackles raised. "Leave my sister out of this," he nearly growled.

"What. Do. You. Know."

Aiden hung his head, and Skye could still hear the frantic thump of the earth mage's heart pounding like a drum between them.

"I first noticed something was off when I was treating Taly for the harpy venom." The words came out in a rush, and Aiden's eyes darted about the room, then to the wall of air magic that still surrounded their booth. "It didn't make sense for a human to have that kind of reaction, and no matter what I did, she just kept getting worse. So… I did something I probably shouldn't have done." He swallowed hard. "I gave her faeflower."

The glass in Skye's hand began to crack, and he forced himself to let go, sliding it across the table.

"I know," Aiden said, taking in Skye's thunderous expression. "I already know what you're going to say. Faeflower is one of the most potent poisons known to mortals, and believe me, I agonized over that decision. I treated her with every mortal remedy I'd ever learned; I pored over every book on human health and anatomy I could find. But the symptoms, the progression of the disease—it was harpy venom poisoning. *Textbook* harpy venom poisoning—from the fever to the pain, the confusion... Everything, right down to the blue rash on the bottom of her tongue.

"She was *dying*, Skye. She was dying, and since I couldn't stand by and do nothing, I made the decision to give her the draught, figuring that, at worst, I would at least be able to ease the pain of her death."

Aiden ran a hand through his hair. "It only took an hour before she started to improve. So, I kept giving it to her, increasing the doses gradually, and she just kept getting better and better and... it wasn't long before she was back on her feet, going on like nothing had ever happened."

Skye forced himself to take a breath. Then another. "But that would mean..." He stopped. "No," he said with a shake of his head. "You must have made a mistake."

Aiden huffed out a joyless laugh. "Believe me, I was confused too. Because if it looks human, it *is* human—that's always been the rule." A pause. "But then Aimee—I think she made a connection. I think that Taly might not have been human after all. It would explain the magic."

"Magic?" Skye asked, a note of hysteria creeping into his voice. The world was crumbling right out from underneath him, and he couldn't find his footing. "Taly doesn't have magic. I've known her my entire life, and she's *never* had magic."

"Not your entire life," Aiden countered hesitantly. "As I recall, she was just some unknown child Ivain took in after the Sanctorum destroyed an entire village. She had no family, no past, no memories. Under those circumstances, I'd say it's very possible there might be things about this girl you never knew. Things *she* never knew."

Skye's heart may have actually stopped beating at that point. It was true. They had known very little about Taly when Ivain decided to take her in. The trauma of the fire had wiped away most of her memories—she'd barely been able to give them a name. Truthfully, they weren't even sure how old she was. Sarina had assumed she was closer to four years of age based on her size. Ivain had insisted she was too smart to be that young. The healers had finally told them she was probably closer to six.

The only thing they had known for sure was that she was human. She had human features, human traits. She had iron in her blood, and when she reached maturity, she had bled on a standard human cycle. It was unheard of for a fey female to bleed 12 times a year, but...

Skye's mind began to race, trying to assimilate this new set of facts. What had Kato said? He had found shadow magic, a water glamour?

And if he assumed she was fey, enough to give her an immunity to faeflower…

A simple memory alteration spell could account for the amnesia. And aether suppression spells could've dampened her magic. A desecration rite would alter basic aether metabolism, and there were even enchantments he had stumbled upon over the past few days that could be used to alter bodily functions and physiology.

It wouldn't have been an easy task to turn a fey mortal—even temporarily—and it would have required an exceptionally powerful shadow mage as well as someone adept with water magic. But it was *possible.* The Genesis Council had done something similar when they still sent their prisoners to the mortal realm to live and die. And back during the Hunt, the Sanctorum had even...

Skye's stomach dropped as the realization began to set in. The question that still stood out was *why.* Why go to such lengths to hide a fey child? Why take away their magic? Why make them appear mortal?

The answer, unfortunately, was starting to become clear.

"You mentioned magic." Skye had to fight to keep his voice steady. "What kind?"

Aiden's throat bobbed, and his breathing hitched. His pulse beat out an unsteady rhythm.

That was answer enough.

"Tell me," Skye demanded. He needed to hear the words. "You took care of her while she was sick. You had to have seen something. What kind of magic did she have?"

Sighing, Aiden checked the air ward, fiddling with the small sheet of metal. Satisfied that they wouldn't be overheard, he said softly, "What kind of magic would make someone panic? What kind of magic would make someone fear not only for themselves but those around them? What kind of magic might warrant a complex web of aether suppression spells and a high-level glamour strong enough to endure 15 years with minimal degradation?"

Skye closed his eyes, a random memory trickling through his thoughts. When he was still a child, he had taken the new sketchpad and set of charcoals Sarina had given him for his birthday and climbed the tallest tree in the orchards located at the southeastern edge of the manor grounds. He had been so intent on capturing the way the light glinted off the snow-blasted peaks of the Avondale Mountains in the distance that he hadn't noticed when the tree beneath him began to groan, too thin to support his weight. It was almost twenty feet to the ground, and he had landed flat on his back.

He had cracked a few ribs, likely broken open his skull. It had hurt. A lot. But what he remembered most vividly was lying there, the air knocked out of him, completely stunned and unable to move.

That's how he felt now, sitting there, staring at Aiden and trying to remember how to breathe.

Taly… was a time mage.

And fey.

And a time mage.

And fey.

And… a lot of things suddenly made a hell of a lot more sense.

Like why Taly had suddenly decided she needed to cut ties with her old life. Or how she had nearly bested him in the sparring ring only a few short weeks ago. Why the harpy had gone for her—a *mortal*—when there were three other mages nearby.

And perhaps most importantly, how she had known about the guard rotation. And the tunnels. And the attack that would've inevitably ensued if they hadn't known to reinforce their defenses. She was a time mage. She could see the future. So, those dreams he'd been having, the ones that told him things he couldn't have known—those weren't *his* dreams. They were hers, and he had just somehow… stumbled into them.

Somehow being the operative word. But that was a question for another time.

"You knew." Skye's eyes instinctively darted around the room, noting every face, both familiar and foreign. He was angry now. A hot fire began simmering in his chest, growing, expanding, waiting to explode. "You knew the reason Taly left last year; you knew that she had *time* magic. You knew how much danger that put her in, but you didn't fucking say anything?"

"Skye," Aiden said very, very carefully. He looked scared now. "I had to pry it out of her, and even then, she didn't want to tell me. All I know is that she was having visions—she described them as afterimages showing her events just a few seconds into the future—and that she left the manor last year after they started to manifest."

Skye felt the world tilt, and he placed both hands flat on the table, trying to find his bearings. "Why didn't you tell us?"

"Because I promised her I wouldn't."

"No." Skye shook his head. "No, that's not good enough." Not for a secret like this.

So what possible reason could Aiden have had for keeping this information from the people that could've helped her? The people that loved her? The people that would *want* to protect her.

The realization made him feel cold.

"You were going to hand her over to the Crystal Guard." Skye's voice was barely above a whisper, gaining volume as he said, "The first time mage—human or otherwise—to survive to adulthood in two and half centuries and you were going to hand her over to the Crystal Guard so they could use her to find the Time Shard."

"We would've protected her," Aiden insisted.

"You would've killed her the same way you did the last time mage you managed to get your hands on!"

"That was a child. The boy barely had more than a few sparks of magic, and he was already half-dead by the time the Guard managed to rescue him from the Sanctorum. It would've been different with Taly." Aiden paused, tugging at his ear again. "If I had actually intended to hand her over."

"What do you mean?"

"I was trying to convince her to tell you," Aiden said carefully, regarding Skye the way a fox might watch a wolf. "I had to blackmail her into moving back into the manor—for her own safety—and I think if I'd had just a little more time, I could've persuaded her to tell you. Then, we could've figured out a plan together."

Skye let a growl slip free, and Aiden's own patience finally snapped. "What exactly would you have had me do then? What was the right answer here? She was scared. Terrified, not just for herself, but for *you*. For what *you* would do if the Sanctorum ever found her. One wrong move from me and she would've been out the damned window and our lives before you or me or anyone could've done anything about it."

Skye's anger guttered at that—just slightly. He was right. Taly was stubborn to a fault.

Still… Aiden had known. He had *known* and never said a damned thing.

"You need to leave," Skye said in a low voice.

But Aiden didn't move from his seat. "I think we need to talk about these dreams, Skye. And the hallucinations you experienced down in the tunnels. Regardless of what Taly was or wasn't, she's gone now, and you need to accept that if you're going to start to heal. Why don't we go back to the townhome, sober up a bit, and then I'll examine you? This psychosis could be as simple as—"

"I said *get out*," Skye barked. He pounded a fist on the table, not reacting in the slightest when the wood cracked down the middle. The sound was satisfying and loud, and the air ward flickered as it filtered out the noise. "If you value your life, that is."

To Aiden's credit, he knew how to pick his battles. Holding up his hands in surrender, he kept his eyes to the ground as he slid out of the booth and quietly left the bar.

CHAPTER 25

-From the personal notes of Azura Raine

I always find it amusing how many people still believe in destiny. As if it doesn't have any help.

Skye stalked through the streets of Ryme.

He didn't know how long he'd sat at that table, waiting for the world to make sense again. Anger had given way to shock, then awe, then fear, elation, sadness, fear again.

He'd been feeling too many things at once, so instead of succumbing to the urge to rage and scream and curse the malevolent deity that had decided to shatter every single Shards-forsaken thing he'd ever thought he'd known—he'd clung to his anger, pushing everything else aside.

Because anger—anger was easy. Anger he understood. It helped him find his feet. Gave him the strength to walk out of that bar without crumbling. It was a fire in his blood, a heat that wrapped around his very bones.

It kept him moving forward.

His breath steamed in the chill night air, and from the way people began scurrying out of his way, the look on his face must have been murderous.

She knew, he thought, the heavy wool fabric of his overcoat billowing out behind him as he turned another corner.

Taly had known how much danger she was in, but she hadn't told him. Not when the visions started. Not during the *year* she'd spent on her own. Not when she was attacked by the harpy. Not even when they had found themselves under attack, holed up inside a compound with spies lurking within their ranks.

Every single time, she had just left him behind.

Skye bared his teeth and snarled, desperately clinging to that bright, burning anger. He was going to throttle her when he found her—shake some sense into that empty head of hers. And then he was going to yell at her for using her magic to come back and torment him in some damned tunnel. That had obviously been some future version just getting in one final laugh. Why else would she have said those things and worn that *dress* if not to mess with his mind?

To pick you back up, some small rational part of him said. He had been so close to giving up in those tunnels, and she had kept him moving forward.

Skye shook his head, trying to refocus his thoughts. The variables had changed. *Again*. Why did it seem like he was always working with an incomplete set of information?

Taly was a time mage, but it was worse than that. She was a time mage on an island full of dimensional gates, and while they still didn't know who they were fighting or why, with a time mage, their enemy would be unstoppable. They could go anywhere. Do anything. They could infect countless worlds with nothing to stop them.

The third moon was already shining high above him by the time Skye found his way back to the townhome. He kept his footsteps quiet as he came in the kitchen entrance, taking the servants' stair back to his quarters on the top floor. He packed a bag, then slipped out of his suit and into a plain shirt, trousers, and a comfortable pair of boots. His armor was still downstairs, but he would grab it on his way to the workshop.

It was time to go. If Taly was a time mage—if that truly was the reason she had left him in Ebondrift—then he didn't have time to wait around and see if Kato's offer of help had been sincere. He needed to leave. Tonight.

Skye was halfway down the stairs when he heard his name being called from deeper inside the house. He debated ignoring the voice, but—

Shit. There it was again.

His feet started moving. Better to take care of this now than risk being followed.

The carpets muffled his steps as he found his way down to the third floor, to a small, sitting room he and Taly used to call the "Painted Room." It was a circular space, flanked with ivory columns, every wall filled with art. Sarina had always said the paintings were supposed to symbolize the soul bond, but, truthfully, he'd never really seen it, even if he had always nodded along with her explanations.

The doorway stood open, spilling light into the darkened hallway. As soon as he stepped inside, his stomach sank.

Ivain and Sarina were standing by the fireplace—both dressed in their usual black. But they weren't the only ones waiting for him. Aiden and Kato were milling about the room as well, both dutifully avoiding his gaze.

It took half a second for Skye to realize he had just landed in deep shit.

"Skye." Ivain waved him forward. The hardness in his eyes had softened since the last time they spoke. "Come inside. We need to talk."

"I'm fine where I am," Skye said carefully.

"This isn't up for debate," Sarina said, her voice calm but lethal. She didn't turn to watch as he slowly stepped inside, already knowing that habit—and maybe a bit of childhood fear—would make him obey.

The door clicked closed behind him.

"Aiden," Ivain began, glancing at the healer and then back to Skye, "has just told us something very troubling."

"I can think of a lot of troubling things Aiden could've told you." Skye gave Aiden a pointed look. He'd known this would be an issue, but he didn't think anyone would try to confront him tonight.

"I had to tell them, Skye," Aiden said in his defense.

"No, you didn't," Skye replied coldly. "We both know how good you are at keeping secrets."

Aiden flinched at that.

Skye turned to go. "I'm leaving. Right now. But I assume you already knew that. Otherwise, all of you wouldn't have assembled at such a late hour just to tell me goodbye."

"You won't get very far without a horse," Ivain said, arms crossed as he leaned against a small writing desk. At Skye's questioning glance, he added, "I've already instructed the stable hands to turn you away. With force, if necessary."

Skye smiled grimly. "I don't need a horse." He could run faster, farther. A horse would just slow him down.

Ivain shared a look with Sarina, who still stood beside the mantle, stony and silent. "Boy," he said, "I know you're grieving. And I take full responsibility for not realizing just how much. For letting things get this bad. Hopefully, you haven't done anything yet that can't be undone."

"What are you talking about?" Skye asked.

"They know about the books," Kato said. He looked contrite, dragging his hands through his hair and shifting from foot to foot. "Ivain came looking for you in the workshop and..." He hesitated, eyes pleading. "I'm sorry, I just... I didn't know what to tell them. Those books were scent tagged—he sniffed them out immediately."

Skye shook his head. In a room full of friends and family, Kato was the only one on his side.

Maybe he really had gone mad.

"I'm leaving," Skye said for the final time.

"I will throw you in a cell if that's what it takes to stop this lunacy," Ivain hissed.

"Then do it. Arrest me. Throw me behind bars if it makes you feel better about leaving her to die!" Ivain winced, but Skye couldn't bring himself to regret the words. Not when that thread, that tether, perked awake.

Taly. Always there when he needed her.

A gentle tug in the darkness that would lead him home.

Ivain stalked across the room, cutting him off before he could reach for the door. "I will not allow you to throw your life away over dreams and hallucinations. I have already had to say goodbye to one child. I refuse to make it two."

I'm not yours. Skye almost said it, but stopped himself. Ivain had been more of a father to him than his own sire, and he wasn't that far gone. Not yet.

"I won't leave her," he said, reaching for that thread. "I don't know how she's doing it, but the dreams are real. *She's* real."

Something warm and fuzzy brushed against his mind.

And he let it in.

That thread pulled taut, wrapping around him, twisting and tightening its grip. "If you don't believe me, just ask Aiden! He knows why she left last year. All this time, he *knew*—"

"Skye, please," Sarina cut in. "Listen to yourself."

"You're not in your right mind," Ivain added.

"I don't care." That thread tugged so hard it nearly jerked him forward. "I don't care if it is madness, you can't—"

"*Skylen*."

The raw command in the old man's voice brought Skye up short.

"Enough of this!" Ivain continued. "We all want her back, but you have to accept the truth. She's gone."

"She's not!" Skye nearly shouted. Because she couldn't be. He wouldn't allow it. "I've *seen* her. I see her every night. She's not gone!"

"Skye." Sarina's voice was full of pity. "I know how hard it is to accept the loss of a—"

"She's not gone!" Skye bit out. He frantically searched the room, but his brother was the only one that would look him in the eye.

A moment later, he hung his head.

"She's not gone," Skye repeated, hating the way his voice began to crack. He grasped at the thread, but…

No.

No no no

It was fraying. Fluttering out of reach.

What had happened? While they had been standing here arguing, had she… Was it possible?

"Surely, you know what this looks like," Ivain said, his tone a little gentler. "We're worried about you."

"What's wrong?"

The voice was soft but unmistakable, and Skye's head turned.

His body moved without thought.

The sound of footsteps followed him, along with a clatter of movement, a din of voices. But he had stopped hearing. Stopped caring. The world around him had faded, and all he could see was *her*. Covered in blood. Slumped on the floor. Panting and holding her sides, obviously in pain but still completely and utterly *alive.*

Taly was alive.

A small, broken sound cracked out of him as he fell to his knees in front of her, reaching for her.

But his hands passed right through her shoulders.

"No," he breathed. He tried again, but… Why couldn't he feel her? Touch her? Why couldn't he hear the sound of her heart beating? "No, no, no."

"Shards." Ivain was on his knees beside him, eyes wide as he tried to assess the situation. "*How…?*"

And that's when he saw it. A shimmer of aether covering her body like a veil.

Skye reached for her again, but it was like trying to catch a shadow. Her body began to fade—flesh and blood turning to smoke and mist. The color leached from her cheeks; her eyes drooped shut. It was as though something vital were being drained away.

"Stabilize her!" Ivain's hands glowed with shadow magic, and tendrils of aether snaked through the air, trying to grab at the fading image. But she was just that. An image. A facsimile. Not quite real, and yet— "It has to be you, boy!"

Skye pulled at his own magic, letting it fill the air around him with a violet glow. If he searched for it, he could still feel the *tug, tug, tugging* of that thread. Weak but—

Not knowing what else to do, he grasped at the rapidly fraying edges, wrapping his own aether around it as he began weaving the strands back together. Stronger. Tighter. Adding bits of himself to fill in the gaps.

The image began to resolve itself. Slowly. The next time he reached for her, Skye managed to grip her shoulders. She was like smoke in his hands, and he gave her a shake, nearly sobbing in relief when she gasped awake.

Her eyes found his and—

Skye blinked. Her eyes… weren't the right color. They were too bright, too… *fey*. And now that he was looking more closely—her cheeks were too angular, the arch of her brow too high. Every feature had been sharpened and refined until there was nothing human left.

But then again—she wasn't human. She had never been human. That's what Aiden had said.

Sarina's gasp from beside him confirmed that he wasn't the only one that had noticed the change.

"Taly?" Skye tried to control the tremble in his hands as he gave her another gentle shake. "Taly, where are you?"

She reached up to grasp at his wrist, and Skye couldn't help but shiver at the buzz of aether that swept across his skin. She was still staring at him when the first trail of blood rolled down her cheek.

"What's happening to her?" Sarina snapped as the blood began to leak from the girl's eyes like crimson tears.

The image began to stutter.

"Hold on to her!" Ivain clapped a hand to his shoulder, and Skye felt a wave of aether being forcibly injected into his veins. It was like pure adrenaline, and he grabbed onto it, pushing it into the spell.

Taly flashed in and out of focus—once, twice, three times—before she finally stabilized. There was more blood on her face now, trailing from her eyes, her nose, even her ears. She touched a finger to her cheek, smearing the perfect lines of crimson that marked her skin.

"C'mon," Skye whispered, holding tight to that thread. "Stay with me. Just a little longer. Where are you? Are you still on Tempris? Are you at the palace?"

"Oh, my little one," Sarina sobbed. She tried to wipe at the blood on Taly's face, but it was like trying to touch a ghost. "What have they done to you?"

Taly was still staring at the blood dripping down her fingers like it was a puzzle she couldn't figure out how to solve. Skye gently wrapped a hand around her wrist, and her eyes finally snapped to his.

"I don't know what's happening to me." Her voice was distorted and garbled, as though she had already stepped one foot out of this world.

"Where are you?" Skye asked again. "Please. I know you're hurt; I know you're tired. But I need you to tell me where you are. Tell me where you are, and I'll come get you."

"I found the relay," she said, her brows nudging together in confusion. "I talked to Ivain."

"Taly, I know, but—"

The thread was starting to pull taut.

"She's fading again."

"He needs more aether."

"Move."

"Hold her."

The voices were swirling around him, and he vaguely felt Kato's hand on his shoulder, followed by another surge of aether. The power was almost too much for him now—a flaming maelstrom of energy that skittered across every cell, threatening to burn him up from the inside out.

But Skye tuned out the noise, pushed away the pain. "Taly, please," he said when her attention began to flit around the room. He grabbed her chin, forcing her eyes back to his.

That invisible string was pulling tighter and tighter. He was losing his grip, and she was starting to fade. "Please, Tink." He couldn't hold on. She was going to slip away no matter what he did. "Come back to me. Just stay alive."

And then... Taly smiled. It was weak and edged with pain, but so, so beautiful.

"I'm glad I got to see you one last time, Em," she said, and the words sliced right through him.

Skye began to shake his head as the first tear rolled down his cheek. She was telling him goodbye. Again.

He opened his mouth to speak, but her eyes had already broken away from his, taking in Ivain first, then Sarina, Aiden, even Kato. "All of you," she whispered.

And then he blinked, and she was gone.

Silence settled over the room.

Nobody moved.

Nobody spoke.

Skye had to force himself to breathe, in and then out. He didn't bother asking how, or why, or when. With time mages, *when* became a very important question to ask.

But he didn't care about any of that. Those were questions he could answer later. All that mattered right now was that he had been right. The dreams were real. *Taly* was real. He wasn't crazy.

And Shards, that felt good. So, *so* good.

Slowly, Skye rose to his feet. "Now, do you believe me?" His voice shook, and his eyes were damp—but he didn't care. "She's out there. She's been out there this entire time."

Ivain and Sarina still kneeled on either side of him.

"Was that...?" Sarina rose, turning to her brother.

"Give me a moment," Ivain murmured, standing to his full height. "Just let me think."

"How?" Sarina went on. "How could she possibly—"

"I don't know," Ivain murmured. "But did you see—"

"Yes."

"And—"

"I know."

"And what about—"

Enough of this, Skye thought. He was just wasting time now.

Skye turned for the door, only to find Kato blocking his way.

"Move," Skye said, an edge of warning in his voice.

But Kato didn't move. He didn't even flinch. "Skylen," he said carefully, like he was trying to pacify some sort of wild animal. "Let's just take a moment. It's late, and there's very little that we can do tonight. I promised you allies, remember? I'm not going to be able to hold to my promise if you don't at least give me until morning. That gives us plenty of time to talk. I don't know about you, but I'd like to know just how your little human friend managed to ghost her way in here."

Skye's jaw clenched, taking in his brother's wary stance, the way he held his hands out in front of his body. Placating, but also… defensive.

They still think I'm crazy. After everything… they still thought—

"I believe you." Ivain's hand landed on his shoulder, and Skye couldn't stop the near-sob of relief that shuddered out of him. "I'm sorry I didn't believe you before, but I understand now. I know why you can't let this go."

"She's alive," Skye said feebly.

"I know." Ivain began pulling him away from the door. "Has this happened before?"

Skye shook his head. "No." His eyes drifted to the hand at his shoulder, still wary. Ivain abruptly let go. "I saw something in the tunnels, but not like this."

"Would somebody please explain what just happened?" It was Aiden who finally voiced the question on everybody's mind. He sagged against one of the columns, eyes still wide with shock. "What did we just see?"

Ivain gave a heavy sigh, shooting a careful glance at Sarina, who nodded. "That was a projection," he said.

"I've never heard of that," Kato said, his back to the door. He had armed the silencing wards, and they flickered behind him.

"It's rare," Ivain said. "And dangerous. The soul is not meant to exist outside the body, and can only be projected outside of the physical form if properly anchored. I only know of a handful of individuals capable of pulling it off, and most of them have already been soul bonded for centuries, if not longer."

Skye swayed on his feet. *What?*

He must have asked the question aloud, because Ivain said again, "A soul bond. Not complete—not yet. That takes centuries. But the dreams, the projection… That *was* Taly." Ivain's voice cracked on her name, and he glanced at the spot where she had been only moments before. "That was her anima—still tethered to her physical body, but also… to you. The anchor. Somehow, she pushed her soul outside of herself, and then you pulled her through. Pulled her down the bond forming between you."

Skye staggered back a step, only to run into the couch. Sinking down, he was only half-aware that every eye in the room had settled firmly on him.

A soul bond—a bridge between two people that loved so deeply, trusted so completely, their very souls began to reach out, desperate to intertwine.

Marriages expired. Lovers separated. Even mates could fall out of love.

But soul bonds were permanent, lasting even beyond death.

Skye pressed a hand to his chest, feeling for the tug of that thread and smiling when it gave a tiny spark of recognition.

Taly. Not just a friend. Or a mate. If they continued down this road, accepted the bond and cultivated the love and trust that already existed between them—even calling her his wife would be an insult.

She would be his *élan*. His beloved. His partner and equal.

He probably should've been more surprised. A soul bond—that was big. But then again, this was Taly. The girl who had slipped into his heart so slowly and so quietly, he'd loved her without knowing. It made sense that she had stolen a piece of his soul too.

Skye blinked, and the voices around him snapped into focus.

"How is this possible?" Sarina had moved from her position by the fireplace and was now standing over him, a motherly hand on his shoulder.

Kato barked out a laugh, the back of his head hitting the door with a thud. "Is anyone in this room really surprised by this news? Anyone at all? Granted, I only knew the little human for all of five minutes, but I can't be the only one that wanted to hurl when they started up that tap-tappity thing."

"That is not helpful," Ivain said, even if he quietly shuddered at the memory of their not-so-silent code.

"And beside the point," Sarina added. "Regardless of the desire, mortals can't form soul bonds. They can't carve out a piece of themselves and give it to someone else. It would kill them."

"But she's not mortal," Ivain countered. "Sarina, you saw—"

"I know." She shook her head, raising a hand to her throat. "But *how*? How can that be possible? She's human. She's always been human."

"Not always." Skye stared down at his hands. The ones that had just been holding onto her. "Taly had secrets. Good ones too. Whoever has her right now—they're not going to kill her. Not if they know what she is. They're going to do something far, far worse. To her and to us. Which is why I need to go. Right now."

"You're going to wait." The look Ivain gave him was stern but kind, his own curiosity, anger, confusion all carefully restrained. "I didn't believe you then, but I do now, and I know why you have to do this. An *élan* comes before self, before sanity and reason, and I won't stop you. But we need to figure out some answers first.

"Now then." Ivain clasped his hands behind his back as he surveyed the room. "I get the feeling that everyone here has been working off an incomplete set of information. I think it's time we fixed that."

"Majesty?"

Azura looked up, a glass of red wine in one hand, a book in the other. It was late, far later than she would normally stay awake. But dreams had chased her from her sleep, and she'd just needed to be sure.

"And?" Azura asked as Leto drifted into the kitchens, her soft blue light bouncing off pots and pans and glass-lined cupboards.

"We are still on schedule," Leto replied, her voice low and soothing. The woman had always been an unwavering force of calm, even in life. "They will be here within the week."

Azura closed her book, sighing as that coil of dread that had been slowly tightening around her chest since the moment she awoke finally began to ease. *Thank goodness*, she thought. Taly was a strange one—the timelines were always tangling around her, getting so snarled it was hard to make sense of anything.

It was absolutely infuriating. Made trying to divine the future with any sort of accuracy nearly impossible. *If that girl knew just how many of my plans are starting to come together... or the consequences if they fail...*

She wouldn't still be complaining about those pistols or that damned dagger. A time mage couldn't dream without the proper tethers. She should know that.

Azura let out another soft sigh as she rose from the table, plastering on a smile and pushing back the ever-present exhaustion. It would do little good to let the others see how this place was beginning to wear on her.

"What a relief," she chirped, but from the way Leto tilted her head, she knew she'd used just a tad too much enthusiasm. "I just love it when a plan comes together, don't you?"

"If I may, Majesty?" Leto's light dimmed in that telltale way Azura had come to identify as worry.

"Yes, of course," Azura said. "Speak freely."

"This plan is quite dangerous," Leto said without missing a beat.

"I'm aware."

"For Lady Caro."

"Yes."

"And Lord Emrys."

"I know."

"And for all of us here." Leto paused. "Including you. Are you sure this is going to play out the way you intend?"

Azura glanced down at the book on the table—Taly's journal. She made it a habit to review the girl's dreams. They were often bloody and full of terror, and it was getting harder and harder to dissuade her from seeing the truth in them. There were things she couldn't know yet. For her own good.

"I'm not sure," Azura said softly, letting her fingers graze the leather. "I've never coddled my students, but this..."

This would be one of the cruelest things she'd ever done.

Azura took a breath, steadying herself. "It's the right decision," she said, looking to Leto, her oldest and dearest friend. "Skylen must die. It's the only way we'll ever know if she's ready."

CHAPTER 26

-An excerpt from the Arylaan Times

Coming on the heels of last week's controversial victory at the Pytchdrive Worlds Championship, time mages will no longer be allowed to compete at the professional level.

"This decision has been a long time coming," Interspecies Pytchdrive Federation (ISPF) Commander Sterling Roe said. "Even with the special regulations put in place for time mages, their magic gives them an unfair advantage."

The ISPF has not made any accusations regarding the Worlds Championship game, though foul play is still suspected. While a time mage's skills allow them to assess the field, predict an opponent's actions, it has not been confirmed whether the current Pytchdrive format would allow for a 623-point score within a 4.2-second period.

As one commentator noted, "Time mages are a bunch of cheats. The whole lot of them."

To which Queen Raine responded directly, "That is accurate, yes."

The orange glow of dawn brightened the long oval windows, and even the fairies that liked to haunt the upper floors of the palace library hushed their tinkling laughter, watching the light stretch towards the sky.

Taly yawned and turned the page. The bookshelves were dusty, and the floating platforms that would take her to the highest shelves had been grounded. The crystals in the reading lamps flickered, making the light dim and inconsistent. The entire area was rundown and just a little grimy, and yet this forgotten corner on the 32nd floor of the main library had become her sanctuary. She had always loved the smell of books, the whisper of paper. Although the palace boasted dozens upon dozens of libraries—most hidden away in their own little pockets of spacetime—this one was her favorite.

Long, ivory staircases reached into infinity, spiraling up among countless rows of books that contained more secrets than could ever be learned in a single lifetime. There were comfortable seating areas scattered about, and the reading rooms were still stacked with journals and papers, as if the librarians had only just stepped out and would be back presently.

Over 100 floors of unlearned knowledge. Over 100 floors of forgotten alcoves and darkened corners where neither the Queen nor Leto would be able to find her.

Even the fairies left her alone when she was "studying," always hovering around the periphery, always curious, but polite enough to stay out of sight.

Taly stared at the page, the words and letters blurring together. Sometimes, if she tuned out the chirps of the fairies that floated listlessly through the stacks, she could almost pretend she was back at the Harbor Manor library. This one had the same feel. The silence was heavy but comfortable, completely free of expectation. The outside world and its problems had no power here. It was a place to just *be*.

And the only place she would allow herself to just sit and think of home.

There were so many things she missed, things that almost made her glad for the year she'd spent as a salvager, if only because it had prepared her for the times when the longing would suddenly sneak up on her. Sitting in the kitchen while Eliza cooked breakfast, walking through the gardens with Sarina, smoking cigars with Ivain—those were some of the things she missed the most. She even missed the way Skye would tug on her hair just because he knew it irritated her.

Calcifer bumped his head against her leg from underneath the table, and she reached down to idly pet him. He was still getting bigger, and Azura said that he would get larger still. His head came up to her hip when he was standing, the tips of his ears reaching to her breast. His canines were the length of her palm, and his tail was long enough to swing over the edge of the table, swatting at the pocket watch she'd placed near the edge.

"Is it time to go?" she asked him, finding a particularly itchy spot that made his leg start to twitch. He gave an annoyed huff when she removed her hand to reach for the watch. "It seems it is. Thank goodness one of us was paying attention."

With a sigh, Taly closed the book in front of her with a thud, sneezing when a plume of dust puffed into the air. A wave of her hand sent the scattered piles of books and papers that littered the desktop flying through the air, each individual item rewinding through time and neatly re-shelving itself with a hiss and a thump. She felt the slightest drain on her aether, but after countless hours of meditation, her body was already compensating for the loss.

There was a part of her now that was always keenly aware of just how much aether she had left, how quickly her reserves were regenerating, and how either of those two variables could affect her spellcasting ability at any given moment. It was like another sense, as crucial to her now as sight or scent or sound. She wasn't sure how she had lived her entire life without it.

Gathering up a small pack and slinging it over her shoulder, Taly began wandering through the stacks, Calcifer loping beside her. His feather and fur-tipped wings dragged behind him, as did the leash that was hooked to his new golden collar. He was too big now to stay cooped up in her tower all day, so Azura had started letting Taly take him out for daily walks. After all these months, the Queen still insisted that he was going to kill them all, but the leash seemed to make her feel better.

At the end of every row, the dust on the shelf was streaked: one line for left, two for right, three to go straight, and a dot to switchback. She'd come up with the system shortly after she'd arrived at the palace—it was always good to have some place to hide those things you didn't want found—and she followed the marks, occasionally dragging her finger through the dust if she saw a line that was beginning to fade.

After several minutes, she arrived at her destination. The bookcase was identical to the thousands of others inside the library—old and dusty, stuffed from end to end with books bound in leather, paper, even wood and sometimes gold. She had to climb a nearby ladder to reach the top, count three spots to the left of center, and—

There, Taly thought, using a finger to tug the old book of mortal fables from where it was wedged between two other books on the same subject. The inside had been hollowed out, and she smiled as she began stuffing the contents into her bag.

She'd been working on her plan for weeks now, slowly gathering materials and hiding them away. She'd have to work quickly and quietly, avoiding detection and making sure to slip back into bed before Leto came to fetch her. It was a risk, but if she succeeded…

Taly's grin widened. Azura had told her that if she wanted to beat the fairies, she'd have to get creative. And that's exactly what she planned to do.

She was tired of playing that damned game. Tired of losing. Tired of knowing that it wasn't a fair fight.

Today, however—today, she was finally going to win.

"Are you ready?"

It was a beautiful afternoon—warm and sunny, with just the right amount of breeze to ward off the summer heat. Each cloud, each subtle variant of color, each golden ray of sun was exactly the same as it had been the day before and would be the day after.

Beautiful. Picturesque.

Stifling.

What she wouldn't do for a little snow. Or maybe a hurricane. Even a tornado. She wasn't picky. Any violent force of nature capable of sweeping in and wiping the board clean would do.

"Yes," Taly called back, giving the Queen a lazy smile. She rocked back and forth on her heels, listening to the dirt crunch underfoot as she scanned the perimeter of the training yard.

Another day, another game of tag.

Shards, she hoped this worked.

Azura sat in her usual seat wearing her usual regalia, sipping at her usual cup of tea. "Are you sure?" she asked, crinkling her brow. "You don't look ready."

Taly stuffed her hands in her pockets. It was a fair assessment. Usually, she would be checking her weapons, making sure that the shadow crystals were fully charged and probably taking up position next to the tree where her back would be protected for the first few minutes of the game.

But today—today, she stood dead center, no weapon in her hands. Instead of trousers and armor, she'd chosen a thin pair of blue leggings that breathed in the heat, and her tunic was sleeveless and made of matching cambric. She had even left her hair down, only bothering to tie off the sides.

"I'm sure," Taly confirmed. After all, everything was in place, and if she didn't do this today, she wouldn't get another chance. The explosions would come, the world would reset, and all her hard work would be destroyed right along with it. "Let's get this over with."

"Well, alright then." Azura glanced at Leto, who stood just off to the side, and shrugged in confusion. "Begin," she trilled, clapping her hands.

The familiar rush of adrenaline shot through her, but Taly held it in check. The sound of bells tinkled on the wind as the first 20 wisps charged the arena.

Taly nudged her aether, and her Sight painted the landscape in a heavy wash of gold. There was a ripple to the north, a slight wrinkle to the east. The fairies were scattering, making decisions only to immediately change their minds. It was a common tactic when fighting a time mage with the Sight. If the variables were always changing, it became harder to predict the future.

Not that it mattered.

Taly had been studying their tactics for weeks now.

Yawning and giving a long stretch, she sunk to the ground, leaning back on her hands and turning her face to the sky.

"What in Shards' name…? Did the girl hit her head?" she heard the Queen mumble to Leto.

There was a tickle at the back of Taly's mind, an unscratchable itch that crawled across the skin of her neck. The fairies were in range now, and they circled the perimeter of the arena, confused, chittering back and forth in that strange language of windchimes and bells. Their bodies flickered with faint pulses of light and energy.

Please work, please work, please work

Because Shards this was going to really hurt if it didn't.

The fairies began to laugh, and she bit her lip hard enough to taste blood, forcing her shoulders to relax as she closed her eyes.

Complete, absolute boredom.

She still had her eyes closed when she felt the first spell snap and release. Several other pops of magic followed in rapid succession.

The tinkling laughter that had been circling her, strangely predatory as it drew closer, abruptly ceased.

Taly opened her eyes.

Twenty orbs of fairy fire stood frozen just inside the perimeter of the training yard, fenced in by a slight shimmer of magic that circled the area. The world beyond swayed and shifted, and through the veil, she could see the Queen. Unmoving, eyes wide, mouth agape. It was the same expression the woman had made the day Taly had not-so-accidentally eaten all Azura's favorite cakes at teatime.

Taly grinned, a manic giggle bubbling up and out. Her trap had worked!

It had worked, and Shards, it had all been so irritatingly simple in the end. Don't use crystals, the Queen had said, which for the longest time, she had taken to mean that she wasn't supposed to rely on crystals to help her cast.

But crystals, Taly had finally realized, could be used for more than just focusing talismans and spell training. They could be charged with active spells.

So, she had spent most of her morning tethering spells to crystals and burying them at key points, each one chosen after several weeks of studying the fairies' movements. A simple ceasing spell was all she'd needed to capture the fairies, but triggering the release... that had been more difficult.

Air crystals, stolen from the armory and then wired together in such a way as to create a thin, nearly imperceptible wall of air around the perimeter of the arena. It was crude, and Skye and Ivain could've done far more in far less time. But she'd still managed to rig something together—an invisible snare that would trigger her trap when the fairies crossed into the arena.

The brief shower lasting exactly four minutes and 13 seconds that occurred every morning at two minutes past the fifth bell had quickly washed away any evidence that she'd been digging, making her trap virtually undetectable.

Simple. Easy. And she hadn't even had to cheat.

"I win," Taly chirped, hopping to her feet and dusting herself off. "And technically, I didn't break any rules. You said I wasn't allowed to use crystals *during* the game. You didn't, however, say anything about using them *before*."

When she turned to the Queen, Azura's lips were pressed into a thin line, and Leto still stood off to the side, head tilted, shoulders shaking with barely suppressed laughter. The fairies that had come to watch the daily beat-down were whispering amongst themselves.

Taly gave a mocking bow, delighting in the low growl that carried across the training yard. "I beat your game."

Azura's anger was all the evidence she needed to confirm that she'd never meant for her to win.

Azura closed her eyes, and when she opened them, that heaviness, that depthless power that Taly knew the Queen commanded, even if she'd only seen it demonstrated a handful of times, settled over the arena.

The fairies whispering hushed.

"That means I've earned my freedom," Taly said, still standing in the middle of the arena, her feet set defiantly.

"Does it now?"

Taly nodded—confident. She hoped. "We had an agreement. I earned my third seal. I'm an Acolyte now. It's time for you to hold up your end of the bargain."

"An Acolyte? You?" Azura chuckled, low and mocking. "What in Shards' name makes you believe that?"

"I passed your test."

"You passed *a* test. You finally figured out that time mages cheat. That we're always thinking at least ten steps ahead. However, that is far from the last lesson I have to teach you."

Taly's heart seized. No. No, she couldn't— "You said that stupid game of tag was my test for the third seal."

Azura's smile widened as she rose from her chair. "Oh, my dear," she said, her voice lilting as she sauntered into the ring. Every movement was calculated and lethal, limned with ancient grace. She held up a hand, and the veil of air and time magic evaporated in a hiss of aether. "You poor tiny little slip of a thing. I said you needed to beat a game of tag before I would let you leave, but I never said *when* that would be. You really should've been listening more carefully."

Taly began to shake her head, hating the tears that burned her eyes. This was supposed to be her way out. This had been her only way out!

"You lied," Taly whispered.

"No, I didn't," Azura claimed. "To quote a very dear, very *old* friend: *'I did not lie. I simply did not correct you when you made certain assumptions.'*" Azura winked. "Spoken like a true time mage."

Taly visibly winced. Those were her words, said to Skye that night at the tavern. The night before their entire world had changed.

How the Queen knew them…

"There is still one more trial you must complete," Azura said. "One more game. If you win, I'll send you home. *Immediately*. You'll be an Acolyte. A student I can be proud to call my own."

The Queen had finally made her way to the center of the ring, standing only a few feet away. "That's it?" Taly asked.

"That's it."

"One game?"

"One game."

"And you'll give me my freedom?"

"I'll give you your freedom."

"Immediately?" Taly pressed. "Not next week, not next year—"

"Yes, yes, yes," Azura muttered. "That's exactly what I said."

Taly hesitated. "What's the catch?" There was always a catch with this woman—even if she couldn't immediately see it.

The Queen's smile was positively feline. "If I told you, it would ruin the surprise."

CHAPTER 27

-*From the personal notes of Ivain Castaro, Marquess of Tempris*

My wife is dead.

My daughter too, gone before she took her first breath.

I still have their blood on my hands, and the healers keep asking me questions. They keep saying that it was an accident. That there was nothing anyone could've done. Both mother and child were healthy—up until they weren't.

They just took my daughter away, wrapped in a black cloth. My wife is still in our bed. I can feel Sarina watching me, like she's afraid of what I might do.

She's right to be worried. Because I think I know a way to bring them back.

You're a hypocrite.

How many years had it been since Breena spat those words at him?

You think I don't know what you did?

Ivain knelt on the floor, staring into the old trunk.

The basement vault was dark. He'd only bothered to turn on a single light overhead, knowing exactly where to go in the maze of boxes and trunks, all dusty with age. He had bought the townhouse originally for Sarina and her new husband, but after Madoc died, taken during the Schism, it was mostly used for storage. For pictures and books and old clothes, things they didn't need but couldn't force themselves to throw out.

And in a forgotten corner, Ivain had hidden those things he wished he could forget. Notebooks speckled with blood, manuscripts written in his own hand, each one filled with forbidden spells he had refused to relinquish even when the Genesis Council had given the order. It might have been safer to bury them away behind magical seals and locks, but that would have been too conspicuous. It would have only taken one moderately intelligent shadow mage to see the traces of aether and wonder what exactly he was trying to protect.

Better to hide the forbidden in plain sight.

Although, if Breena had ever found these... she'd have never let him live it down.

Because she had been right.

He *was* a hypocrite.

He had warned her against the dangers of bloodcraft, chastised her and turned his back when she had used illegal magic to win a tourney in front of the full assembled Council. And yet when his wife and child had died only a few years prior, he'd convinced himself he could overcome death. That he could take the horrors he had witnessed during the Shade Rebellion and turn them into a force for good.

Thank the Shards Sarina stopped him before he went too far. Both his sisters—they brought him back from the brink, though they hadn't been able to help him save Breena from herself.

And now here he was again, with another student lured in by the seductive power of bloodcraft. It was pain and passion that compelled one to take these sorts of risks; the folly of those blinded by their own desperation.

Ivain reached into the trunk, already knowing which books he would need.

The humans had a saying: history is doomed to repeat itself.

And he believed that—to an extent.

Breena had been *desperate* in her need to prove herself in a family of mages that had already accomplished great things.

And now Skye—he was also *desperate*. To find Taly. To rescue her. His bondmate.

History was doomed to repeat itself. But only if they kept making the same mistakes.

"Come here," Ivain said, sensing the boy standing at the door to the vault.

Skye stepped further into the light. His expression was carefully blank, and Ivain mourned the trust that had been lost between them. He should have believed him. After everything he'd seen in his too-long life, he should've just believed the boy when he said that Taly was still alive. He shouldn't have been so afraid to embrace that spark of hope.

Ivain rose to his feet, a stack of books in hand. "I saw in your notes that you've been dabbling with simulacrums." He waited for Skye to nod before continuing, "I know they don't seem dangerous, but they will continue to draw on your aether until you dismiss them, even tapping into your anima. It's a passive spell, one you must monitor constantly."

Navigating the stacks of boxes and junk, Ivain made his way to the door, placing a hesitant hand on Skye's shoulder. He had grown to love all his students in some way, but Skye had been different. So smart but so quiet—when he first came to them, it had taken months to get the boy to open up. To finally understand how his family had kept him sequestered with only nannies and tutors in the place of friends. People who believed that children should remain silent and unseen.

Watching that quiet, lonely boy grow into a man, teaching him, seeing the light he and a little human girl had brought back to a house that had experienced so much death—it had been one of the greatest joys of his life.

And he wasn't ready for it to be over.

So, he would do better. Be better. This time, he wouldn't make the same mistakes. If this was the path Skye was meant to take, he wouldn't be traveling it alone.

"Show me what you've learned so far," Ivain said as he pushed Skye towards the door. "We'll go from there."

The townhouse armory was on the first underground floor, and it was here that Ivain found himself just before dawn, preparing for the day ahead.

Skye was sleeping. Or should've been. Instinct told him the boy was likely still awake, practicing the spells they'd spent the early morning hours rehearsing. He had a natural talent for bloodcraft, and a curiosity to rival even Breena's. He still needed to learn moderation, but that would come with time.

Ivain scanned the arsenal of steel lining the wall. He couldn't fault Skye for his restlessness. There was still so much to do before they could mount a proper rescue and very little time to do it. Although, he supposed, *time* had suddenly become a very tenuous construct.

They actually didn't know *when* Taly had projected—*when* she had managed to shove her soul outside of her body, following the bond to Skye. Time mages were tricky, and novices were even worse, sometimes shifting through the Weave at random. The image they had seen that evening—that had just been the destination. Where and *when* she was coming from was another matter entirely. It was impossible to know if she had been moving backwards or forwards through the Weave, or if that projection had been months or minutes out-of-sync.

For now, it was easier to let everyone think that Taly was still alive. That the projection was irrefutable proof. Hope was a powerful thing, after all.

Footsteps approached from down the hall, and Ivain didn't need to glance over to know who had come looking for him. He had expected her to find him eventually.

Crossing her arms, Sarina leaned against the doorframe, watching as he moved between the racks lining the walls, pulling swords and daggers and piling them on the long table that split the room. Though her face was lined from lack of sleep and worry, she had changed out of that awful black into straight gray trousers and a green silk tunic. It seemed he wasn't the only one who had seized on to this new hope, and he had no doubt she had been making her own preparations. Taly was a time mage, and while it was his job to get her back inside the city, his baby sister had likely already started thinking through just how they would keep her concealed.

"What are you doing?" Sarina finally asked.

"Exactly what it looks like," Ivain replied gruffly. He held up a dagger for inspection, then replaced it on the wall. They had better weapons. "I'm preparing to leave the city."

"That's illogical," she said tiredly. "You know you can't do that."

"I can, and I will." He lifted a long broadsword from the wall. The wiring was rusted, but it was a quick repair. This one would go. "Even if we manage to hold this city, that won't mean a damned thing if we can't get the Aion Gate to open. We need a time mage. Desperately."

Sarina gave a sad sigh, looking down then back at him. "We need *you* more," she insisted. "I want to find Taly as much as you do, but if you leave, you're risking the entire city."

Yes, he knew that. And yes, he had been over the variables. But at this point, he was allowed a bit of selfishness. Until now, he had held himself back, but with this new information— "Taly is Breena's daughter."

"I'm aware."

Ivain threw her a glance.

She shrugged. "The resemblance is there, and there's only one bloodline that produces that color of eyes. The age is correct as well. Taly was six years old when she came to us. The healers confirmed that, and it still holds despite whatever kind of magic was used to conceal her appearance. And then if we consider how few highborn children are being born now—there were less than twenty during Taly's birth year. Only one didn't survive to adulthood. A girl with blonde hair and gray eyes, whose mother kept her sequestered and away from the public eye. Breena's first and only child." Another shrug. "Our sister was a powerful time mage, and Breena was her granddaughter. It's no surprise Taly is what she is."

He closed his eyes, gripping the sword in his hands a bit tighter. "Taly is Breena's child," he said again, still not quite believing it. "And if we know that much, we can begin making other assumptions."

"Such as?"

"Well," he said, grabbing tools and wiring from the bins along the wall, "Breena never announced the sire, but at the time, her household wasn't enforcing the use of breeders. That leaves only one viable candidate. Her husband."

Ivain figured only he knew his sister well enough to see the slight widening of her eyes before it was immediately concealed. It seemed this was one variable she hadn't yet considered. Or its consequences.

For indeed, shortly after joining the Crystal Guard, Breena had married Atlas Venwraith, the High Lord of Water.

Sarina began to shake her head. "No," she breathed. "Atlas *can't* be the sire. Why would he have sent Breena back to Lycia if she was pregnant with his child? They would've been completely unprotected if his political enemies ever decided to move against her."

"Not completely." Clearing a place on the table, Ivain laid out the sword and began stripping the wiring. "Esmund was in Picolo, and he would've gladly given his sister refuge. Especially considering that the continent would've been a far safer place to birth a child. The mortal cities are stable enough for adults, but all it would've taken is a single aether blackout, and she likely would've lost the pregnancy. They wouldn't be the only family to resort to such measures."

Sarina looked slightly dazed as she began to walk toward him. "A High Lord's daughter," she murmured, arms crossed protectively around her body. "All this time, our little one, our Taly… she was a High Lord's daughter."

Ivain pounded a fist on the table, aether flaring around him. "Taly is *my* daughter," he growled, low and dangerous. He didn't often give in to his instincts, but considering the night's events, his hold on his temper was becoming tenuous.

Sarina merely arched a brow, eyeing the dent in the metal tabletop. "I think you mean *our* daughter."

Finishing the repair, he shoved the sword off to the side, then stalked back to the wall. "I mean that while Atlas may be her sire, he is only important because of who he is and what she likely inherited from him."

"You mean his aether pool?"

He nodded. Breena had been powerful, but bonding with a Shard required a truly massive capacity for aether. Most mages that tried were burned up from the inside. "If Taly's aether pool is even a fraction the size of his, every shadow mage within a ten-mile radius is going to be able to sense her. Kato said he could find men to help with the retrieval, but I don't trust anyone else to do this. It has to be me. I'm going."

Sarina stopped in front of the table, running a finger along an old dagger that had been too rusted to repair. It had belonged to her husband, he realized just a moment too late. The flash of long-buried sorrow was brief but acute. "What is this really about?" she asked.

"I've told you." Skipping the onyx warhammer—it was too heavy for the horses—he selected a thin rapier with a line of earth crystals embedded in the grip. This one would be good for the boy. He needed to start using his off hand.

"I mean it." Sarina caught his eyes when he turned around. "I don't blame you for wanting to go. Right now, there's nothing I want more than to find our girl and beat some sense into that stubborn head. But we can't. Neither of us. I have helped you unite these people, but I can't lead them the way that you can. I can't oversee the Watchers or force dimensional gates to open. If you leave—if you *die*—this city falls with you. You know that, Ivain. You know that you couldn't be the one to find her before, and it can't be you now, so what is this really about?"

Ivain felt something in his chest cave as he tried to find a place for the rapier on the overcrowded table. She was right, of course. Power always had a cost, and in this case, it was freedom. The freedom to take care of his own. To only consider his personal priorities.

It couldn't be him, and he hated that realization. Hated it so much that for a moment, he had almost convinced himself otherwise. He had almost let himself be taken in by the fantasy that he could be the one to make his family whole again.

Unable to find space, he tossed the sword onto one of the piles. It landed with a clatter. "Breena was here," he said, not quite trusting himself to look his sister in the eye. "Living in Vale of all places. She was on my island, in my territory, and she didn't come to me for help."

Sarina snorted softly, slipping her hands into her pockets. "One of these days, you're going to have to forgive yourself for what happened with Breena. It wasn't your fault that she did what she did. She chose to use illegal magic in a public arena, and you did everything you could to mitigate the consequences short of dragging your own name through the mud.

"Towards the end, she saw that. She knew that you didn't abandon her in her time of need, and if she didn't come to you, it wasn't because of some old grudge. It's because she wanted to protect you. Harboring a time mage is an executable offense. Our lives here on Tempris would've been over."

With a sigh, Ivain leaned against the table, pressing a hand to his chest as that old ache ripped open. "Maybe," he said. "But I still should've known. I should've known she was here, should've realized that Breena would never take her own life, even when faced with the death of a child. I should've seen what Taly was. Just once, I should've looked closer. I've spent my entire life studying magic, but what was the point of it all if I can't even protect my own child?"

Sarina chuckled grimly. "That's a lot of *shoulds*," she said, rounding the table and leaning against the edge beside him. "And you're neglecting the fact that you were not the only one that failed to take a second look. I was there, and so was Skye, day in and day out. There were the healers that tended to her, the household staff that doted on her, the people on the island, even the mainland nobility we've hosted throughout the years—no one ever looked closer because the magic was *flawless*. Breena was a powerful mage—one *you* trained. If anything, you should take it as a compliment."

He huffed. "Breena didn't do this alone. Taly was glamoured—Kato confirmed that. Which means Esmund was helping her. He's the only water mage that Breena would've trusted to protect her child."

"But then…" Sarina closed her eyes, hanging her head as the weight of that realization settled over her. "Oh no," she murmured. "Aiden and Aimee."

Ivain nodded tiredly. "Yes. If I'm correct, their father's last mission, the one the Crystal Guard had no record of, was to protect a time mage. Taly, specifically. He died so that she could live."

"That has the potential to become a very big problem."

"I'm aware. Taly's not at fault for the way the world is, but whether Aiden and Aimee will choose to see it that way..." Ivain shook his head. "I just don't know." Footsteps sounded from the darkened hall, and he looked to the open doorway. "Speaking of..."

A moment later, two figures emerged from the shadows, marching towards them.

"Aimee—"

"No," Aimee said as she blustered into the room, Aiden close behind. "I was right." Whirling in place, she jabbed a finger into her brother's chest. "*I – was – right.*"

Aiden slapped her hand away. "I've admitted that. I've said the words, *'Aimee, you were right,'* many times now. That's not in question anymore."

"What's going on?" Ivain asked, and both siblings turned.

"I was right," Aimee said, somewhat breathless. "Look." She was smiling as she came forward, waving a stack of papers.

No, not papers. Glamographs, he realized as they were shoved into his hands. One of Taly and the other of a fey child he'd never had the privilege of meeting, though he could hazard a guess as to who she might be. It seemed Aimee and Aiden had already done their own sleuthing, and come to the same conclusions. "Corinna, I presume?"

Aimee nodded eagerly. “I found these last week, but *Aiden*” —she shot him a poisonous glare— “told me I was grasping at straws.”

“Well, if all you had was pictures,” Ivain said, giving the glamographs to Sarina when she held out a hand, “I can see his hesitation.”

Aiden let out a visible sigh of relief. It had been a hard night for the boy, but thankfully, Ivain had been able to stop Sarina from tearing into him too badly. He may have been keeping secrets, but he had also been acting in the service of a friend. The same as he had been earlier that night when he had come running back to the townhome afraid that Skye was about to go off and get himself killed.

Aimee looked undeterred. “It still doesn’t change the fact that I was right. Talya is our cousin—Corinna. And if you’re going to get her back inside the city, you’re going to need my help to conceal what she is.”

It was true. Particularly now that they knew Taly’s sire. They couldn’t bring her back in as she was. Even if they could keep her appearance concealed, there was the issue of her scent. She would likely reek of aether. Every shadow mage in the city would be able to scent her coming from a mile off.

And unfortunately, there wasn’t a political solution. Even if he could figure out a way to bring the Sanctorum to heel, tensions were running too high to broadcast the arrival of a time mage. The Hunt had left an ugly stain on this island’s memory, and while the people here may have been more sympathetic to the time mages’ plight due to their own bloody history, there was no trust there. Taly would still be seen as an enemy.

Which meant they needed a glamour. A damned powerful one.

Ivain shared a look with his sister, then found Aimee's eyes. "This glamour," he said, "it's going to have to do more than just mimic the human form. It's going to have to conceal aether—possibly more than even I possess."

Both Aimee and Aiden faltered at that, paling slightly.

"Do you think you can do it?" Ivain asked. "Would you be willing, considering the possible connection to your father's disappearance?"

Aimee took a breath, squaring her shoulders as her resolve hardened. She smiled as she reached into the pocket of her dressing gown, pulling out a plain silver ring and offering it to him on the palm of her hand. "Will this do?"

Dawn came and went, and they spent the rest of the morning packing supplies and reviewing plans. By that afternoon, Ivain was still trying to gather resources. As far as the rest of the city was concerned, this was a rescue mission for a human. A very special human, but a human nonetheless, so he had to be careful. While he now had a compelling reason to recover her—apart from his own personal affection—there were other considerations.

Unsurprisingly, the nobility had divided into factions inside the city, and with Sarina's help, he'd managed to unite them under a tenuous alliance. But that partnership would quickly unravel if they began to question his leadership, which many of them would if they believed he was putting this city's safety at risk out of mere sentiment.

It would be so much easier if they could just say what Taly was. Maybe, one day, they would be able to. If the situation ever became more stable. But for now, that simply wasn't an option.

"Brother," Sarina called as she swept into his office. The fire in the mantle immediately began to spark, and he braced himself for his sister's temper. "Would you mind terribly if I murdered Lord Holfax?"

"Personally, no." Ivain never looked up from the duty roster. He'd been staring at it for ten minutes now, but unfortunately, no new names had suddenly appeared. "However, it wouldn't reflect terribly well on us if I let you execute members of the nobility based on contempt alone. What has that Shard-sucking bastard done now?"

Sarina was growling as she claimed the chair in front of the desk. "Eliza says she overheard him in the market this morning. He was moaning on about how we were wasting our time trying to rescue some shardless *filth*, and very conveniently ignoring the fact that the only reason he's still alive and free to make an ass of himself in a public street is because our Taly made it to the Vale relay." As she spoke, she clenched her fists, a thin coating of fire rippling across her skin.

"Please don't set my office on fire," Ivain said flatly.

The flames immediately extinguished. "Sorry," she muttered.

Ivain waved her off. "I think the bigger issue here is just *how* he learned of our plans. Less than a day, and it seems like the entire city knows exactly what we're trying to do. Both Eula and Harin have already been in and out of my office—both volunteering to accompany Skye and Kato."

"You told them no?"

Ivain nodded. Kato would go. He was Skylen's brother, and despite the outward animosity between them, family protected family. That sacrifice was justifiable. Even his most vocal opposition wouldn't think to question it. His other mages, however… Each one was indispensable. Each one even more desperately needed in the absence of his two strongest fighters. The enemy had breached their walls once, and despite his personal feelings, he had to think beyond the short term. He was responsible for the citizens of this city and he owed them a duty to ensure that they were protected. As much as it pained him, he had to plan for the possibility that Skye and Kato wouldn't return.

"I wouldn't worry about how news of the rescue spread," Sarina said, rising from her chair and moving to the mantle. Fire mages were always attracted to fire. "We're all stuck inside these walls together. There's nothing to do but gossip and point fingers. No one outside of this family knows what Taly is—that's the important part. If they did, the people in the market would be whispering about time mages instead of humans."

She was right, of course. His sister was always right. "I don't know what to do," he said, glancing at the duty roster. "Skye and Kato can't do this alone, but I'm already taking too big a risk just sending them. If I try to mobilize any of our other forces, I'll just be giving Lord Holfax and his allies additional ammunition. I have to keep the public sentiment on my side. I can't hold this city without it."

Kneeling, Sarina waved a hand through the fire, the flames turning blue as they danced between her fingers. Her brow furrowed in a look he knew well. She had an idea, but the way her lips pressed together told him he wasn't going to like it.

"What about Kalahad Brenin?" she asked.

"No," Ivain replied immediately. "I already said no."

But Sarina went on, "Kato mentioned that they were on friendly terms, and I have it on good authority that Brenin has been maintaining his own personal guard."

And there was yet another problem. Since the siege began, the nobility had been hoarding resources, food, *mages*. In a time when they all needed to be working together, certain factions were still trying to make this about personal gain. It made planning difficult, and if he tried to conscript those otherwise idle hands... well, he suspected he might have a full-fledged mutiny to contend with then.

"I don't trust him," Ivain muttered.

"I don't either. But he's popular in the circles where you're not. You can't give anything more to this mission. Not without coming under scrutiny. But Lord Brenin—he could spare a few mages. And he might be willing. I overheard Kato telling Skye that the man has a fondness for mortals. The Savior of Ebondrift might be a worthy use of his guard, and if he we can get him to publicly back

Taly's rescue, then the other nobility can't condemn you for misallocating resources."

Ivain considered her for a moment. His baby sister was smart—he'd give her that. The woman could charm water from stone, and if she hadn't cut all her ties on the mainland in favor of an ill-advised marriage, he had no doubt that she would've conquered the world by now.

Sarina rose to her feet, eyeing him. He knew that look too. She could see that he was wavering. "We need him," she pressed. "I know how much you hate asking for outside help, especially when it comes to family matters, but if it brings Taly back..."

Then it was worth it. His own prejudices aside.

With a heavy sigh, Ivain pushed himself to stand.

"Where are you going?" Sarina asked, watching as he pulled on a coat.

"To speak with Kalahad Brenin," he muttered as he moved toward the door. "And before you say it," he added when she opened her mouth to speak, "I will watch my language. I might not be as well-versed in courtly manner as I once was, but I'm no fool."

Sarina's eyes followed him as he stepped out into the hallway. "I've never accused you of being a fool. Stubborn, yes. Set in your ways, certainly. But never a fool."

Ivain resisted the urge to roll his eyes. "To my face, you mean. Or did you forget that I'm a shadow mage? I can hear all those things you're always muttering under your breath."

She smiled unapologetically. "Things you hear on account nosiness don't count."

Ivain shot her one final glare over his shoulder. Her laughter followed him all the way to the stairs.

CHAPTER 28

-An excerpt from the Della Daily Life

Witnesses have reported hearing strange sounds coming from within the gates of Infinity's Edge every night this week. One man described the disturbance as "a low growl coming from deep within the earth." Another woman claimed that at certain hours of the night, "even the ground seemed to shake."

These allegations come on the heel of Queen Raine's unprecedented decision to recall all members of the Time Guild to Della, an order which experts say could threaten political negotiations in gate worlds where tensions have been on the rise.

Despite repeated inquiries from the press, representatives at Infinity's Edge still have not made a formal statement regarding the recall, and when asked about the noise, one official, who has asked to remain nameless, stated, "The Queen has decided to redecorate."

Early the next day, Kato had come through on his promise.

Five horses were lined up outside the public stables, and the stableboys were finishing with the supplies. The sun felt warm, a welcome reprieve from the lingering morning chill, and there was no sign of rain on the horizon.

For better or worse, they'd be off within the hour.

Ivain leaned against the paddock fence, arms crossed, lips pressed into a thin line. "I should never have agreed to this."

Skye snorted. "Haven't we already been over this?" he asked as he finished strapping a bandolier of knives to his chest. He was armed to the teeth this morning, with a sword at his back, two more blades hidden in his boots, a collapsible staff buckled to his thigh, and a set of pistols holstered at his waist—both modified with Taly's crystal chit system. "I'm going. There's no use trying to talk me out of it."

"That's not what I mean."

Skye snapped, "Then what do you mean?" It came out more harshly than he intended. Ivain didn't deserve his anger. He knew that. They had all been struggling to cope with the consequences of Taly's actions, and Ivain had taken the rational approach. He had tried to deal with the loss and move forward despite the grief. He had tried to encourage Skye to do the same.

Eventually, he would come to see that. Eventually, he would be grateful for the people that had cared enough to try to pull him back when they thought he'd been standing on the brink of something terrible.

Eventually—but not yet. The pain was still too fresh, and Taly was still out there. His... bondmate.

He was still marveling at that word.

Ivain sighed, glancing at the man that stood on the other side of the yard, speaking with Kato. He was slender and fit with moon-white hair and a narrow face, and his fancy frockcoat and white tie looked too clean for a stable yard.

"Ah." Skye pulled on his coat, smoothing the fabric over his armor. "You don't trust *Kalahad*." The High Lord of Earth's younger brother, whom Kato had introduced them to earlier that morning.

"Not a lick," Ivain admitted without shame. "He was a good kid when he was younger, but now—"

"He kidnaps Feseraa," Skye finished. "Presumably. There are rumors, but no evidence, and Kato claims he's honorable."

"Perhaps," Ivain conceded—grudgingly. "But he's still been vocally anti-mortal the few times I've met him, which makes me wonder why he was so eager to dedicate resources to a rescue mission for a human. I just can't figure out what he stands to gain."

"What makes you think he's trying to gain anything?"

Ivain snorted. "I've been around a long time, boy, and I know a snake when I see one. He's given us three of his strongest mages during the middle of a siege, and fey aren't that generous. Not where humans are concerned."

"You were that generous," Skye pointed out. "You took in an unknown human just because she needed you."

"I was old and lonely," Ivain grumbled. "Not to mention, Sarina had already spent half my fortune buying new clothes for the girl before the end of the first week. This Kalahad, however… He's hiding something. I can feel it."

Yes, Skye had been having similar worries, but— "We're not in a position to turn down help right now, no matter the source."

"Believe me, I understand the variables," Ivain said, even if he still looked distinctly unhappy. "My sweet sister has explained them to me at length. I am well aware that Kalahad is our only option, but that doesn't mean we shouldn't be cautious.

"Watch what you say and do. His men will be watching every move you and your brother make, looking for information that could be used against you. We may be in the middle of a war, but don't think for one second that's going to stop those with more ambition than sense from trying to seize power."

Skye nodded. It was good advice, and while he trusted his brother—something he was still trying to come to terms with—Kalahad was an unknown.

Ivain reached into his pocket. "A gift from Aimee," he said, pushing a small, nondescript box into Skye's hands. "She said it will last up to three days once activated. When you get back, we can figure out something more permanent."

Skye quickly pocketed the box. "Understood."

"And—"

"I know." Skye watched as Kato began to approach, followed by four other highborn fey Skye only vaguely recognized. "I'll make sure I'm alone when I set out to look for her."

Because while Kato might've known what Taly was, the other members of their party didn't. He would need time to create the simulacrum, time to find her, and then time to get her disguised before integrating her into their party.

"Skylen," Kato greeted. "Lord Castaro." And then he began introducing the men and women trailing behind him.

There was Lord Kalahad Brenin—the High Lord of Earth's younger brother.

Followed by Asher Venwraith—a lanky man of middling height with pale blond hair and grass-green eyes. According to him, he was the second son of nobody cares, and his only notoriety stemmed from his very distant relation to the High Lord of Water.

Then came Carin Fenmar. Her eyes were a startling shade of carnation pink, and her hair was the color of pale honey. She stood just a step behind Asher, shoulders hunched, arms wrapped tightly around her body. The shirt peeking out from beneath her leather armor looked strangely shabby compared to the newness of her gear.

The last man Skye knew by reputation only: Vaughn Adamaer. He had a hooked nose, and his hair had been shaved at the sides. He kept rubbing at his chin, like there was still some kind of pain there that had yet to fade. The man's most striking feature, however—the one that sent a chill slithering down Skye's spine—was his eyes.

Deep-set and hooded. *Yellow*. They had a sickly gleam, and it was a struggle not to look away.

"Vaughn," Kalahad said, throwing a pained smile to the yellow-eyed shadow mage at his side, "was put in charge of my protection detail." Neither one of them looked too happy about it. "My older brother—Shards bless his soul—will one day worry himself into an early grave, and despite my insistence that I was perfectly capable of taking care of myself, he insisted that I take his Captain of the Guard along with me. Now, I give him to you."

"That's very generous," Ivain said, his expression schooled into that perfect mask of serene indifference that some nobles never truly mastered.

"Sire," Vaughn said gruffly, ignoring Ivain and Skye as he turned to his master. "I must insist—"

"You insist on nothing." Kalahad crossed his arms imperiously. "My brother may have sent you, but you're mine to command. We still have literal *months* until the first predictions say we might be able to escape through the Aion Gate, and until that time, this village needs hope. It needs a beacon. And that girl—that human the villagers have dubbed their *Savior*—she will be that beacon."

"It is noble of you to pledge your men to rescue a girl you barely know," Ivain said. "You have my *gratitude*." The last word felt forced, but Skye had a feeling he was the only one that noticed.

Kalahad smiled at Ivain. "I only seek to help support the morale in Ryme. For better or worse, we're all in this together now, and it pains me to see so much fear and hopelessness. Although," he added. "you do raise a fair point. We know very little about this girl."

Kalahad looked to Skye. "The two of you were close, yes?"

Skye gave a slow nod. He felt Ivain shift beside him. Kato just sighed.

"What was she like?" Kalahad asked. Too eager. The man was far too eager. "I'm not ashamed to say that I've been dying to meet her. Ever since I heard the Vale transmission. I hear she's a smart little thing. Resourceful, surprisingly ingenious, pretty too." A *merciful* pause. "For a human, that is."

The words shouldn't have gotten underneath his skin so quickly, but the blatant curiosity, the interest in the man's eyes coupled with that stitch of arrogant dismissal had something deep, something primal bubbling to the top and—

"We can't thank you enough," Kato said hastily, clapping a hand to Skye's shoulder. That thing inside him quelled. "Taly was very dear to us all, and we're looking forward to having her home."

"You should've asked sooner," was all Kalahad said in reply. Skye wanted to slap that smile right off his face.

Kato and Kalahad exchanged a few more friendly pleasantries, and when they retreated, both Asher and Carin trailing along after them, Ivain said, "I still don't like him."

"Me neither," Skye muttered, glaring daggers at the man's back. "But help is help."

Ivain loosed a heavy sigh. "I would go with you if I could." There was regret in his eyes.

"We both know you can't." The Gate Watchers were already spread too thin, and while Skye's death would be felt, the village would recover. If they lost, Ivain, however—the entire island would be lost.

Ivain cleared his throat noisily, and Skye pretended not to see the moisture that rimmed his eyes. "Remember," the old man said, "if you don't come back, Sarina's threatened to burn her way into the afterlife just to scream at you, and that's a mess I'd prefer not to clean up. I'd be sweeping up ash for weeks."

Skye chuckled, leaning into the old man when he clapped a hand on his shoulder. "Oh, I wouldn't dare die and risk her anger. I might be crazy, but I'm not stupid."

"Good." Ivain gave his shoulder a firm shake. It was obvious there was more he wanted to say. More he would've said if there had been time. But there wasn't, so all he said was another mumbled, "Good," before letting his hand drop and walking away.

They took the main road, steering the horses into the densely wooded forest that dominated the central part of the island. The air was mild and humid, warming when they moved into the sun, and everything around them was green—the trees, the giant ferns blanketing the forest floor, the moss growing on every surface and in every nook and hollow.

It would've been lovely if not for the flickering wardline along the side of the road, the crystals and wiring dug up and strewn across the pavement—evidence that the barrier had been broken. That meant that the shades had access to the highways, and while the faint scent of rot now mixed with the smell of the forest, they saw neither shade nor beast.

Not until a few miles past the main river crossing.

Skye held up a hand as they approached the clearing, stopping a few feet inside the tree line.

"What are they doing?" Carin murmured, her voice nearly inaudible even to a shadow mage's senses. It was the first time she had spoken all day, though Asher had made up for her silence with a near-constant stream of chatter. He kept poking at her, trying to make her laugh. There was history there, though Skye couldn't quite tell if it was good or bad.

"Is it a trick?" Kato asked. He looked to Skye.

Who just shook his head. "I don't know," he said. He'd never seen shades act this way. The ones he'd encountered had been wild and vicious, desperate for any amount of flesh or aether they could find. They were constantly on the move in search of sustenance, and they would tear a mage apart if given the chance.

These, however—they looked almost… calm.

There were five of them wandering listlessly around the glade. Two men, two women, and a single child. They seemed to have no direction, no purpose. It was unnerving.

Kato pulled up his horse beside him. "Just when I thought I'd seen everything—"

"Never assume you've seen everything," Vaughn said gruffly. "It's childish."

Kato and Skye shared a look. The man was unpleasant, to say the least. There was likely a reason Kalahad wanted to be rid of him.

"Should we find a way around?" Kato asked. "It may be best not to alert these. Shards know what they're doing out here. Or how many more could come running."

"Is there an alternate path?" Vaughn asked.

"Not by road," Skye said, tightening his grip on the reins when his horse tried to kick. The shades were making them antsy. This entire area smelled like death. "We'd have to double back to Ryme to find another highway, and while there are trails that cut through the forest, it would be slow. We'd lose what little protection the wardline is still giving us."

Vaughn let out a low hum, grazing a finger across the amulet at his neck—a single shadow crystal encircled by a carved ouroboros. Skye had seen that symbol before. He knew he had, though he couldn't quite place it.

"Let me take care of this," Vaughn said after a moment. He swept aside his fur-lined cloak, revealing a set of fine gold armor. He reached for an equally exquisite sword.

"Look," Kato said, one hand going to his own sword. His horse skittered back a few steps as the child stumbled closer—a small girl with tangled black hair. Half of her face had been shredded down to the bone, and when she spotted them with a single brown eye—

Tilting her head back, she *screamed.*

And it was like nothing Skye had ever heard. Shrill and piercing, it echoed into the distance and nearly made his ears bleed. Birds jolted from the treetops overhead as the shades began to scramble.

Heart lurching into a gallop, Skye just... reacted.

He dropped from his horse and reached for the dagger in his boot in a single fluid movement. His legs surged, his aether flashed, and then he was flying, a flurry of dirt and gravel streaming in his wake.

All shadow mages could use aether augmentation. They could move magic around their bodies to increase their already-enhanced abilities. Bolstering immortal strength and quickening immortal speed—boosting the superior reflexes they'd been granted solely because they'd been born fey.

But bloodcrafting—that allowed him to *alter* his body. To examine the way his muscles flexed and snapped; the way his heart thundered in his chest, pumping blood and magic through his veins. If he could see it, he could *change* it. He could make it better. He could re-weave his muscles and strengthen his bones.

He could become something that was no longer completely fey.

His dagger found its target as he cut the throat of that screamer. And before any of the shades had begun to react, he'd already started moving through the crowd. A slice here, a cut there—the crystals in their chests shattered. They fell to the ground. It was almost a relief to finally be able to let loose. To give himself over to the moment. For a little while, there was only the dance of metal and the spray of flesh.

Seconds later, Skye skidded to a stop, grabbing his horse's reins before it could panic. He ran a hand down its nose, cooing at it the way Taly had taught him. She'd always had a natural way with animals. He could feel his heart pounding, the fire of his aether still burning in his limbs and only just beginning to recede.

That had felt... *good.* Better than it probably should.

The others were staring at him. Gaping.

"What in the nine hells—" Vaughn began.

"And here I thought I was the faster brother," Kato interjected, shooting a meaningful glance at the others. "Pureblooded bastard... You don't think you could've *shared* a bit of the glory."

Skye forced a smirk. He knew what his brother was doing. Kato was covering for him. What he'd just done—it was unusual, to say the least. "I guess you just need to work on your reflexes."

Kato muttered something under his breath, then looked to Vaughn. "You wanna know what's sad?" he said in a conspiratorial whisper. "Our great-great-great-grandmother could still hand him his ass. The woman was already ancient when she was conscripted to fight in the Shade Rebellion. She ran messages between the Council and the front line, and rumor says she once ran from Tempris all the way to the Arunea outpost in a single day. *On foot.*" Kato looked to Skye, sneering. "What do you think, golden boy? Think you could beat that?"

Skye made sure to scoff, refusing to pick up the bait.

Vaughn hesitated just a moment longer, then let out a derisive snort. He still eyed Skye suspiciously, but for now, he seemed placated as he urged his horse forward, grumbling something about shadow mages from House Ghislain.

Carin, though… she just stared at Skye like she'd seen a ghost. He could still feel her eyes on him as he swung himself back into the saddle.

As they urged the horses forward, through the clearing. It was almost like she knew. Like she could see each spell he had used, the magic still entwined beneath his skin, meshed with flesh and bone.

But then her eyes shifted to the bodies littering the clearing. Their mouths gaped, and their limbs tangled. She paled even further when her horse stepped over that little girl with the slit throat and black hair.

"Hey," he heard Asher murmur to Carin. Turning slightly, Skye saw the water mage draw up his horse beside her. "Look at me."

So, she did.

"It's okay," he said softly, reaching over to place a hand on hers, still clutched around the reins in a white-knuckled grip. "*You're* okay. We'll get through this, Cee. Nod if you understand."

She gave a shaky nod, and Skye suddenly felt guilty for eavesdropping. Whatever this was—it was personal. They were fighting an army of dead men, and it was impossible to come away from that without a few demons. As he looked back at Carin Fenmar now, he could see each one of those monsters and their gnashing teeth.

Thankfully for her—and this mission—Asher Venwraith seemed more than willing to fight them.

Evening came and went, and Skye was grateful for the brief but heavy shower that pounded down on them somewhere outside of Della. Asher and Carin had grumbled out a few choice curses, complaining about visibility, but the downpour helped wash away some of the sweat and rot that clung to them as they began piling up a mound of shades.

It was a precaution as they drew nearer to the palace. Shades fed on flesh and aether, and they didn't want anything that would draw them into their camp.

Kato began directing the others to gather wood and kindling for the pyre, and Skye checked each body, retrieving arms and legs and heads and trying to piece them back together. There were humans and fey, even an old draegon man whose scaly skin, once a vibrant blue, had faded to a dull gray. After the Schism, most of the otherworld races had retreated to Lycia, but with the impending Aion Gate connection, the merchants had started to return to the island.

Shards, please don't let them have nephilim.

With their paper-white skin and bat-like wings, those cranky bastards were already unsettling. If they'd been turned into shades, however… Skye shuddered. That was something he didn't even want to imagine.

"The palace is just ahead," Vaughn called to the group. He was still atop his horse, and the flames from the nearby pyre glinted in those yellow eyes. "As far as I can tell, the area is clear, and if memory serves, the stables should still be intact. We can make camp there."

There was a chorus of grumbled agreement, and then they were moving forward again.

The last of the sunlight began to fade, and Skye channeled more aether into his eyes, blinking as the darkness of the surrounding forest bled away. He could already hear the rapids that flowed beneath the palace roaring in the distance, and as they drew nearer to the main gate, they had to slow the horses as the terrain flowed from dirt and moss-covered roots to broken pavement.

Infinity's Edge loomed in the distance, a behemoth of a building that, even in its current state of neglect, still managed to outshine any of the palaces in Arylaan. The spires, though crumbling, still stretched towards the sky, and the veins of golden crystal that swept through the white marble stone glittered in the moonlight. Despite the fighting that had taken place shortly after the Schism, the palace had been treated with surprising gentleness, and most of the destruction had been contained to the area just outside the fence line.

"The ground has been disturbed," Kato murmured as the horses carefully picked their way through the scraps of armor and refuse littered along the black iron fence. "And I don't think this was Aiden. The destruction is too widespread, even for an earth mage."

The old cobbled drive was cracked and overgrown, and there were several old Mechanica suits lying in pieces around the main gate. The helmets had been crushed, the torsos dented. For some, the brightly colored metal was so twisted and bent, it was no more than a tangle of scrap and wiring.

And all around, the ground was littered with shards of crystal. *Hyaline*, Skye realized. The closest relay tower—what used to be a shining colossus that dwarfed everything around it—was now a jagged pillar of cracked stone jutting from the earth.

That was recent, he thought, shivering. He couldn't even begin to imagine the force it would've taken to bring down one of those towers.

The stables were on the northeastern side of the palace grounds, and Skye kept his hand on his sword as they skirted around the edge of the property, cataloging each building, each trail. The gardens were overgrown, but he could still pick out what had once been rolling lawns with winding walks bordered by long rows of evergreens and colorful exotic flowers.

Everything around him had an aura of abandonment, of hushed despair. And though he had never believed in ghosts—not in the way that Taly did, though he was more inclined to now after those little blue bastards had terrorized him down in the tunnels—he couldn't deny that this place *felt* haunted. Like there was something here, watching from the shadows.

As Vaughn had predicted, the stables were intact, and they began the process of cooling the horses and setting up camp.

"I'm going to go scout the area," Skye said to Kato as they both stood to the side, watching Asher and Carin building a fire beneath a hole in the stable roof. "There are too many places to hide inside the palace, and I'd feel better if the main entrances were warded."

Kato gave him a look that said: *Do you really expect me to believe that?*

To which, Skye just shrugged, meeting his gaze and refusing to back down. He could feel the tug of that thread more clearly now, and if Taly was anywhere nearby, he didn't want to wait until tomorrow morning to find out. He wanted to know tonight.

Plus, this would be the easiest time to break away from the group. When they were tired and less inclined to question his motives.

Kato sighed. "Don't go outside the fence line. It's not much, but it does give us some protection from the forest beasts."

Skye frowned at what almost seemed like genuine concern. "Why are you really here, Kato?"

Kato's brows rose, but Skye didn't back down. He hadn't asked the question out of malice—just curiosity. His brother had always been a capricious, sometimes hateful presence in his life, and yet now he had somehow become his most ardent defender. *Now* he suddenly cared.

It didn't make sense.

Kato was the first to look away, stuffing his hands in his coat pockets. "I already told you—you look so pathetic, I'd rather let a shade take a bite out of me than have to watch you piss and moan about your lost love for even a second longer than I have to.

"Now go," he muttered with a jerk of his chin. "I'll make something up to tell the others since we both know there's no point warding an empty kitchen."

With a final glance at the stable and their makeshift shelter, Skye gave his brother one last look before making his way towards the palace.

Skye followed the tug of that invisible thread inside the palace, walking from room to room, hallway to hallway. There was no smell of rot here; no sign of anything more dangerous than dust and cobwebs. And when the paintings began to repeat, and he realized that thread had just led him in a circle, he stopped, crouching in the middle of what used to be the throne room.

The black-and-white marble tile was cracked, and the long rows of windows that lined either side of the massive hall were coated with slithering, leafless stems so thick, they had become little more than a dense mat of foliage that gobbled up even the faintest trace of moonlight.

Atop a large dais, the throne loomed at the farthest end of the hall. Crystal roses were ensconced between coils of gold and silver, and every swirl, every petal, had been obscured by a thick layer of dust.

"Alright," Skye said, shivering at the way the empty hall seemed to absorb the sound of his voice. He pulled a small flask from his pocket and frowned.

Aiden had collected several samples of Taly's blood while she was recovering from the harpy, but the healer had used most of it up during his own search. There were only a few drops left now—barely enough to cast a single spell.

He would only get one shot at this.

Holding his breath, Skye tipped the vial and let those few precious drops *drip, drip, drip* onto the tile. He bit the flesh between his forefinger and thumb and let his own blood mingle with hers.

Where and when, he thought, and that part still made him nervous. In his dream, Taly had said that *when* had become an issue, but this spell was supposed to account for that. There were breaks in the veil between worlds all over Tempris. It would just be an issue of figuring out which one she had fallen through.

Skye began to pull at his aether, shaping the spell in a way that felt so unlike anything he had ever cast before. It twisted his magic, made his heart flutter. It felt *wrong.*

You're just not used to casting this way, he tried telling himself even as the sweat began to bead on his brow. Even as his aether recoiled, seizing in his veins. *Bloodcraft is an extension of your magic. Just another application. You can control it.*

Slowly, *slowly*, he felt another presence curl through his thoughts, wrapping around his bones and tugging at that bond.

And he did his best not to panic as the pool of blood spreading across the floor began to undulate and roil, peeling away from the tile and rising into the air, glowing a faint red.

The light pulsed. And flickered. His own magic glimmered beneath the smooth, milky surface—violet pinpricks of light inside a sea of blood.

Cautiously, Skye plucked at the molten orb, shaping it with sure, quick motions. He kept an image in his mind, something that reminded him of the person he wanted to find.

When he was done, the tiny animal rolled over, shook itself, and then stared up at him with eyes that looked like little purple jewels.

A rabbit—perfectly formed. A miniature version of the animal Taly hadn't been able to bring herself to kill. After he had brought the little beast home, Eliza and the rest of the kitchen staff had adopted it, claiming for themselves that final link to Taly. The plump little monster now lived inside the townhouse kitchen with its own little bed and its own little collar and its own little bowl emblazoned with the name: *Marshmallow*.

Skye sighed. The things that he did for that woman… He really did have it bad.

The rabbit shook its head, throwing off a spray of blood that evaporated mid-air. The bell at its neck tinkled, and it twitched its nose, almost annoyed that it had been made to wait.

Clearing his throat, Skye said, with purpose, "Find your donor." The words were carefully crafted, taken from a list of commands. Simulacrums could only follow a limited set of orders, and the slightest mistake, the smallest blip in pronunciation, could burn away the aether powering the spell.

Shards, he hoped he didn't mess this up.

The little rabbit gave another shake of its head. It still floated mid-air, and as it began to hop away, it left tiny footprints that slowly faded and disappeared, washed away by some invisible force.

Something groaned from deep within the palace, and Skye paused, letting his hand drop to one of the pistols at his waist as he turned in a circle.

His nostrils flared as he scented the air, and he blinked, channeling a bit more aether and watching as the shadows turned just a little brighter.

But there was nothing out of place.

It's probably just the wind, he told himself, though it did little to banish the trickle of dread that had managed to push its way in.

Still, there was no going back now. Chanting a silent prayer to anyone that might be listening, Skye followed the simulacrum deeper into the palace.

The palace was a twisting labyrinth of marble and gold hallways, and Skye's heart began to beat just a little faster as the simulacrum led him not up, not out, not into the forest—but *down.*

Down and *down* and *down.* Until the air turned musty and the sound of running water began to pound against the walls.

Down and *down* and *down.* Until he knew that he was underground. How far, he couldn't be sure. The wide hallways lined with mirrors and tapestries and paintings had given way to tight corridors made from rough-hewn rock. This was likely some sort of old tunnel system built so that in the event of an attack, the Crystal Guard would be able to smuggle the Time Shard to safety.

The scent of aether began to permeate the air, faint at first but growing stronger the farther he descended. It stung his nose and made his skin feel clammy. It even began collecting on the backs of his hands, shimmering like someone had soaked him with violet paint.

A light shone up ahead. After what felt like hours of walking in darkness with only the glitter of aether and the dim glow of that tiny rabbit to show the way, the blazing halo was almost blinding.

At last, Skye stepped through the arched doorway, and he felt his breath catch as he glimpsed the room beyond. The chamber was round, with high ceilings and crisscrossing bridges, each one terminating in a carved, stone doorway identical to the one in which he stood. Below him, the ground dropped away, disappearing into infinity. There were no lamps or torches, only a ridge set into the wall that glowed with a soft, unwavering golden light. And in the center of the room, elevated on its own platform—

Skye's eyes went wide, and he took a step into the room, holding tightly to the railing and trying not to think about that steep drop. Even with a shadow mage's senses, he couldn't discern the bottom.

It was smaller than any he'd seen on the island, and the control panel looked strange, flickering with a set of runes he didn't recognize. But there was no mistaking those smooth, flat planes of crystal.

Skye took another step, dazed. Because there in the center of this strange cavern, surrounded by columns of violet and gold-crystal stood—

"A gate."

But not just that.

Shards, not just that.

Between the two pillars of hyaline flanking the portal stood a room lined with giant screens and flickering control panels and long tables stacked with tools and papers and crystals.

It was a *room*. With doors and windows that showed a land of rolling hills and colorful gardens and impossibly blue skies.

Not underground. Not a cavern.

The gate was open.

And that little rabbit that had become Skye's lifeline in the dark continued to hop ahead of him, across the bridge and up the steps of the dais.

As it approached that shimmering wall of magic, it paused, looking over its shoulder and twitching its nose before disappearing through the portal.

CHAPTER 29

-From the personal diary of Talya Caro

I've had the same dream for almost a week now, and even though it's been months since I had a vision that made me feel like that first night, this one—this one I can't seem to shake.

Not because of the dream itself—this isn't the first time I've dreamed of Skye at the palace. It's more because of how rigid *it feels. I've never had a dream that felt quite like this. Where no matter what I do, how many variables I change, it always ends the same. It's like I'm marching through a set of events that have already been decided—set into immovable stone and immune to alteration.*

It haunts me now, even in my waking hours. I blink, and I see Skye lying in a pool of his own blood. I'll turn a corner, and the air will suddenly reek of pain and death.

"See the timelines and choose your path."

That's what the Queen is always saying. If time is a tapestry, then I am the weaver. I control my dreams.

But what do I do when there are no more threads to cut? What do I do when Skye is already dead, and there's blood on my hands?

For one moment—one single breathless moment—Skye allowed himself to doubt.

Going through that portal would be the stupidest thing he'd ever done. Crazier than believing in dreams. More reckless than learning a handful of illegal spells.

He had no idea where it went or if he'd even be able to get back. There were no assurances here. All he knew for certain was that Taly had gotten herself into some deep shit, and that for some reason, as always seemed to be the case, it was up to him to pull her out of it.

And Shards, how was that even fair? She had lied to him for months on end, threatening a bond, a *trust*, that had been cultivated and nurtured over a lifetime of friendship. She had fucked up, and yet *he* was the one risking *his* life to bring her home.

It wasn't fair. None of it. And he would be insane to go through that portal. Completely and utterly mad.

But that thread was still tugging him forward. The evidence of a love so deeply ingrained into every living, breathing part of him that even his soul had started to reach out, desperate to keep her close.

He loved her. No matter what she had done or why.

Though when he did find her, he might just kill her himself. After the hell she'd put him through, he was certainly reserving the option.

His moment was up. And so, Skye took a deep breath, gave that thread a small tug in return, and then stepped through the portal.

Taly was dozing, drifting somewhere between wakefulness and sleep, when the door to her apartment creaked open. The clatter of dishes accompanied by the smell of food had her blinking, blearily staring around the room.

"Who's there?" she mumbled, lifting her head off the desk. A scrap of paper stuck to her forehead, and she frowned as she peeled it away from her skin, squinting at the notes she'd scribbled the night before. She yawned and rubbed at the ink that was surely smeared across her forehead.

"It's only me," Leto replied, drifting into the small tower library, a silver serving tray as well as a flat, wooden box balanced in her ghostly hands.

Calcifer immediately rose from his "bed," which instead of a palace now vaguely resembled a stately coin throne with a blue velvet pillow as the seat. It had eventually just been easier to disassemble the entire structure than trying to adjust for his increasing size, repurposing the coins into something new. His long gold-tipped tail swished back and forth as he went to inspect their visitor.

Taly rubbed the sleep from her eyes. "What time… Shit." She looked to the window, noting the position of the sun. "Shit!"

Ever since she had beaten Azura's game almost a week ago, the days had started to blur together. Her lessons had stopped, and they no longer played tag. The Queen no longer insisted that she attend tea or come down for dinner. So, with nothing else to do—and not knowing just when Azura planned to test her or what that might entail—she had started studying.

Every hour of every day, learning every spell she could get her hands on.

"Ma'am," Leto said as she zigzagged through the haphazard stacks of books and journals that littered the floor. Calcifer tried to nudge the box from her hands, and she raised it higher. "Could I perhaps—"

"No." Taly began flipping through the book in front of her, trying to find her place. She vaguely remembered sitting back and watching the sun start to rise, which meant she had to have fallen asleep sometime just after dawn. "I know where everything is."

Calcifer gave an annoyed yowl as he reared up, reaching for the box with two big black paws. That tail knocked over one of the stacks. Then another. A quick freezing spell saved the third.

"*Calcifer*," Taly warned. She snapped her fingers, and he gave up the box, trotting ahead of Leto and over to where she sat at the desk. His wings were gone today, and only that large, slightly gangly feline form remained. "Veet." That was Faera for sit, and he obeyed, plopping down beside her and patiently waiting for the cloud of golden aether that she manifested on the palm of her hand. He breathed it in languidly, licking his lips.

It was hard to express just how glad she'd been to finally wean him off blood.

"Sorry." Taly shot Leto an apologetic glance. "He's been antsy lately. I need to take him for a run."

Leto just nodded, finally giving up on trying to find her way through the stacks and instead floating over them. "Surely, I can return some of these to the main library. Juniper has been complaining about the books that have been going missing."

Taly scowled. She hated that old fairy. Even if he was just an amorphous blob of blue light, she still got the sense that he was glaring at her every time she visited the main library.

"He would only let me check out two books at a time," Taly said, finally finding her place. "Obviously" —she gestured to the many, many, *many* books she had pilfered and brought back to her tower— "that wouldn't do. The Queen hasn't told me anything about this final test, which means I need to study everything."

Without ceremony, Leto plucked the book from Taly's hands and set the serving tray in front of her, not bothering to move aside her notebooks and journals.

"I'm not hungry," Taly said, even as her stomach growled. She tried not to look too desperate as Leto pulled off the dish covers, revealing eggs and bacon and batter cakes as well as several thick slices of still-steaming bread that had already been slathered with butter and jam.

She reached for her book, but Leto held it just out of reach.

"You did not come down for dinner last night," Leto pointed out. "And you skipped lunch as well."

"I was studying."

"You still need to eat."

"Can I eat while I read?"

Reluctantly, Leto placed the book on the desk, only moving her hands away when Taly picked up a fork and began shoveling food into her mouth.

Leto peered over her shoulder. "I did not know you were studying Relin."

Taly shrugged. "I thought it might help me with my Sight," she said around a mouthful of food.

"Perhaps," Leto conceded. "However, I find his work to be rather… unscientific. I would recommend Adrunn or even Ilu. Their studies on chronal field theory are far more in-depth."

Taly paused, her fork hovering mid-air. "You know chronal field theory?"

Behind Leto's blank expression, she could've sworn she saw a flicker of amusement. Taly still hadn't told the fairy she knew what she was—what any of them were. And she didn't plan to. The fairies were freer with their words when she acted dumb.

"Good afternoon!"

Taly groaned, reaching for her coffee as the door to the apartment opened and shut.

Azura was every inch the queen as she strutted into the library, dressed in a heavy white velvet gown that hugged her tightly at the waist before exploding into a voluminous mass of skirts.

She wore a matching robe edged with silver, with a high stiff collar and long stately sleeves that grazed the floor. For the first time that Taly could remember, there was a crown nestled inside the coil of dark curls piled atop her head.

"You're in a good mood," Taly grumbled into her cup.

Azura practically floated over to the windows, beaming from ear to ear as she effortlessly maneuvered the maze of books. Her skirts swished and sighed, swirling around her like a cloud. "Well, it's a beautiful day!" she exclaimed, waving a hand at the window. "The sun is shining, the sky is blue, the gardens are in bloom—"

"It's like that every day," Taly pointed out. "It's literally the same day. We're in a loop."

"True," Azura conceded. "But that doesn't mean that today isn't special."

Taly snorted. "Let me guess—Rhanna invented a new teacake."

"No," Azura chirped. "Although that would also be cause for celebration."

Taly had to rein in the urge to roll her eyes. If she never saw another crumpet, it would be too soon.

"Today," Azura went on, "is examination day."

Taly choked on her coffee. "What?" she asked, wiping away the liquid that dribbled down her chin.

"Examination day, my dear!" Azura stooped, examining the piles of books, occasionally picking one up, nodding, and then setting it back on a *different* stack.

Taly made a note of each misplaced book, irritated that she would have to go through and reorganize later.

"You know," Azura sighed, a dreamy look on her face, "I envy you sometimes. What I wouldn't give to be a student again. To feel the rush of victory, the agony of defeat. Always walking that razor-thin edge between—"

"Stop." Taly held up a finger, ignoring the Queen's pout at being interrupted. Azura's speeches could get lengthy, and it was best to stop them early. "Let's go back to the part about the exam. That's today?"

Azura turned to Leto. "Why do I even bother? Everything I say just goes in one ear and out the other."

Taly gulped down the rest of her coffee. Her final test—the thing she had been dreading all week. And it was today. "I take it you're not going to tell me what it is you want me to do. Or what happens if I fail."

The Queen's lips twitched. "No and no."

Taly grimaced, picking up her fork, and then setting it down. She'd suddenly lost her appetite.

"Oh, don't look so stricken," Azura said. "I'm sure you'll manage. There's a bloodthirsty little imp hiding somewhere deep inside of you, just waiting to come out. Never be afraid to bathe in the blood of your enemies, my dear. It's highly underrated. In fact, the nephilim believe it has certain health benefits."

Pushing the tray aside, Taly rested her head on the desk. "I just… I don't even want to know."

"Leto." Azura snapped her fingers. "I want her ready in an hour. And make sure the beast" —she waved a hand at Calcifer, who had retreated to his golden coin throne— "remains contained. I don't want him to come running if he hears the girl scream."

"Yes, Majesty," came Leto's cool reply as Taly gave a loud groan.

"Oh, and did you remember—"

"They are right here, Majesty." Leto picked up the flat wooden box she'd brought in with the breakfast tray, drifting over to the side of the desk. When she pulled the lid away, Taly's eyes widened.

Her hand darted out, snatching the air dagger from the bed of crimson velvet and pressing it to her chest. "Zephyr," she breathed, savoring the familiar press of the shadow crystal against her palm. It was a simple little blade, completely worthless and yet so very dear. She'd been carrying it when she was first brought to the palace, but she hadn't seen it since.

Her eyes snapped to Azura. "You said you lost my weapons," she said, not bothering to hide the note of accusation that edged her voice.

Azura shrugged. "Just because something's lost doesn't mean it has to stay that way."

Taly frowned as she reached for one of the two pistols still inside the box. The Queen was lying. Crazy as she was, everything she did or didn't do always had a purpose. "Why are you giving these back to me now?" she asked, because even that was likely strategic.

Azura threw her hands into the air, doing a very impressive impersonation of someone who had just been insulted. "Can't I do something nice? I merely thought you might like to have them today as… I don't know. A good luck charm? A totem? We have far better weapons in the armory, but I know how sentimental you get over your kills."

Taly looked up, her hand hovering over the second pistol. "Did you just say *kills*?"

But Azura didn't answer as she turned on her heel, flicked her skirts in a swirl of velvet, and marched out the same way she had entered, calling over her shoulder, "Throne room—one hour. Don't be late."

Skye couldn't believe his eyes. The hallways and rooms he passed were open and airy, not a speck of dust to be seen. And even though it had been night when he left Kato and the others, the midday sun streamed through the windows, casting everything around him in a warm, golden glow.

Everything was new and clean, and... none of it made sense.

He hadn't stepped through time. He was pretty sure of that. If this was the past, there would be courtiers loitering in the halls. But then what was this place? An illusion? Possibly. He had also heard that the time mages used to be able to create pocket universes, but a place like this—he couldn't even begin to imagine the amount of magic it would've taken to create a place like this.

Not even the near-limitless power of the Time Shard would've been able to pull it off. Not alone, anyway.

The rabbit still bounced ahead of him, but its light was starting to fade. Soon, it would go out entirely, and then… he didn't know what he'd do. Follow the bond? The tug of that thread was stronger now, but indistinct, leading everywhere and nowhere all at once.

Skye turned the corner and found himself at an intersection that diverged into four paths. Taly's scent was all around him, but it was old. She hadn't passed this way in at least a day. Maybe more.

The rabbit hesitated, fat crimson drops of blood peeling away from its body and dripping to the floor.

Skye bit his thumb. "Rest now," he said. It was another command taken from a very small list, and he held out his hand.

Immediately, the little rabbit hopped over, alighting on his palm. Its nose twitched as it began to lick at the single drop of blood pooling on his thumb.

When it was done, Skye placed the simulacrum on his shoulder, snorting when it scurried down the lapel of his coat and into his front pocket. Its head poked out, and it blinked up at him, seeming to say: *Hurry up. We don't have much time.*

A light glinted in his peripheral vision, and Skye slipped his sword from its sheath, hesitating when he thought he heard… *windchimes?*

He listened closer and looked around, his eyes going wide when he saw three pale-blue orbs melt from the shadows.

"I remember you," he whispered. From the tunnels. They almost looked like… "Fairy fire."

That was fairy fire. Just like Taly had claimed she had seen outside her window so long ago.

Shards, she was going to be intolerable now. She always was when she was right.

They were at the far end of the corridor, and they gave a little hop when he moved forward and let out a chime-like warning when he turned away.

Before he could question his own sanity—after all, these were the same little bastards that had tormented him with Taly's voice—he forced his feet to move, one in front of the other, following the flicker of that soft, blue light.

The palace seemed endless, so much larger than it appeared from the outside. Left, then right, then straight ahead. Deeper and deeper he went, keeping his footsteps quiet, trying to breathe over the tightness in his chest.

Finally, they entered a corridor longer than the rest, dark save for the thin strip of light shining from beneath a wide, arched doorway at the opposite end of the hall.

That chime-like laughter ceased.

The doors opened on silent hinges.

The very air seemed to hold its breath.

"Yeah, yeah," Skye said to no one in particular. "I can take a hint."

Muttering the foulest curse he knew, Skye continued moving forward. For better or worse, he knew where he was now. Knew where he was meant to go.

It was a struggle to relax his grip on his sword, to push down that instinctive urge to run as he continued to move forward, down the hallway and through that door into—the throne room.

The place where this journey had begun.

Like everything else he had encountered, the room was resplendent. Shafts of warm, buttery sunlight streamed through the windows, and roses coiled around ivory columns, each perfect petal somehow delicately edged with gold.

Skye turned in a circle, his eyes darting first to that great golden throne gleaming up atop its dais, then to the three massive chandeliers tinkling high overhead.

Where are you, Taly?

She was close by. He could sense it in the way the bond thrummed, almost whispering in his ear.

A door slammed, and Skye whirled, raising his sword and backing up as the sound of footsteps echoed from the hallway. Someone was approaching, but it wasn't Taly. The stride was too long, the footfall too heavy.

A figure loomed in the doorway, and Skye recognized the broad shoulders and gold-plated armor well before he heard that all-too-familiar voice drawl, "Well, well, well—what do we have here?"

Skye's blood ran cold. "Vaughn," he said as the yellow-eyed shadow mage stepped further into the room. "What are *you* doing here?"

Vaughn didn't answer as his eyes slid over the room, a muted sense of awe evident in his expression.

Skye eyed the sword at the man's waist, the line of daggers strapped to his chest, some streaked with what looked and smelled like fresh blood. Was it Kato's? He had said he was going to make up an excuse. Keep them busy.

Shards, where was his brother?

"You followed me," Skye said. Ivain had been right not to trust this man. But what did he want? Why was he here?

"We were worried when your brother said you were going off on your own," Vaughn said gently.

Bullshit, Skye thought, retreating another step towards the throne. Vaughn blocked the main doorway, but he knew that most of these throne rooms had a door behind the dais—just one more security measure.

"And where is my brother?" Skye asked, trying to buy time. Vaughn was older, a brawler. He had focused his training on the physical attributes of shadow magic—prioritizing raw strength at the expense of everything else. He was a living weapon crafted of flesh and bone rather than crystal and steel, and if it came down to a fight, Skye would lose.

"Your brother is back at the camp," Vaughn said lightly. As though they weren't inside a palace that shouldn't exist. As though he hadn't followed him here in secret.

"I gave an order not to be disturbed," Skye pointed out. "One I'm sure Kato passed along."

"I do not follow your orders, boy."

Skye gave up another slow, cautious step, quickly schooling his features when he felt the distinct sigh of water magic itch across his skin.

Fuck.

Of course, Vaughn didn't come alone. Asher was, after all, a water mage, and the only one in their party capable of tracking a shadow mage without giving himself away. Even a simple glamour could obscure sound and scent and sight, making him and anyone standing in his radius effectively invisible.

Which meant that both Carin and Asher were likely standing behind him now, concealed behind a veil of water magic. And though Asher would be easy to take out—he was weaker, slower—Carin could be a problem. She was a shadow mage. Not as strong as Vaughn, but still formidable.

Skye kept his eyes pointed straight ahead. This was a trap, and Vaughn was the distraction. If he gave even the faintest hint that he'd figured it out—this would be over before it had even begun.

"So if you don't follow my orders—" Skye began, letting his magic fan out, feeling for the edges of the water glamour. Just behind him and to the left, and Vaughn was still advancing—herding him. "—then who holds your loyalty?"

Vaughn chuckled darkly. "That is none of your concern."

"I'm afraid I have to disagree with you there." Skye glanced over his shoulder, pretending to trip as he looked for the ripple of water magic he knew would be there.

Shards, think. Think!

They didn't want him dead. That was a safe assumption. After all, Vaughn had already had plenty of opportunities to gain the upper hand. He could've struck without warning at any point, but he hadn't attacked, hadn't even drawn his weapon. Instead, he had set a trap, putting his men in the perfect position to jump out and disarm him as soon as he stepped into range.

Which meant they wanted him alive. For what reason—he couldn't be sure. But that did give him a slight advantage.

"Come, Skylen," Vaughn said, holding out his hands in a gesture of friendship. "Let's talk. You must have questions—questions that I can answer."

"Why don't we start with why you're really here? It's not to help me, that's for sure."

"We want the girl, of course."

Skye snarled, body shaking with rage.

Another step. Another glance—it was a good glamour, practically invisible. But not completely. He could still see a shimmer in the space beside the dais, where the light shifted and bent as though it were being directed through a prism. And truthfully, if they had expected him not to notice the faint itch of water magic permeating the air, then they must truly believe him to be a novice.

Which was fair. With only twenty-five summers to his name, he was a child in their eyes. How could he match hundreds, perhaps even thousands of years of experience?

The simple answer was that he couldn't. Not in a direct fight. They had more training, a more complete command of their magic. But that didn't mean he couldn't use their assumptions to his advantage. He was young—that was true. But he was still a member of House Ghislain—one of the most powerful houses in the history of the Fey Imperium. He had more raw aether at his command than most fey could ever dream of possessing, and he had been schooled in the art of magic since birth.

A plan began to take shape, and he pulled at his magic, letting his aether curl around the crystals embedded in his armor and clacking together in his pocket. With the dense ambient aether swirling all around them, Vaughn was unlikely to notice this subtle shift.

"I'm sorry, Vaughn." Skye plastered on his best smirk when Vaughn angled his head, confused. "But I don't think this is a fair fight."

Whirling in place, Skye ducked as a sword shrieked overhead. There was no one in front of him, but that water glamour still itched.

Find the water mage. That's what Ivain had always said. It was easier to fight if you could see what you were facing.

Skye scanned the area—saw the ripple, the subtle shift in the light.

He lunged, immediately slamming into a body. The man barely had time to grunt before Skye had planted his feet and swung his sword in a wide arc.

Blood sprayed, wet and warm, as a head with wild blonde hair rolled across the gleaming marble tile. Asher's body slumped to the ground as the water glamour evaporated in a hiss of mist and magic.

Carin slowly faded into focus, eyes wide and swiftly filling with tears. She was only a few steps away, her attention riveted on that head as it continued to bounce and roll, leaving a trail of blood across the tile.

Less than a heartbeat of hesitation, but Skye seized it, launching himself forward.

Carin recovered, her own aether pulsing as she let out an enraged scream that bounced off the walls, echoing with a pain that was all-too-familiar. Asher had been a friend, maybe more.

And now he was dead.

Skye swung his sword, but she met his blade with her own, sinking the dagger in her off-hand into his side, then his gut, rage fueling each blow. The pain was sharp, but he didn't let himself falter. He'd been expecting that blow, as well as the next, and the next. She was fast, striking with lightning-quick precision.

But Skye was still larger.

And now she was close—close enough for him to end this fight.

Clenching his jaw, Skye dodged the knife, feinting left, then right. Her dagger sliced through nothing but air, throwing her slightly off-balance, and he hooked a foot behind hers, tugging at her ankle and sending her hurtling towards the ground.

Bone crunched, and metal clanged. A second head rolled to join the first.

The altercation was over in seconds, and Skye panted, gritting his teeth against the pain. The air reeked of blood, but he forced back the bile as he stepped over the body and the rapidly spreading pool of crimson still gushing from the neck of the corpse. He raised his sword and fixed his attention back on Vaughn.

One-on-one. He liked those odds a bit better. Granted, Vaughn was stronger, but at least he stood a chance now.

"Well now," Vaughn drawled, re-sheathing his own sword without any sense of urgency. Skye's eyes tracked the movement. "It seems I underestimated you." A glance at the bodies that still twitched, the two heads that lay only a few feet apart, twin expressions of slack-jawed shock distorting their delicate, fey features. "Not that it matters. This is an irritation, but hardly a setback. They were far from important."

Traitor, traitor, traitor. The word was a chant, pounding in his blood. This man had been in their city. He had worked with their guards and their people—and they'd had no idea.

Skye adjusted his grip on his sword, groaning when the tendons of his arm sparked with pain. Carin had stabbed him twice in the ribs and once in the gut, but the wounds should've healed by now. He channeled a bit more aether, but—

Why wasn't he healing?

"It will be a slight inconvenience replacing Lady Fenmar, but" —Vaughn smiled— "I suppose we have you now, don't we? The simulacrum was a bit crude, but as long as you have the aptitude for bloodcraft, the rest can be taught."

Skye didn't reply. Merely kept his sword raised as Vaughn began to circle him. The pain was spreading, and he was still bleeding. He could feel his aether start to dip.

"To be honest," Vaughn said, "we were starting to think you weren't going to look for the girl. We knew you were the key, of course. One more week, however, and my master was going to have you seized, and I doubt your pretty little bondmate would've liked that very much."

Skye's stomach churned. There was no way this man could've known about the bond. No way he could've known who or what she was.

Unless…

"I was there," Vaughn clarified, no doubt reading the shock in his expression. "When she projected. Little thing probably thought she was dying with so much magic pouring out of her. I suspect she went to say her goodbyes."

Vaughn was still circling. And Skye let him, keeping an eye on the door. Trying to ignore the rising pain.

"Whether you know it or not, we are at *war*," Vaughn said, hands clasped behind his back. "There is a plague moving through our ranks. A sickness that could kill us all. Fewer and fewer of our kind are born each year, and yet the Genesis Council has done nothing. They sit on their thrones, watching as we allow our fellow fey to breed with those shardless *beasts*, all in some vain attempt to pad our ranks with half-blood imposters."

Those yellow eyes flared. "My master is the only one willing to do what must be done. He has given us a way forward, a promise for the future, and your bondmate is going to help him deliver us. With a time mage, we can solve this problem once and for all."

"Taly will never help you," Skye bit out. The pain continued to blaze, setting his blood on fire and pulsing like a second heart. "And neither will I."

"Are you sure about that?"

A beat of confusion, and then—

Skye's grip on his sword began to slacken, the strength leaching from his body.

That snake's smile widened. "Let me put it this way."

Weakness pulled at Skye's arms and legs, rapidly spreading into every cell and fiber. His sword clattered to the ground. *Poison,* he thought, trying not to let the panic take root. The pain, his wounds—Carin's dagger must have been tipped with poison.

So he began to push back. It was eating away at his aether, but he pushed back. There were ways to clear poison from the blood—with bloodcraft. He only needed to figure out how to shape the spell, how to—

Vaughn kicked the sword away, and the clang of metal against tile thundered in Skye's ears as he tried but failed to rein in his aether. His magic was crushing in on him, lurching out of his control and threatening to devour every shred of sense.

Vaughn said, "You only have two choices, boy."

The pain spread beneath his skin like a living fire, and the world went in and out of focus. Skye stumbled, swaying on his feet. But still pushing.

"One," Vaughn continued, so calm, so collected, "you come with us, and convince your bondmate to do the same."

The blood was flowing out of him in a steady stream, draining his magic and leaching the color from his skin. It pooled on the floor around him, so garishly red against the snowy white tile.

No.

He kept pushing. Against the pain, against the poison.

Somehow, he found his feet. Somehow, he pulled a pistol from his belt.

Only to double over, groaning at the fist that slammed into his gut. He fell to his knees, but Vaughn caught him, twisting his fingers in his hair and jerking his head up.

"Or two," Vaughn said, still smiling that small, horrible smile as he wrenched Skye's head back so far that he was sure he felt something snap. "We ascend you." He held up a vial filled with something sickly and red.

Skye sputtered as the vial was tipped into this mouth. More poison. He felt his remaining strength stutter.

"I will personally carve out a piece of your soul," Vaughn went on, "placing you under my thrall, and then we'll use you to make sure that little chit of a girl doesn't give us any more trouble."

Taly. They wanted Taly.

But he would never give her over to them. He would die first.

Skye snarled, and then spat in the man's face.

To which Vaughn responded by giving him a shake so vicious, it made his vision blur at the edges.

"It seems you need some time to think on the matter," Vaughn said.

The world was going dark now.

"We'll see how you feel when you wake up."

Vaughn was still talking, but the words became garbled and twisted as Skye finally gave himself over to the pain.

I'm sorry, Taly.

Skye closed his eyes, knowing he wouldn't find the strength to open them again. He had come so close. So close to finding her…

But in the end, he was the one that had led the wolves straight to her door.

Two figures watched from the shadows.

Watched as the burly shadow mage finally released the boy.

Continued watching as he slumped to the floor, unconscious and barely breathing.

The burly mage's afterimage began to flicker, and Azura decided it was time to intervene. *Before* Vaughn managed to beat Skye's unconscious figure to a bloody pulp.

Taly would be very unhappy if she allowed that to happen, and Shards that girl was bothersome when she was unhappy.

And loud.

Bringing her hands together, Azura began to clap, slow at first but gaining speed as she stepped from behind the throne, Leto following close behind.

"Oh, that was marvelous," she trilled, enjoying the look of befuddlement—and yes, *fear*—that quickly twisted the mage's expression. It had been far too long since anyone had properly feared her. The fairies tried, but it wasn't genuine.

Smiling a bit wider, she loosened the damper on that power she usually kept leashed so tightly, letting it expand to fill the space around her.

"How...?" Vaughn stuttered, blinking furiously. As though he could make her go away. "This is impossible. You're dead."

"My dear, you really shouldn't listen to rumors." Azura stepped around... what was her name again? Carin? Yes, she stepped around Carin's body, and a slight tug on her magic had the head rolling back across the floor and reattaching itself. She *could* have put the poor girl's anima back in her body, but considering the things she had been made to do... She had wanted to die. And Skye had given her a painless death.

Vaughn reached for his sword, only to find that his arms had been frozen in place. He tried to back away, but she had already snared his legs as well.

"That was a lovely monologue, by the way. Very evil. And it's been quite a long time since I heard a proper evil speech. I especially liked the part about personally carving out a piece of his soul. Gave me chills." She circled him, mindful of the blood on the floor. It would be a shame to ruin her shoes.

"However," she went on, "and this is only if you're open to feedback—it was a bit brief for my taste. You see, I was expecting you to wax poetic about your evil little plan and your evil little master for just a little while longer, which means we're now running ahead of schedule. So, with that in mind, I'm afraid I'm going to have to *pause* things. Just for a bit."

The spell snapped into place, completely entangling Vaughn within her web of frozen time. Only his eyes moved now, tracking her movement as she practically skipped the last few steps toward him, hopping over the puddles of blood.

"Just for now," Azura said, waving a hand in front of his frozen form. Another quick tug on the spell had his eyes glazing over as she fully halted his timeline. "I do hope you don't mind. And if you do—well, I don't really care. You were already a right bastard back when I knew you, but apparently, you've moved on to brutalizing young women in addition to other atrocities I won't even mention. As far as I'm concerned, you deserve everything that's coming to you.

"Although..." Azura murmured, noting the way Vaughn's eyes had gone wide, the way his mouth hung open. "This won't do at all. You look a bit like a carp—not terribly menacing if you ask me."

Pressing a finger to his chin, she closed his mouth and began rearranging his features into something a little more intimidating.

Azura turned, frowning when she saw Leto floating over the water mage's body. She had retrieved his head, and her hands glowed with faint wisps of golden aether as the shredded muscles and tendons of his neck began to slowly weave themselves back together.

"Why do you waste your magic with such foolish things?" Azura huffed. "You have so little left."

But Leto didn't stop. "I am simply granting him the same courtesy you gave Lady Fenmar."

"Lady Fenmar was ascended," Azura pointed out. "This man was not."

"Asher Venwraith only joined this war to protect his mate—because he blamed himself for her abduction. He did terrible things under the banner of an enemy he despised. Perhaps he went too far in the name of love. But now he is dead, and the least we can do is show him the most basic respect."

Grumbling under her breath, Azura waved a hand. The boy's body instantly reassembled. "You always were the romantic."

"You used to be as well," Leto replied, then turned her head, listening. "I just felt their souls pass." The dead could always sense the dead. "They were together—both happy to be free."

"Satisfied?" Azura drawled.

Leto's light shivered. She gave a stiff nod. "I will have the bodies moved to the crypt before the Lady Caro arrives."

"Good." They would only detract from the scene she had envisioned: Skye lying prostrate on the floor in a pool of his own blood with Vaughn standing over him.

There was just one thing missing.

Azura began patting down Vaughn's pockets, producing a cloth-wrapped bundle from inside his coat.

"What is that, Majesty?"

"Just a little extra motivation." Azura unwrapped the bundle, revealing a small viridian dagger with delicate swirls of metal and pearl swimming across the scabbard.

Leto glanced at Skye, then back to the Queen. "Majesty—I feel I must once again protest. We cannot undo what has been done, but if you'll allow it, it would be my pleasure to dispose of Lord Adamaer. I will make sure he suffers appropriately given the nature and frequency of his transgressions."

"As much as I like watching you work," Azura said with a sigh, "this kill belongs to Taly. I know you don't agree with my methods concerning the girl, but believe me when I say that this is necessary. That trick with the crystals was clever, but Taly's still holding back, and I will not have that be the thing that gets her killed. She needs to know what she's capable of."

"But Majesty, the odds that the young Ma'am survives this trial—"

"Yes, I know."

"She could destroy herself."

Azura hesitated. It was true. That was always the problem with powerful mages. Pushing them to their limits inevitably meant endangering their lives, and today, Taly would be pushed to her limit.

If she lost control of her aether for even a moment—it could consume her.

And this place.

And everyone in it.

Though at least that would finally take care of the mimic.

"Please," Leto said urgently. "There must be another way to test her. If she fails, if Lord Adamaer manages to escape—"

Azura waved a dismissive hand. "Yes, yes, I know. We'll all die, evil will reign, and so on and so forth." She forced a smile. "However, that's a problem for tomorrow. For now, I want you to move young Skylen over just a smidge. That gorgeous face needs to be visible from the door."

Leto's light pulsed, but she said nothing else as she moved to follow the Queen's command.

"Perfect," Azura said, taking one final look at the room. "Now, all we need to do is wait for our young heroine to arrive."

CHAPTER 30

-An excerpt from the Essential Fey Survival Guide

Rule #1: Never piss off a time mage.

They won't just kill you. They'll do it creatively. And then, after they resurrect you, they'll do it again. Over and over. Until they've decided that you've suffered enough to quench their thirst for blood.

No matter how hard she tried, Taly couldn't keep her hands from shaking as she hit the bottom of the stairs, making her way towards the throne room.

This was it.

Today was the day she might finally earn her freedom.

She had come so far since that first lesson when she had so badly botched her first spell. She had learned to control her aether, memorized enough enchantments to turn her brain to jelly. She had covered nearly two decades of practical training in one grueling hell of a year, and this one trial—whatever it may be—was the only thing standing between her and home.

Breathe, she told herself. *Just breathe.* The Queen had insisted that she complete this test in full armor, and the set of enchanted leathers she had found waiting for her in her closet fit like a glove—tight but comfortable enough that she could still move.

As to why the Queen wanted her dressed and ready for battle… well, she was still trying very hard not to think too hard about what that might mean. Or how much it was going to hurt.

Taly finally came to the main hall, and the fairies peeked from behind the rows of columns flanking each side, darting out of sight as she approached. Their voices were hushed, their light soft and subdued.

They were nervous.

Fuck. Just what the hell did Azura have planned?

The doors to the throne room loomed ahead, and Taly threw her body against them, heaving until the heavy slabs of gold and pearl and polished wood began to move.

"I'm here!" she announced, trying to muster some swagger. "So let's—"

The words abruptly died on her tongue. The world bled away.

She blinked. But the room didn't change.

There was blood *everywhere*. Smeared across the tile, even splattered on the steps leading up to the throne. It oozed and eddied. Some of it had already started to dry, fading from red to black.

And in the middle of the room, surrounded by all that blood, stood a man. He looked different than she remembered. His hair was shorter, and his beard was gone. But the eyes, the thick cords of muscle, the ruddy skin—

Taly's eyes slid to the floor, and though something inside her tugged her forward, some small, still-sane part of her kept her feet firmly planted, not wanting to get too close to that man with the knife that still shone with the sickly sheen of poison.

Something was cracking inside of her, but she couldn't move, couldn't look away from the second figure in the room. The man with dark hair and the symbol for House Ghislain stamped on his chest. The man lying on the floor, lifeless and pale. He couldn't be here. Not like this.

She couldn't breathe. Not as an aching, ageless void quietly slashed her open, pulling her apart seam by seam. Dazed, she placed a hand to her heart, surprised to find smooth armor rather than shredded sinew and flesh.

She had tried so hard to find her way back to him, but now, here he was. Broken and bleeding. Unmoving as the glint of poison mixed with the steady stream of blood oozing out of wounds that refused to heal.

Skye. Her Em that she had dreamed about countless times, even her magic responding to the visceral need to keep him alive. To keep him safe.

But here he was now. Dead.

One of those nightmares had finally come true.

The man with the yellow eyes was looking at her now, but he didn't advance. Instead, his gaze flicked to the fairies that gathered behind her, assessing.

"Well, hello there, little mage." That voice was as thick and oily as she remembered. "I was wondering if I was going to get to see you again."

Taly slowly lifted her eyes. Away from the blood. Away from Skye. "Vaughn," she said a bit breathlessly, still trying to figure out just how the world was supposed to fit together now.

"And you're Taly, yes?" Vaughn chuckled darkly. "I've been doing some research on you, as well. Found this one." He kicked at Skye's motionless body. "He was quite fond of you, you know. Even I was surprised at what he was willing to do just to get here."

Was. That word hit her as surely as any blow. Skye had become a *was*—something to be spoken of and remembered fondly.

Vaughn shifted, taking a cautious step around Skye's body. Her eyes fixed on the dagger in his hand, still dripping with blood.

Her dagger. Vaughn had used *her* dagger… the dagger Skye had made for her…

That tear ripped open, every piece of her having to shift to make room as that hole that used to be her heart began to widen and expand. In an instant, all of her doubt, all of her hesitation dissolved, leaving only a depthless ocean of white-hot rage to fill the empty space.

This man had come here. He had hurt Skye. Made him bleed. Taken him from her.

As her eyes shifted back to Vaughn, every cell and fiber and molecule of her being—her very aether—seemed to hum in a pulsing discordant rhythm, demanding a single goal.

Revenge.

Again, that voice of reason spoke up, thin and tinny, growing ever distant. *Careful*, it said. This enemy was still a shadow mage. If she wanted her revenge, she would have to be smart. She would have to plan.

She would have to wait—if only briefly.

"I'm going to kill you." Taly was surprised she was able to get the words out. Tears streamed from her eyes, dripping from her chin to the floor—a stark contrast to the mask of lethal calm that veiled her features.

Vaughn looked her up and down, taking in the fighting leathers, the pistols at her waist, the dagger at her thigh. He gave a snort of dismissal.

"I'm going to kill you," she repeated, and that rage inside her turned vicious, focusing her senses. A plan began to form. "And if you believe in the Shards or any god at all, then I suggest you begin to pray. *Pray* to your gods for mercy—for I will show you none."

He took another step, but she had already seen the flash of aether, anticipated the sharp blur of movement. Half a thought had a wall of frozen time rippling out in front of her.

He skidded to a stop, nearly slipping in the blood pooled on the floor. His eyes went wide as he flattened his palm against the spell. It was sloppy and crude, shimmering there for all the world to see. He could break through it in an instant.

But that wasn't the point. She didn't want to stop him. Not yet. She had only wanted him to hesitate.

Part of being a time mage is knowing when to fight, when to run, and when neither one is necessary.

The Queen's words. She finally understood them now. Because even though she couldn't take this man on directly—he was far too strong—that didn't mean she couldn't *crush* him. Drag this out until he was begging for death.

She was a spider, and he was her prey.

She simply needed time to build her web.

The wall of time shattered, but Taly had already used those scant few seconds to turn, look ahead to her own flickering afterimage, and *pull*.

To Vaughn, it would've looked as though she disappeared.

Vaughn tore around another corner, letting loose a roar loud enough to make the chandeliers rattle.

She'd just been there. He had seen the glint of that bright, golden hair just ahead, but…

Vaughn forced himself to breathe.

There.

Her scent was just around the next corner. He didn't know how she'd managed to evade him time and time again, always slipping away just before he could reach her—but he would find her eventually. He had no other choice at this point.

He'd made a mistake at the relay—one he'd paid for dearly. And if he failed to deliver the girl to his master again, he'd end up like the Lady Fenmar. Ascended. Trapped inside his own body while someone else moved his arms and legs and used his voice. He'd likely be assigned to one of the contingents controlling the shades, and… Vaughn shuddered. He'd do anything to avoid that stinking, rot-filled pit.

Vaughn growled and set off in a sprint, siphoning his aether and forcing his legs to move faster. His mages were gone, and that damned Queen was going to be a problem. She was likely protecting the girl—her last living subject. And while he didn't know how she was alive or why she was here, he didn't care. All he knew was that if the Lady Raine was resorting to these means—skulking in the shadows rather than just facing him like any Genesis Lord would—that meant she had been weakened. As long as he worked quickly and carefully, he could still grab the girl without having to confront the High Lady of Time.

He was reaching the southeastern edge of the palace now, and he slowed his step when he came to a long hall of mirrors. They were every shape and size, lining the walls in gilded frames polished to their own mirror-like shine. Some were foxed, others nothing more than smooth planes of silver. They dotted the aisles in haphazard stacks that spiraled up to the ceiling, and there were even statues made of dense piles of shattered glass, the largest of which was a massive dragon perched upon a glittering mound in the center of the room.

Its scales were made of shards as big as his hand, and it had a long tail that wound through another nesting of those strange spiraling columns. Its teeth were jagged and sharp, only slightly less intimidating than the glowing, red eyes that seemed to focus in on him as he moved farther into the room.

"Taly," Vaughn called, following the winding path between the pillars. Fractured patterns of light flickered all around him. Her scent permeated the room. "Come now, child. Let's talk, you and I."

"What do you think about Draegonian art, Vaughn?"

The voice came from up ahead, but when Vaughn turned the corner, all he saw was the girl's reflection slinking off the edge of an old oval mirror.

"I've never liked it personally," he said, keeping his footsteps light as he emerged from one row and edged around the dragon. Its head followed him, a strange, tinkling groan echoing through the room. Steam began trailing from its nostrils.

"I didn't understand it at first," she conceded. "But then it came to me. The Draegon embrace their vanity, whereas most species don't like to be confronted with that aspect of their nature. We like to think we're above such worldly things, that we can't become victims of our own pride."

A pause. The light around him shivered as her image flashed in and out of focus around the next turn.

"But then," she continued, "I suppose I shouldn't have to say anything to you about vanity. I saw that cosmetic glamour on your finger.

By any chance, are you trying to hide those scars I gave you at the relay? As I recall, you made a lovely torch. Very flammable."

Vaughn leashed his temper, refusing to study one of the thousands of reflections that shimmered at him from every angle. The healers had done well, but there was still some discoloration along his jaw. When the time was right, he had every intention of punishing her for that little stunt. "This will be easier for you if you don't struggle. You only got hurt last time because you struggled."

"Oh, you are a gem." Her faint chuckle echoed through the hall, bouncing off every surface. "I can see now why my mother chose my father over you."

With a snarl, Vaughn slammed his fist into a nearby pillar, sending it toppling and filling the room with the crash of shattering glass.

All around him, his own reflection shifted and flashed, but just ahead—

Vaughn shoved the next pillar and the next, sending them hurtling to the ground as he chased the flicker of an image. She moved from one mirror to the next. In front of him, and then behind.

He began swinging his fists, shattering the mirrors on the walls, the tables, knocking over statues and sending splintered shards of glass spraying into the air.

Until the room was empty, filled only with the echo of that deafening clash and clatter of tinkling glass. Until he finally saw her, standing beneath the dragon's head.

She held a dingy little air dagger at her side, and her eyes were as murderous as those of the glimmering monster that loomed over her, so close that the steam curling from its nose fell down around her like long, white ribbons of smoke.

Glass crunched beneath his boots as he made his way across the now-empty room. "You," he said, reaching for her, "are coming with—"

Vaughn barked out a curse when his hand passed right through her shoulder. He tried again, but the image sputtered and faded.

"What do you think about Draegonian art, Vaughn?"

He whirled, only to see the girl standing in the corner of the room.

"I didn't understand it at first."

This time, she was hovering mid-air, standing on a platform that now lay in pieces.

"Clever girl," he murmured to himself, turning in a circle and surveying the room. A glint of gold sparkled from beneath the dragon's mirrored perch. He stooped and dug out three time crystals, each as big as a thumbnail.

Despite himself, he began to laugh as he easily snapped the spells bound to the stones. The apparitions blinking around the room instantly faded.

A trick. He'd forgotten just how loathsome time mages were with their traps and games. He turned one of the crystals over in his hand, grazing his thumb over the sloppily penned rune engraved into the surface.

He had been chasing a wraith—a moment in time captured and replayed over and over again. It was little more than a party trick, but the way it had been tied to the crystal—that was advanced magic, if a bit crudely executed.

Not the Queen's work then. Even without the full extent of her powers, she was better than that.

Vaughn smiled as he rolled the crystals in his palm. Perhaps the Queen wasn't trying to protect the girl after all. Granted, the little bitch he'd met at the relay had been barely more than a child—utterly unaware of her power and abilities. During the few weeks she'd been hiding in this place, she'd likely found some books and cobbled together a few spells, hoping to fill in the cracks with a bit of cleverness and sleight of hand. But that wouldn't protect her for long. Not from him.

Chuckling softly, Vaughn gave each crystal a tiny nudge with his magic, searching for the slight tether that still connected them to their caster.

His smile widened. He had a location now. The girl had made a mistake.

Satisfied, he pocketed the handful of crystals and set off in the direction of the Water Maze.

Taly watched the main doors of the palace.

She had felt the spell for the wraith snap, which meant that Vaughn had finally figured out that she was no longer inside. He had chased around a flicker of an image—a few moments in time easily captured and replayed—for nearly an hour, goaded on by the fairies who had been planting her scent all over the palace, always just a few steps out of reach.

Taking a breath, she soothed that simmering rage that had begun pulsing in her ears like a second heart. There was no reason to wait any longer.

Her trap was ready.

A figure appeared in the distance, and Taly waited just long enough for him to get a good look at her before turning, dropping a time crystal and hastily kicking some dirt over it before approaching the Water Maze.

Winding ribbons of white stone slithered across a wide, reflecting pool, but instead of following the path or giving the command to move the stones to the side, she tugged on her magic and watched as the pathways collapsed into dust. She'd never been able to execute that spell, but now—

Her aether responded to her so easily.

It was an entity unto its own. A fiery maelstrom howling through her veins, snarling and snapping and thirsting for blood. Something had been taken from her—from *them*. Something precious. Something dear.

Now! it demanded.

"Soon," she soothed, stepping onto the surface of the pool. Beneath her, the water that used to gently gurgle between the snaking pathways hardened, each molecule as stiff and immovable as though it had been turned to ice.

Bells tinkled on the wind.

"You did fine," she said to the fairy that zipped past, little more than a ribbon of light. "It was more than enough time."

The fairy chirped a reply.

Taly shook her head. "Don't bother. While I'm not sure what the Queen has suddenly decided is more important than a fucking shadow mage intent on kidnapping me" —she stepped over a pile of dust still hovering on the surface of the water— "if you see her, make sure she stays out of the way. This is my kill."

Taly was halfway to the hedge maze at the center of the pool when the fairies gave another chime. She glanced over her shoulder, checked her Sight, and when Vaughn stepped behind a copse of trees, momentarily obscuring his line of sight, she turned, looked, and then *phased.*

Only a moment later, she neatly stepped onto the platform of the hedge maze, at least a hundred yards away from where she had been less than a second ago.

She wasn't supposed to know that spell. It was seal five, at least—a more advanced version of the enchantment the Queen had ordered her to learn: *celerity.*

Celerity could give a time mage the appearance of speed, allowing them to accelerate their body and its movements. But it also came with the problem of needing to adjust for the added momentum when the enchantment ran out. Shadow mages could toughen their bodies to cope with the physical strain that came with moving faster than the eye could track, but time mages... well, Taly had quickly discovered that she didn't have the coordination to exit the spell without breaking an arm or a leg, sometimes both.

But if she *phased*—looked ahead and gave her timeline a yank—she didn't have to worry about the problem of momentum. She just stepped and phased and stepped and phased—as easy as walking down the street. Even the Queen had been reluctantly impressed that she'd managed to learn it.

Her aether gave another flare, coating her skin like a veil as she dropped another time crystal, hiding it beneath one of the hedges. Then, throwing a glance at the shadow mage that was now wading into the pool, she disappeared inside the maze.

Walls of blue ivy arched up and over as Vaughn stooped, picking up yet another time crystal. As expected, the spell attached to the small stone was crude and easily broken, and he slipped it into his pocket before moving forward through the maze.

The girl had left him several more traps to collect, each one poorly concealed. It was a valiant effort on her part, and to his surprise, some of the spells even managed to detonate before he'd finished digging them up. The leaves would start to shiver as time distorted, and the vines would attempt to crawl off their trellises and obscure the path. But the magic was weak—so adorably undeveloped—and all she had done was leave him a trail to follow. Each crystal had a tether, rapidly fraying but bright as a dying star to those that knew how to look.

Which he did, though even without the crystals, it wasn't hard to guess where she had run. Not as he circled closer and closer, finally emerging into the labyrinth's heart.

The center of the maze was nothing more than a wide circle of white stone flanked by marble benches and fountains that swirled and eddied, defying gravity and its laws. Vaughn took a cautious step out of the shade of the hedges, letting his aether fan out across the area, searching for any more of those piss-poor excuses for traps. When he found none, he straightened, turning his attention to the girl kneeling in the center of the circle.

Something that might have been pity tightened his chest. She looked as though she had been hollowed out, as if something vital had been drained away. Even the bright highborn gray of her eyes seemed muted as she stared at him, making no move to run or fight as he continued his approach.

She thinks the boy is dead.

Good. He could use that to his advantage. Perhaps, if he made a show of giving him some sort of antidote or helped her "revive" him using her own powers, she'd come willingly.

His master wanted her willing.

"You killed him," she whispered listlessly. The wind whipped at her hair, freeing a few wild strands from her coil of braids. "Why did you have to kill him?"

"All may not be lost, little mage," Vaughn cooed gently. His eyes darted around the clearing, and he took slow, cautious steps. She had *phased* in the throne room, and even though he doubted she had the technical ability to replicate the spell, he wasn't going to risk losing her again. "Young Skylen made the mistake of fighting back. He took out two of my mages in cold blood, and then he pointed his sword at me. What else was I to do?"

The girl tilted her head. "Why did you have to kill him?" she repeated. "Why am I still here when he isn't?"

"He might not be gone." Vaughn was halfway to the center now. "There might still be some hope.

Time mages have the power to revive the dead. I could show you how."

Her eyes widened slightly, then dropped. She stared at her hands, as though she could find the answer there. After a moment, she shook her head. "I don't believe you."

Something pricked against his neck, like an insect bite, but he ignored it. "Come with me, Taly. Come willingly, and my master may even allow you to see your family. He may show them mercy."

Taly rose to her feet, still staring at him blankly. "I'll come with you," she whispered, "if you answer one question."

"Anything you want, little mage," he said, still holding out his hand. He was so close. All he needed was a physical connection to dampen her magic, and then it would be easy to get her out of here, out of this place before the Queen could interfere.

Her lips twitched. "What's in your pocket?"

Something else snapped against his skin. Then again. And again. Over and over in quick succession.

He realized too late that his legs had stopped responding. And when he tried to summon his aether and break free, his magic felt like sludge in his veins, vague and unresponsive.

The girl was smiling now, and that hollow look had been replaced with something cruel and deadly.

Panic edged in.

Still heaving at his aether, he began to thrash, launching every bit of raw strength he possessed at the coil of phantom chains that were starting to tighten around him.

No.

His arms were fixed in place.

No, no, no.

Even his lungs felt tight.

There were too many spells all bunching and tangling together, and the panic dulled his wits, making it hard to think. He couldn't pick his way through the web. He couldn't find his way out.

"*Bitch,*" he rasped. Even his vocal cords were starting to become stiff and unyielding.

The girl's smile widened, the only warning she gave before her aether erupted in a bright flash of light. It gilded the stones, the plants, even the vibrant blue of the leaves. And then faded in an instant, leaving only a soft shimmer that coated her skin.

She took a step, then another, glowing like freshly forged steel.

He tried once more to throw off the magical bonds that chained him in place, letting out a low whine when he failed. Something tightened—but not enough to ease the fear, to let in that darkness that came with being completely frozen in time. He had been trapped in a time mage's thrall before. He knew that they could control pain and consciousness, playing with a man's timeline like a child might play with a bit of string. And if he could still see, still feel pain, it was only because she wanted him to see and feel. She had left him his mind, left that small part of him outside the influence of her magic, because she wanted him to witness the punishment she had chosen.

The boy, he tried to say. *The boy is safe.* But he couldn't make his mouth form the words that might've saved his life.

She stopped in front of him, still smiling through the glow of aether. "Let's talk now, you and I?"

It was at that moment that Vaughn began to pray.

Taly circled the man, watching impassively as he tried to get free. His magic writhed, beating against her mind like a hammer and doing him very little good as the enchantment continued to creep up his body like frost on glass.

Her aether licked at her skin, content to finally be free. She could feel its giddiness, sparkling and effervescent, bubbling through her blood like champagne.

Soon this man would be dead. They would repay blood for blood.

Taly grinned as she completed another turn, still monitoring the spells. She'd set a trap for this man, knowing just how much magic he commanded and just how little she could do against him in a fair fight. Any individual spell she threw at him would've been easily rebuffed, so she'd decided to get a little more… creative.

Taly picked one of the time crystals he'd collected from his pocket and tossed it into the air. She'd left thirty-five crystals, all poorly concealed with sloppily penned runes, the active spell still half-tethered to her own magic. Novice work. And even though it had pained her to make such inaccurate representations of the runes she'd been practicing for months on end, to leave that nearly-imperceptible trickle of aether that would lead him straight to her—it had paid off. Because Vaughn had picked up every crystal she'd dropped and disengaged the spells, never thinking to look for what was lurking underneath.

Taly tilted her head back, letting that glittering rage stretch and flow beneath her skin. It had been difficult given the time constraints, and she'd never have been able to pull it off without the fairies helping her lead Vaughn around in a circle. But despite the odds, she'd successfully managed to enchant thirty-five crystals, each one layered with no less than *three* enchantments.

The first—something basic and easily disarmed. Little more than a decoy to hide the second enchantment—a slowing spell, all identical and seemingly dormant. She had intended for Vaughn to find the first spell, maybe even the second. But the third enchantment... it was such a tiny little spell, barely noticeable. And its only purpose was to moderate the release of that second spell.

She was the spider, and Vaughn was the fly. And by the time he had finally sensed the web that was slowly tightening around him, it was too late.

"You know what your problem is, Vaughn?" She stopped in front of him, enjoying the way her aether flickered in those yellow eyes. He was nearly frozen now. He couldn't even blink. "You're arrogant. You let your prejudices blind you, and you never think to look deeper. You underestimated me back in Vale because you thought I was just some pathetic little human, and you underestimated me today because you thought I was just some pathetic little mage."

Taly pulled the dagger from his waist and held it up to the light. Snowdrop—it was still just as beautiful as the day Skye had given it to her on the front steps of the manor. A birthday present made just for her.

Letting out a vicious snarl, she gave the man a hard shove, knocking him to the ground. "I'm going to kill you now," she said, using every ounce of fey strength she possessed to slam her heel down on his knee. The joint shattered beneath his armor, and he let out a strangled whimper of pain. "And I'm not going to be gentle."

She crouched over him, drawing the tip of her blade across his cheek. The cut welled, but the enchantments caught the blood, keeping it from dripping. She sketched a matching cut on the opposite cheek, and then waggled her fingers, watching as the cuts vanished and then reappeared, over and over until tears began to leak from those yellow eyes.

Feeling another pulse of aether thrash against the back of her mind, she began removing the pieces of his heavy plated armor, unfastening the buckles and letting them drop to the ground until she had stripped him from the waist up. He wore an amulet around his neck, and though the symbol looked familiar—a single shadow crystal nestled between the coils of an ouroboros—she pushed it aside.

She went on, "As much as I would love to stay here all day and make sure you suffer, I don't have time for that. I can already feel you pushing back, and unfortunately, even though I managed to catch you, I'm not strong enough to keep you down for long."

She pressed her blade to his chest, carving out an "X" over his heart. "You killed the thing I loved most." And for a moment, that raging grief threatened to overwhelm her. But instead of letting it crush her, break her down into a countless number of pieces that might never fit together the same way again—she used it, siphoning off every ounce of anguish and despair and feeding that bright, burning fury.

"You took him away from me," she murmured, tracing that "X" with a gentle finger and smearing the blood that bubbled around the wound. "So instead of lopping off your head or carving off your limbs and waiting for you to bleed out, I thought I would show you how that felt. I thought I would show you what it feels like to have the thing that you would kill for, the thing you would *die* for, ripped away."

Leaning back, she lifted Snowdrop high into the air—and then slammed the dagger into his chest, smiling when she heard the crunch of bone. Her aether practically purred, and despite the spells holding him in place, Vaughn flinched. She twisted her blade, and the blood began to bubble. "It feels like having your chest cleaved open."

She wrenched her dagger free, and this time, a low whine slipped past the man's gaping lips. His eyes had finally gone wide with fear—true genuine terror. He was breaking through the spells, one by one, and his hands tried to grope for her, the faint pulses of shadow magic around his fingers burning like violet embers.

But it was too slow.

Every movement, every flicker of shadow magic, was too slow. He had underestimated her and her abilities, seen her as nothing more than a child.

And he had been wrong.

Giving her dagger a twirl, Taly placed Snowdrop off to the side and pushed apart the bits of severed cartilage and tissue that were already starting to mend. She felt two more spells pop, and he actually managed to blink.

"You invaded my island," she said softly. "You killed my friends and neighbors and turned them into monsters. You attacked the only remaining piece of my mother while she did everything she could to save me."

Taly's eyes found his as she continued to list off his sins. "You tried to *rape* me. You tried to turn me over to my enemy. And now, you've killed my friend. You've killed the man that I love." She viciously blinked back the hot, angry tears that welled in her eyes. "And that feels like hell, Vaughn. It feels like everything is falling apart with no way to ever put it back together. It feels like drowning in a big, black ocean that has no bottom and no shore and no sun."

Wrenching back her arm, Taly summoned that fey strength and plunged her fist directly into his chest, between the fractured ribs and shredded flesh. "It feels like having your heart *ripped* from your body."

She gave a sharp tug, and something tore. She held up her quarry, gripping it between fingers that still shimmered like molten ore.

Blood for blood, she thought, admiring that tiny pulsating rhythm beating against her palm. *A heart for a heart.*

She looked back at Vaughn. Normally, he would've died almost instantly. But under the effects of her spells, the blood hadn't even begun to spray. His eyes were wide and frightened, his mouth slowly twisting into a mask of pain and terror.

She held out his heart, letting the blood drip onto his face. "You broke my heart," she whispered. There was still fear in his eyes—but also a realization. He was going to die. It was decided. "And now I'm going to break yours."

With that, she squeezed, her fingers still glowing with aether as the rhythm stopped, as that small yet vital part of him turned to dust and scattered on the wind.

And when it was done, she rose to her feet, stumbling back a few steps before releasing the spells. Blood abruptly sprayed from Vaughn's chest, staining the ground around him, and his body gave one final jerk before going still. The arms that had been slowly reaching for her dropped to the ground, and his last breath gurgled from his chest, speckling his lips with red froth.

A warm breeze whipped through the hedges, rustling the leaves. Whipping the dark strands of hair away from Vaughn's unseeing eyes.

Taly panted as the rage began to recede. Her aether dimmed, contracting in on itself and seeping back into her skin. That voice that had been hissing in her ear finally quieted, allowing the pieces of her and who she was to settle back into place.

Exhaustion slammed into her, and flames erupted in her lungs, searing her from the inside out. Every breath was more painful than the last as she glanced around the clearing, slightly disoriented.

There was blood splattered on the white garden stone, blood staining her hands, her face, her hair.

So red. So warm and sticky.

And Skye…

Skye…

Falling to her knees, Taly began to scream. And when she ran out of breath, she screamed again and again and again.

She screamed for what she had done. For how easy it had been. How much she had relished that man's pain. And all because of Skye. He was gone now. Taken from her. And now that she no longer had that rage and fury to keep the grief at bay, all she could do was scream and curse and beg for the Shards to take her too.

Her voice grew hoarse, but she continued to silently wail, doubled over and clutching her sides as her tears soaked the ground. All this time, he had been the thing pulling her forward. The chance to see him smile, to hear his laugh, to tell him things it had taken her far too long to understand—that's what had kept her from crumbling. That's what had kept her going day after day, and without him… without him, she was—

Something tugged at her braid, but she waved it away, too lost to care. Because how was she supposed to go on? How was she supposed to live in a world that didn't have him in it? She didn't like that world. She didn't want it.

That thing nipped at her ear, and she lashed out, snarling as she—

Stopped. Frozen as surely as if she'd been caught in one of her own snares.

A tiny red rabbit with violet jewel-like eyes blinked up at her.

She blinked back.

As if in answer, the rabbit gave a tiny squeal of joy, then a hop, before evaporating in a cloud of mist.

"Taly?"

Taly's breath left her in a whoosh, and the pain and anguish dissolved, replaced by something more tenuous. A fragile, sparkling ember of hope.

She turned, slowly, as though in a daze.

And then somehow, she managed to stagger to her feet, staring with wide eyes at the figure that emerged from a break in the hedges.

Dark hair, green eyes, lean but powerfully built. The crest for House Ghislain stamped into his armor was speckled with blood.

"Skye?" She had to mouth the word, unable to find her voice.

His eyes found hers, and that smile, small and disbelieving at first but quickly widening, had her racing forward, running as fast as he was running to meet her. They collided somewhere in the middle, and he lifted her up, wrapping his arms so tightly around her she could barely breathe.

But she didn't care. Because she was holding onto him just as tightly, relishing the feel of his racing heart pressed against hers. He was here. He was alive. And she wasn't sure if she was laughing or crying as the full weight of those long months apart, all that time spent missing him and worrying about him and watching him die in a countless number of ways, finally crashed into her.

They were both shaking when her feet finally touched the ground, and it was an effort not to pull him back to her when he leaned away slightly. Some of the blood on her hands had rubbed off on him, staining his cheeks and mixing with the blood that had already soaked through the leather of his armor.

Leaving one arm banded around her waist, he brought a hand up and gently tucked a strand of hair behind her ear. There was a faint look of wonderment shining in those impossibly green eyes, and Taly held her breath as he traced the arch of her ear, then her cheek, noting each change. He even touched the tip of her nose, and she couldn't help but snort. There was nothing different about her nose. It still had that damned bump right in the middle of the bridge from when he had tripped and sent them both tumbling down the stairs as children.

"Don't tell me," Skye said at last, and Shards that voice. Oh, how she had missed that voice. "You changed your hair."

At that, she was crying again, and he pulled her to him, letting her bury her face in the crook of his neck as he held her.

"I wouldn't get too sentimental," he said, pressing his nose to her hair and breathing her in. She felt his whole body relax, as if he'd just been relieved of some great weight. "After all, you still have to explain this mess to me, and I plan to be quite furious."

Taly cried harder, and Skye had to pry her away far enough so that he could look her over. "Are you hurt?" he asked.

She shook her head, saying tearfully, "No."

"Are you sure? I heard screaming and—"

"Believe me, my dear," a new voice drawled, "she's perfectly fine."

Skye's reaction was immediate. In a blur of motion, he twisted his body, shoving Taly behind him and reaching to draw his sword in a single, fluid movement.

Taly grabbed his wrist, staying his hand. "Don't worry about her," she said, looking up at the woman that sat on top of one of the hedges, merrily dangling her feet. "That's just the Queen."

"What?" Skye glanced at her over his shoulder.

"It's a long story," Taly muttered.

Azura grinned and hopped off the hedge, a wisp of aether curling around her body as she gently floated to the ground. Her skirts puffed around her like a cloud. "Now, my dear, what sort of introduction is that?"

"Fine," Taly snapped. "Skye, this is the woman that's been holding me captive for the past year."

Skye sucked in a breath, but before he could say anything, Azura groaned dramatically, saying, "There you go again with that *'I'm a prisoner,'* and *'Az, why won't you let me go?'* nonsense." She turned to Skye. His expression was cold and cautious, but Taly knew him well enough to see the confusion in his eyes as he glanced between the two women. "You have no idea just what I've had to endure all these long months. After everything I've done for the girl, and not even a thank you."

"You shot me with an arrow," Taly barked.

"You healed," Azura snapped back. Then, to Skye, she said sweetly, "As for you, I apologize for the confusion. You see, I know you, but you don't seem to know me—at least not yet. And, if we're being honest, that's Taly's fault. She never brings you here in the right order."

Azura dropped into a curtsey, and Taly was pretty sure the look of bewilderment on Skye's face was a perfect match to the one she'd worn that first day at the palace gates.

"I believe introductions are in order," the Queen said, rising. "I'm—"

"I know who you are," Skye cut in, pushing Taly more firmly behind him. "You're Azura Raine. You're the woman responsible for the Schism."

CHAPTER 31

-From the personal notes of Azura Raine, High Lady of Time

Breena came to the palace today. Not here, of course—inside the loop. She came to the real version that even those upstarts at the Dawn Court were too afraid to touch. The fairies report that she screamed and cursed at my empty throne for hours—things like "Why would you curse my child?" and "Did you even think of the world you were creating for those that came after?"

Since there is nothing I can do for the child until the time is right, I had the fairies deliver a small gift in my name—a necklace. Breena wasn't pleased, as indicated by the vulgar gestures she made on her way out, but the fairies said that she did stop screaming.

Taly frowned when Skye pushed her back another step. He was growling deep in his chest, bristling with that innate fey instinct to protect and defend. She didn't know how he recognized the Queen; how he had gotten here; how he was alive and not still lying in a pool of his own blood, unmoving, unbreathing—but right now, none of that mattered.

The Queen glided across the clearing—a spot of pure white in a world full of blood. "How disappointing," she muttered. "And here I thought today was going to be a day for introductions… All these men and no one has said a thing about my dress…" She picked at her skirts. Despite the spreading pool of blood at her feet, the fabric was still unstained. "But then again, I don't know why I even bother to be surprised anymore. You were always the more even-keeled of the pair, Skylen. Taly would've gotten herself killed multiple times over without you there to cool her heels."

"Taly?" Skye dared a glance over his shoulder, one hand still resting on his sword. Taly could see the question in his eyes: was this woman a threat? One word and he would stand down, even if he didn't like it.

"She won't hurt us." Taly placed a hand on his shoulder, breathing a sigh of relief when she felt him relax, if only slightly. "And even though I know it doesn't make any sense, she does know you. And me. Like I said—it's a long story."

"One that you are more than welcome to tell him *later*," Azura said as she began circling the still-cooling corpse in the center of the clearing. "Right now, I want to talk about this, because *this*—"

Guilt twisted in Taly's gut. There was too much blood. It itched as it dried on her skin.

"—is *marvelous*." Azura clapped her hands, laughing as she daintily hopped over a puddle of blood. "The timelines are always twisting and tangling around you—I had no idea what was going to happen when I brought Vaughn here, so naturally, we all started making bets."

On cue, the fairies began to peek over the tops of the hedges, their soft blue light nearly disappearing against the cloudless sky.

"Leto—" Taly followed the Queen's gaze to a softly glowing orb floating just inside a break in the hedges. It seemed Leto had given up her feminine shape, and her light pulsed, dimming in shame. "—thought that when you walked in and saw Skye on the floor, pale and bleeding out, that you would just fall to your knees, weeping. She said this was a terrible idea; that it was going to end badly. Most of the fairies were on her side, though *I* had a *little* more faith in your abilities. Not much, mind you. I did still have the fairies make some emergency preparations just in case this all went south."

Taly's heart was beating too quickly, her breath coming too fast. There was a high-pitched ringing in her ears, faint at first but growing louder with each piece that clicked into place. "You planned this?" she whispered. Vaughn... Azura had *meant* for her to kill Vaughn—taken her worst fears and constructed a series of events to ensure it.

The stab of betrayal should've left her bleeding.

"I trusted you." This time when Taly went to step around Skye, he didn't stop her, though she did feel his aether spark, perhaps in warning. Perhaps reacting to her pain. "I told you about my dreams, and you used that. You used the things I told you to make me believe that..."

Taly couldn't bring herself to even say the words. She'd thought Skye was dead, and her entire world had shattered.

"Yes," Azura said. Unconcerned. Smiling like this was some grand joke. "Don't worry, though—I was never far away. I saw the whole affair in all its delightfully vicious glory. I especially liked how you used the mirrors to slow Vaughn up a bit. Top marks for that bit of cleverness. Though you did destroy an entire collection of priceless art."

Taly wobbled, and Skye was there in an instant, placing a steadying hand on her waist. Shards, he must have been so confused, and he was so pale. He'd been wounded—that part had been real. She could see blood still leaking out of the rips in his armor.

Taly swallowed back the bile that began to rise. There was so much blood. On her, on him. The air reeked of it. "You planned this. You said that..." The realization ripped right through her. "This was my test?"

"Yes, my dear. Your final examination was to kill Vaughn," the Queen confirmed. "And I'm happy to say you passed! Congratulations, *Acolyte*—you're a student I can be proud to call my own." Azura seemed practically giddy as she continued to circle the corpse, holding her skirts in one hand. "This really is brilliant work, by the way. Better than Leto in her prime. Maybe that's why she kept trying to dissuade me. She knew just how vicious you could be with the right... *motivation*." Azura gave a small secret smile.

Taly began to shake her head as that ringing became a dull roar, as the pain and betrayal began to pound inside her, keeping time with her frantic heart.

Leto had known. The fairies had known. Everyone in this damned place had *known* what the Queen had planned, and not even one had cared enough to tell her.

Betrayal swept into grief, then sickness, then back again.

Over and over—until something inside her snapped.

Taly didn't realize she'd launched herself forward until Skye's arms were around her, lifting her off her feet as she struggled against him, wild with rage.

"*Let me go!*" she snarled. Her aether flared, and then hit a wall as Skye's own magic wrapped around her like a vice.

"I don't know what the hell is going on," he hissed in her ear, "but I didn't come all this way just to watch you die. That's a Genesis Lord. She could kill you with a thought."

"You should listen to him," the Queen added. And that smile...

That stupid, smug *smile...*

Taly let out a shriek of rage. "You—"

"Gave you a test worthy of your skill?" Azura arched a brow. "Allowed you to take revenge on a man that had not only wronged you, but your family, your island, your home, and countless others? A man that would've made you wish you were dead had he succeeded in capturing you?" This time when the Queen laughed, it was humorless. "Yes. That is exactly what I did. And now, this man is dead, slain by your own hand, and the world is better for it. You're better for it because you've finally realized what you can do when you finally stop hesitating."

Skye's magic continued to tighten around her, and the flames reignited in Taly's lungs as he slowly took control of her aether, holding it just out of reach.

Giving one final jerk, Taly sagged against him, her heart twisting so viciously in her chest that the world went sideways.

"Why?" Taly whispered. Then louder, gaining strength: "*Why?!* Why would you do this?"

The Queen smiled a bit, reaching down to pluck the amulet from around Vaughn's neck. "When faced with their worst fears," she said, "many people fall down and never find the will to get back up. I've seen it happen many times before. To good mages. Brave men and women that allowed their sorrow to cripple them. Before I let you leave this place, I needed to know that you weren't that kind of person. I needed to know that even in your darkest moments, you had the strength to get back up."

The Queen passed the amulet from hand to hand. "This test wasn't about how many spells you've learned, or how much magical theory you can recite. This test was about getting Talya Caro out of her own way. This test was about finally getting you to embrace what you are and what you can do and to force you to let go of that girl that got tossed at my feet a year ago wounded and confused. You keep holding onto her, but that girl was destined to die. Maybe not today, maybe not tomorrow, but eventually. Everything I have done has been to keep that from happening. To keep you *alive* because that is the promise I made to your mother when she came to my palace, desperate for a way to keep her child out of the Sanctorum's eye."

The Queen stepped around the body, making her way across the clearing. Her face was impassive, her eyes serene, and when she was close enough, she reached for Taly's hand and pressed the amulet into her palm. "A gift." A glance at Taly. Then Skye. "Given as a symbol of my everlasting friendship. Lord Castaro will know what to do with it."

Taly stared at the amulet. Quiet. Unmoving. Blood had caked beneath the scales of the ouroboros.

The blood of a man she had killed.

"Now then," the Queen said, straightening her cloak, "you are free to go whenever you wish. I would, however, recommend staying until tomorrow morning, perhaps the next day—take some time to rest and recover before going back to a shade-infested island full of people that want to kill you both." She looked to Skye, her expression softening a bit. "I'll keep an eye on Kato in the meantime, so there's no need to worry. He'll be a little rattled when you return, but, otherwise, unharmed."

Skye let out an audible sigh of relief that Taly didn't quite understand. He and Kato hated each other. When had that changed?

The wind picked up, and the fairies began to whisper.

Azura was watching her, but Taly had nothing else to say. She was too numb, too exhausted. Despite the warmth of the sun, she felt cold.

The Queen turned, disappearing into the hedge maze without another word; the whispering of the fairies began to fade.

Still, Taly didn't move, only stared at that amulet. At the blood, already flaking on her skin.

"Taly?" Skye's voice was gentle as he closed his hand around hers. "Is there a place where we can get you cleaned up? You would feel better."

She almost laughed. Typical Skye. Here he was, bleeding and wounded—Shards only knew what he'd gone through to get here. Yet he was still putting her needs before his own.

Taking a breath, she let her fingers trail down his chest. There were three rips in his armor. The leather was black with blood. "You're hurt."

"Bruised and sore, yes." Skye caught her wrist, the movement making him wince. "And I think Vaughn had his mages using mistlewick venom—it's painful but hardly lethal at such small doses. I'll be fine."

Taly gave a jerky nod, her eyes drifting back to Vaughn and that ever-widening pool of blood that was slowly devouring the circle of white stone.

Skye followed her stare, taking in the corpse, the pieces of armor lying off to the side, the crystals scattered on the ground. He was looking for the heart, she realized. The one she had turned to dust.

"You probably have questions," she said softly.

"A few, yes. The least of which being just how you managed this." She couldn't read the emotion in his eyes, if it was judgement or pride. "But that can wait." He removed the amulet from her hand, replacing it with his own. "C'mon. I know that palace has to have at least one shower."

Taly gave another nod, too numb to do anything else. And when Skye gave her hand a tug, she allowed him to pull her away from the center of the maze.

To lead her out of this place of death.

CHAPTER 32

-From the personal notes of Ivain Castaro, Marquess of Tempris

The 2nd day of the month Janus, during the 236th year of the Empty Throne

Of all the villages hit by the Sanctorum's raid, Vale suffered the greatest losses. In Plum and Bago—the destruction was centralized, as though the Sanctorum came, realized there was nothing there for them, and then retreated. In Vale, however, the damage was pervasive. The village wasn't just burned—it was razed, reduced to nothing but ash and cinders.

We're still not sure what brought the Sanctorum to the island. There are so many rumors circulating. Some are saying they were looking for time crystals while others claim there was a time mage hiding amongst the townspeople—a child. I do not know if this is true, or if the Sanctorum was successful in their quest. I can only hope that they failed. The death of a child would not validate the lives that have already been lost. It would only show how far we as a people have fallen.

The next few hours passed in a blur, and Skye might have thought he was hallucinating, that he might've actually lost his mind this time, were it not for the warm, steady weight of Taly's hand in his.

They were both silent as she guided them back to the palace, and by the time they came to a large, well-stocked infirmary, he was thoroughly lost.

She helped him with his armor, lifting his breastplate and ruined shirt over his head when the pain got so bad that he couldn't raise his arms. And while she worked, tutting and fussing and rubbing all manner of foul-smelling herbs and salves on his wounds until the bleeding finally stopped, he tried not to stare.

As a human, she had been beautiful.

As highborn fey, even covered in blood and sweat… she was hypnotic. Still Taly, but with the tang of aether clinging to her scent now instead of mortal iron, a more graceful arch to her ears. And those gray eyes that seemed to almost glow, as if her body couldn't quite contain the sheer force of her magic…

He had definitely been staring.

While they were in the infirmary, she told him a little about this place—where they were and *"yes, that really was fairy fire."*

She also explained that during the four weeks she'd been gone, a year had passed for her. One full year in which she had lived and trained with a woman the world thought dead, honing the skills that had allowed her to hunt and kill a man thousands of years her elder.

He had been expecting the time differential, of course. She had said as much during those few shared dreams. But hearing her say it and seeing it firsthand, feeling every single one of those long months open up like a gulf between them and suddenly realizing the *reality* of it…

The girl who couldn't kill a rabbit.

He wondered if there was anything left of that girl now. Wondered how it was possible to grieve her loss but also still find excitement in the obvious skill she had displayed—the raw intelligence and power he knew she had always possessed but now wielded with such vicious efficiency.

He wondered if there was still a place for him beside this new, fascinating creature—or if she had already left him behind. Again.

A *year*…

He probably should've said something. She had looked at him like she was expecting him to say something. But when the words wouldn't come, she had just sighed and taken him by the hand, not letting go until they came to a large tower apartment. That's where she had left him, mumbling something about going downstairs to clean up as she shoved him into the washroom and closed the door.

There were clothes waiting for him when he emerged: a shirt and trousers, both finely made and sewn from light summer fabrics. How they got there—or how they fit so well—he wasn't sure he wanted to know. This day had already been strange and exhausting, and it wasn't over yet. He would focus on the less important questions later.

Skye completed another circuit of the apartment. It had been almost an hour since Taly had left him here, and in that time, he'd explored every room and peeked into every drawer. With nothing else to do, and already hurting now that the pain tonic was starting to wear off, he padded into the bedroom on bare feet and eased himself front-first onto the mountain of blankets and pillows piled on the bed.

They still hadn't talked—not about the things that mattered. There were questions he needed to ask, things she needed to explain. It wasn't going to be an easy conversation, but… it had to happen.

He needed her to look at him and tell him why she hadn't trusted him to help her.

Why she had lied. Why she had run away.

Why she had used the things she knew about him, those vulnerabilities it had taken a lifetime to learn, to hurt him again, and again, and again.

Skye winced as he turned over onto his back, holding a hand to his ribs.

At least, there was the bond. It was proof that she cared. Proof that even though his faith had been shaken, that trust wasn't gone. At this point, the link between them was still incomplete. It wouldn't take much to sever it, so the fact that it was still intact, even after the lies, the separation—that gave him hope.

Enough to quiet the doubts still churning his thoughts as he hoisted himself to his feet and began another circle of the apartment.

Taly stood in front of the mirror, willing her heart to stop beating so damned fast.

She had scrubbed the blood off her skin and washed her hair. She'd even rummaged through the small case of cosmetics that had been left in the washroom, using just the barest trace of rouge on her cheeks and lining her eyes with kohl. She couldn't use a glamour—that would be too obvious, especially to a shadow mage. But if applied with a delicate hand, human cosmetics looked natural enough to escape immediate scrutiny.

She fiddled with her hair. Pinched her cheeks. Despite the rouge, she still looked pale. And her hands—her hands wouldn't stop shaking.

"Just breathe," she whispered, wiping her palms on the front of her dress and watching with detached fascination as the girl in the mirror parroted the movement. Her reflection still caught her off-guard sometimes, and considering that she'd had nearly a year to adjust her own perception, she couldn't begin to imagine what Skye must be thinking right now. How different she must seem from the person he'd last seen. How different and how strange…

It was probably why she'd caught him staring.

With a growl, Taly grabbed a nearby cloth and scrubbed her face before yanking out the twist of hair she'd tried to pile on her head in that way that Leto made look so effortless. She began weaving it into a long, ropelike braid.

She'd spent a year wondering what it would be like to finally see Skye again, trying to picture his reaction, what he would say when he finally saw the eyes and the ears and the perfect features. She'd planned out what she'd wear (something pretty but familiar), how she'd arrange her hair (braided to hide her ears). She'd imagined the things she might say to help him see beyond the stain of her magic, to still see *her* beneath this new, strange thing she had become.

But that chance was gone now. The first time he'd seen her since she'd left him in Ebondrift and she'd been covered in blood, still out of her mind with rage and grief. She'd been every horrible thing the Sanctorum had ever claimed time mages to be, and no amount of rouge or lipstick was going to erase that image.

Taking a breath, she placed both hands on the ceramic vanity, still warm from the steam of the bath.

Their friendship would survive. She knew that. They had spent their entire lives fighting and making up, and they would find a way to move past this. Maybe not the same as they were before, but they would have a tomorrow.

The only problem was… she wasn't sure that was enough anymore. She wasn't sure it had ever been enough. She wanted more than his friendship, but what if she had missed that chance? She had lied to him. Hurt him. And even though her intentions had been noble, that didn't change what she was. It didn't change the fact that loving her meant that his life on Tempris would be over.

That he would never be able to go back home.

Taly wiped at the tears welling in her eyes, then tugged her dress into place. It was simple and light, the skirt falling in gauzy layers to just below her knees. She had found it waiting for her in her closet, along with a note from Leto that simply read: *I'm sorry*.

"Too late to change now," she murmured, throwing her braid over her shoulder. She had thought the dress looked pretty at first, but now she just felt silly. She should've worn something more familiar, like trousers and boots, maybe her favorite tunic. She'd hardly ever worn dresses as a human. Skye was probably going to think she looked strange.

"Just go," she breathed. Before he figured out that she was avoiding him and the conversation she knew was coming. She couldn't run anymore. Didn't want to.

So, Taly closed her eyes and counted to three. And when she opened them, she gathered what was left of her pride and swagger, wrapping them around her like a shield. By the time she reached for the doorknob, ready to face the man that now had the power to break her heart beyond recognition, her hands had finally stopped shaking.

"What are you doing in there?"

Skye looked up from the dresser drawer to find Taly leaning against the closet doorframe, arms crossed.

For a moment, he forgot how to breathe. She looked so devastatingly lovely, dressed all in white with the late afternoon sunlight flooding in behind her. And those eyes, that face, the way her dress was at once modest and yet somehow still teased at every curve and—

I should've shaved, he thought suddenly. And tucked in his shirt. Found shoes. Granted, Taly wasn't wearing shoes either, but he'd been killing time for over an hour now. He could've at least combed his hair.

"Well?" Taly prompted when he didn't answer. A smile hovered at the corners of her mouth. "Is there a reason you're snooping through my closet?"

Boredom. Curiosity. What had begun with a cursory glance inside an open doorway had become a full-fledged investigation once he had seen the sheer number of ballgowns, and jewels, and formal wear—all of it covered with her scent. As though it had been worn and not just shoved into a dark corner to be forgotten like every other dress she had ever owned.

It was just dumb luck that she had walked in the moment he opened this particular drawer, and since death was now inevitable, he decided he should at least have some fun before she ended him.

Skye finally found his tongue, and despite the danger to his person, plastered on a smirk. "This is not what I would've expected," he said, holding up a small scrap of lace that didn't look large enough to cover much of anything, much less the area for which it was intended. "Considering your hatred for all things satin and lace, I figured you probably wore men's shorts. I'm pleasantly surprised."

Taly's cheeks turned a very fetching shade of pink, but she didn't rush forward, didn't squeal and start pummeling him the way he'd expected. She simply pushed herself off the doorframe and began making her way towards him, skirts swishing with each feminine sway of her hips.

When she was close enough for him to feel the heat from her body, she murmured, "I like the way satin feels against my skin." The teasing smile she gave him made his heart pick up a beat. "It makes me think of sex."

Heat rushed through him. But before his brain could formulate a response, Taly snapped the drawer closed.

He jumped back, barely escaping with his fingers still intact and laughing when she snatched the pair of undergarments away. The look she gave him—he saw his death there.

"Since when are you this nosy?" she grumbled, tossing the bit of lace on top of the dresser before grabbing his arm and shoving him in front of her.

"I was left unattended for a really long time. I figured rummaging around your closet was safer than trying to clean your study, which" —he turned, and she was still glaring at him as she pulled the closet door closed— "looks like a tornado tore through it. And I'm not even going to touch on that coin... throne... thing. I thought you were supposed to be the organized one."

She shrugged. "Just because you don't understand a system of organization doesn't mean it's lacking. I know where everything is in that room."

Skye was almost embarrassed by the stab of knee-wobbling relief that shot through him. What she had, of course, meant to say was that she had some overly complicated system of organization that only made sense to her and other like-minded basket cases, and... it was nice to see that not everything had changed.

He looked her up and down, noting with no small amount of satisfaction that the color returned to her cheeks. "I like the dress, by the way," he said as he turned back down the hall. "You look nice."

There was a small gasp, and he heard her heart stutter. After a moment, she followed, pushing past him. Even the tips of her ears were red as she led them back into what looked like a dining room. There was a set of silver serving dishes on the table, all covered.

"Dinner," Taly explained. "I found it waiting outside the door."

The smell of chicken and potatoes and spices hit his nose. Simple, hearty food. His mouth was already watering, but he shook his head. He needed to get her talking first. For his own sanity. "Did you really think that was going to work? That you could just wave a plate under my nose, and my mouth would suddenly be too full to ask questions?"

"I never said that," she mumbled, though from the look on her face, the thought had crossed her mind.

"Tink—I got stabbed three times today. I think that's earned me an explanation."

"For which part?"

Skye pretended to think. "How about… all of it? Let's just start with all of it. The magic, you running away from the manor, the spells Kato found, that time you ran away for a second time in Ebondrift, the Vale relay, Vaughn, how you managed to become a resident of a homicidal Genesis Lord and her court of ghostly minions… Do I really need to keep going?"

Taly picked at her skirts, refusing to look at him. "That list could take a while. Are you sure you don't want to start with something easier?"

His temper flared, but he stopped. Then took a breath. His ribs ached at the movement. Taly had done a decent job patching him up, but mistlewick venom was painful and long-lasting. It would take a few days for his aether to fully regenerate and his body to heal.

She saw him wince, and her face fell. "I should've told you."

"Yes."

"A long time ago."

"You could've told me at any point, Taly, but you didn't. Instead, you spent a *year* digging through gate rubbish. You nearly died because we didn't know how to treat you for the harpy venom. You've had countless opportunities, and the closest you ever got was in Ebondrift, but even then—you didn't. You ran away. *Again.* You decided you didn't trust me—"

"Skye, I—"

"You should've trusted me." Taly hung her head. "I shouldn't have had to find out that you had *time magic* from Aiden when I accidentally got him too drunk to keep his mouth shut."

She attempted a smile. "I suppose that explains a few things. Aiden always was a chatty drunk."

She had a point, but— "Stop deflecting."

"I'm not, I..." But then her voice trailed off, because yes, she was—deflecting. "I just wanted to protect you," she said softly. "That's all I ever wanted to do."

His brows rose.

"I know it doesn't make sense, but I... I don't even know how to explain any of this anymore. Everything got so out of hand, and every time I try to think of what I need to say, I just..." She sighed, slumping down into a chair at the table. "I wish you could see inside my head sometimes. Everything I need to say is in there, but I just can't get it out."

There was a decanter of something red and fizzy in the middle of the table. Shard wine by the smell of it. Taly never would've been able to drink this as a human. Two sips and he would've been holding back her hair while she retched.

Though he supposed that wasn't a concern anymore as he reached for the decanter, filling both their glasses.

"Just start at the beginning," he said and claimed the chair across from her. "Start with the day in the training yard. Tell me what happened when I discharged your dagger. Tell me why you started screaming."

And so, she did. She told him about how she suspected now that the encounter in the sparring ring had weakened the hidden wards inscribed on her arm. How the visions had started soon after. She told him about how panic had taken over once she figured out what they were and the fear that had ruled over every moment of every day for nearly a year.

And even though he'd already guessed at most of the story, hearing how the pieces fit together—it left him speechless. And heartbroken. He hated every lingering fragment of pain he could still read in the lines of her face and the tension in her body. The specter of fear he could still see looming behind her eyes.

When she came to the subject of Ebondrift, however, even though he could still see that same pain and fear, it was all he could do not to reach across the table and shake her. She was scared, she claimed. And her magic was becoming more uncontained. And then, when Kato confronted her, she was *sure* she'd been discovered, *sure* that he was going to reveal her, *sure* that she was what their enemy wanted.

So, she ran.

There was no mention of the way she'd left him or those few kisses they had shared, the promises she had made that she never intended to keep.

I'll get some rest, and then we can talk.

But that had been a lie. Just one of many.

His anger must've shown because she started babbling, circling back around whenever she seemed to remember a point.

The relay, Vaughn, how she had come to meet the Queen and the year that came after—she explained it all.

It was dark when she finally stopped explaining.

The food had gone cold, the dishes still covered and forgotten on the table. He needed to eat. So did Taly—she had used a lot of magic today, and her movements were sluggish, her skin too pale.

Neither of them reached for their plates.

In the distance, explosions growled, and light flickered beyond the windows like lightning. She had told him about that too, how this single day had been carved out and set aside, cursed to replay the same set of tragic events night after night.

He still wasn't sure how that made him feel. Wasn't sure how he felt knowing that was the Schism or that she had been here long enough to catalog each blast.

"So," he said finally, "I guess I'll just come right out and say it. You fucked up."

"Hilarious," Taly muttered from across the table.

"I mean it. You fucked up so badly, you redefined the standard by which we will judge all other fuckups from now until the end of time."

She snorted into her wine glass. "I wouldn't go that far."

"*Really*? You wouldn't go that far?" He pinned her with a disbelieving stare. "Vaughn and his master didn't know about you before you basically walked right into their base and said, *'Hey, here I am! A time mage. You needed one of those, right?'*"

She took another sip of wine. "You don't know that."

"I *do* know that," he said as he pushed himself to stand. "I know because how else would Vaughn have known about you? How would he have known about your magic? Ivain and I lived with you for 15 years, and we never sensed a damn thing."

"Kato knew."

"Kato didn't know. He thought you were a traitor, not a time mage. He discovered a glamour and a little bit of magic underneath. Just enough to make him suspicious."

She didn't reply. Just pursed her lips in that way she always did when she'd been proven wrong but didn't want to admit it.

Skye began to pace. His body protested every step, but he was too restless to stay in one place. "You gave yourself up," he said. "You ran away. You hid one of the most important parts of yourself from the people you pretended to call family, and you gave yourself up."

Tipping her head back, Taly finished off her wine, setting the glass to the side. When she looked up, it wasn't shame or remorse simmering behind those bright highborn eyes.

It was anger.

He'd hit a nerve.

"I was *protecting* you," she said through her teeth. "I protected my family."

"You're a fool if you believe that."

"And you're a fool if you believe anything different."

The words were said with such conviction—Skye hesitated.

Long enough for her to say, "Leaving Ebondrift was the right decision." She rose from her place at the table, and even the way she moved was different now. More fluid. More sure. She stepped in front of him, halting his pacing. "You said it yourself. You would've died at the canyon if Ivain didn't know to come. *I* made that happen."

"That was a decision we should've made together."

"I gave you a chance. I told you exactly what I planned to do, and you said no. Telling you the real reason *why* I wanted to leave wouldn't have made any difference."

Skye snarled at that, but she answered with a growl of her own. It was a purely fey sound, one that caught him off guard.

But only for a moment. "I would've helped you," he seethed. Her eyes widened slightly. "I would've tried to talk you out of it, but if you were truly intent on going, I would've helped you. The same way I have always helped you with every terrible idea I've never been able to dissuade you from. We could've planned *together*, worked *together*. But instead, you decided for the both of us, and then you left me behind with nothing but questions and lies and a giant Taly-sized mess to clean up."

Taly flinched.

And he knew in that moment that she had never considered the aftermath. What her leaving would look like. If his loyalties might be called into question.

"It hurt when you left," he said, not to be cruel, but because he needed her to know. "It hurt, Taly, and I'm not talking about just Ebondrift. I'm talking about last year when you left home. Climbed out your fucking window in the middle of the night and then just disappeared. Do you know how many nights I heard Sarina crying after she'd thought everyone had gone to bed? Do you know what a gut-punch it was every time Ivain would pull two cigars after dinner, only to realize that you weren't there? You left a giant, gaping hole in our lives, and if you want to know why I'm so pissed right now, it's because I'm half-expecting you to do it again. The next time you decide you're right and I'm wrong, how can I trust that you're not just going to leave me behind? That you're not going to lie to me, tell me how much you hate me, all for my *own good*?"

"Skye, I..." But she didn't finish. Couldn't.

Taking a shaky step back, Skye resumed his pacing. His skin felt too tight; his aether flared, reacting to his anger. There was still one thing that didn't make sense. "You let Sarina and Ivain back in."

"What?"

"You let them back in." Skye's voice was raw. He hadn't realized how much this particular betrayal still hurt. "You keep saying that you left home, pushed us all away to keep us safe, but you let *them* help you. You talked to *them* in the street rather than walking the other way. You let *them* back into your life but not me."

His eyes met hers, angry. Demanding. "Why?"

Some other emotion flickered in her own eyes—guilt. "I never asked for Sarina or Ivain's help. I told them to get lost, and they didn't listen."

"Don't lie to me."

"I'm not," she insisted weakly. "You try telling Sarina *no*. See where that gets you."

Still lying. She was still *lying* to him. As if he didn't know that she had tried to push him farther away than anybody else. "Maybe you should've told her that you were '*tired of being treated like a possession, so go find some other shardless pet. You are not my friend, Skylen. You were never my friend, so get the hell out and forget you ever knew my name*'."

Taly winced, but he didn't care. Those were her words, the ones that had kept him away for almost a year the first time she had run away. They hurt just as much now as when she had first hurled them at him in that bunkhouse in Ebondrift. After she'd collapsed in the training yard, screaming and clutching her arm, he'd spent three weeks chasing her across the island. Three anxious, sleepless weeks where all he could do was hope she wasn't dead or dying because of something he'd done.

"Did you try that?" His voice cracked. He didn't bother to wipe away the tears stinging his eyes. "Because it certainly worked on me."

"I..." She took a breath, blinking back her own tears. "I just wanted to protect you."

"Stop saying that," he hissed.

"*No,*" she barked back at him. "I will not stop saying that. I made mistakes, and knowing what I know now, I may have done some things differently. But I'm not sorry for wanting to protect your stupid ass."

"Then give me a reason, Taly. Give me a *better* reason. Tell me that you didn't trust me enough or that I did something to make you question my loyalty because I don't understand why you keep leaving me behind—why you would shut me out when all I have ever wanted is to stand with you. Why did you take away that choice? Why did you try to *break* us?"

"*Because!*" she spat.

"*Because why?!*" And Shards, it felt good to finally scream out his frustration. "*Why Taly*?! Stop fucking around and *tell - me - why!*"

He could almost hear her own temper snapping from across the room as she screamed back at him, "Because I'm in love with you, you stupid idiot!"

Skye went still. Even his heart forgot to beat.

"It's because I'm in love with you," she said again, panting, sobbing, he wasn't quite sure. One hand pounded against her chest, fingers digging into the fabric of her dress. "But I am a death sentence, not just for the people I care about, but anyone unlucky enough to be within spitting distance. Why do you think the Sanctorum came to Vale when I was only six years old? Why do you think they concentrated on that village over any of the others?"

A pause.

She gave a wet, miserable little laugh. "It's because *I* was there, and yes, it took me all of five fucking minutes to figure that out once I started seeing *ghosts*. People have already *died* because of me, so if you want to know why I let Ivain and Sarina back in—that's it. It's because you mattered more. It's because you weren't letting go even after I said those *awful* things, and I knew if you kept at it, I'd cave and tell you everything. So, I singled you out. I sent back your letters, made sure you saw me turn around in the street. I accepted Sarina and Ivain's offers of help even though I knew it put more risk onto them. I wanted you to be angry, because I knew if you were angry, you would stay away. And if you stayed away, you would be safe.

"If I managed to keep just one person alive, I wanted it to be you. Just you, Em. Because if you died, there wouldn't be anything of me left."

The windows rattled as a particularly violent explosion split open the sky, and it continued to growl for several long moments after.

Taly was panting, that hand still pressed to her chest. The tears were streaming freely down her cheeks as she stared at him from across the room. He could once again see every one of those long months apart filling up the space between them, each one spent dwelling on her own mistakes. Trying to piece together an impossible situation.

She was waiting for him to respond, he realized. And though he tried, he couldn't.

She loved him.

And just like that, his anger slipped away, leaving him dangling, hanging over the edge of a cliff.

She loved him. And how many crazy things had he done for that same reason? How many times had he endangered his own life for a chance at saving hers?

Not just a friend or a lover. Not just a partner or even a wife.

A bondmate. The person on the other end of that thread. Always with him. Always tugging him forward.

Taly was still waiting, shifting awkwardly as her eyes dropped to the floor. And since he still couldn't find the words to say what he so desperately *needed* to say, he did the only thing he could think to do.

Crossing the room in a few, quick strides, he took her face in his hands—

And he kissed her.

She stiffened, and for one terrifying moment, he thought she might pull away—that he had overstepped or misunderstood.

But then she was kissing him back.

She was kissing him back with the same fierceness and longing that had been building inside him every day since Ebondrift. When he'd kissed her for the first and final time. When she'd told him goodbye.

He could hear the frantic beat of her heart, sense the shift in her scent. That thread—the bond—thrummed between them. Her mouth opened so easily to him, and at the first brush of her tongue—

Snarling softly, Taly pulled back and slammed a fist into his shoulder.

Skye immediately crumpled, not sure if it was pain or shock that had him staggering back a step. Maybe both. She hit way harder than she used to.

"What the hell was that for?" he sputtered.

"I'm still angry at you." She sniffed back a fresh flood of tears, and her aether pulsed like fireflies in the space around her. "You're an empty-headed jerk with absolutely no sense of self-preservation, and see if I ever do anything ever again to try to protect you."

Skye began to laugh, ignoring her protests as he pulled her back into his arms. Her aether gave a violent flare, but he drank it in, letting his own magic spark against that bright veil of gold that rippled between them.

"I love you," he whispered onto her lips. She immediately softened against him. "I am *in* love with you, even though you are a stubborn" —a kiss, quick and brutal— "pig-headed" —then a harsh nip to her bottom lip— "*brat*."

That earned him a slap on the chest.

Then another when he just laughed and kissed her. Again and again, until his lips were wet with her tears and he felt drunk off the taste of her. It had been a long, hard road, but she was finally back in his arms, finally back where she belonged.

Though there was still one final thing.

"Don't do this again." He had to force himself away. "Don't run, don't lie, don't leave me behind. You don't get to decide that my life is more valuable than yours. Even if you were human, that handful of decades would be worth everything to me. *You* are worth everything to me. Understand?"

Taly nodded, closing her eyes as he kissed her brow. "I understand," she said. "And I won't. I'm done wasting my time trying to save someone who doesn't have enough sense to save himself. You're stuck with me now."

Skye's lips twitched. "Good."

"For a lot longer than a few decades."

"I already did the math," he said, smiling softly into her hair. They would have forever now. The entirety of their immortal lives.

The world outside continued to rumble and growl. Ash pelted the glass.

From somewhere inside the apartment, a clock began to chime the hour.

"Are we done fighting now?" Taly asked. Her voice was small and tentative, and she pulled back, craning her head to look up at him.

Skye huffed. "About this? Yes." He nudged her nose with his. "But don't worry. I'm sure I'll do something to piss you off here soon, and then you can be the one to yell at me."

Her answering smile made him feel giddy. He couldn't have stopped himself from kissing her if he tried.

He wasn't sure when they moved to the couch, only that she was still in his arms. And if asked, he wouldn't be able to say whose idea it was to move their dinner to the bed. Everything was cold, but it all tasted fantastic spread over thick slices of crusty bread.

There was more wine, and the decanter never seemed to empty—some time magic enchantment that he didn't care to question. And at some point, after they'd exchanged more words and more kisses—after she'd curled into his side and her limbs had become tangled with his as she drifted off to sleep, he finally allowed himself to close his eyes, safe in the knowledge that this wasn't a dream.

That the nightmare had finally come to an end.

CHAPTER 33

-An excerpt from the Rhyming Alchemist's Book of Verses

Mistlewick venom, more painful it grows

You'll wish for sweet death, till free of its throes

The morning after Vaughn died, Taly found herself in the kitchen, rummaging through the pantry.

The fairies kept their distance, and for that, she was glad. They had known about the Queen's plan, and she didn't want to hear their excuses for not warning her. Wasn't ready to accept even Leto's apologies.

She didn't want to acknowledge the hurt she felt knowing that the Queen had manipulated her, or that somehow, at some point, she had started to trust that she wouldn't.

Those were things she would think about tomorrow. Perhaps the next day. When the memory didn't feel quite so raw.

Skye had still been asleep when she slipped out of the apartment, completely dead to the world. He had lost a lot of blood, and with it, aether. He'd also said he'd been dosed with mistlewick venom, a nonlethal but still very dangerous poison. It would take his body longer to heal, his magic longer to recover. Which meant he would be needing faeflower. And food—a lot of it. Shadow mages were absolute pigs even when they were healthy, and while she was no cook, she could manage a decent breakfast.

So, that's what she focused on. There was fresh bread and butter—already brought in from the outdoor larder that reset at the beginning of every day—and she found eggs in the cold box along with sausage and bacon and leftover corn cakes. There was even a pot of hydra and potato stew bubbling on the stove, so she grabbed that too.

Taly was just finishing loading everything onto a tray, trying to find a place for a pot of Skye's favorite tea among the stacks of plates and covered serving dishes, when the Queen found her.

"This is a first," Azura said, coming to stand in front of the long kitchen prep table that bisected the room. "In all my years, I don't think I have ever seen you wield a spatula. I take it last night either went very well or very poorly."

Taly didn't answer. Didn't even look up as she balanced the porcelain teapot on the top of the pile.

"Are you not speaking to me now?" Azura asked, chuckling softly. "That seems a bit juvenile."

Taly carefully picked up the tray.

"Everything I have done was to make you stronger."

Bullshit. *Bull - shit.*

Azura had tricked her, lied to her. She'd been pushed *beyond…* Well, not beyond, but *up to* her breaking point.

And she hadn't broken.

She'd come close, but…

Taly shook her head. She wasn't ready for this conversation. Wasn't ready to think about Vaughn. Wasn't ready to forgive the Queen for using Skye to test her.

Back rigid, she aimed for the door.

Azura said nothing as she watched her go.

Skye awoke that morning and immediately wished he hadn't.

Everything hurt. Every muscle, every cell.

Mistlewick venom was painful and long-lasting, so when Taly immediately began fussing, he let her. She brought him trays of food and made him take faeflower and pain tonic, and when he asked if her new mender training had come with a uniform, and could she wear it (please), she just rolled her eyes, telling him that if he kept talking, she would start lacing the tonics with sleeping draught.

And then, of course, there was Calcifer. The mimic—whatever the hell that was. All Skye knew so far was that it was large and grumpy and had been shadowing Taly around the apartment ever since she returned from the kitchen.

Oh, and it didn't like him. At all. It growled every time he so much as looked at Taly and kept trying to push her away when she sat down beside him to check his bandages. And then when she had coaxed it up onto the bed beside him, it had *"yawned."* Which was to say it had opened its mouth just so he could see what massive teeth it had.

"I think it wants to eat me," Skye said, lying flat on his back—that was the position that hurt the least—and eyeing the gangly cat-thing lounging on the opposite side of the mercifully large bed.

"Why does everyone keep saying that?" Taly asked from beside him. She was resting on her side with one leg slung across his beneath the blankets. Over her shoulder, the beast glared at him, its large bat-like ears folded against its head.

"Other people have said this?"

Taly shrugged and turned the page. "Only Azura. And to be fair, he does feed on time aether, but he's never taken more than what I give him."

"Wait. What?"

"Time aether," Taly said as if it was perfectly normal and not something utterly bone-chilling. Behind her, the beast twitched its long tail. "He prefers straight aether, but sometimes I give him spells linked to crystals."

Skye just gaped until she looked up. "I think you might be crazy."

"He's not going to eat you."

"No, it's going to eat *you*, and then it's going to kill me out of pure contempt."

"You're being dramatic."

"Taly, it's growling at me." And then just to prove his point, Skye lifted the hand she'd been resting on his bare chest, setting it off to the side.

The growling stopped.

Picking her hand up again and cursing every part of him that still ached, he placed it back on his chest.

The beast gave a dangerous snarl.

Taly reached behind her and scratched behind one of the monster's too-large ears, and it immediately gave a huff and settled, resting its head in the crook of her neck. "He's just cranky," she said and turned back to her book. Skye felt her bare foot graze his calf beneath the blanket in a way that was meant to be soothing. "After all, he had to sleep downstairs last night, and now there's a strange man in his bed."

"His bed?"

"Yes, and you're on his side."

Well, that explained the black fur on his pillow.

"Taly—" A yawn cut him off as a sudden wave of exhaustion crashed into him. "We're not taking that thing home with us." Even if they could figure out a way to get it back into the city, he wasn't sure how comfortable he was bringing along a creature that fed on his mate's aether.

Looking up, Taly gave him a small smile—the one that let him know that he had already lost, and there was no use fighting. "Why don't we talk about this tonight after you've gotten some rest." Translated, that meant the issue would never come up again, defaulting her a victory.

Skye gave another yawn, every muscle in his body protesting the movement. Why was he so tired? It's almost like— "You gave me sleeping draught."

She smoothed the edge of the bandage taped to his abdomen. There was blood leaking through the white linen. "Just a little," she said unapologetically. "You keep moving around, and I went to a lot of trouble trying to patch you up. I can't have you undoing all my hard work."

Skye relaxed into the pillow, humming contentedly when Taly leaned over and brushed a kiss to his mouth. The one good thing about sleeping draught was that it also numbed the pain. "Shards, woman," he mumbled. "It's like you've been taking notes from Sarina."

By the next morning, Skye's aether was still close to depleted, and his wounds were only newly healed, still scabbing though it looked like there wouldn't be any scars. His torso was covered in bruises, and every part of him ached. Which might explain why Taly had just stared at him like he'd grown a second head when he asked where to find the training grounds.

Though slower to provoke, fey females were as protective and territorial as their male counterparts, and even more impossible to negotiate with once those instincts had been triggered. But after he'd explained that exercise would help him metabolize the remaining toxins in his system, she'd pointed the way. Grudgingly. And with a promise that if he collapsed, she wasn't going to drag his limp body back to bed.

And that was fair. He still couldn't take a step without wincing. But he didn't want to spend another day in bed. He was antsy. Restless. And there were too many thoughts, too many worries swirling around in his head.

Too many things he still needed to tell Taly but wasn't sure how.

About her family. The shared dreams. When she projected. The bond. All were important, though none were the reason he now found himself in a training arena surrounded by stone arches, mercilessly beating the shit out of a wooden dummy.

THUD.

His fist slammed into the wood.

It hadn't been a lie, what he'd told Taly. Not exactly.

Exercise increased his pulse, his bloodflow. And while that usually wouldn't have done anything for him—besides make him wish he'd stayed in bed—thanks to Ivain's new training, he could alter his body chemistry on a cellular level. Channel what little aether his body had managed to recover directly into his liver, thus isolating the poison. Making it easier to sweat out.

THUD.

After only an hour, the pain was gone, and his wounds had fully closed. The air here was so rich, his aether reserve was already close to full.

THUD.

He hadn't even had to meditate. Hadn't needed but the barest whisper of magic to pull at the ambient aether in the air, pushing it into his blood, his cells, and jump-starting his body's already-accelerated healing.

It had all been so easy once he'd been able to think about the *how* and the *why*, to figure out the ways his body fit together.

If only he'd been able to think this clearly when he'd been facing off with Vaughn. To feel the mistlewick venom as it saturated his blood. Its edges were rough. It was something *other*, something that had no place inside him.

Why was it so easy *now*? Why not then? Why couldn't he have figured this out when it had actually fucking mattered?

He spun and kicked the dummy, then brought up a fist.

The wood cracked.

Wood that had been reinforced to withstand a shadow mage's strength.

His knuckles split, but he used aether to immediately heal the wound, pushing calcium into the skin as it regrew and hardening the surface of his knuckles to the consistency of bone in an instant.

Shards, why was it all so easy now?

THUD.

It felt good to hit something.

THUD, THUD.

He'd had far too much time to think over the past day. Too much time to imagine Vaughn's face. To remember that sneer, that knowing smirk.

The things he had said. About *using* Taly.

THUD, THUD, THUD.

The dummy went flying, shattering as it skidded across the red dirt.

Skye stood there for a moment, panting. Sweating beneath the midday sun.

He kept replaying that fight in his head. Kept trying to figure out what he could've done differently.

Should he have rushed Vaughn? Gone for Carin first?

The water mage had seemed like the natural target, but he'd still been beaten. He'd played right into the Queen's hand, and Taly had been forced to take a life.

A life that had needed to be extinguished, but...

Skye moved to the next dummy in the row.

THUD.

He could see it eating away at her. Even if she wouldn't say as much.

And he should've been able to protect her from that.

The girl who couldn't kill a rabbit.

If he'd just been *stronger*... Maybe that was why he hadn't been able to bring himself to tell her about the bond. Why would she want to permanently bind herself to a man so easily beaten, who had almost given up on her?

A man who couldn't even defend a bridge over a fucking canyon?

"Well now, isn't this a surprise."

Snarling, Skye sent a second dummy hurtling through the air. It smashed against the large silverleaf oak in the center of the arena, bursting into a shower of wooden fragments.

Barely a foot away from where the Queen now leaned. Smiling.

He felt a muscle in his jaw begin to twitch. This woman—Taly had told him about what this woman had made her do. The training, the sadistic games of so-called *fairy tag,* all of it leading up to that final test.

It had been effective. That he couldn't deny. Taly had accomplished remarkable things in an absurdly short period of time. But why keep her separated from her family? Why use him to try to break her?

This woman had manipulated them both. She sent her fairies to taunt him—to exploit his weaknesses, his pain, just to see if that wound would fester.

He would have killed her if he was able. If Taly would have allowed it. For reasons he couldn't begin to fathom, she had developed some sort of affection for this woman. Perhaps even trust.

Which made the rage he felt at seeing that trust broken cut even deeper.

A few splinters flecked the gray silk of her dress, and the Queen brushed them away, still smiling as she said, "You look like you're feeling better."

"Oh yes," he drawled, moving to another dummy. "After being manipulated and led here." He threw a punch. "After being poisoned." Twisting, he kicked. "After having some genocidal tyrant attempt to orchestrate my death and use it to terrorize my mate." Getting close, he grabbed the dummy's head in his hands, wrenching it off the joint before turning to face Azura.

"I'm doing quite well. Thank you for asking." And with that, he crushed the wood between his bare hands, never letting his eyes break away from hers.

The Queen's smile vanished. The fairies that had followed her, chirping overhead where they hid in the branches of the aged silverleaf oak, hushed. "I'd watch how you speak to me, boy." The words were clipped. Cold. A response to his implicit threat. "I have been generous up until now, but I am still your superior in both power and years. Do not test me."

A dangerous line—he could feel the power roiling inside this woman. The majesty of a god checked only by the limitations of flesh and bone.

But anger made him bold. It gave him clarity.

The Queen was unmoving as he simply dropped the wooden fragments to the ground. "It's Azura, right?" She arched a brow at the familiarity, the audacity of using her given name without her expressed permission. There were rules to be observed with such very important persons, but he just smirked. "That's what Taly says she calls you. You see, we've been doing a lot of talking, and she's told me a lot about you. And while I can't quite figure out what your intentions are, one thing is clear.

"Taly is important to you," he went on, dusting off his hands. "And I'm important to her. So, if I were a betting man, I'd say that you're bluffing. That if you were going to do something, you'd have already done it. Given those odds, I'll speak to you however I damn well please." He dropped into a mocking bow. "Your *Majesty*."

The Queen stared at him for a long moment. So still. So cold. There was a heaviness in the air. A weight of power that made even the birds stop singing.

But Skye didn't cower. Didn't break away from that regal golden stare. He'd met Genesis Lords before. He knew how to play their games.

And just like he'd expected, once she realized that there was no fun to be had at his expense, the coldness cracked, vanishing in an instant. The birds resumed their singing.

"Oh, I knew there was a reason I liked you," she crooned, that half-mad smile returning. "Of all the men Taly has brought to me over the years, you've always been my favorite."

Obvious bait—and a piss-poor attempt at stoking his jealousy. Skye made a small disgusted noise in the back of his throat. "You don't know a thing about me," he said as he moved to the next dummy. A clear dismissal.

But the Queen just laughed and pushed herself off the tree. "On the contrary," she said, "I know everything about you. I've been watching you through the Weave since before you were born. I've seen every iteration your life could've taken. You're Skylen Emrys, the golden child of Ghislain, the pureblooded heir your mother always wanted. A boy born to power and wealth, who's been afforded every luxury, every comfort. Whose very blood grants him privileges, ones that have cost your brother more than you've ever been asked to give up."

That made him turn.

From the way the Queen's smile widened, she knew she finally had his attention. "Everything has always come so easy to you, hasn't it, Skylen? Language, mathematics, magic, statecraft, *women*." He didn't miss the suggestive lilt to her voice, as if to say she knew about that reputation Taly had once accused him of having. Perhaps rightly so.

"You have *everything* you've ever wanted," she went on, "and everything you've ever needed. The world is yours. It has been promised to you on a jewel-encrusted platter, and yet you're unhappy. Because you don't want the world. You want everything that you have right now. You want your life on Tempris, but you realized a long time ago that it has an expiration date. One that, despite current events, you can still feel approaching. You dread the day when your mother will finally call you home, yet you've resigned yourself to it. You've never had to struggle, so in the face of hardship, all you see is looming inevitability."

Skye remained silent, clenching and unclenching his fists. Anything he might've said to the contrary would've been a lie.

With a snap of her fingers, wood flew, groaning as the dummies reassembled. Unmarked. Whole.

Except for a single head that landed in her waiting hands. Coming closer, she placed it gently back upon the dummy's shoulders.

"That is until recently," she went on. Her fingertips glowed gold as she secured the head in place. "When the world went to hell, you finally gained some clarity. The same clarity that all men gain when faced with an end. You realized that there was something you wanted. Enough to buck your family's reins. Enough to kill for, to die for. And the longer you lived with that truth, the more you wanted it. Wanted *her*—a human, then a time mage. The want consumed you, so much that you stopped seeing the struggle it would take to stay with her and forged a new path."

The Queen stepped back to inspect her work, the pale jewels in her black hair glimmering in the summer sun.

Skye felt as though he'd just been opened up, the pieces of him laid bare. "What do you want with us?" he rasped. The weight of that power was suffocating as she came to stand even closer to him, barely a handful of feet away. "With me, with Taly? Why that test? Why did you bring me here the way you did? Why did you send your fairies to torture me?"

The Queen gave a delicate shrug. "You needed a push," she said simply. "Without encouragement, there was a chance that you would've done nothing. That you would've stayed in that city and followed Ivain's command, obeying his every order and never thinking for yourself. It would've been easier. It's always easier to let other people make your decisions. And then when I sent Taly back, you would've been the same man that you were when she left. A man that saw hardship as inevitability. Who faced defeat on a bridge and nearly let it cripple him. That man would not have been strong enough to protect her. He would not have been able to face those that would see her dead, but *you*—"

Her eyes flicked up and down, looking him over. As if she could see through him, to what lay beneath his skin. "You might have a chance. If you keep going down the path that's now opened before you, you might just be strong enough to stand at her side."

If he kept learning bloodcraft. If he kept experimenting, kept getting stronger. Kept sacrificing for that forbidden power.

Leaves rustled overhead, fairies peeking from between the branches.

Skye's heart was hammering in his chest. The Queen watched him as he backed away, those eyes following him as he turned to go. He needed to see Taly. Needed to get away from the Queen and that suffocating gravity of power.

"It's feels good, doesn't it?" she called when he passed under one of the arches.

He glanced over his shoulder, waiting.

That smile was back. "Taking ownership of your life," she clarified. "Doesn't it feel good?"

Skye didn't bother to reply as he exited the arena. The Queen already knew his answer.

Taly dove beneath the water, swimming down to the bottom of the pool. Fire and water crystals swirled across the floor in nonsense patterns, shimmering softly, and when she reached the deepest part, she hugged her knees to her chest and exhaled slowly. Streams of bubbles raced for the surface.

Here she stayed, listening to the gentle roar of the water as her hair whorled around her, pushed by the gentle current.

After Skye had left to go do whatever it was he planned on doing, she had spent her day sorting through clothes and books, trying to figure out what would stay and what would go. She had come to the palace with nothing, so it was a little astonishing just how much *stuff* she had managed to accumulate in only a year.

Clothes, jewelry, trinkets from the fairies, gifts from the Queen, and so many books.

At least that last one was easy. Azura had given her a list, slipped beneath her door that morning. It detailed every reading assignment and spell she needed to complete before she returned to the palace—which Taly had no doubt that she would at some point. The future was a weird, tangled mess, and even if she hated the Queen right now, forever was a long time to hold a grudge.

Home.

That word had been chasing her all day.

They were going home tomorrow. Back to Tempris. Back to an island full of shades. And even though this was what she had been working towards for nearly a year, desperate to get back to her friends and family, now that the time had come…

Taly craned her head, looking up at the light as it danced across the surface of the water. She wasn't sure how to finish that thought. If she even wanted to.

Being in the palace had come with an assumption of safety she had taken for granted. True, the Queen's methods had been brutal, sometimes cruel. But Taly had never feared for her safety. She'd never wondered if she'd live to see the sun rise. Never doubted she'd live to see it set.

It had taken nearly a year, but she finally understood the gift she'd been given.

Azura, for all her eccentricities, had given her time. Time to train. Time to get stronger. The Queen had given her a chance against the Sanctorum—one she wouldn't have had otherwise.

Taly's lungs were starting to burn. She was out of air, so she unfolded her body and kicked off the bottom of the pool.

She surfaced a moment later, gasping in a breath.

It was dark, the only light from the crystals flickering in the pool and peppering the rough-hewn rock that curved overhead. She had found this grotto early on, and it was still one of her favorite places to come when she just needed to think. The water was warm, fed from a natural hot spring, and the air was fragrant. She could hear the roar of the rapids that fed into the palace like a distant growl, soft enough to be soothing.

"I know you're there," she said to the shadows. She wasn't sure how, but she could feel him.

There was a soft huff, then Skye stepped away from his place in the arched open doorway. Taly looked him over. His shirt was clean but untucked. His hair was wet, as though he'd just showered. There was more color in his face than there had been that morning, and the limp was gone.

Noticing her assessment, he smirked, as if to say, *See, I was right.* Apparently, all a shadow mage needed to overcome even the most egregious of injuries was a few laps around the property, and she was going to remember that the next time he was moaning and whining and asking her to spoon feed him all so he could get a look down her shirt.

"Five minutes," he said. His voice sounded strangely hushed as he came to stand by the edge of the pool, hands in his pockets.

"What?" Taly asked, treading water.

A shadow passed across his face. "You were underwater for five minutes," he said too softly. "After minute three, I… But then I remembered..."

"Oh," Taly mouthed silently. For a fey, that was hardly impressive. But for a human… "Sorry," she mumbled.

He shook his head, watching as she swam closer. "Don't be sorry. It's just… all our lives, you've always been so much more breakable than me. It's going to take me a little while to realign my thinking."

Ah. That she could more than understand.

Taly reached the side of the pool and hoisted herself up, water sluicing off her body as she turned to sit on the stone ledge. Her blue and white swim costume was copied from a human design. Form-fitting but practical, though far from revealing, especially by fey standards—his eyes still sparked as they slid across her body. Slowly taking in the flash of her back, her bare legs. Brazenly lingering on every curve.

Her toes curled in the water. He gave her a wicked smile as he eased himself down beside her, as if to say that, *yes*, he knew the exact effect he had on her now, and *yes*, he planned to use it against her in the most delightful way.

Jerk.

Even in her head, the word lacked bite. She could hardly look at him without thinking of that mouth. Without wondering just how long it would be until it was back on her own. And considering that he was staring back at her with that same desperate hunger reflected in his eyes, with longing and lust and more love than she knew she deserved, she found that she didn't really mind.

"I'm still human in my dreams," she said when she remembered how to speak. His brows rose slightly. "Azura calls it a fabricated self-image. When we dream, we don't appear the way we are but rather the way we perceive ourselves."

"And you still perceive yourself as human?"

She shrugged. "I guess a part of me does," she said softly, turning to stare at her toes in the water. "Or maybe... maybe I just don't want to forget that face. Sometimes it feels like the girl that walked into the Vale relay died that night, and someone else came out in her place. I haven't felt like me in a long time. After the Queen's test, I… I'm not sure if I ever will again."

She could feel Skye watching her as she leaned back on her hands, tilting her head so she could see the crystals flickering above. "You know," he began, hesitant, "you can talk to me about Vaughn. If you want to, that is."

Of course, he'd see that wound. Of course, he'd try to fix it.

"I don't regret it," she whispered up to those crystals that glistened like stars. "I feel like I should, and I keep waiting for the regret to finally settle in. But I don't think it's going to. I killed a man, and if given the opportunity, I'd do it again. If given a thousand second chances, I'm pretty sure I'd kill him every time, and I'd never feel regret."

She turned her head, finding those green eyes in the flickering dark. "What does that say about me, Em?"

Skye sighed and looked to the water, then back to her. As if he couldn't figure out just how to tell her that becoming fey had turned her into a monster incapable of remorse. That human girl would've felt regret. She had been kinder.

"I think…" he began, but then stopped.

She didn't speak, waiting.

"I've had to kill a lot of shades in the past few weeks," he said slowly, as though feeling out the words. "Some of them I knew; some of them looked like they could still be alive. But Carin and Asher—killing them felt more personal. More real, somehow. We traveled together, fought together. But if I found myself back in that room, I would kill them again. Without hesitation. They were going to hurt you. And me. I don't think we should feel regret for protecting ourselves against our enemies. Sadness at the necessity of taking life, perhaps. But not regret."

Taly stared at him for a long moment, something easing in her chest. If he was right… Maybe she wasn't tainted then. Wiser, yes. Aware of things about herself that she'd never wanted to know. But maybe the world wasn't quite so black and white as it had once seemed. Maybe she could feel sadness but not regret, and maybe not every good thing about that human girl was gone.

Leaning over, she gave him a gentle kiss. "You got smarter while I was away."

He snorted at that, kissing her again. And again. One hand lifted to tangle in the hair at the base of her neck. "Maybe I was always this smart, and you just didn't listen."

"No," she said, her breathing growing ragged as his tongue began to tease at her bottom lip. "That's not it."

"It could be."

"It's not."

Her hands slid up his chest, gripping him by the collar as he slipped an arm around her waist and pulled her closer. She smiled against his lips, and he went still as death. He knew this game as well as she did. If there was a body of water nearby, they both knew what the rules demanded.

"Shit," was all he was able to say before she threw her arms around him and sent them both hurtling into the pool.

Taly surfaced a moment later, almost cackling with laughter as she blinked water from her eyes. Skye had always been bigger and stronger, and she never got to be the one to do the dunking. But the king had been dethroned! And he didn't look too happy about it as he emerged a few feet away, shaking the water from his hair like a wet dog.

"You're going to pay for that." Mischief lit his eyes as he ripped his sodden shirt over his head and tossed it to the side. "And here I was being nice—"

"Oh please." She let out a little squeal, backpedaling through the water when he lunged for her. "The *'sadness at the necessity of taking life'*? You actually expect me to believe you came up with that on your own? You stole that."

"Nope." He tried again. Missed. "That was all me."

"Yeah, right." She splashed him, but he shielded his face. "You're not that eloquent."

A flare of aether was the only warning she got before he snatched her wrist—

And then she was gone, halfway across the pool.

Water dripping from his hair, Skye stared at her, slack jawed.

Shit.

She'd phased.

And she'd been doing such a good job of not casting in front of him. Knowing she was a time mage and seeing her cast were two different things, but now—

"Do it again."

It was Taly's turn to gape. "You're not..." Frightened. Disgusted. The words seemed too silly to say aloud—this was Skye, after all. And he loved her. But fear wasn't always logical.

He swam to her, that powerful body moving through the water with a grace she had always envied. A natural ease of movement that only a shadow mage could muster.

Strong hands slid around her waist when he was close enough, pulling her against him so she wouldn't have to tread water.

"Show me more magic," he commanded softly. He was grinning from ear-to-ear, almost giddy. It was impossible not to smile back.

Impossible not to give him exactly what he wanted.

So, lifting a hand, she let the water drip from her fingers between them. But instead of dribbling back into the pool, the droplets hung suspended, each one glittering in the flickering crystal light.

His eyes were wide, but she wasn't done yet. Taking one of those droplets between her thumb and forefinger, she dragged it through the air. Then she took another and another, pushing them up toward the ceiling until—

"Stars," he breathed.

She nodded. The explosions always began before sunset, and even when they ended, the smoke would obscure the night sky. She hadn't seen stars in such a very long time…

So, she had started making her own. Using her magic to reform the shape of reality.

Skye squeezed her tighter, looking on in wonder as she continued to drip water in the air, forming starbursts and constellations and little comets that shimmered in the dark. And because he was a menace, he began to pepper soft teasing kisses along her jaw, then her neck. The spell shuddering when he would nip her with his teeth.

He found a place beneath her ear, and one droplet fell. Then another.

"Concentrate," he murmured against her skin. The water did such wonderful things as he slid his hands along her body, over the swell of her hips and up her waist. His thumbs just grazed the undersides of her breasts before beginning their journey back down.

Such slow, wicked torture, and Taly was aware of every place their bodies touched, every bead of water he licked from her skin. And when he finally found his way back to her lips—he wasn't gentle. The way he kissed her—it was a kiss that made a vow. That said he belonged to her and she to him, and that no matter what, she could never leave him behind. Not again. Not ever. Not even if this thing between them crumbled, and they spent the rest of their lives as just friends. They went together now. Into the future and into the unknown.

Until the end.

So, Taly kissed him back, hard and wild. She made that promise as the delicate patter of rain filled the grotto, the stars falling down around them as the last of the spell unraveled.

CHAPTER 34

-An excerpt from the Book of the Faera

Beware the firstborn child of Magnus. For he is beloved. He is the Judge.

And now, he is Death.

Taly and Skye walked side-by-side, their footsteps echoing down the long, mirrored corridor. Leto drifted ahead of them, followed closely by Calcifer and his great loping strides. The fairies peeked out of doorways, whispering amongst themselves. It seemed that nearly every resident of the palace had come to see them off, and Taly couldn't help but smile at the way Skye's eyes would follow every fairy that skittered across their path, chiming out a laugh as they disappeared into the shadows.

They were showing off for him, transforming into butterflies and birds, cats and snakes. Some were little more than ribbons on the wind, and there was even a little spectral bear following a few paces behind.

Smiling over her shoulder, Taly gave the tiny bear a wink, giggling softly when its chest puffed up with pride. Most days, Lucan would drift listlessly through the ballrooms, humming songs she only vaguely recognized. Where he found the energy to pull off the transformation, she didn't know.

"You like them." Not a question. Merely an observation from the man walking at her side. Leto had managed to clean the blood from his armor and even produced a new surcoat and cloak for him to wear—both black and nearly identical to the layers of heavy fabric she wore over her own armor.

It was still spring where they were going. Which meant it would be cold and wet, and honestly, Taly couldn't wait.

"Some of them," she replied, turning to look ahead. Others, like the old cuss that roamed the main library, she could do without.

"And are they really… spirits of the dead?"

She nodded. "They're the time mages," she said, answering what she was sure would be his next question. Leto glanced over her shoulder, but Taly just smiled as if to say, *Yes, I figured it out.*

That day in the training yard, when she'd dreamed of a time when this palace had been filled with life and learning, she'd finally discovered one of the secrets of the Schism. The time mages were dead. All of them. The great disaster had claimed them, and while she couldn't say how or why, she knew their staying had been a choice. Instead of passing on, they had stayed behind, still loyal to their Queen.

They rounded another corner, and Leto announced, "We've arrived," as she pushed at a mirrored panel that looked like all the rest.

The glass slid to the side, and a narrow stairwell stretched up, spiraling out of sight.

"Where is *here* exactly?" Taly asked as they began to ascend. This was the Queen's private wing, and she had never spent much time in this part of the palace.

"Her Majesty has been making preparations for your departure," Leto replied. Her soft blue light provided the only illumination. "Due to the events surrounding your initial arrival," she said to Taly, "we had to use emergency protocols to bring you here directly. For most visits, however, you will come through the bridge room."

An open doorway appeared at the top of the stairs, a light in the dark. Calcifer bounded ahead of them, and as soon as they stepped across the threshold, a familiar voice chirped, "Well, look who finally decided to make an appearance. I was starting to think you'd decided to extend your stay."

The Queen was sitting at a long table at the center of a room that was easily the size of Taly's entire tower apartment, sipping a cup of tea while her free hand flew across a glamour interface.

Giant screens lined the walls, each one covered with scrolling lines of Faera and complicated calculations. Some of the equations were familiar—she'd learned a fair amount of multidimensional mathematics over the past year—while others were entirely foreign and incomprehensibly complex. Each time the Queen tapped the interface in front of her, the equations would shift, more numbers clicking into place. The screens almost seemed to ripple as waves of information cascaded around the room.

Taly moved further inside, her attention immediately drawn to the massive sheet of violet crystal that spanned the entire length of the back wall. A long strip of gold punctuated the center, and two pillars of translucent hyaline flanked it on either side, flashing in time with the staccato tap of Azura's fingers against the interface.

It was a gate. Fully functional. And suddenly, the screens and the interfaces made sense. Azura was programming the gate, aligning the timelines, stabilizing the bridge that would take them from this world to the next.

"How did I not know about this?" Taly asked, still staring at the gate.

"Because I didn't want you to, dear," Azura replied simply.

And that was that. Because even though Taly had explored every inch of Infinity's Edge and its grounds, she knew there were still places left unexplored. Rooms and corridors that had been hidden away in their own little pockets of space and time, only to be revealed at the Queen's discretion.

Azura was dressed in soft yellow chiffon, the color a perfect match to the jewels woven into the nest of dark hair piled atop her head. "Feel free to look around," she said with a distracted wave of her hand that set the sheer fabric of her sleeve to shimmer. "I'm still working on the coordinates, but I'm hoping to be able to put you back just a few hours after Skye left. Sunrise, I think—or close to it."

"You can control that?" Taly asked, wandering over to a control panel. Skye followed close behind. He kept a wary eye on the Queen.

Azura shrugged. "To a degree. This was the original prototype for the dimensional gates."

"Really?" Skye asked with genuine curiosity, and Taly almost rolled her eyes. Leave it to a Gate Watcher to be interested in, well, gates.

"Yes." Azura frowned at the interface. "I've modified it, of course, but the controls aren't nearly as sensitive as Aion." A sigh. "If I had the Aion Gate, I could program your destination down to a tenth of a second, but we work with what we have."

Taly approached one of the screens, watching as it flickered between worlds filled with lush forests and barren deserts and cities surrounded by nothing but water.

"That's Dromeda," Skye whispered when a dark world of stars flashed by. "And Eya." The Draegon homeworld.

"The Fey Imperium used to be a vast and wondrous place," Leto said from where she drifted nearby. Calcifer batted at one of the flickering screens behind her.

"It's still a wondrous place." Pushing the interface aside, Azura rose from her chair. "When those idiots at the Dawn Court aren't mucking it up, that is."

Azura moved around the table, only to lean against it. She looked to Taly. "You're angry at me."

There was nothing but ice in her tone as Taly replied, "I'm more than angry at you."

Crossing her arms, Azura chuckled, dipping her head before she said to Skye, "Be careful with this one. She holds grudges. And judging by just how quiet your room has been the last few nights, it seems you haven't quite figured out how to uh… How shall I put this delicately? *Talk* your way out of trouble. I hear you have a silver tongue."

Taly's cheeks immediately burst into flames. Was she implying… She looked to Skye, the way his brows rose, a hint of a smile playing at his lips—yes, that's exactly what the Queen was implying.

And she and Skye… well, they had only kissed the night before. A lot. In the grotto, and then late into the night as they were lying in bed. But that's it. He hadn't pushed for more, and she hadn't known how to ask. That was still very new territory.

Azura looked to Skye, smiling wickedly. "She's loud, you know. I can't tell you how many times—"

"Azura, I *will* kill you," Taly ground out, sure that if her cheeks got any warmer, she might combust.

"Alright, alright…" Azura gave a dismissive wave of her hand. "What the two of you do behind closed doors is none of my business. Although" —a glance back at Skye— "I am well-versed in all the ways that time magic might be applied… in the bedroom? Just let me know if you'd like me to add anything to her future lessons. Left to her own devices, she can be a bit of a prude."

"That's it," Taly snapped. "Skye, give me your sword."

Skye caught her hand, then wrapped an arm around her shoulders and yanked her body against his, tightening his hold when she squirmed. "Please don't murder our way home," was all he said.

He had a point, so Taly settled for growling at the Queen while glaring daggers over her shoulder.

Azura just smiled serenely back. "You really do make it too easy," she murmured, reaching for her teacup. Even Skye's lips twitched.

"Majesty." Leto inclined her head, gesturing towards one of the screens.

"Yes, yes…" Azura picked up a portable interface, keying in another series of commands. "You're angry at me," she said again, then tossed the interface aside, not looking where it landed. "So, as my own attempt to land myself back into your good graces, I'll give you one question, Taly. Ask me anything, and I'll answer to the best of my ability."

Taly waited for her to rescind the offer. This couldn't be real. Azura never answered questions. Or if she did, it was in a way that only led to more confusion. "Any question?" she asked, stepping out of Skye's grasp. With the Queen, it was always important to be clear.

"That's what I said." She splayed her hands, as if to say she had nothing to hide. "So? What will it be? Will you ask me about the fairies? Who's attacking your island? Why the Sanctorum continues to exist despite an apparent lack of time mages to hunt? Or perhaps you'll ask me how I managed to hide a dimensional gate beneath my palace and then keep it hidden for over two centuries? I know Skye has already told you about his journey here."

Taly glanced at Skye, but he said nothing. This was her question. And while there were so many she wanted to ask, so many things she still didn't know, if she only got one answer… "Why did you close the gates?"

Azura tapped a finger against the side of her teacup. "Why didn't you ask the other question you've been considering? Why didn't you ask me why I took it upon myself to train you?"

"Because I already know the answer," Taly said, meeting those golden eyes. "You need me."

"And don't you want to know why?"

"Of course. But I have a feeling the two questions are related."

Azura's expression sobered as she carefully placed her teacup to the side.

"Why did you do it?" Taly asked again. "It's the question every single citizen of the Fey Imperium has been asking for nearly two and a half centuries. Why did you close the gates? Any time mage with a heartbeat would've been able to predict the devastation you caused."

Azura crossed her arms protectively around her body, letting her eyes scan the room as she gathered her thoughts. After a moment, she said bluntly, "The last time the full Genesis Council met, a man came to see us. He wasn't on the docket, but since it would be another ten years before our next scheduled congress, we gave him the floor."

Azura's eyes dropped. "He told us such horrible things. Too horrible to ever be considered, and yet… I couldn't shake them. We adjourned that day, and I spent the next year in deep meditation. And when I could no longer deny the truth of his words, I called my mages to me, hoping that they could see something that I could not."

"I'm assuming you're referring to the final meeting of the Time Guild?" Skye waited for Azura to nod before continuing, "At the time, no one could figure out why you recalled your mages. They were serving as advisors and teachers, politicians and ambassadors. You threatened fey relations with multiple gate worlds by forcing an assembly."

"We kept that information to ourselves," Azura said. "We kept a lot of things to ourselves as we began picking apart the timelines, using our collective power to make a map of every possible future. Secrecy was vital to our endeavor—even the smallest change in a person's actions can have a cascading effect on future events. In the end, however, all we managed to prove was the truth of this harbinger's message.

"Which only left one question: what to do about it?"

Azura frowned, flicking her skirts behind her as she began to idly pace. "I called an emergency session of the Council, and we debated. We went back and forth, analyzing every variable. And after weeks of arguing, we split. Auberin and Nissa went one way—they formed their Dawn Court and entrenched themselves on the mainland and would eventually use my actions to seize more power than they were due."

Taly blanched. "The Sanctorum," she breathed, and Skye placed a hand on her shoulder.

Azura only nodded. "As for Zion, Heleus, and Atlas," she continued. The remaining three members of the Council. "They moved their courts to the mortal realm, hoping to escape the devastation that was to come. Perhaps they even planned to learn the ways of that world, a way to survive should we ever need it. I'm not sure. We stopped talking to each other after that meeting—stopped trusting each other. Which is, I think, exactly what that man wanted. To divide us."

"What were the Council Lords in the mortal realm running from?" Taly asked, grateful for the hand that was still resting on her shoulder. The warm, steady reassurance. "The shades?"

Azura shook her head. "My dear, the attack on Tempris is only the beginning. The opening act in a war that's been building for longer than even I am able to comprehend."

"You still haven't explained why you closed the gates," Skye pointed out. His tone was steady, but even he looked a bit pale at this point. "You claim that you found out war is coming, but you didn't try to solidify power or escape—you shut down the gates. You killed the people you were sworn to protect. *Why?*"

Instead of answering him directly, Azura found Taly's stare and held it. "Everyone else is always dealing in possibilities," she said softly. "But *we* can see when those possibilities fall away. The others—my fellow Council members... they didn't want to believe in a future without hope. They didn't believe me when I said—when every time mage with the Sight and even those without—confirmed the inevitability that was slowly creeping towards us.

"No matter how many times I altered the variables, no matter how many scenarios I ran, I saw only two viable futures. In the first: blood and death swept the land, wiping out every people and race, regardless of creed or religion. Life continued, but not in the way that we knew it. Not in a way we would even want it.

"It was such a terrible future," Azura breathed. The sadness in those words made Taly's heart clench. "Not for the horrors that awaited us, but the certainty of our demise. I spent months, maybe years, in that timeline, trying to learn its intricacies, trying to find a way forward should the worst come to pass, and sometimes… sometimes, I think I can still hear the screaming, still feel the sting of the whips, and the cold bite of the chains. I'll turn a corner, and all I'll see is smoke and blood and…" Azura's voice trailed off, eyes wide with some distant terror.

"Az," Leto said kindly. Any other time, Taly would've marveled at the informality.

Azura drew in a soft gasp, seeming to come back to herself.

"In the second future," she continued hoarsely, the hand she pressed to her chest trembling, "I saw a possibility. A whisper of a chance. There were no guarantees, of course. There never are. But that's what I chose. It's what I and every soul haunting the corridors of this palace chose. *Life*—no matter the cost. *Survival*—if not for ourselves, then for those that might come after. The world thinks me mad. That my actions were unprompted and unprovoked. That I acted alone. But that is a lie. A calculated *lie* spread by those that know better.

"We were at war, and I did what was necessary." Azura's throat bobbed as she sank down into a nearby chair, cradling her face in her hand. "I gave us a chance. In a war we were never meant to win, I bought time. And now—now that time is up."

Taly couldn't breathe. Couldn't speak. Couldn't move.

War.

They were at war with something worse than shades. Something that made the sudden and abrupt deaths of millions of people worth the sacrifice.

Something that would drive them to extinction. That's what Azura had just described.

And what did this have to do with her? With why Azura had trained her, brought her here—

Skye slipped his hand into hers, and Taly jumped. He'd been so quiet, she'd almost forgotten he was there.

Skye cleared his throat. "Alright," he said, and damn him. Damn him for still looking so calm. "You felt the destruction of the gates was for some greater good. However, what does this have to do with Taly? What role could she possibly play in a war that's been silently raging longer than anyone in this room has even been alive?"

The flicker of devastation that flashed across Azura's face was like a punch to the gut. "That is information you neither need nor want."

"Tell us anyway," Skye demanded.

Azura shook her head. "I am done answering questions for today. I have already given you more than you need."

Skye turned Taly to face him, and it was only then that she realized she'd started shaking. He took her face in his hands, forcing her eyes to his, and… there was so much love there. More affection than she knew she deserved. "You're not alone," he said with such quiet ferocity. "Whatever happens, you won't be alone. We go together. Even into this."

Taly gave a jerky nod. “Until the end,” was all she managed.

“The gate is ready.” Azura looked to the shimmering portal that spanned the back wall. A dark room lay beyond, rippling at the edges. “And as I promised, Kato is safe and sound. Although, perhaps a little frazzled, so you might go easy on him.”

Leto placed a rucksack on the table filled with food and water and other supplies.

“Skylen.” Azura rose from her chair, her dress giving a soft sigh. “If you would. I need a moment alone with my Acolyte.”

Skye hesitated, unsure.

“I’ll be fine,” Taly said, giving his hand a squeeze. “Really.”

He still looked conflicted but made no argument as he pressed a kiss to her head and moved to gather their supplies. “She had better come through that gate before it closes,” he said to the Queen, his eyes sparkling with something dangerous and unfamiliar. “If she doesn’t…”

He let the words hang, and Taly shivered at the implicit threat.

Azura merely smiled. “Skylen, it’s always a pleasure. And be sure to take the beast with you.” She threw a glance at Calcifer as he loped toward the gate. “Shards know I’m not going to miss having a mimic in my palace.”

Skye let out a low growl but said nothing else. His footsteps echoed on the metal plating surrounding the gate, and the rippling sheen of magic slipped across his body like water as he disappeared through the portal, Calcifer close behind him.

The gate hummed in the resulting silence. The Queen made no move to speak. She simply waited, hands clasped, knowing exactly what she had done and the things that still needed to be said.

"I should hate you," Taly breathed.

"But do you?"

"No." And in that moment, Taly realized it was the truth. Though this woman had created a nightmare tailor-made to each and every one of her darkest fears, she had learned something about herself.

She was strong. Stronger than she had ever allowed herself to believe. Stronger than she would ever have allowed herself to be.

She had set a trap for a man thousands of years her elder, mastered grief and panic and finally embraced that vicious, brutal part of her that was and had always been unmistakably fey.

That had been the Queen's final lesson, and Taly was grateful for it.

Taly turned to Leto. "If you need us," was all the fairy said as she reached for Taly's wrist, fastening a small bracelet with what looked like little bells attached to the clasp.

"I'll never take it off," Taly said, tears welling in her eyes as the fairy's form began to shiver, evaporating into mist. She was going to miss Leto—the one voice of reason in all this insanity.

Taly toyed with one of the bells, the sound like windchimes. Like the fairy's laughter. "Are you really not going to tell me anything else?" She lifted her eyes to Azura's. "You said we were at war, but who are we fighting? And why did the Council split when we would've been stronger together? Why did the Genesis Lords run to the mortal realm? Why would the Dawn Court waste resources hunting down time mages when they could be preparing to fight?"

Azura sighed, taking Taly's hands in hers. "All knowledge has its time, and for now, you have what you need."

"That's horribly cryptic and incredibly annoying," Taly muttered.

Azura smiled—a real, genuine smile despite the tears that shimmered in the corners of her eyes. "I'm aware. But I'm also a time mage—we are, at our core, horribly cryptic and incredibly annoying."

The tears flowed freely from Taly's eyes and... Damn it. Why was this particular goodbye so hard? She'd always thought she'd be glad to be rid of this insane woman.

Azura let her hands drop. "I haven't told you this enough, but you've done well. Better than I expected. You'd think I would've learned to stop underestimating you by now."

Oh. That felt better than Taly wanted to admit.

Azura went on, "I have one more thing to tell you, and if you only retain one lesson from your time here, remember this. You are going to be asked an important question very soon. And though I cannot tell you what it will be, I need you to say no." Azura's voice caught. "Do you understand me, Talya? When the question comes—and you'll know it when it does—it is imperative that you say no. Promise me. You have to promise me. Swear it."

"I swear," Taly said, and meant it.

"Good." Azura wiped at her eyes. "Good, good... And I suppose, if there's nothing else, it's time to send you home. Before Skye comes back through and decides to commit regicide." Her lips quirked. "It's not the first time he's made the threat. Not the first time he's meant it either."

"I imagine not," Taly said dryly.

Azura snorted at that, then placed her hands on Taly's shoulders. "Good luck, Talya Caro."

With that final statement, she gave Taly a slight push, through the gate. Multi-colored swirls of energy danced all around her, cascading, growing, expanding, and condensing as Azura faded from view.

And for the first time in a year, Taly felt a pull, like a current flowing past her, dragging her downstream, as time once again began to move forward.

EPILOGUE

He could not remember who he had been. There was no room for those memories now. The creature that lived within him had pushed them out to make space. Pushed *him* into the shadows and trapped him in the darkest corners of his own mind.

He had fought back in the beginning. Until he had forgotten how to fight.

He had felt frightened for so long. Until he had forgotten what it was to be afraid.

Little by little, the pieces of him had fallen away, until there was nothing left but fragments.

Sometimes, the creature would pass a mirror, and he would catch a glimpse of his face. He couldn't remember it, no longer had the words to describe the color of his eyes or the shape of his chin. It was like looking out a window as a stranger passed by, and yet he somehow knew that face had once belonged to him.

He could see that face right now. Tonight, the creature was resting. It reclined in a soft leather chair, its head tilted back as it watched the woman sleeping on the bed. It was distracted, and that gave him more freedom to creep out of his dark corner, to peer out those windows at the world beyond. There was a mirror on the wall. The frame was gilded. Expensive. The creature liked extravagance. It liked rich fabrics and fine clothes, and when it had come to the city that its followers called Ryme, it had found itself a grand house with servants to tend to all its needs.

It had been wealthy once, it had told him. Though wealth was not what it sought now.

Death is what it had become. Death is what it craved.

Just as the woman on the bed would soon be dead. Her lifeblood drained through the tubing running out of her and into this weakening body.

An earth mage. He had once been an earth mage, his magic connected to the ground itself, to every living thing. So at odds with this creature and its strange magic that festered inside him like a wound.

But it had come inside anyway. Shoved its way in and latched onto the part of him that was mortal—his mother's human blood. That's what allowed it to cling to him day after day, even as this body began to get sick.

Indeed, the arm it had extended, tubes running out of its skin, was streaked with lines of decay. The magic it stole from other earth mages would sustain it for a little while longer, but this vessel was dying. Just like the vessel before it had died. That was the inevitable outcome when death itself attempted to mimic the living.

"Sire."

The creature looked up to the woman standing in the doorway. She had soft black hair and bright brown eyes. She was one of the mages that had followed the creature willingly, fear and hatred blinding her to its lies.

The creature nodded its head. "Speak," it said in its stolen voice.

The woman took a tentative step forward. Even the willing ones were afraid of this thing and how unnatural it seemed. "Vaughn," she began, voice quavering slightly. "We just got word that he—"

"I'm aware." The creature had felt the shadow mage's passing. Fey souls were made of aether, and it always felt the loss of aether as it passed from this world. As more of itself, more of death and nothingness prevailed. "I warned him that someone else might be better suited to retrieving the girl. Someone with less history. But he insisted. Arrogance, it seems, was finally his downfall."

"Yes, Sire." She ducked her head. "What—" It held up a hand, and the woman paled. "Sorry," she breathed. "Aneirin."

That made the creature happy. That had been its name long, long ago, before its brothers and sisters had tried to erase it.

Out of everything they had done to it, that was their most egregious sin. It did not want to be forgotten.

"What are your orders, Aneirin?" the woman asked, glancing nervously at the unmoving body on the bed. The latest sacrifice—she wouldn't die tonight, but... soon. And then they would have to find another.

The creature plucked the tube and needle from its arm, rolling down its fine sleeve to cover the corruption marking his skin. It rose to its feet. "The same as they were before. I want the time mage." It could not let her go to another. She was a new variable. An advantage in this war it had not believed it would ever find again. "Give the generals her description and Vaughn's final coordinates, but also begin briefing the city agents. If Castaro gets his hands on her, he will try to hide her away. We cannot allow that to happen."

"Of course." The woman raised a fist to her chest in a salute, then quickly exited. Like a cornered animal that had just been given a path to freedom.

The creature didn't mind. It enjoyed their fear. It had not enjoyed such things before its fall, but after so many millennia spent sleeping in the dark, of having its power exploited, it had changed. Was still changing. It had no idea what it was yet to become.

The creature moved to the window, pulling back the curtain so it could see the city lights twinkling in the dark.

He felt that eye turning inward. It was no longer distracted, so he crept back to his corner. He did not remember his name. And he was already forgetting the few bits of memory he'd managed to recover during that brief glimpse into the outside world.

Soon, there would be nothing left of him.

And then only the High Lord of Death would remain.

Thank you for reading!

Here we are at the end again, and I hope you enjoyed the story! As usual, this book took twists and turns that even I wasn't expecting and really forced me to grow as a writer. I've already started putting words on the page for book 3, so stay tuned!

Please leave a review!

I can't overstate how important these reviews are to ensure other people get a chance to read my books. I would also love to hear your thoughts—good, bad, or anything in between. At the end of the day, it all helps me write a better story.

Feel free to email me directly at sfisherbooks@gmail.com if you have any questions, comments, or suggestions. If you see any errors, please let me know, and I will fix them immediately.

For updates on my writing projects, you can find me on Facebook as well as Patreon if you'd like to help support me—this is where I typically publish early chapters of whatever I'm currently working on.

Until next time, happy reading!

Made in the USA
Monee, IL
23 November 2020

49233918R00377